TARGET TROJAN

The author asserts that in no way was this book inspired or altered in the light of the recent tragic murder of a British soldier in Woolwich. The entire manuscript existed and was completed significantly earlier.

TARGET TROJAN

ROGER GRAY

Matador
9 Priory Business Park
Kibworth Beauchamp
Leicestershire LE8 0RX, UK
Tel: (+44) 116 279 2299
Fax: (+44) 116 279 2277
Email: books@troubador.co.uk
Web: www.troubador.co.uk/matador

ISBN 978 1783060 818

British Library Cataloguing in Publication Data.
A catalogue record for this book is available from the British Library.

Typeset in Minion Pro by Troubador Publishing Ltd
Printed and bound in the UK by TJ International, Padstow, Cornwall

Matador is an imprint of Troubador Publishing Ltd

AUTHOR'S NOTE

There is an unusually broad spread of characters depicted in this book. This is the nature of the teams that are the firearms dept. Embrace them as you read on. You will come to know and enjoy them all.

RG

CONTENTS

INTRODUCTION

Let there be no illusion, this book is a fiction. I hope though, that you will find a realism that is beyond the norm. May you feel the depth of the characters, the emotion and the danger that this very real task encompasses.

Characters like these really do exist. I know because I worked with them. Events like these can, do and have occurred. The sights, sounds and smells I have striven to bring you are in my head and my heart. These people are out there now. At the moment you read this text it goes on still.

I carried a gun for a number of years in one form or another, both as a Constable and then as a Sergeant. Many things happened even then. Early in 1991 I was accepted into SO19, The Metropolitan Police Firearms branch. As a Sergeant in what was then a new concept, the strain was enormous. As the years went by much was to change. Before I was done and injury ended my career, I would touch the widest of experiences. I would carry the first responsibility for any immediately occurring firearms incident in the whole of the Metropolis. I would go on exercises with the S.A.S. Be privy to their briefings, watch them assault an aircraft, abseil on to buildings and rescue hostages.

On the streets of London I would experience anti-terrorist patrols and tactics, stare into the eyes of a man dying of gunshot wounds at the hands of my own men. I would have my own officers shot and seriously injured, face a man confronting us with live, primed grenades. At times I would stand alone in the midst of all this.

Even now when I close my eyes I see it still. The whirling blue lights, the screaming horns and racing engines. The sound and smell of the guns. I still hear the radios and the voices of men for whom my respect and affection is undimmed. I feel the close bonds that were forged in adversity, and will remain with me forever.

I hope that I can convey just a little of that to you my reader, that I can take you there, make you laugh, make you sad, make your heart beat just a little faster. Remember though, that after all…

It's only fiction…

Roger Gray

GILHOOLEY'S EYES

Small beads of sweat ran down Gilhooley's forehead and into his eyes, interrupting his concentration, misting his vision. Along the carbine's black, lethal and predatory body, his master eye sought its mark. He focussed on the single pole of the foresight. With the fingers of his left hand, he rotated the back sight until it presented the smallest aperture. This was no rapid combat shoot. This would be a sniper-initiated assault. Drawing his eye back and forth until the two concentric rings were perfectly matched, he placed his aim centrally in the doorway of the small suburban house, that single pole now perfect for a chest shot. Centre of mass. In his mind, the words of the instructors, heard so many times, spoke loud. *'Foresight clear, target blurred, keep pulling, keep pulling. Wait for the bang.'*

Stealing a moment he wiped the sweat away as the sun beat down on his cropped head, burning his scalp. But it didn't matter, nothing mattered. The breeze played tormenter again, making the blue and white cordon tape buzz in short bursts of cooling air and he thought for moment how as a boy his kites had sounded so similar, pivoting and turning above the cliffs and an Irish sea. Dragging his mind back to grim reality, he steeled himself again.

In concert with the tape, net curtains billowed free from the open windows of the house, clinging here and there to the rough brickwork. Through his earpiece, he heard Cravetts's voice at a whisper. 'Control and all units from point seven, I see smoke. He's firing the house.' Gilhooley responded 'received at point six.' Then Cravetts's voice again, now loud, echoed across the empty street. 'Samuel…Samuel Richards. We are armed police. Put down your weapon and come out. You will not be harmed. Samuel…' Cravetts's voice tailed off. Now just distant sounds, the radios, traffic, the tape.

The small pieces of gravel that ground his knees and elbows were as nothing. The thirst, the dry mouth were forgotten. In a moment, a second he might end a

1

man's life. Northern Ireland, the desert all meant nothing now. So close, so personal. Suddenly he felt vulnerable, like a small boy.

*

The yard at Croydon had been full. The big blue security gates had swung respectfully open as the silver BMW approached. At the far end of the yard Gilhooley turned the steering wheel sharply right, occupying a bay marked 'Supt' in large white letters and the only one available amongst a mix of marked and unmarked cars. 'Always the rebel then,' grunted Cravetts. Gilhooley exhaled in a cross between a sigh and a growl, adding, 'The lazy bastard won't get out of bed for a night deployment, so he won't be in here for an early turn, will he?' Cravetts smiled, 'Well they all give him a wide berth, but I guess they have to live with him and we don't.'

In the rear seat Sally Galloway watched as the early turn ritual of an ARV crew was played out. She saw the tail of another ARV, a Vauxhall, tucked into the wash bay. As Gilhooley stepped out, she watched as his left hand atop the steering wheel made it look like a toy. This was the beginning of her rite of passage, her entry into a world so different from the rest of the job and so predominantly male. The next few hours, days, weeks, months, would be crucial. The desire for acceptance, no excellence, drove her.

The three burst through double doors into a long corridor, leaving them flapping to and fro as Cravetts strode ahead, his dark, compact figure cutting a swathe through the milling crowd. Sally decided to take the conversation forward, to trespass into their private lives. 'So have you got any kids Kieran?' She had taken full note of the thick gold band on his left hand. 'Course he has,' cut in Cravetts. 'He's a good catholic boy, ain't you son? None of that unholy contraception lark for our Kieran.' A wry smile spreading across his face. Just outside another set of doors leading into the canteen, Gilhooley stopped. 'Is this how it's going to be today Mark? Shall I tell Sally why your hair is thinning on top? See we reckon he's worn out a little patch against his girl friend's headboard.'

Footsteps echoed on the stairs behind them, grippy soft rubber soled boots squeaking on the surface.

'That'll be you being jealous,' John Munney's soft Welsh accent broke in. 'His girlfriend's gorgeous. If he was a real team player he would share her around with us lesser mortals, selfish bastard.' He pushed through the group and opened the doors.

Beyond them, sat around two tables pushed together, were the crews of several ARV'S. The rest of the local officers sat respectfully apart, eyeing the guns that hung from every hip.

'Welcome to bacon and beans mountain,' grinned Munney.

Gilhooley smiled at the girl. 'If Colours knew we were all in here he would freak.'

Cravetts smiled, 'and do you really think he doesn't?' For Sally the test had begun.

The body armour was left draped over the backs of the seats, staking a claim as the crews formed a queue at the counter. It was time to broker friendship. As the aroma of coffee and bacon assailed her senses, she turned to Gilhooley again.

'So how many children do you have?' she asked once more.

'Three,' Gilhooley smiled. 'A son taking his A levels, a girl of twelve going on eighteen, and a baby girl not yet one.' He smiled broadly. 'We called her Caroline, but I think we should have called her hiccup, if you see what I mean.'

The girl's laughter lit her pretty face. She watched as Fudge balanced a tray full of tea and coffee toward the waiting tables. His round shape rocking in a failed attempt not to spill the contents, as little rivers of caffeine ran zig-zags around the cups.

Near the counter a small black woman was swapping obscene suggestions with Benny, his gold tooth glinting in a furtive grin as plates loaded with huge fried breakfasts emerged and were ferried toward the morning ritual.

Three or four of the crewmen were settling in to their meals as a black hand-held radio dominating the table crackled into life. The harsh, clear voice of MP, the Met control room. 'Trojan 552 or any Trojan unit take a call Zulu Delta section, uniform units require urgent armed assistance, shots fired.' Munney was on his feet, spilling coffee. Grabbing the hand-set he said 'MP from Trojan 553 and 552 running from Croydon with a full location please.' Fudge grabbed a serviette as he teased a pen from his pocket, nodding at Munney. The voice over the radio began again.

'Silver End Road, Thornton Heath, number 74, man with a shotgun holding his family hostage. Local units on scene are being fired on. Message ends 0710 on CAD 241, MP over.'

'Rolling MP,' continued Munney as Fudge frantically scribbled. 'ETA four minutes,' Munney barked as he ran toward the door, a radio in one hand and his body armour over one shoulder. All around the scene galvanised, as men threw on body armour and ran to the cars. Hot steaming cups of coffee and meals were

3

abandoned. Suddenly the girl found herself in the eye of the whirlwind she had joined.

Transported almost hypnotically she felt herself running amidst cursing swearing men, her ears ringing to so many alien sounds. Kit rattling and Velcro ripping. Over the radios the voices of desperate and fearful fellow officers, some almost hysterical. At the car Cravetts was making an MP5 carbine ready, knocking the action forward with a loud 'clack'.

'Well you're in at the deep end here girl,' said Gilhooley, dropping like a stone into the driver's seat, the suspension yielding beneath him. 'Baptism of fire,' The blue security gates were already open as the convoy of three ARVs burst screeching and bellowing into the traffic. In the windows all around, the shops, the windscreens of cars flickering blue strobe lights reflected back to disorientate sleepy commuters.

A mixture of horns, high and low, long and wailing, assaulted her senses, desperate voices on the radios, and messages between the car crews already beginning to plan. She heard a voice that said, 'What should I do?' It was her own.

Cravetts flashed her a glance as he wrestled with his kit and the radios, frantically scribbling snippets of information in his log. 'Geographia!' he shouted, holding her gaze. 'We need to know exactly where we are going, we need to know the route. Kieran's alright for now, but we need specifics.' Momentarily she stared blankly back at him. 'Sally for fuck sake. You're maps man *Come on!*' She snapped back, suddenly assertive 'okay,okay. I'm on it.'

Behind them two more cars pitched back and forth through the commuter traffic, their blue lamps and headlights creating a nightmare kaleidoscope, the horns confusing all the other sounds. They were following and she was the navigator. She looked down at the black map book now on her lap, and the motion of the car made her feel nauseous, the tiny print dancing about in the map light. Her hands shook uncontrollably.

*

Chief Superintendent Eduardo 'Eddy' Seredemigni sat behind his desk framed by the light of an oval window that looked down on the busy city traffic three floors below. A centre pane hinged horizontally to allow a breeze to pass through that was as hot as the room itself. In the corner an electric fan pivoted back and forth, left and right, threatening to disrupt the paper and files on his desk, its whirring head performing a continuous negative that reflected the man it served. 'You're long over-due to go training Roy, so I'm insisting you make the move at the next turn around.'

Colours sat impassively as the pudgy man rose to his feet. 'Look,' he went on. 'You could do a lot of good there, a man with your management skills. It could be a real career move for you.'

Seredemigni turned to stare at the traffic below. 'Now I don't want to order you to go, but I must insist.' Colours winced as the smoke from the man's illicit cigarette stung his eyes. He rubbed them and stared down at the green-corded carpet at his feet, rubbing his palms softly together, containing his rising anger.

'Sir! You know my heart's with my relief, and I want to stay operational. I'm a soldier learning to be a copper with a gun. I believe I've done some good with my relief and I want to stay with them. I won't go without protest.' Seredimigni turned to confront him, his eyes widened and a reddened flush appearing at his cheeks. 'Look Barras, don't be so selfish. Others need your talents and I need to bring in fresh blood. Now I won't hear any more of this.'

Colours rose quietly to his feet, turning toward the door. Seredemigni's face grew blank with consternation as Colours quietly closed it the last few inches, daring a glance at the Sergeant waiting outside, disgust dripping from his features. He strode back to the desk.

'I believe they call this *hats off below decks* in the navy, Mr Seredemigni. If you think I'm going to give up my relief so that you can bring in some fucking lackey of yours, you're dreaming.'

Seredemigni began to bluster, his bloated face flushing. 'How dare you, you have no right. I'm a Chief Superintendent'…but Colours cut him off, suddenly dominating the exchange.

'You don't give a shit about this department. I hate people with no faith but their own ends. I've pulled my relief together from the pits, nursed them through shootings, car crashes and trauma, and now you think I'm just going to hand it over to one of your pious cronies, so that they'll look good. Well brace yourself for an eruption. I'll make more noise than a stuck pig, and I'll make sure that everyone knows that you can't honestly pass a straight day on the range.'

Seredemigni paled and spoke. 'Call your Sergeant in here now,' he choked. The door suddenly swung open. Barry Mankowitz stood red-faced holding a mobile phone, anxiety etched on his face.

Colours cut in 'It's alright mate,' but Mankowitz stopped him mid-sentence.

'No guvnor, the south crews are on way to *shots fired*.' A domestic in Thornton Heath. Occupant of a dwelling is firing on police. It's a hostage situation'.

Colours turned on his heels. 'Sorry *Sir...* more important business,' and exited with Mankowitz at his heels.

As they tumbled down the staircase toward the car, the Sergeant blurted between snatched breaths. 'Car's kitted, Omega estate and I've a copy of the message.' They ran to the car as Colours dropped into the passenger seat and Mankowitz cranked the starter.

'Know where we're going?' asked Colours...'

Yup,' came the Sergeants reply. 'And not down the tubes, continued Mankowitz with a grin.

'So what did you hear?' asked Colours as the car bumped and swerved its way into the traffic, the horns echoing ever louder around them.

'Everything or fuck all,' grinned Mankowitz, flashing a glance upward toward the senior officers office. 'Just depends what you want. Anyway we have more important matters right now than that wanker.'

Colours thumbed open the map book and fingered his mobile phone, desperate now for more information. He stretched the message out across the page and read it again. 'Do you know, they ruined a good arsehole when they put teeth in that man's head.'

*

'Are you feeling inspired?' asked Cravetts as the BMW drifted sideways through a sweeping curve. It left long black, burned rubber tyre marks in its wake as traffic around braked and swerved to avoid them. The tumult of noise was undiminished as Sally fought for control. The violence of the ride threw her bodily across the car, scattering pen and paper. 'Wedge yourself in,' advised Cravetts as the girl fought to keep her seat. 'Put your back in the corner and your feet against the door and seats. You won't be able to function unless you do. Pin the map against your knees.'

She pinned the map down with her forearm, matching the grid reference with the page and tracing her finger down it. To her huge relief as if by magic the soft shine of her fingernail fell upon Silver End Road. She saw that her hands no longer shook as she blurted out, 'At the traffic lights ahead, go left, left, left.'

With only yards to go Gilhooley trod hard on the brakes then threw the nose of the car into the centre of the road before turning violently left. On the kerbside a mixed group of young boys shouted, 'Nineteen, nineteen,' while making gun gestures in the air.

Gilhooley smiled. 'Well informed, aren't they?' he said, as the headlights of the second ARV danced in his mirror and he squinted. The horns echoed in the narrow confines while angled bay windows turned into kaleidoscopes of reflected blue light scattered from every facet.

'Two hundred yards and right into Morley Road. Then fifty yards to the junction with Silver End. Should see the target premises on the left.'

The girl was getting into her stride now, reading the information and feeding it on. Cravetts glanced at Gilhooley. He raised his eyebrows as the car slowed, then he nodded.

Nearby a huddle of marked police cars identified the rendezvous point, where panic and chaos ruled. Beyond them blue and white cordon tape fluttered in the light breeze, marking out a no man's land in which only those involved or the foolish would go. The street was long and descended gently away from them between terraces of older houses with short front gardens.

The houses were broken only by the occasional hip-high brick wall, punctuated by pairs of gates, some of which were now missing. Where perhaps a wartime bomb had cut a swathe through them stood a low-rise block of flats two stories high.

Diagonally, and opposite, stood what was once an ecclesiastical hall, now used for some commercial purpose, but with eves and windows that echoed its first calling.

Cravetts ran to the boot of the car. He began to extract kit methodically. ballistic shields and blankets; heavier body armour; binoculars and whatever he thought might be required. Gilhooley walked forward toward a young Inspector crouched behind a Vauxhall Astra. Its reflective markings played mischief in the light of a strengthening sun. Gilhooley felt its first heat as he walked.

He could see no gunman, hear no shots. In the street several local officers were hiding behind the brick walls of the houses, apparently pinned down. Their positions and attitudes hinted at where the gunman might be. He calculated that he was pretty safe at such a distance and angle.

Calm was needed and calm he would be. He walked onward. The young Inspector held his eye, questioning. Gilhooley winked at him. As the distance closed the young man took a breath to speak but Gilhooley's brogue was there first.

'Mornin' guvnor. What've you got for us?'

*

'Seagull, that's what they call him.' Mankowitz restarted a conversation that Colours reflective mood had diluted and the noise around them had drowned out. Colours finished a call on his mobile phone and responded. 'What?' leaning closer to the Sergeant as they negotiated the 'dog leg' junction and traffic lights at the approach to London Bridge, he strained to hear.

Frantically spinning the steering wheel through his hands, Mankowitz shouted again as the squeal of tyres and the insistent radio traffic added yet more to the rising tumult. 'Seagull, they call him Seagull,' he said again, swerving right to overtake a red double-decker bus as oncoming traffic tucked into the kerb, or mounted it to give him way.

'Because,' he began again 'he flies around at a great height, and shits on everybody.' It worked, and the spell was broken as Colours's face softened into a smile. 'Oh Seredemigni you mean! Yes, I've heard that reference to him used once or twice before.'

'That was the base-man on the phone. 552, 553 and 554 are there and deploying. I'm waiting for an update.' He flipped open the atlas he had spread on his lap but Mankowitz shook his head. 'No need boss, I know where this one is. Got an uncle who lives real close.'

The Sergeant continued. '552 you say? That's Gilhooley and Cravetts. The new recruit is going to be tested here. I hope they don't make her control. She'll flip.' Colours turned his head and looked at the man beside him. The Sergeant's eyes were fixed on the road ahead as he span the steering wheel back and forth through his hands, pitching the bellowing car in and out through the heavy traffic.

The heat was intense as the transmission worked close to its limit, conspiring with the rising power of a summer's morning to slowly cook them. The engine note rose and fell as the auto-box wrestled with the incessant acceleration and braking. The smell of hot oil and brakes began to pervade.

'If I know those two, they won't. It would be too much for a first deployment, and this one is going to roll.' At the Elephant and Castle Mankowitz threw the car wide and around the back of a stationary black cab now in the east-bound lane.

As he passed between it and the island, the rear door flew open and the fare stepped out. He threw the car wide and braked as they squeezed through in a cloud of acrid tyre smoke. '*Fucking idiot*,' he bellowed, knowing no-one would hear. 'Guess you're right!'

'Yeah! Usually,' Colours concurred, bracing himself as the car slewed screeching through a second roundabout, 'as right as you are about that pratt *Seagull*.'

Trojan 553 slewed to a halt beside Cravetts and Sally. Behind them again a third car braked heavily, its roof lights competing for attention. From the driving seat of 553 Raffles caught Cravetts's eye knowingly.

He chanced a glance at the girl in the back seat now frantically wrestling with kit and body armour. 'I'll do control,' he sighed. Cravetts acknowledged, touching his eyebrow with a forefinger.

'Okay Ray, you're a good egg.' Raffles settled sullenly into the role of control muttering to himself 'me and my big mouth.' He would be the hub of the empire now. Every one would ask him the questions, feed him the 'intel' and expect him to record it all.

Gilhooley's bulk presided as he ran back to brief the crews as they were preparing.

'Right, IC1 Male armed with a shotgun and a handgun.' Gilhooley began. 'Two hostages, wife and son aged maybe six. Several gunshots from within and at police. No police injuries, kid's still okay, but haven't seen Mum for a while. Three at the front, two at the back. That's Fudge and Benny. There's a network of alleyways so get in, find a safe back route in. Get it contained and the safe route marked. I'll update you on the hoof. *NOW GO.*'

He turned to Raffles. 'Teams, paramedics, dogs, ambulance, India 99, ...' But Raffles cut him off.

'The guvnor, the Queen and God almighty, old uncle Tom Cobley and all. Go Kieran, I can cope.' Gilhooley sucked in some air. 'Okay Sally, This is your moment. Let's go.' He called back to Raffles 'Brief the other car.' Cravetts joined him as they ran forward, laden with kit, radios and shields.

Raffles called after them. 'Send the local duty officer back to me, and ask him for a local PC to be my oppo.' Cravetts raised an arm in acknowledgement, and they were gone.

*

Blood ran thick from the cut above her eye. It traced a line across her trembling cheek, down the side of her nose and into the corner of her mouth. The olive skin of her face was smeared with it and her clothing wet and sticky. Her breath came in short gasps as she swallowed hard, trying to stay conscious, trying not to vomit.

Each breath seemed to herald another gush of blood from the gaping shotgun wound in her right thigh. It diluted in the spreading pool of urine beneath her, as her body slowly lost all control.

She clasped the bunched material of her Sari to the wound, desperately trying to staunch the flow. A small boy clung to her left arm as she lay on the bare boards, her back against an old, tiled fireplace.

The hazed vision of her young eyes watched his burly shape. The blue boiler suit he wore was smeared with her blood. From his right hand hung the shotgun, the butt sawn down roughly and rounded, its twin barrels shortened and pugnacious like flared nostrils.

He paced back and forth across the floor, between the two old sash windows. At his feet was a small holdall. Inside lay a self-loading Italian pistol, ammunition and a huge bowie knife.

Acrid smoke misted the room from a small fire burning on the stairs. He spat and muttered as he moved, rising menace in his eyes. 'I told you. You wouldn't believe me you bitch. I warned you.'

*

A voice rang out from the street below. 'Samuel…Samuel Richards. We are armed police. Put down your weapon and come out. You will not be harmed. Samuel…'

'You hear them. Every fucker's against me.' Suddenly Richards strode across, dropped to one knee and placed his face close to hers, her laboured breath brushing his cheek.

'Dying are you? Now you know, now you understand.' He stood up and turned away, his voice now loud and booming, his face contorted with anger and the insatiable lust for revenge.

He shouted toward the window, wanting his tormenters to hear.

'You want to take my boy. Your family hate me, they always did. I'm not good enough, am I? Just some fucking thick squaddy that you've defiled yourself with. That's what your old man said, wasn't it?' Then he took the bewildered child's hand. He pulled him firmly but gently away, turning toward the light. There was no anger for the infant, just a terrible resignation.

He stood facing the road below, holding the boy in front between him, the small squares of glazed window framing the armed police officers as he watched impassively. Tucked in behind garden walls or black ballistic shields

10

were Gilhooley, Cravetts and Sally Galloway. His eyes flicked from one to the other, as the rage grew again.

His hands contorted twisting the boy's tee shirt until the child winced. He didn't cry out. The fear silenced him. Gilhooley had worked his way along the front gardens, demolishing every vulnerable obstacle, covering with a carbine for Sally and Cravetts whenever they were exposed. Cravetts hoisted the shield as they leapt low walls until they were opposite the house.

Gilhooley dropped to the prone, tucked himself in against the brick pillar of the gate and settled in. To his left Sally squatted behind the same wall about six feet away. It's castellated features giving her a 'firing slot'. Following Gilhooley's example she adjusted her back sight as he spoke in a deep, clear whisper. 'He has the height. He can fire down at you. Stay low.' Cravetts began to call out. 'Samuel…'

*

At the RVP Raffles was sweating heavily. The centre consul of the car buzzed with incessant radio traffic. Below it the Trojan link between the cars, the base and Information Room sporadically interrupted. In his hands a back-to-back radio allowed him to speak to his crews now deployed around the house, while a mobile phone rang to add to his torment. The young Inspector leant against the side of the car, his face strangely untroubled, staring in at the sweating man. Raffles looked up and spoke.

'Sir, can I have one local PC in here with me. I need a scribe and some good local knowledge.'

The Inspector's smile broadened as he beckoned a portly middle-aged man in uniform hiding comfortable and safe in the driver's seat of a nearby police van. He pointed at the passenger seat of the ARV and said,

'Tom, you're aid to SO19 comms.' Sullenly the overweight man dropped into the seat beside Raffles, who handed him the log.

'Write down every communication, every occurrence.' Raffles began. 'Remember you will be giving evidence from this one day.' The newcomers face hung with trepidation.

Over the radio, Gilhooleys voice. 'Control from Kieran, receiving over?' as he began to build the picture.

'I'm at point five on the white, Sally is at six and Mark is at eight, received so far?' In the car Raffles grabbed a flip chart and pens, starting to draw outlines. 'So far okay Kieran,' Raffles acknowledged through the radio link.

Barry Mankowitz was sweating profusely. Commuter traffic was at its height as they hurtled passed Streatham Common and onward. In the passenger seat Colours fought to stabilise himself and collect every snippet of information. 'Red team are on a digout in North London. Orange are training, so the base has assigned them both. We won't get either for a while though.'

The radio barked through the chaos and noise as they barrelled into the narrowing confines of their route. 'Trojan one from MP, what is your ETA at Silver End Road? The Scene Commander requires your attendance A.S.A.P.' Colours looked at the Sergeant and shook his head, as Mankowitz raised his left hand, daring for a moment to release it from the busy steering wheel.

'Five minutes MP. Do we have 99?' Colours went on.

The voice of the information room operative replied in clear and measured terms.

'Trojan one from MP, India 99 has refuelled at Lippits. Flying time to venue... MP out.'

*

Fudge had stumbled along a rancid alleyway, ducking low to get to the back of the house. A high but flimsy slatted wooden fence marked out the boundaries at the rear garden of scrub grass and nettles, hemmed in both left and right by others of a similar description. In one corner an ageing garden shed intruded, obstructing part of their view. Benny followed, labouring under the considerable weight of the blue ballistic blanket. He muttered and swore as he progressed. Behind him came Arthur's gnome-like presence, waddling toward them and picking his way.

'Don't you help me out will you, you fat little bastard,' Benny berated Arthur who looked up with a mixture of offence and humour. 'This alley's full of dog shit mate. Don't want that kind of good luck thank you.' A sudden explosion rent the air and all three ducked.

The garden shed erupted in a shower of broken glass as a shotgun blast blew out the windows. A second blast blew apart some panelling between Benny and Fudge, splinters of wood flying in their faces.

'*Fucking hell,*' spat out Benny as Fudge screamed down the radio, 'Shots fired on the black, shots fired. We are being shot at now.'

Arthur became suddenly calm. As over the radio Raffles acknowledged he spoke in level, even terms. 'He could've hit us easy. What's he doing? It's a diversion.' They could hear Raffle's voice over the radio as they hoisted the blanket over the fence, now finding super human strength.

'Any injuries? Benny? Fudge from control, receiving?'

At the rear door of the house strange scraping sounds reached their ears. Arthur chanced a glance through a gap in the panelling.

'What the fuck is going on?' whispered Benny.

Arthur slumped down beside him, sucking in a deep breath.

'He's dragged a little Honda motorcycle in through the back door,' he sighed heavily.

'So what,' said Benny angrily 'What's he going to do with that? Throw it at us, or fucking wheelie his way out of here?'

Fudge was up and covering with a carbine now. There was a long pause and then he spoke. 'Don't you get it mate? The info is that the bloke's an ex-soldier. Now he's got a few gallon of petrol.' Benny fell silent for a moment, then uttered 'Shit...'

*

Mankowitz allowed the car to roll into Morley Road. He let the pace drop off, as Colours killed the noise from the horns. He left the blue strobing lights to lance ahead, announcing their arrival to the array of uniformed police officers now strung along the outer cordon. Against their ranks and separated only by the tenuous line of blue and white tape, the throng of onlookers grew.

Inevitably the press were there harassing anyone they thought might know what was going on. As camera flashes invaded both their eyes, Colours grunted.

'The hyena's are here.' Mankowitz smiled and responded

'They're up and about early today.'

Beyond the line stood a paramedic ambulance and an assemblage of police vehicles. Territorial Support Group personnel carriers, traffic cars and local vehicles parked close into the protective flank of the terraced houses.

In the mirror more blue lights appeared as the fire brigade vehicles made their noisy presence known. 'This is going to be a bigger carnival then Notting Hill,' Colours mused.

Like the Red Sea, the crowd parted. A uniformed officer lifted the tape high as they passed below. In the distance a blue lamp flashed just once as Raffles, now too busy to speak, guided them to control.

13

As the car rolled to a halt Colours was already getting out, clipboard and papers in hand. The last rocking motion of the car echoed his footfalls as he strode toward Raffles, now standing by the bonnet of his car. Across it was taped a large 'flip chart' upon which a mass of information had been penned. Descriptions, deployments, manpower and events were laid out as Colours went smoothly into action, the Sergeant standing coolly at his shoulder.

Running on 'auto' Raffles began to relate all he knew, his finger tracing the maps and drawings he had so hastily compiled.

'First thing you need to know guvnor, is that he has fired on containment units, and we think he may be constructing incendiary devices.' Colours ran a forefinger across his brow, conceding just a hint of his rising concern. 'Any injuries?' he barked.

'No boss,' Raffles smiled. 'Fudge, Benny and Arthur are at the back and they're expendable.'

Colours met the Sergeant's eye. 'You know what I want? An I.A. now, D.A. almost as soon and hostage and prisoner reception sorted.'

With no more than a nod, Mankowitz was gone. Colours laid his hand on the shoulder of a young ARV officer standing nearby. This was Chris Harding a sharp-featured and agile-minded new face on the relief. 'Be ready to relieve on the containment, but for now help Raffles. He's getting swamped.'

The young Inspector closed with Colours as local politics became an issue. The man smiled at him and spoke.

'I know it's my ground, that I'm scene Commander and I have to consider my seniors. Truth is though, it's your game, and I'll back you all the way.'

'Thanks,' Colours replied, and continued 'These are your options.' His counterpart raised a hand and stopped him, a boyish smile invading his features.

'I think I just chose them.'

*

Feverishly the overall-clad man rummaged through aged kitchen units, discarding all that was of no use, while the boy watched, cowering in a corner of the dirty and sparsely furnished room. His wide-eyed gaze followed his father's every move as the man seized upon an old and wide-necked bottle and ripped open a box of soap flakes. He allowed a grunted hiss of satisfaction to pass his lips, as they turned to a thin smile.

In the corner of the room a single tap fed an old Butler sink. He drank the last

14

of the beer that had occupied the bottle for some interminable time, then spat the residue from his mouth in disgust. Regularly he paced from the rear of the house to the front, checking that his adversaries had not moved. From the table he picked up the petrol tank he had ripped from the small motorcycle opened the tap and allowed the contents to trickle into the bottle. When it was almost full, he topped up the mixture with soap flakes stuffed an old rag into its neck, shook it and grunted with satisfaction.

*

Pikey's lank form appeared to Arthur's left as in his earpiece and through the radio, the man spoke.

'Coming up on your left Arthur, got an extinguisher.' Catching his eye, Arthur nodded as he watched the tall man stooping difficultly low, dragging a large fire extinguisher with him, while the rest of his kit and his guns conspired to obstruct his progress.

'We've got a right nutty bastard here,' hissed Pikey, his breathing laboured. 'Colours asked me to bring you this. Teams are on their way. He wants to know if you're okay here?' Fudge turned his head to speak, his eyes still fixed on the house through the sights of a carbine.

'Seeing as you can't get an armoured Land Rover up here, another shield would be helpful.'

'None left,' said Pikey nonchalantly. 'I'm going to the front. No room left here,' he said with wry smile. 'Anyway this alley stinks. Was it like this before you got here?'

Benny flicked his eyes away from the sights for a microsecond. 'Why don't you bugger off, you long streak of piss.'

*

'Sir!'... Colours concentration was broken by the approach of a tall and heavy-set police officer. He wore the shoulder markings of the Territorial Support Group. Beside him walked a well-dressed Indian man. The Green turban complimented a sports jacket over a lighter green shirt, above khaki trousers and polished brown shoes. His lower face was masked by a greying beard, intricate twists and plaids drawing it close to his jaw line. His dark eyes shone with both intelligence and concern.

15

'My Inspector sent me down with this man sir.' Began the PC. 'He say's he's the girl's father, the girl in the house.'

Colours thanked the officer and turned toward the Asian man. Before Colours could utter a word, in impeccable English, the man spoke.

'Sir, I am Marwinder Singh. I am a Consultant Oncologist at St Mathews hospital. I heard of the incident when the emergency services were mobilised to this address. I'm terribly afraid that the woman who is being held hostage is my daughter.'

Colours stood suddenly upright from his position leaning across the maps and diagrams fixed to the hot car bonnet. 'I'm so sorry sir,' he began. Beneath darkened eyebrows flecked with grey, a hint of tears filled the man's eyes.

'The man you have cornered, Samuel Richards. My daughter married him against my will.'

As the man began to sway Colours took him by the arm, leading him toward the back seat of the car. He looked at the fat man scribbling frantically in the log, ensconced safely in the passenger seat.

'Write this down, every word and get it exactly right,' Colours said firmly.

He turned to the Asian man again. 'Tell me all you know sir please, every detail.'

Mankowitz appeared at Colour's side and began. 'Right sir. Got an I.A. sorted...' but Colours stopped him. 'Yes Barry, but listen to this first.'

The Asian man looked up again wearily, tears now descending his cheeks, losing themselves in the complex workings of his beard.

'My son was in the army with Samuel Richards. He introduced him to my daughter Saria. I didn't approve but he got her pregnant and they eventually married. He has her and the children in that house.'

Colours took a deep and sudden breath. '*Children?*...We have only seen one child, a boy.'

The old man began to sob. 'There is a baby, a new baby girl. She is in there.' Unable to contain himself, Mankowitz broke in.

'Are you sure there's also a baby in there? How d'you know?' Reaching into his pocket the old man produced a mobile phone.

'I spoke to her on this. Don't you know? He's shot her. She will bleed to death soon. Please do something. Kill him, he is mad.'

Colours turned and faced the Sergeant, folding his arms and shaking his head. 'Frontal assault, pick a team.'

Mankowitz frowned. 'I'll lead, Roy,' he said.

16

'Behind me,' replied Colours. 'It's my call, my relief and my responsibility.' He paused for thought 'Distraction?' he said quizzically.

'Okay, something from the rear perhaps, but what about the S.F.O. teams?' asked Mankowitz.

The heavy beat of helicopter rotors suddenly filled the air above them.

'Unless they are going to abseil down from that,' said Colours wistfully 'There ain't going to be time buddy.'

*

At the back of the house Fudge, Benny and Arthur were shuffling uncomfortably about.

'What the fuck's he doing now?' groaned Arthur as shifting, scraping sounds reached their ears.

'Control from point twelve…' began Fudge, about to report the movements.

In the house the boiler-suited man dragged an old mattress close to the window. Then he placed the petrol tank on it and opened the taps. The fuel was hungrily absorbed by the thick material.

'Point twelve from control, go ahead Fudge.' Raffles responded.

'Odd movements heard on the black,' began Fudge. He made to speak but his voice trailed off as Fudge broke in again loudly.

'Fucking hell…*petrol bomb*.' At the control a loud 'whumph' was audible.

Benny saw it first. Mesmerised he watched the bottle arc from the upper window, its strange crackling accompaniment bemusing him.

The tiny filament of light that was its crude fuse drawing lines across their sight. It seemed to hang momentarily in the air. Then the bottle descended sharply to smash on a concrete path.

A wall of searing hot flame reached out for them, stealing all the breathable air as they ducked low behind the protection of the fence and the ballistic blanket. Instantly the whole garden was engulfed in flame, the wooden fences and the old shed succumbing readily to the inferno. At full tilt the three men ran headlong into the street. From the window above, Samuel Richards watched in bitter glee.

'Run rabbit run. Want to play soldiers, do you coppers?' he whispered to himself. Pushing the boy out of the door he dragged the petrol tank onto a landing while its contents drew a wet trail across the floor. Then holding it chest high he tossed it still spiralling fuel, back on to the mattress and closed the door.

17

Colours had left Mankowitz to care for the old man while he ran headlong to where Fudge, Benny and Arthur stood heaving and breathless in the safety of a side road. 'Are you boys alright?' he called, barely now in control of his own emotions.

'Okay boss,' responded Fudge, as they coughed and choked. 'There's a ballistic blanket back there that would pass for a breakfast waffle though. He won't be coming out of that way for a while boss, too much heat.' Colours felt his self-control returning.

'Can you get some kind of rear containment back in place as soon as possible boys?'

Benny grunted an acknowledgement and turned to Arthur. 'Here Arthur, have you shit yourself mate 'cos there's an awful stink?' Arthur looked up in disgust.

'No I fucking haven't.' he snapped back. Benny's chuckling voice was punctuated by coughing.

'Well in that case, you remember all that dog shit you missed on the way in? Well sorry mate but you got it on the way out.' Colours shook his head and walked away.

At the control Barry Mankowitz struggled to keep order, watching as Colours reassuring presence jogged steadily back toward him. In the car Raffles spoke in fast-forward down the radios, updating Gilhooley and the front containment, placating MP and fending off endless incoming enquiries. In the passenger seat the fat uniformed man sweated. The morning heat was rising inexorably.

*

She had drifted into a state of calm as unreality preceded unconsciousness. The light from the window invaded her eyes as a mist and shapeless forms moved disembodied around her. For Saria there was no hope, she knew that. A distant sound filtered through her fading thoughts. At first like a bird song as it repeated again, and again.

'No answer boss'? asked Mankowitz. 'Let it ring. Maybe he'll answer, maybe it'll distract him.'

In the house Richards stared at the mobile phone lying in her limp hand. He drew his face close to hers again, pinching her cheeks brutally between finger and thumb as he knelt to mock her.

'You can still hear me, you bitch? Is this your rich daddy d'you reckon? Can't take you now can he? I reckon the devil himself will have us all soon.' He laughed, an ugly grimace of a laugh. Then he took the phone and answered it.

'Samuel Richards?… This is Inspector Roy Blagden-Barras. Please don't put the phone down. Please keep talking to me.' There was a long silence before a hoarse reply.

'Not your normal punter Mister Blagden fucking Barras. I know too many tricks for your boys. Why don't you come in and talk to me? D'you think I will keep chatting nicely to you while you plot and manoeuvre? Bollocks will I.' The phone went dead.

'Fuck it!' Colours couldn't restrain himself. 'He won't talk to me.'

The Sergeant stared at him, smiling softly.

'Keep trying boss. The assault team will be ready soon. Gilhooley, Cravetts and Harding. Pikey off the back and you and I. Got dogs nearby if we need them. Benny and Fudge will smash back windows with bricks as a distraction as we go for the front door. We can get close along the front of adjacent houses. Gilhooley will do the door. Sally can cover from where she is.'

Colours looked up. 'Take the Remington.' Mankowitz stared at him. *'Only for the destruction of dangerous animals boss?'*

Colours responded, 'He is a fucking dangerous animal. A shotgun full of double 'O' buck is about right. Anyway, if he has set booby traps, I want him down and dead first hit.'

The mobile phone in Colours hand rang. In his eyes was a look the Sergeant had not seen before. Mankowitz turned to the sweating operator, still writing furiously.

'You didn't hear any of that,' he whispered close 'and you certainly won't write it down.' The man dropped his eyes.

'No sarge, 'course not.'

*

'What the hell was that?' Cravetts had exclaimed as the sound of the petrol bomb reached their ears. Moments later Raffles voice crackled sharp over their radios. Now they knew their colleagues were safe, at least for a while, and how dangerous and violent their adversary was. Over the radio Barry Mankowitz directed Gilhooley to ring his mobile phone. Cravetts and Sally covered as he rolled away into merciful shade, and dialled the number.

'Barry, it's Kieran.' Gilhooleys unmistakable brogue whispered in the Sergeants ear. 'We're going in, aren't we?' Slowly and methodically, the Sergeant laid out the plan. He scribbled out notes and grunted acknowledgement here and there.

Then Gihooley replied 'Got it sarge. Anything's better than frying in this heat.'

He crawled and shuffled forward to relay the plan. Cravetts placed a hand on Sally's shoulder. With a soft smile he said, 'soon enough Sally, but today is too soon.'

The girl smiled and nodded in gentle admission.

'I'm know I'm not ready for this yet,' she said. 'but not too long.' Her expression hardened her pretty features.

'Royston Blagden-Barras. Colour Sergeant Blagden-Barras. I've heard of you.' The phone in Colours hand had suddenly rung. It was Richards. 'You should know what this is about. You were a soldier.'

Suddenly disarmed, drawn personally into the depths of this confrontation, Colours found himself lost. 'Yeah, that was me. I was a soldier and now I'm not. Neither are you.'

There was a long pause, then Richards spoke again.

'Is that what it means, all those years. Is that what being in the mob is worth… nothing? What happened to Brothers in Arms? What happened to all the bright promises?'

Colours fought to clear his mind. He tried to bring the trained negotiator in him to bear, but this was all happening too quickly.

'Look Samuel, this is a permanent answer to a temporary problem. Please stop and think. No-one has died. There's still a tomorrow,' but Richards cut him off.

The old man rose from the back seat of the car, knowing or sensing who was calling. Mankowitz restrained him, staring at Colours, the anxiety etched there in his face. Colour's phone rang again.

'Don't treat me as stupid Mr Bloody Blagden-Barras. She's going to die. It's too late. Pass a message for me will you? Tell that miserable old bastard that I really loved her once. But you can also tell him I hate her now as much as I hate him. Tell him this is payback.' Colours fought for words, his mind seeking focus. He must not lose this link. He must keep Richards talking.

'The kids, the children. They haven't done anything wrong.' He continued. The silence that followed chilled Colours to his very soul. The phone went dead. His heart sank. He turned to his Sergeant and spoke, a shudder in his voice.

'We go in now.'

*

His eyes were dark. They were so large and innocent that their very darkness seemed to lift them clear of his flawless olive skin.

The thick, dark hair that lay smooth across his forehead was jet black and shone with every hint of light. The clothing that he had worn so new and proud to school just a few hours before was dirty and torn, stained and now sticky with his mother's blood. The bright maroon of his blazer darkened with a more sinister shade.

The small bundle at his feet stirred. She had slept for hours, but now hunger tormented her. The longing for her mother's breast grew stronger, but that breast would be denied her and she began to cry. The small boy pulled the bundle close to him, embracing the only human being in his universe that he did not now fear.

He stared at the boiler-suited figure that sat now desolate in the corner by a bay window facing the street. Distantly Cravetts voice called vainly again and again. 'Samuel Richards. We are armed police…' Far away sirens sounded and the relentless whump-whump of the helicopter rotors intruded, while the more subtle murmur of distant radio transmissions was subdued.

The heavy smell of smoke filled his nostrils, while the inescapable and powerful aroma of petrol was everywhere. He stared at the figure until the man raised his eyes and met his own.

'Daddy, please let's go home.'

The first words the boy had spoke for hours cut him like a knife.

'Daddy please, *please.*' The boy began to sob, quietly at first, and then more deeply until his chest heaved, and his breath came in halting snatches.

In her ears the loud buzzing sound subsided and she heard the bird song, and his voice.

'I really loved her once.'

Why didn't he love her now? The terrible cold was fading as a more gentle warmth comforted her. Through a misted tunnel she could see the boy, his hand stretched out toward her infant child. She drifted as the feeling of a gentle warm sea bathed her feet. The sand rising between her toes. The sound of her child's laughter warmed her, and she smiled. Then the sun was on her face and the man she had so loved embraced their new-born child as the warm sea churned at his ankles. She watched him smile as the brilliant sun was dimmed by a passing cloud. Then a cloud slowly blotted out the light and life faded away.

From where he sat Richards stretched out and touched the woman's face. She sat quite silent now, the grip on the sari released. The blood no longer pulsed but spread slowly and relentlessly across the wooden floorboards. He drew his fingers gently down her cheek and she rolled softly to one side, seeming to exhale just once. Then she was silent.

In the furore of preparation the mobile phone should hardly have been noticed, yet its ring was shocking. Colours raised his hand and all around him fell silent. There was no voice, but he knew.

'Samuel, this is Inspector Bagden-Barras, ex-Colour Sergeant Blagden-Barras. Please talk to me.' He looked at Mankowitz, seeking help to somehow get this man to speak. A tremulous, subdued voice responded.

'I was a good soldier you know. Decorated and all sarge. Never put a foot wrong me. Liked a drink but there you are!'

Colours broke in, hoping at last for a resolution.

'Come on brother, there's no good to this. I'll meet you at the door. Neutral ground eh? Soldier to soldier.'

There was a long pause, a silence and then Richards spoke again.

'She's dead. I know dead when I see it and she's dead. She was all I ever wanted but I should have known. Her family are all achievers, but brown skin or white, it makes no difference. I was never good enough.'

Colours's thoughts span. What could he say, what could he do to stop this now. The terrible depth, the dread that was palpable in the man's voice chilled and exhausted him. What could he, just another human being, say to undo all of this, to end it? To even limit it?

'Samuel,' he began. 'You could have shot my blokes at the back, but you didn't, and you didn't mean to kill her. What about the kids? I'll try to help, but you must give yourself up.'

Barry Mankowitz watched the agony on Colour's face, felt his emotion. He willed with every ounce of his being for a surrender. The subdued voice on the phone spoke softly again.

'I think sarge, that this patrol is compromised.'

Desperately Colours cut in.

'Don't Samuel… Private Richards I am ordering you.'

The voice was there again, now harsh, loud and aggressive.

'No more orders, no more patrols, no more bloody officers. No more second-class citizen. Watch them take notice now sarge.'

Colours felt something akin to panic as all reason left Richards words.

'What are you going to do?' Colours asked, almost pleading, breaking every negotiating rule.

There was a terrible silence. In the background Colours could hear the boy quietly sobbing, and the baby's plaintiff cry. In the street outside the sound drifted to where Gilhooley, Cravetts and Sally sweated in the hot sun. Along the dirty alley way to the back of the house Fudge, Benny and Arthur settled in again beside the charred and smouldering fence. Throughout the exchange Raffles had broadcast the content, updating all and sundry.

A terrible stillness fell. Only the sound of distant radios intruded, the more distant sound of traffic and the crackling cordon tape. A single bird song echoed strange and loud. Colours held the line open, daring not to speak, listening to the children and holding his Sergeant's gaze. The voice on the mobile phone spoke once more.

'Watch and learn Mr Barras.' Then the line went dead.

As Colours face fell, Raffles saw his expression, knew what it meant. Through the radios he gave a general alarm. 'All units stand by.' At the back fence the three men were shocked, thrown almost off their feet by the force of the explosion.

Arthur winced and fell to the ground, blood streaming from a cut on his forehead. Fudge and Benny were peppered with a thousand tiny missiles as hungry black smoke and red flames licked at the roof from a first floor rear window. The smoke billowed and turned as the helicopter closed with them again. Flying glass tinkled to the ground all around them.

The scene was galvanised. A nearby house-alarm joined the chaos, wailing loudly as radio traffic multiplied and every eye, every gun focussed on the house. Colours and his Sergeant ran forward, knowing what must certainly now happen. Gilhooley raised his voice.

'Watch your front. He will come this way. It will be a grandstand, I just know it.'

The heat was unbearable as from fume and flame a relative calm fell again. The stifling air was riven with stinging smoke, the morning sun multiplying its heat. The concrete below Gilhooley's body was almost too hot to touch and yet he could not, he dare not move. Cravetts called again.

'We are armed police. You in the house come out with your hands raised. Leave your weapons behind.'

From somewhere in the now smoke-filled house, a voice replied.

'Oh I'm coming out copper, I'm coming.'

Cravetts looked momentarily at Sally. The carbine she held was gripped so tightly her knuckles were white, and her hands trembled slightly. The sweat on her brow though, did not match his own. It dampened her cheeks as if a tear would fall at any moment. He looked at his own hands and saw that he was trembling too. In Colours's hand the vibrating mobile phone intruded as the baseman spoke. 'Mr Barras. Red team's ETA is three minutes to the RVP.' Colours sighed deeply and then replied. 'They won't make it.'

Inside the house slowly he stood up, then turned and looked at her. The pain had gone from her face and only a blank serenity resided there. He allowed his head to fall forward as he uttered,

'Forgive me. They would never let us be.'

Then he drew his hands down her bloodied clothing, and turned again toward the terrified boy.

Outside the heat grew unbearable, searing their skin, burning into cropped scalps. Cravetts pushed ever more into the scant protection of a thinning hedge. Sally's thick hair gave her no relief from the heat, but shielded her skin. For Gilhooley there was no relief. He dare not move and expose himself. He felt the burning sun tormenting him, little rivers of sweat trickling down past his ears, between his eyebrows and into his eyes.

The boy watched as his father broke open the shotgun, and dropped two fresh cartridges into its gaping, hungry breaches. With a chilling 'clunk' he snapped it closed. Then he took the pistol, racked it and along with the huge knife, stuffed it in his belt. The boy flinched as the man drew his moist hands over both their faces and clothing.

The child watched uncomprehending as his father tipped the contents of a plastic bottle into his own face and body, spreading it with his hands. Then he dropped on one knee beside the boy.

Gently he whispered,

'Please forgive me.'

He turned and fired each barrel successively, blowing out the windows. Beside them the infant girl began to wail. Gilhooley blinked repeatedly as the salted sweat burned his eyes. As the rending crash of the shotgun blew fragments of glass all around he flinched, managing the words 'Gunfire on the white,' haltingly into the radio. In the car the sweating man scribbled on furiously.

Sally squinted while the shock set her trembling hands to work again. Cravetts threw himself to the kneeling position and targeted the front door. A brown glass bottle span through the air and splintered on the roadway in a sheet of fire, setting dry grasses on the verge aflame. Through the sights of the carbine Gilhooley watched with misted vision.

In the shadows of the hallway their tormenter moved back and forth, the opaque glass denying them truth. Then the door swung slowly open. The boy stood in front, the man knelt, glistened in the sunshine as he broke the gun and loaded it again.

'Tell mister Barras it's my rules, my game and my moment.'

Then holding the boy ahead of him, his left arm around his waist, defiantly he stood up. Again he spoke, a weak smile thinning his lips. He extended a wet palm that reflected the sunlight, as did his whole form.

'Do you know what this is coppers. It's blood…blood and fucking petrol.'

*

In the car, the force radio at Raffles knee interrupted.

'Suspect is out MP, has a child hostage as a shield, India 99 over.'

The fat operator scribbled furiously as a deluge of information overwhelmed him, his handwriting reduced to a desperate scribble. Raffles stared at him through the windscreen across a sea of paper and diagrams spread out across the car bonnet, nodding and shaking his head as he spoke into a mobile phone.

'I can't, I'm too busy. I'm sinking here mate. You're on your own and I don't think you will make it in time.'

There was a pause, then Raffles went on.

'Suspect is out. Child hostage and shots fired. You'll never get here Brendan.'

He leaned in through the window above the sweating figure.

'Enter it in the log. Red team at Thornton Heath roundabout. ETA two minutes.'

He returned to his 'desk', muttering under his breath,

'Might as well be on the moon.'

Nearby in an unmarked police car, the Asian man rocked gently back and forth, as the young Inspector tried vainly to console him.

'Go wide toward the green aspect Mark. Prevent a breakout.'

Gilhooley whispered through the radio.

'The guvnor and the skipper are on the other side.'

He heard two clicks through his earpiece and glimpsed Cravett's exit away from them. He heard the girl breathing hard nearby, but dare not allow his gaze to stray.

'Get a loudhailer.'

From behind the cover of a brick wall Colours sent the young Chris Harding sprinting back to the cars, while in the garden of the small terraced house the tension spiralled. Gilhooley thumbed the moisture from his eyes, the very

25

movement burning the salt deeper into his skin, but he could not stem the flow. He cleared his throat but the dryness cracked his voice, distorting his broad accent.

'Don't do this Samuel, please. Let the boy go and put the guns down.' There was an awful calm in which every movement, every sound was magnified. Young Chris Harding, the loudhailer in his hand, broke his returning run and stopped, a length of his fair hair plastered now to his sweating brow. He sensed as did they all, that this moment was everything. That what happened next would decide who lived, who died.

'A permanent solution for a temporary problem Mr Barras said.'

From the front garden the boiler-suited man's voice rang strong and clear. The distant sounds barely intruded.

The wail of a police siren stopped abruptly as down a radio Raffles called desperately 'Kill the noise… *Red team kill the noise.*'

A tall white Mercedes Sprinter van emerged through the cordon. It sidled to a halt as blue-suited armed men rushed from it. Raffles gestured frantically and the van driver had abruptly stopped, knowing the next few seconds were crucial. In the car the fat PC scribbled on, even the rustling of his paper now an intrusion. From the garden his voice echoed, carried along the street.

'Well tell Mr Barras that this is a permanent problem and there is no solution.'

His voice was an agony, almost a cry in a raised, breaking pitch.

'I can hear you. If there is no tomorrow then there is no hope. Give yourself, give the children a chance,' Colours replied.

A sudden crack emitted from the house, where the rear room still quietly burned, a pall of smoke rising. The beat of the helicopter grew loud again as it closed with them once more. Down the radio the Sergeant frantically called in a raised whisper,

'Nine nine…stay away, stay clear'. Instantly the helicopter pitched to its right and powered away. The distant crowd fell totally silent.

'There is no hope, there is no tomorrow. They took it away.'

His left arm was around the boy's waist clamping him close, his sinewy forearm a litany of tattoos. With his right Richards allowed the shotgun to drop and hang from a sling on his shoulder. He reached into his belt and drew the pistol. Colours sensed what was next and stood up, calling loud and forceful. 'No Samuel, no. Let the boy live. *For God's sake no.*'

Sally felt herself sobbing and yet it was remote, as if it were another's voice. She could see only the child and his dark innocent eyes, lost and terrified. Her mind blanked out all else. Cravetts took careful aim through the carbines ringed sights. Gilhooley shifted a little to perfect his sight picture around the brick pillar as his target began to shuffle slowly forward. In his ear piece Cravetts desperate voice whispered.

'Kieran I'm losing him. There's a car in the way and he's moving behind it.'

They watched in horror as the pistol rose until it touched the back of the boy's head, it's ugly snout lost in the thick, black hair.

'This is my moment then.' From the garden his voice was a sob. Suspended in time he stood there, gleaming and blooded. He called loudly.

'Tell the old man I'll see him in hell.' Then he turned suddenly to face Colours.

Beads of sweat joined to form a sudden thick rivulet that ran instantly into Gilhooley's eyes, blinding him. A shocking concussion assailed all around him and a shell case struck his hand.

Then another bang. He blinked to clear his vision and saw the man stagger. He dropped the boy then turned toward them raising the pistol. There was another bang and yet one again and the man fell back.

Seated on the path his back against the wall, he seemed to fight for breath. The acrid smell of gun smoke filled an air that was suddenly silent again, until Colour's voice broke in loud and strong.

'Medics up...'

For a terrible moment no-one moved. The boy stood alone on a patch of scrub grass near a small tree. Behind him on the pathway sat his father, rasping breaths issuing from his lips. The pistol lay on the paving, loose in his grip. The footfalls of the para-medics grew louder and the boy began to cry, his arms held wide from his body. Behind him the house burned.

Barry Mankowitz was suddenly at Colour's shoulder. 'Come on boss,' he urged and they broke cover. With handguns drawn they closed with the figure, now so diminished against the wall. He made no move to resist, lifting his hand clear of the gun. At the gate his eyes met Colours's. In them a weight of ages lay, an awful, empty resignation. Beneath him a pool of blood began to spread, and bubbles of saliva flecked with crimson descended from the corner of his mouth.

Cravetts followed them through the gate, snatching up the child and carrying his sobbing form away. The Sergeant lifted the hand-gun clear, placing it on the grass, while the shotgun remained trapped beneath the bleeding man. With laboured words he began to speak.

'Hello Mr Barras.'

'Don't talk now,' Colours responded, the tone of his voice now kind.

'Better while I can sarge.'

A trickle off brighter red blood ran down and hung pendulous from his chin. He took short deeper breaths as the para-medics cut open the boiler suit, desperately seeking veins in his arms.

'The baby's downstairs, in the front room,' he whispered. 'Saria's up there.' He cast his eyes toward a front upper window.

'Don't let her burn...*please.*'

Behind Colours, Gilhooley's fearsome bulk stood with Chris Harding. Without bidding they strode toward the front door. As the medics tore the boiler suit away, bloodied areas surrounded holes in the white tee shirt below. One just below the right armpit, the other in his stomach just above the belt.

'There's more lower down,' he whispered ever fainter. He coughed shallowly, bringing more blood to his lips. 'Fucking awful grouping sarge.' Then his eyes rolled back and his breathing turned to a shallow pant. Colours looked into the face of the medic beside him, fighting to get lines and saline into the dying man. Softly the man shook his head.

A shadow relieved the sun's relentless heat and Colours turned. Sally Galloway stood above them, the carbine limp by her side and instantly Colours knew the shots had been hers. Her face was a mask of despair. Turning on his heels the Sergeant stood rapidly up from the path and sped her away. Within seconds the injured man was stretchered up and gone. Only the guns and the blood bore witness.

Gilhooley was at Colour's side, his arms filled with a crying, swaddled child. 'Baby's okay. Woman's upstairs, dead as a do-do.' Colours was beyond emotion as he called. 'Get the brigade up here now.' Together they walked back to the cars, where the young divisional Inspector waited. The smile was gone from his face as he nodded toward the desolate Asian man. 'I'll tell him now,' he said and turned away.

Colours nodded to Raffles and then turned to the sweating man in the passenger seat. 'I think you can stop writing now.'

THE RECKONING

The murky water lapped at their feet. High on the embankment above them the car creaked gently as it cooled. Above it again a canopy of plane trees threw shadows on the waterline. Couples ambled by, enjoying the evening air and a riverside walk. They stared quizzically at the two policemen seated at the base of the concrete ramp that descended to the water's edge.

Few noticed the Glock pistols strapped to their waists. Small craft bobbed gently at anchor in the wake of a passing power boat, while inquisitive wildfowl closed with the two men, curious about the white paper cylinder that Barry Mankowitz was unwrapping.

'We used to come here a lot.' Colours broke the silence. 'When we were courting, you know, me and Beth. We used to drink in the Star and Garter over there. We would walk down here when I was in Putney section house.'

Mankowitz pealed the white and silver wrapping paper from the packet in his hands. 'Extra strong mints. Good for clearing your head after a long day.' Colours took one, prompting a large and inquisitive swan to become ever bolder. It waddled free of the water toward them, cursing and softly fluttering its wings. 'Cheers Barry. Give one to that stroppy bastard. He won't be so eager next time,' he said, a weak smile on his lips.

'It's not your fault. You did all you could. You can't put right half a lifetime's calamities in just one day, let alone a few moments,' said Mankowitz, throwing the white disc of a mint at the swan's feet. The bird greedily snatched its prize, shook it's head and threw the mint into the water, cursing in disgust. 'See, you're not the only one whose day's been a bucket of shit.' Mankowitz continued.

Colours sat with his elbows on his knees, tossing small pebbles into the shallows, as he inhaled sharply and then let out a long sad sigh. Beside him the Sergeant looked for a way to lift his morale. 'Look boss, nobody could have

29

foreseen all of that. He did it all on purpose. How could you know? The cooking oil, the ammunition, the replica. How *could* you know?'

Colours stood up and began to walk slowly along the water's edge, his height contrasting the seated figure of the Sergeant beside him. He folded his hands behind his back and spoke, a bitterness in his tone. 'I've seen all of this before, one way or another. You take an ordinary man, you mould him, sometimes beat him into a soldier. You teach him loyalty and fraternity. You give him skills and responsibility, give him some pride in himself.'

His voice was rising with emotion 'Then one day they just show him the gate, y'know...*just like that.*' He stopped suddenly and picked up a large stone. He turned and hurled it with uncharacteristic force across the water.

'When I joined this fucking job, we had to learn the Vagrancy Act of 1824. D'you know what one section dealt with? Begging, an offence of exposing wounds. These were the poor bastards that had just come home from Waterloo and the Peninsula war, crippled and on the streets. They were persecuted then, treated like scum. I reckon Kipling had it right!'

The Sergeant looked up and saw a boat crew that were launching beside them. They had seen and heard every word, but turned respectfully away. 'Back to the base now boss,' the Sergeant interrupted. 'Down the Barley Mow and a debrief for you.' Colours expression eased, slowly smiling. The smile broadened as he softly replied 'Sure thing mate.'

*

The locker room was quieter now than Gilhooley could remember, but still cruelly hot. He wrapped the white towel around his waist and turned toward the shower room. Arthur's naked and rotund form shuffled pendulous toward him, towelling himself as he approached, a pair of rubber sandals flapping beneath his feet with every step.

'How's the head Arthur?' Gilhooley asked. Arthur fingered the plaster on his forehead. 'Fine thanks mate, just a couple of stitches. It was worth it. The nurse that stitched me up had a magnificent pair of tits, and she stuck 'em right in my face.' Gihooley listened as Arthur's cackling laughter echoed after him.

In the warm embracing steam, Fudge and Benny were washing off the soot and smoke of the day, their forms barely visible. Other anonymous shapes were lost in the fog. Cravetts outline faced a far corner, his head bowed in a torrent of hot water that plastered the thick, dark hair to his muscular body. The Star of David he wore swung gently from his neck, a conduit for a stream of water.

Fudge looked up. 'Hello Kieran. How's the girl?'

Gilhooley shrugged. 'Don't know mate. After the post incident procedure, welfare just whisked her away.'

Benny was listening intently. 'I think she did really well. If I had to deal with that on my first day, I might have freaked. Good shot too. If he hadn't of turned there wouldn't have been much of a chance.'

Gilhooley sighed. 'You know it was suicide don't you.' There was an ominous pause as Fudge and Benny stared at each other.

Out of the steam, Pikey's lank form emerged. 'Don't make no difference boys, does it? Dead's dead and that's it.'

'Take no notice of him,' ventured Benny, fearful of Gilhooley's response. Gilhooley threw his towel on to a slatted wooden bench and stepped into the shower, his bulk dominating. He allowed the soothing water to cascade over his head and bent neck.

'I'm just pleased to see you near soap and hot water, you smelly unsanitary bastard,' he responded, his breath throwing droplets from his lips.

Pikey paused, his face a mask of offence. 'You know how to hurt a girl, don't you big guy,' he replied passing close behind the huge Irishman. Then with one deft movement he reached out to the temperature control and span it to its coldest extreme. Gilhooley bellowed as the icy water struck his hot skin, and Pikey scampered off down the corridor leaving wet footprints on the faded brown lino. Benny retreated to a corner of the tiled room, muttering to Fudge, 'Oh fuck! There'll be tears before supper. Mark my words.'

*

The huge green steel gates impacted noisily with the walls of the old building. Colours pinned them back until his Sergeant had piloted the car through. Soon they were climbing the stairs again laden with kit at the end of a very long day. The guns slept in the armoury, and the responsibility was behind them, just for a while. The relief's favourite pub was calling.

Colours stared for a moment at the precious photographs, taped to the inside of his locker door. Beth's face smiled back at him from the deck of their boat. Dark hair framed her face, and flicked up at the jaw line. 'Pretty,' he thought. 'Classy and pretty. Much too pretty for me.'

He remembered the last time he had seen her, flitting naked from the shower, the smallest of towels clasped to her breast. He remembered the last time they made love. How he had floated away in the soft warm fantasy of her body, and he smiled. It was a warm, private, and intimate smile.

Below Beth was taped another photo. A tangle of arms and legs. Six belonged to his young daughters. The other four to a brown and white bulldog. Next to the photo were scribbled notes in a child's handwriting. He smiled again at their happiness, remembering the day of the great summer barbecue. Their faces looked back at him and he longed to see them.

The squashed face of the bulldog also looked up at him with a silly kind of canine grin. 'Stuka, you smelly old bastard,' he whispered to himself. He flicked open his mobile phone. Moments later he heard his wife's voice. 'Why can't you come home?' Her voice had a laughter in it. 'You should have been here hours ago.'

'I can't, not yet sweetheart' he replied. 'There's been a shooting and I must spend a little time with the boys.'

She heaved a great sigh into the receiver. 'The boys, the boys, always the boys! I think you're married to them, sometimes I think they're your real family.' The laughter in her tone had gone. 'Watch the news,' said Colours gently. 'It'll be on there. I'll be home in a couple of hours.' There was a silence.

'Okay' she said suddenly. 'I'll tell the girls.'

He wanted to be with them at that very moment, to be home with his family. Then the words of an old friend relating time-served wisdom and long since retired came back to him. 'You sort of have a second family now.'

*

As the door to the Inspector's locker room swung closed, Barry Mankowitz was already on the landing, waiting. Even in his own clothes, there was still a crispness to his appearance. With an exchange of smiles they began to descend the staircase. Mankowitz's voice competed with the echo of their footfalls and the squeak of their shoes on stair treads polished with years of use.

'There's a memo in my tray that's worth noting,' he began. 'Apparently a maverick group of Middle-Eastern origin is infiltrating some of the criminal elements in the southern counties, using crime to create funds.'

'SO13 don't yet know why, but they fear it's a prelude to some new campaign. There was an armed robbery of a bookmakers in Balham. One of the staff came from a Muslim background. He identified some conversation between two of the robbers as Saudi Arabic language or dialect. I wonder what this will mean?'

Colours took a breath, his brow creasing as he replied. 'In this current climate who knows what's next. But it's trouble in the making I'm sure. It sounds like the I.R.A. tactic of using crime to create funds. Okay until someone gets greedy.' His reply was cut short as their footfalls became confused with another sound, a voice. 'What was that?' said Colours as he stopped in his tracks, seeking silence.

Distantly Pikey's voice could be heard. 'I can't understand him, but I think he's in some kind of trouble,' replied the Sergeant. They turned and ran back past the first landing, and on again to the very top of the building. Colours pushed open the green wooden door to the Constable's locker room, where they both fell victim to helpless laughter.

Pikey was sitting on the floor near the fire exit. His face was etched with black felt tip pen in the shape of a full beard and moustache. Both hands were secured by handcuffs to the lower feed pipe of a heating radiator. He had a pair of grubby underpants pushed down tightly on his head. Otherwise, he wore no clothes at all.

'Gilhooley sir,' muttered Pikey. 'I upset him'. 'Why the underpants on the head then Pikey?' said Colours.

Pikey shrugged. 'He said he didn't want me to feel naked.'

*

The two men crossed the road, dodging through the city traffic, along a footway until the pub was in sight. Outside were tables thronged with drinkers, driven by the incessant heat. Loud voices and laughter filled the air, at odds with Colours preoccupied mind. Mankowitz pushed through the crowd ahead of him and they passed into the main bar, its fabric historically patinated a kind of beige by countless drinkers and innumerable cigarettes.

The spotlights over the bar highlighted the haze. City whiz kids occupied every stool, sweating into pin stripe shirts, jackets abandoned everywhere. In the far corner, laying siege to a huge wooden table the relief gathered, laughing and drinking in the face of the trauma of the day.

Colours thrust paper money into the pint mug on the table, lifting the reserve by twenty pounds. Gilhooley rose from his seat, swaying slightly and spilling the pint of Guinness over his hand. 'Always there for the boys aintcha boss,' he began, a glassiness in his bloodshot eyes. 'You ain't always right,' he went on, his brogue deepening, just a little slurred. Then leaning heavily on the table he spoke again, his face inches from Colours 'But you ain't often wrong.'

Barry Mankowitz stepped forward as if to intervene, but Colours caught his eye, gently shaking his head. Benny reached up grabbed the big Irishman's shoulder, only the alcohol allowing him the edge. Gilhooley slumped back on to the corner of the bench, falling silent and reflective.

Through the door Pikey's ranging form appeared. Above the old tee shirt he wore, his face was shadowed blue and grey, remnants of the marker pen still visible. Low laughter ran through the group. 'Hey Pikey,' struck up Fudge. 'I hear you wear your underpants on your head, is that because you always talk out of your arse?' Fearful of further retribution Pikey merely muttered 'Okay, very funny.'

Gilhooley raised his eyes 'I'll get this one,' he said, thrusting his hands into his pockets 'as you're such a good sport.' Pikey smiled. 'Fair enough Kieran.' He stared intently into Gilhooley's face. 'Christ, your eyes, they look like piss holes in the snow.' A sudden silence fell that held them all, while Pikey stood uncomprehending, bewildered by the stunned silence that befell the group.

Cravetts stood suddenly at the bar, pushing a city suit to one side, the man's impotent displeasure plain. 'Landlord, drinks for my men, the guvnor's paying,' he said, looking for a way to break the spell. There was a sudden clamour as the glasses were recovered, drinks ordered. Only Gilhooley remained unmoved. Colours caught Cravetts eyes. 'What?' he said, closing with the sallow skinned teetotal man.

'He feels bad sir, about the shooting. He feels he should have taken the shot, not the girl.' Cravetts said quietly.

Colours sighed deeply, but did not speak. Cravetts went on. 'The shot wasn't on for him any more than me. I had a car in the way, Kieran was blinded.' The pitch of his voice was rising as Colours gripped his arm. '*I know,*' he quietly confided. 'You all did right, but this is for tomorrow. Right now you're doing enough.' Cravetts sighed and then smiled weakly. 'He's right by the way…you're a good man boss.' Then he melted into the crowd.

'Always the same isn't it Roy,' said Mankowitz gently.

Colours nodded and replied 'But tomorrow is another day. Let them stick together tonight and cry in each other's beer. Like my ol' man used to say… '*Manyana.*'

*

34

'Oh, the boy's gifted,' croaked Benny, rubbing the back of his head and wincing with pain. The maps lay on the floor at his feet where they had fallen moments before as his head had impacted on the window frame. Ahead of him the man span the steering wheel through his hands, drifting the heavy car through a roundabout. The engine note hardened as the pace rose higher.

In the front passenger seat Arthur braced himself against the dashboard, while with his free hand he barked into the radio, 'MP from Trojan 521, re your CAD 3841 to the petrol station, rear of City Limits, Juliet Lima section, an armed robbery, we are one minute away.' He was competing with all the road noise, the howl of the siren. The nose of the car lifted as it accelerated along the motorcyclist's 'Mad mile', a long stretch of road before their destination. Green forestry passed in a blur.

Over the radio a voice intruded. 'MP from Juliet Lima two. On scene at City Limits, all seems quiet. Tell the Trojan unit not to break their necks.'
'Fucking typical,' raged Arthur from the operator's seat. Picking up the handset his gruff voice contributed again to the mass of radio traffic. 'MP from Trojan 521, message received. Please ask the local unit to standby at the scene.' He turned his head toward Chris Harding. The tension etched on the man's face momentarily eased Arthur's anger. 'Nice drive young man.'

Arthur smiled as the lines on Harding's face softened, his tension eased. The need to favourably impress the 'old sweats' was huge for him.

He turned to Benny, who was still grimacing with pain. 'Good drive Benny, don't you think?' and he winked.

Rubbing the back of his head again, the 'maps man' responded. 'Superlative, fucking superlative.'

The ARV swung on to the garage forecourt where the local police van driver stood beaming by his vehicle, a young girl sat in the passenger seat, the door open. The bright markings along the van's sides at odds with her dark uniform, making her fresh face seem ever more pale.

Barely had the car stopped as Arthur's rotund form rolled out of the passenger door, resolve and anger in fragile containment. Other local cars swarmed in, uniformed police officers flooding into the garage foyer. Inside an animated young Indian man gestured wildly.

'Nothing for you boys,' grinned the van driver, his hatless form made more irreverent by the open jacket. Gripping a pair of black driving gloves in his left hand, he went on triumphantly. 'Suspects decamped, local units on scene and dealing.'

35

'Watch this Chris,' whispered Benny from the back seat, 'this is going to be a classic.'

Arthur rounded on the van driver. He had sauntered up to the ARV and was now sitting on the bonnet, his ankles crossed. 'I thought you ARV blokes were the bollocks?' he mocked, sarcasm etched on his face, in his voice. 'My granny...' He went on, but Arthur cut him short. He placed his hands palm down on the bonnet, either side of the van driver and lent forward until their noses touched. The man was forced back into an uncomfortable retreat.

'You total fucking knob,' Arthur began. 'Do you think we scream half way across London to help you, so that you can sprint a couple of miles to show off to that little bit of fanny.' In the car Benny smiled, his gold tooth flashing...'Oh I wish I had a camera.'

'Now hold on,' began the driver but Arthur would not be deflected. 'It's okay for you to sniff round her knickers and show off to the probationers sonny, but out here in the real world people get killed, *fucking shot*. The next armed robbery you get to first I hope they are still here and you're first through the door, 'cos I wouldn't want you to get that pretty little thing snuffed out on account of your stupidity.' His face reddened, contorted as his anger reached a tumult. 'But if you do get shot I hope I'm first through the door after you. Then I can ignore the first aid issue and piss all over you. *Now get off my fucking car.*'

Local officers stood by at a respectful distance, some hardly able to conceal their mirth. Arthur dropped like stone into his seat. From the back seat Benny expression rivalled a Cheshire cat. 'A virtuoso performance I thought. Would you agree Chris?' Outside the car and red faced, the local officer turned swiftly toward his van.

The young man smiled broadly as he started the car's engine and piloted it away through assembled vehicles. 'I would say world class. For me it was look and learn.' The two men laughed out loud as the trees and forested hedgerows sped by. Arthur raised his eyes from the log where he scribbled furiously. Then he muttered. 'Take me to Lippitts, you pair of bleeding monkeys.'

Chris Harding negotiated another roundabout and turned swiftly left into the tangle of Epping Forest. Soon they were climbing the hill toward the Met's firearm training camp. The barrier lifted as they approached and they passed through between high wire fences.

'I wonder why he always looks so pissed off?' joked Benny, nodding toward the carved concrete figure of the seated man that presided over the entrance. Arthur gestured toward the pub that sat comfortably atop the hill across the road.

'If you had sat staring at a pub from the outside for sixty years, and never got a drink, how would you feel?'

*

Colours winced as the guns crashed. As he walked in through the doors at the rear of the 'A' range, he grabbed at his ear defenders and rapidly clamped them to the sides of his head. The smell of gun smoke filled his nostrils while the voices of the instructors became a blur, his brain trying to separate them from the whistling sounds that invaded his ears. He watched as the detail of officers ran through strict drills. When the firing withered away, and the process of unloading the weapons and making them safe went on, he cautiously removed his earmuffs and approached the range supervisor.

'Show clear to your instructors and then go forward and check targets,' barked the man in a voice accustomed to command. He turned toward Colours. The instructor bore a Sergeants epaulettes on his shoulders, the light blue woven insignia contrasting the dark blue of his shirt and that of the beret he wore. He thrust a hand toward Colours and they shook as old friends. 'Got some of yours for a back to ops shoot on next. I suppose that's why you're here?'

Colours dropped his gaze and then, looked again into the man's eyes. 'Guess I'm a little concerned Paul. Mostly it's about Sally Galloway.' The Sergeant sucked on his teeth for a moment.

'There's bugger all you can do now. Welfare have been all over her. She's had a week's special leave and been away I hear. I guess you've not had much contact.'

Colours sighed. 'None. It's not my way Paul, you know it's not. But because it's happened to a girl and all on her first day they have gone overboard. The relief wanted to close ranks with her, but the establishment have steam-rollered everything. The media's chasing and I'm worried about the effect. They say she's tough, but you and I know that tough is a house of cards.'

The Sergeant turned toward the range. The shouts of 'clear' had faded away and six overall-clad men and attendant instructors were distantly examining targets. 'We are going to break now.' He had turned again toward Colours and was stroking a greying goatee beard. 'She's in the ARV classroom. Go and see her if you like. The girl from welfare is there with some woman Inspector. Don't let Seagull know I told you where she was. He's making as much personal mileage out of this as he can. I think he wants to adopt her.'

'Thanks,' Colours smiled. He turned sharply and exited through the back of the range, through the cleaning area and past a mass of stacked and prepared targets into the sun. He squinted in the bright light, feeling the sudden heat. As his eyes adjusted he saw Mankowitz's crisp outline approaching along the narrow path that led back to the main accommodation, canteen and car parks.

'What's happening boss?' quizzed the Sergeant. The two men stopped, confronting each other. Colours paused, gazing for a moment skywards. 'Seagull, that's what's happening.' They turned and walked to where the girl should be. '*Seagull,*' Mankowitz almost spat out the words. 'Seagull of all people. Great…just fucking great…!'

*

The sweat stung Sally's eyelids. It ran in little rivers down her face, burning the creases in her lids. She tasted the salt on her lips. Her blue tee shirt had turned almost black with wetness and clung to her torso like a glistening second skin. Only the sound of her own breath, the padding of her own footfalls broke the silence. It had always worked for her before, her exercise therapy. No matter how bad things had got she could sweat it off, lose herself, but not this time.

'The loop' was not enough. It was the standard early morning run from Lippitts Hill, but Sally wanted something more, something to exhaust her, to drain her and demand everything. Then perhaps also this feeling would be expelled. She had run through woodland and over roads until she was spent.

As she emerged from the woodland and her feet found the asphalt, the sight of the ARV ahead of her with Chris, Benny and Arthur aboard passing through the gates made it all once more so real. The knot in her stomach tightened.

Her legs became disobedient and remote as she walked trembling through the gates, past the concrete figure and on toward the shower block, looking down at her feet, not wanting human contact.

As she passed the classroom door, she could see Seredmigni drawing heavily on yet another illicit cigarette, the smoke offending her open lungs. He talked and gestured toward a uniformed woman Inspector. Sally slipped by toward the shower room when the slim figure of another woman joined her from the entrance behind. The woman was wearing shorts and a camouflage vest and sweating heavily. Across her chest was a regimental insignia. The woman pressed a finger against her lips, inviting silence and nodding toward where Seredemigni lurked. Then she gestured onward.

The changing area was empty, save for the two women. There was an awkward moment of silence, and then the woman spoke.

'You run hard and fast.' She was younger than Sally had at first thought, and looked quite toned. The woman began again. 'I like to run two or three times a week, get to the gym when I can. You know, keep things going.' Sally smiled and pulled a towel from her locker, but she did not speak. Inside her the knot in her stomach had control, like a grip of iron.

'I'm sorry, I'm intruding.' She turned away and opened a sports bag. From inside she pulled a large white towel and draped it across the bench. She pulled the sodden tee shirt over her head, released the clasp at her waist and allowed the shorts to fall. Then she walked naked into the communal shower, jets assailing her from all sides. Sally listened to the hiss of the water, watched the steam rise and then undressed and followed.

'I don't mean to be rude,' began Sally. The woman's skin shone in the subdued light, glistening water defining her fit body. 'It's just that I have rather a lot on my mind.' She turned and faced the wall, the jets of water cascading over her face, hiding the tears that she could now safely and unseen shed. Quietly, the sound almost lost to the hissing water, the woman replied,

'I know Sally, I know. That's why I'm here.'

*

Colours and Barry Mankowitz strode along the path behind the bungalow like offices, across the car park and toward the complex of ancient wooden huts that were the canteen and classrooms. A white Vauxhall Omega slowed beside them and the passenger window slid down to reveal Arthur's craggy face. 'I gave a bit of tactical advice to a local PC just now sir. I think you might expect a phone call.'

Colours knew exactly what that meant. 'As always Arthur, *thank you*,' Colours responded as the car sped off toward the canteen and Arthur smiled sheepishly through the glass. 'As if I didn't have enough to think about,' he confided to the Sergeant walking beside him, their footfalls exactly matched.

As the canteen appeared on their right Colours spoke again. 'Get a shit load of coffees will you mate, this could be a long morning.' The Sergeant nodded and peeled off to the right, while Colours turned left toward the classroom where Sally Galloway should have been waiting. He felt his stomach tighten, his mouth dry. These things were never easy, and this for many reasons was so much worse.

The water made it too easy to cry. They sat side by side with their backs to the cool tiled wall, allowing the hot water to cascade over them, the steam seeming to distance reality. 'Clarissa Waters,' the woman confided, cupping her hand over her eyes against the incessant flow. 'I never forgave my parents for that name,' She smiled softly. 'Everybody calls me Charlie.'

Desperate for connection, but slow to lower her guard, Sally responded. 'Who are you? Why are you here?' The woman paused, then spoke again. 'I'm from occupational health…welfare if you like. It seemed like a good way to meet. I had planned to train here anyway, but then I couldn't catch you,' she smiled once more 'You were too fast.' Sally relaxed a little as the woman continued.

'I was in the army, the medical corps before this. I have some qualifications in human affairs and quite a wide experience in dealing with PTSD. I saw a lot of the boys that came back from the Gulf. When I came to the Met, they saw me as perfect for Post Firearm Incident Intervention. So here I am.' There was a long silence while the seated women stared blankly into the steam, their chins perched upon their raised and folded knees, their heels tucked back.

'I didn't realise what it would be like,' Sally's composure finally broke. 'I didn't realise how terrible I would feel. I killed someone, I watched him die. His child stared at me as his father died and I did it, me. I don't think I can ever forget it.'

The older woman extended her hand and placed it on Sally's where it lay curled around her ankle. 'Look at us. No clothes, no rank, no pretence. No men, no people and no eyes to see us. You cry as hard as you like and no-one will know. When you are ready and only when you're ready, we'll go out and face the world.'

The younger woman rolled to her right until her head fell on the other's shoulder. Quietly she began to cry and then to sob as her tears were lost in the torrent of water, her emotion misted into the thickening steam.

*

The stale smell of cigarette smoke betrayed the man's habit. Though he enforced so many rules at the expense of others, he would break them if it suited. As Colours drew close to the classroom these thoughts burned bright in his mind. He hated Seredemigni with a passion. He clenched his teeth so hard the muscle at his jaw convulsed. A sudden tug at his sleeve broke his thoughts.

Barry Mankowitz appeared at his elbow, a steaming tray of hot coffees balanced precariously on a blue clipboard. He wagged a finger at Colours. 'Penny for your thoughts,' he said wryly, and then more sternly 'Hey boss…Be a cool dude, *okay!*' Colours stood motionless for a moment, breathing hard through his nostrils like a sweating horse.

The intense breathing levelled as he collected himself. The Sergeant smiled, nodding his approval. Inside the classroom Seredmigni's toneless voice could be heard through the half open door. 'She's asked to use a gun again. It's a bit unusual so early on, but I agreed.'

Colours paused, glancing at the Sergeant. The woman Inspector responded in a shrill voice. 'You know best sir; it's your department. I'm sure she'll be fine and it'll be months at least before she is operational again.' Mankowitz curled his lip and then silently mouthed 'Bag carrier.' Colours nodded. Then he took another breath and walked in.

'Ah! Mr Barras,' Seredemigni shifted uncomfortably on his feet. 'This is Inspector Bland. She is here on attachment from the DPG.' He gestured toward a portly woman in uniform. She smiled toward Colours, a bundle of papers wrapped in a file cover was lodged firmly under her arm. *Bag carrier…* the words flashed through his mind as he smiled back. 'This is my Sergeant, Barry Mankowitz,' he responded. They shook hands.

'Where's Sally?' Colours asked. 'I understood she was here.' Seredemigni glowered 'So the drums are beating,' the annoyance in his voice palpable. 'No big secret is it sir?' replied Colours, subtly provoking his adversary. 'My boys saw her around earlier, said she might be here.'

A formality entered Seredemigni's voice as he retreated behind his rank. 'PC Galloway has been through the post incident procedures. She has asked go back on the range. I have agreed.' An uncomfortable silence descended. Colours turned and walked to the window, struggling to measure his words, searching for the right response.

'I've always been close to my relief,' he said, staring blankly through the misted glass at the crew that fussed around an ARV parked in front of the canteen. 'I've supported them wherever I could. I want to do the same for Sally… PC Galloway, but I feel I've been excluded.' He turned suddenly on his heels, staring Seredemigni in the eye. 'I wouldn't want her to become a pawn in anyone's game.'

The woman Inspector grew flustered. She excused herself and left, brushing past Barry Mankowitz. The Sergeant sought to catch Colour's eye, to plead silently with him for caution, but he knew it was futile.

'It seems like we have been here before, Mr Seredemigni. I care about the job I do, the people I work with. You care about you.'

Suddenly alone, Seredemigni fell momentarily quiet, sweat now staining his shirt. He picked up a briefcase and walked to the door. 'I will act in the best interests of the service and PC Galloway. I shall also ask to see the Commander today. I don't have to tolerate your behaviour. Don't leave the camp until you hear from me again. Is that clear?' Colours almost spat out his reply. 'Perfectly. That's the whole thing, I understand you perfectly.'

'So how do you think that went?' Colours looked toward the Sergeant, a half smile lurking in the corners of his mouth. Mankowitz raised an eyebrow. 'Frank' he said... 'It's good to have a frank, honest exchange. Delicate? he mused 'I don't think that applied.'

*

Gilhooley towered above them all, the gun looking as if it were a toy in his hands. Cravetts tipped a box of ammunition on to the top of a steel cabinet and the loose rounds rattled on the surface. Only the metallic sounds of the guns, the clicking of bullet after bullet being pressed home into the magazines intruded into the relative quiet.

'This is a ten round shoot,' began the same Sergeant instructor. 'Go forward to your point.' He paused to look down at the diminutive figure of the girl. She was seated on a bench, staring blankly ahead. The instructor stepped closer then sat beside her. His words were for her alone. 'You can wait as long as you like. Doesn't have to be today?'

Sally turned her head and sighed deeply. 'I want to know, *I have to know*. Sooner or later I will find myself here. Please...let's get this done.'

He placed a hand on her shoulder and taking a deep breath said, simply... 'okay'.

Through the partition at the back of the range, Colours hovered watching every move, every emotion. He caught the instructor's eye. The man's forehead creased with concern. Colours nodded, mouthing 'Okay Paul' through the grubby glass.

'This is a ten round supported shoot at twenty-five metres. One shot to be fired on each three-second exposure of the target. The first will be a trial exposure. *Do not shoot*,' Behind Colours stood his Sergeant, while behind them both again stood unnoticed the slim form of a woman. She slipped quietly into the shadows and waited.

The instructor's voice boomed again, louder now. 'Muffs and glasses, and with a magazine of ten rounds, *load*.' Across the line of overall clad figures the click of the magazines locking into the guns resounded.

Gilhooley presided over the far left of the range, his size reduced to the eye again by the huge block wall that flanked him. Between him and Sally Galloway, stood Cravetts, his eyes hardened with concentration. Each stood close to a tall wooden pillar, designed to support their aim. Sally leant gently against hers, knowing that if not with their eyes, with their minds, every one was watching her. To their rear the instructor paced, noting every move.

He began again. 'Make ready.' In unison the three struck the actions of the MP5 carbines forward, checking that the port was closed and that the first round had fed. 'Come up into the aim.' All three raised the weapons, picking up on the point where the target would present, each thumbing the selector lever to 'fire.'

In Sally's head she repeated to herself again and again. 'Target blurred, foresight clear.' Lightly she felt for the trigger. In her stomach the knot tightened. Her breathing was laboured and she began to sweat. She could sense Cravett's muscular form next to her. His body arched and braced, his mind focussed. A feeling of loss swept through her.

Behind the glass Colours fretted, watching her body language and sensing her rising angst. 'Concentrate, concentrate,' he found himself uttering. Above all else the instructor gave his final command, loud, defining the moment. '*Watch...and shoot.*'

The targets turned first once and then once again, a loud clang emitting each time they faced forward. At that same instant she felt a concussion that shocked her. A shell case from Cravetts's gun struck her hand. Twice more the targets turned, a volley of fire splitting the air to greet them until the instructor's voice loudly intervened. 'End ex. Live round unload.'

She sank to the floor, the loaded and un-fired weapon cradled across her folded legs. Gilhooley and Cravetts removed their magazines, racked the weapons to shouts of 'clear.' All at once Colours was there, kneeling at her side. He took the carbine from her hands, removed the magazine and ejected the live round, making the weapon safe.

Behind them the instructor's voice again, controlling it all. 'Line is clear.' Silently he ushered Gilhooley and Cravetts out through the back of the range. Colours sat crossed legged beside the saddened, diminished figure. 'So that's it then.' Staring at the ground she spoke in barely a whisper. 'It's over.'

Colours searched for the right words. 'Give yourself a chance. Wait a few weeks and come back again.' She smiled weakly. 'Hair of the dog, that's what our nice Chief Superintendent called it.' Colours felt the hot flush of anger. 'Well I thought it too soon, but it wasn't my call.' She raised her head and turned to look at him, eye to eye.

'It's not to soon Mr Barras, it's too late. I'm not just leaving the department, I'm leaving the job.' Colours took a sharp, deep breath. 'Sally, don't be so hasty,' but she placed a finger on his lips, silencing him. 'Some things you know in your heart Mr Barras. For me it's over. I can't live this life. Thanks for your concern. Your heart's in the right place, but my head isn't.'

She stood up and turned toward the rear of the range. Looking back she pointed at the carbine, lying impotent on the ground. 'I'll leave that to you, if I may?' Then she walked to where the woman quietly waited in the shadows, and faded from view. Barry Mankowitz appeared at his side as Colours rose to his feet, gun in hand. He placed a hand on the Inspectors shoulder. 'Fuck it, fuck it all,' sighed Colours.

*

'I'm glad it's over Charlie,' said Sally, squinting in the strong sunlight. The two women walked slowly along the path toward the bungalow. The older woman stopped, holding the younger one's gaze.

'It's a big decision to make in just a moment Sally, don't you feel you should think on this.'

'I have,' responded Sally 'I just needed to do this one thing to settle my mind, and now it is settled.'

'What will you do,' asked Charlie.

'My parents have a holiday home in Jersey. I've a qualification as a fitness instructor, so I guess I will go there and find myself something.' She broke her conversation at the sight of Gilhooley emerging downcast into the sunlight from the concrete portals of the range.

'Excuse me for a minute. There's something I've got to do.' Sally turned and walked swiftly back toward the big Irishman, not waiting for a reply. The older woman paused, reflecting on the events of the day. Then quietly to herself she said,

That'll be two of us then.

Colours turned to the Sergeant instructor. 'I guess there's a double problem here. Gilhooley feels guilty about all this. He's beating himself up when there's no point. There was nothing he could do Paul.'

The two men watched as Gilhooley's presence dominated the three men exiting the range, while Cravetts and Mankowitz sought to console him. 'Let him be,' responded the instructor. 'These things have a way of sorting themselves out,' he said, seeing the concern in Colours eyes.

'Hey big guy, show a girl a good time?' Sally stood in Gilhooley's path. The flippancy in her voice evaporated as his eyes betrayed all that was behind them. She took his hand, slipping her small fingers between his and led him away, leaving the other two men to their bemused thoughts.

Colours's mobile phone interrupted his reflective mood. 'Yes, Christ that was quick. I'll be there shortly.' He swung on his heels toward the exit. 'Seagull wasted no time. The Commander's here. He wants to see me.'

The helicopter powered in above them. It turned and descended, the whistle of its engines declining in pitch, the beat of the rotors fading away. They sat on a raised grassy bank above the heliport that higher and wide of the firearms facility giving it almost an air of seniority. Fields fell away before them down to the huge reservoirs below and distantly, London's skyline.

'You've got to believe me Kieran,' began Sally. 'There was nothing you could do, and whatever I feel or do now, you had no part in.' The big man took a breath to speak, but Sally spoke first. 'No, there's no argument and I know you are going to present one. I got myself into this. I thought I was tough, but I'm not. Not tough enough. Not like you anyway.'

She stood up, smiling now at the man's creased expression. 'You're good at your job Kieran, and you're a good man. Don't lose sight of that. Do just this for me, stay that way.' She kissed him lightly on the forehead, stood and turned away. 'Let me give you a lift at least,' he called. She turned back to face him. 'It's a lovely day for a walk in the forest. I walked into this job with my eyes open. Now I'm going to walk out.' Then she was gone.

'Damn you Barras.' The Commander sat across the desk. He was a stocky man with bushy eyebrows and a ruddy face. 'You could at least try to be diplomatic.' Colours felt as if he had been transported back through time. Here he was standing in a wooden building receiving a 'bollocking' from a senior officer. The urge to stand to attention was almost irresistible. Even so 'stand easy' was still in his demeanour.

The Commander stood up. 'Lost for words Barras? Not like you. What have you got to say? Come on, bullshit me or I'll think you've lost the will to live.' He took off his cap and gestured for Colours to close the door. 'Sit down,' he added firmly. 'You've a habit of breaking every protocol,' he went on. 'How you qualified as a tactical advisor and a hostage negotiator escapes me. You rarely negotiate, and career wise, your tactics are appalling.'

'Sorry sir,' began Colours 'but I couldn't stand by and let him destroy a good team, use the department for his own ends without protest.'

The Commander raised his hand, stopping Colours mid-flow 'So you thought throwing a couple of fucks into a vastly senior officer was a diplomatic thing to do, did you?' There was a deathly pause while the Commander walked to the window, staring toward the gate.

'You see that stupid bastard out there, Barras?' he went on, pointing toward the concrete figure. 'Well he's been sitting there thinking for more than sixty years. He thinks too much, you don't think enough.'

Colours felt himself flush. 'Sir, I said I was sorry but I stand ...'

'*No Mister Bladen bloody Barras, you have said enough.*'

The Commander's tone was raised. 'Perhaps a little posting to the DPG would be the way to get you to be *Diplomatic.*' The thought of losing his relief and his involvement appalled him and he began to rise to his feet. 'But then you would probably provoke an international row.'

The senior man turned and walked back to his swivel chair, the steel in his eyes drawing Colours back into his. 'I'm not a fool and I'm not blind,' he continued, his tone now even. 'You apparently used the term *Hats off below decks* to Mr Seredemigni. Here's another Naval term. Privilege posting. It will be a privilege to post Mr Seredmigni with all his aspirations to Royalty protection. He's already cleared his desk. I don't like weasels either so come to me first next time, if there is ever a next time.'

He placed his hands palm down on the desk, and leant slightly forward, as if to confide. 'But don't get your claws out so quickly in future, or I'll cut you off at the knees. Now go and do your job.'

Lost for words Colours stood and walked to the door, managing only to say 'Thank you sir…for your support. Good day.' The Commander shuffled paper across his desk. 'Oh, piss off Barras.'

Colours stepped into the sunshine. Ahead of him he saw the girl walking out of the gates, resolute and alone. His mind dwelt on the events of the day. The seated concrete figure drew his gaze. Then the soft voice of another filtered into his consciousness, rolling back the years and touching his very soul.

'It's been a long time since you bought me lunch.' The woman's slim form stepped clear of the shadows.

'Oh my god!' exclaimed Colours…*Charlie.*'

*

The old woman seemed bent under some crushing weight, an age of suffering. Her once elegant hands now wrinkled with time, were clasped as she twisted them together in an agony of emotion, and small shafts of bright light from her bejewelled fingers lanced out to dance in dark places. Her face was barely visible behind the burqua, but through its narrow window, she suspiciously viewed the world, her eyes glistening with tears. Those eyes now reddened, flicked back and forth in unison with a barely perceptible rhythmic rocking of her whole form. From below the weathered lids they sought an answer. She looked out on a life that had betrayed her every hope, made a lie of her reason for living. Why was her family so riven with pain, with suffering?

But there was no answer. Since her skin had been young and smooth, her loins virgin and her mind open, it had been so. Men fought, governments clashed and manoeuvred. The voice of religion spoke loud of war and then of peace and yet the killing went on.

Now there was the sentence of age to be born, bending her limbs and fingers, dimming her eyes. Anger, sadness and vengeance were to be her companions. The gentle guiding hand she had extended to the children of this wealthy family while she had quietly, separately and alone brought up her own, was rewarded with despair.

Jahwara entered the garden almost reverently, casting the sandals from her feet so that no sound might intrude. She padded silently toward where the sad, diminished figure of her mother sat on the edge of a well-tended flowerbed, her pain and grief palpable as the old woman repeatedly caught her breath. The light reflected from the whitened paving up to highlight her grief, and the younger's

47

bare and beautiful face. She knelt before her mother and clasped the aged hands in her own, as if in prayer.

The morning sun shone in as if to lighten their darkness within the high garden walls, brightening the colours of the flowers and vines that filled the courtyard. Gently lifting the old woman's face, Jahwara spoke, her voice breaking. 'Sweetest Mother, why do you weep so? What can be so bad that you break your heart for all to see?'

The old woman didn't answer, but shook her head and swallowed hard on words she could not yet form. She drew her hands from between those of her daughter's and began to beat them with regular and rising force against her forehead until a small jewel that hung there drew a hint of blood, and Jahwara seized them again. The girl released the cloth from her mothers face and with a small handkerchief, began to softly dab the stains of tears now hinted pink, from her cheeks. Nearby the hiss of an electric door demanded her attention as intrusion threatened.

A short flight of marbled steps led up to glass doors that were flanked by tall pillars studded in gold mosaic and lavishly corniced. Beyond them a wide, galleried expanse of ornate and bordered marble flooring led to more glass partitions behind which staff fussed at desks and computer monitors flicked like distant alien eyes.

Between two further and equally ornate pillars a broad blue richly patterned carpet covered a staircase that suggested much greater opulence lay beyond sight, a stairway to another world where only the invited and the privileged might trespass, and the family to whom the old lady was 'Nanna' resided.

Jahwara's eyes fell on a tall white-robed figure his head covered and banded, his face bearded making the man appear almost biblical. His right hand clasped a telephone while the other a sheaf of paper. A smaller dark man in a belted khaki uniform attended him fussily, as whispered commands sent him scuttling toward the complex of glass-fronted offices.

The robed figure stepped quietly onto the paving and approached the two women with measured steps. He placed the telephone and papers on the low wall, dipped his head and lightly touched his brow. He gestured, opening his hand and un-curling his fingers, and spoke. 'Little sister, you comfort our mother in a time of great sadness. It is well you are here.' His voice though soft and controlled, carried a hint of menace and rang clear above the sound of distant traffic.

Jahwara's dark eyes hardened as with suspicion, she met those of her brother. 'What've you done Nasser, that brings such grief to this house?' He straightened, stretching his chin and jaw upward arrogantly. 'I have done nothing, but the fingers of the great Satan have reached us, even here.' He turned suddenly, working his jaw. His mouth curled cruelly downward at its edges as hatred infused his face.

'Our elder brother is dying. The Americans have bombed the desert camp. Many have died but Wahlid survives for now.' Nasser Medahwi turned sharply on his feet, staring at hills that rose to the eye far distant and above and beyond the enclosing garden walls. 'I shall fly to him. There will be a helicopter to take me to his side very soon.'

'It is always the same,' the heavily accented voice of the older woman intruded as she was driven to her feet. 'Now you come to tell me that my first born son is dying. You who embrace war and hatred as a closer ally than your own blood.' Her voice rose louder, cracking as it did. She began to shake, her extended hands and arms raised upward.

'It is the mothers that grieve, the women that suffer while men posture.' Nasser Medahwi's face contorted, sucking in his pock-marked cheeks. 'It is not for women to meddle in or understand these things. Be silent in your tears old Mother,' he said, his anger rising, but the old woman would not be deflected. 'I ask only for peace, but it can never be,' she continued. She turned to Jahwara. 'Wahlid had another family, did you know that?' she raged. 'When he was a young man he went to Iraq to use the skills he had learned, but the war with Iran meant that he was caught up and he fled for home.'

'Be silent,' Nasser demanded, but she turned to face him. 'I have been silent for many years, what good has that done? I have lost so much,' she sobbed. 'Now I must tell all. Before I die of my broken heart, Jahwara will know.' The young woman's face hung with disbelief, and she could find no words. As her brother stormed away, Jahwara listened to her mother's now tremulous voice.

'Your father died in war, his life wasted. He believed things that had no meaning and went to fight for them. He died in a rotting trench of disease. Then Iran was the great demon. Now Nasser preaches that America and the west are such, when American money supported them in the past. It all means nothing and now it claims my son, a different head but the same monster.' She clasped Jahwara's face between her hands.

'Wahlid had a woman in Iraq that bore him two children, a boy and a girl. They fled through the northern hills to find a better life. The Kurds hated Hussien and tried to help them. When he gassed the villages they died too. Hate begat hate, and now it consumes more flesh. Now you know it all. It has become your burden.

I wish to lay mine down, I wish now that age will soon claim me and I can rest.' Then kissing the girl's brow the old woman stood up and walked slowly away.

*

The power of the helicopter rotors died away curling snake-like rivers of loose dry sand at Nasser Medahwi's feet. He ducked low beneath the barely churning rotors and ran to the craft, dragging himself up through a side door and into the waiting seat. The small, dark and uniformed man that attended him threw a small soft case in at his feet and turned away. Medahwi seized it without acknowledgement. He clasped together a braided harness and locked the buckle with a metallic click.

As he placed the earphones about his head, a slim figure dressed in combat trousers and a grey hooded top appeared at the edge of his vision to drop in an opposing seat. He raised a hand in protest as the hood fell back to reveal Jahwara's defined features.

'The blood that is spilled is the same, yours and mine,' she began. 'That it flows in the brother's veins is no different, for it flows in me. Our brother is dying, our father is dead, our mother's heart is so wounded I fear she may die also. This day I stand with you. Do not try to deter me,'

He cast his eyes down again to the buckle, checking its security, then reached into the soft bag for his mobile phone. To Jahwara, he said nothing as the craft powered up, the rotors beat ever harder, but he did not lift his gaze.

*

The dressings could not cope. Through the window squares of bright sunlight played mischief on the crimson stained fabric lending it an unreality. Every clinical white dimension of this hospital room heightened the stark bloody redness. The dark stubble on the man's chin matched his curly hair, now matted and crushed against his scalp and contrasting his sallow skin. Here and there its surface was punctured, with some wounds sutured while others were left to bleed in the haste to battle for his life.

A network of plastic pipes fed blood and fluids into his remaining arm. The other was amputated below the shoulder. Both his legs had been destroyed in the explosions and were amputated. The left above the knee, the right below.

Through the thick glass Jahwara watched her eldest brother's life force diminishing. The team of doctors and nurses that surrounded him grew ever more intense in their activity, as above them the steady beep of the monitor descended into erratic function.

'Better he had died a warriors death in battle.' Nasser curled his lip as the words seeped through his clenched teeth. His dark eyes would not divert from the prone figure of his mortally wounded brother, whose lifeblood now seeped away. His jaw worked incessantly as he clenched it again and again, the muscle standing proud in scars, the product of childhood illness.

Jahwara turned her head, lifting to one side the respectful black cloth of the Hijab that now surrounded her face. In her piercing eyes the fire of deepest anger burned.

'He wasted his life Nasser, as you would waste yours. While you jeer and posture for the infidels they wipe you away like insects,' she said, her face contorted with emotion.

His mouth took on a terrible twist as he replied; yet he would not avert his gaze. 'Do not presume to judge me woman, she that stands aside, she that hurries for the scraps the Americans leave. You have no place, no pride and no voice here. Do not dare to speak so again.'

Beyond the glass the monitor began to beep ever louder, and the activity surrounding the dying man grew ever more feverish. For long moments the girl did not speak. The tears that she fought to hide welled up in the corners of her eyes, then sprang forth and down her flawless cheeks. Haltingly she found words that carried a force Nasser Medahwi could not ignore.

'When we were children Wahlid cared for me. He would protect and counsel me when to you I was nothing. Just a woman…worthless! When the men of our village would curse and abuse us, he would stand by me. It was your voice that led him to fight, your voice that encouraged him to join the intafada. Perhaps it is your voice that placed him in that training camp.'

'An honourable death? He has plotted and planned, but never lifted a weapon or fired a shot in combat. He lies dying and half a man. Where is his honour, where is your honour now?' Medahwi turned, seizing her wrist his fingers bit deep into the pale skin of her forearm. The anger in his gaze searing as he hissed through clenched teeth. Then he froze as the intermittent beep from the monitor became loud and constant, the pulse on its screen a constant and unbroken line.

Jahwara spoke. 'I do not fear you and I never will. But I will stand with you now for our brother.' Their eyes locked in a bond of hatred and anger. 'Promise me a revenge that will cleanse my soul and I will give it to you or even the foulest demon in payment. There is no price I will not pay, no depth I will not plumb.

51

Say it will be so.' Medahwi released his grip, stunned by her words. 'It will be so little princess. Our blooded fingers will touch their very hearts, then rip them out.'

He took her hand and strode to where the medical staff's frantic efforts inevitably dwindled about the dead and broken man.

Shock registered on their faces as their clinical masks fell away. Nasser Medahwi bent and kissed his brother's blooded brow. Then he thrust his right hand into the sodden dressings of a mutilated arm. Raising his blood stained hand he clasped it around hers, then pinned it to her cheek, cupping her face with his free hand.

'It will be so little sister. With our brother's blood I swear it will be so.' Then he turned and swept out of the room. Jahwara paused for moments, stroking the dead man's face.

Then slowly and softly she echoed *'It will be so...'*

TO CATCH THE WIND

'There was someone else,' she confided 'after you I mean.' It was serious for a while but it didn't work. We both wanted our own careers. This time it was a doctor. What do you think's worse, the creed of a professional soldier, or the Hippocratic oath?'

Colours thought he would remember how beautiful she was, but the memory was not enough. There was something different, something magic that had always captivated him. The wind blew lightly and her long hair, dark with a hint of red scattered across her face. She shook her head until her hair settled on her neck and tumbled onto her shoulders, shining with sunlight. A pit in his stomach opened deep and dark. Her perfume filled his nostrils, and the memory of her soft skin filled his mind.

'Did you tell him your real name?' Colours asked. Her eyes brightened and fixed his. 'I wondered how long that would take,' she said, tilting her head to one side. A smile slowly lit her face and the pit in his stomach deepened. 'Anyway, you can tell your doctor anything. Bound by confidentiality aren't they. Not like you soldier boys.'

Small laughter lines now creased the corners of her eyes, edged her mouth as she smiled. Yet even as she did so, the young girl who had stolen his soul decades ago was still there, sparkling bright. It was as if her smile took him back. His thoughts wandered. He saw her wet limbs splashing the shallows of a Cornish sea, tasted the sea salt on her skin, saw the wind toss that same hair.

'Remember the beach at Porthcurno?' He found himself saying. 'After you left, I used to think of you standing there in the shallows. That pub and the old woman who sat in the corner every night.'

'Mrs Guinness, that's what we called her, do you remember,' she replied. 'And the song?'

He paused for thought. 'What song?... *Oh yes!*'

She tilted her head again, but slowly now. 'You'd forgotten, hadn't you! Donovan...Catch the Wind'. She sighed gently. 'But we let it blow through our fingers, didn't we Roy?'

The spell was broken as the pager on his hip vibrated. 'It's Barry, my Sergeant. There's something happening. This is his discreet way of letting me know I'm wanted.' The weak smile on her face betrayed her disappointment. 'Back to earth I guess. Do you think they will wonder why we sneaked off like that?' Colours smiled back 'No, I'm their Inspector you're from occupational health. Truly cover from fire.'

She stood up, the deep wine-coloured trouser suit and cream open-neck blouse defining her slim form against the light. 'Do you conduct all your case conferences in the beer garden of The Owl?' she asked.

'No,' he replied, 'only the special, the *very* special ones.'

They crossed the road leaving the old pub behind, the distant backdrop of woodland falling away beyond it. The stark wire fences of the camp were a few paces away but a universe from the world they had for a few moments shared.

The tense figure of the Sergeant was profiled in the gateway. 'The shit's hit the fan boss. Armed robbery, car chase and now open country search somewhere near Elstree. Your kit's in Nine-nine, and they are ready to lift off.' Distantly the whine of helicopter rotors, the cough of its engines filtered down to them. She turned toward a black Saab convertible, holding the keys.

Colours thrust a card in her free hand. 'Phone me?'

A sadness clouded her features as he spoke. 'On the mobile?' He ran a few paces and looked back. 'Promise?' he called. She paused, and then nodded.

As the helicopter rose and banked to go north, he peered out and watched her car leaving the gates. As she faded from view and the earth sped beneath them, Mankowitz caught Colours's eye, lifting a quizzical eyebrow. 'What?' said Colours, '*What?*' and then simply...'Don't ask. Okay!'

The taste of the coffee still lingered in his mouth. The smell of kerosene grew stronger, but the perfume still lingered in his senses. It was real, it was her and it had happened, but now this was real also. Men with guns and his responsibilities, contingencies, possibilities, resources and plans flooded his thinking, blanketed his mind.

For now at least...

*

'For fuck's sake'. Pikey loosed an expletive as his head impacted with the roof. From the driving seat Raffles eloquent voice protested. 'Bloody speed bumps old boy. Take it up with Kings Cross and St Pancras local authority. For now please keep your hands inside the car at all times.' Curling his lip Pikey leaned forward and lightly clipped Raffles ear with his fingers.

In the front passenger seat, Fudge was straining his eyes, tipping the mobile phone in his hands left and right, struggling to read the screen. 'They're calling us!' shouted Raffles, his voice now diminished by the reverberating sound of the siren bouncing back from the walls of the tunnel. The radio transmission was lost in a welter of sounds, the tyres emitting garbled squealing noises as they were tortured by the ancient cobblestones.

'Trojan 531, Trojan 531. Can you give your ETA for CAD 4783 to Elstree, MP over.' The anxious radio operator was seeking to reassure unarmed police officers on the ground that soon they would be supported. 'MP from Trojan 531, running time from Kings Cross.' responded Fudge as another voice spoke on the airwaves. 'MP from Trojan 521, we are on the A406 North Circular Road, just crossing the junction with the A10. ETA 8 minutes, 521 over.'

The operator responded. 'All received 521, I will inform units on the ground. Latest update is that we have suspects decamped from a Rover motor vehicle into open country toward woodland. Local units are in close attendance.' Yet another voice broke in as Colours influence began to take effect.

'MP from India 99. We have Trojan 1 on board. He instructs that no unarmed units are to approach the suspects. Can we have an RVP and do I have a clear area to put the SO19 duty officer and his Sergeant down?' The operator paused 'Standby...' Moments passed, then the operator rattled off a map reference. 'Local duty officer will await your arrival. Roof marking Alpha Bravo. Unarmed units have been suitably advised. Dogs and paramedic ambulance on way.'

Back in the car Fudge fought to keep his seat, as he wrote in the log and answered the radios.

While Raffles fought with the wheel, Pikey answered an insistent mobile phone and all the while the attendant sounds of an ARV in full cry strove to dominate it all. 'Okay, Yes...Yes fine. If there is an SFO team downstairs, best you put them on stand by'. Even in the midst of all this he fell momentarily quiet. 'Jesus, I'm sorry to hear that. Thanks Jack.'

Sensing something bad, even beyond that which threatened them now, Fudge pivoted in his seat to catch Pikey's eye. 'So what is it?' he said, bracing himself against the dashboard.

'Sally Galloway,' began Pikey. 'She quit.' Fudge frowned. 'So that's what's on my mobile. What'll she do now? Back to the TSG I guess?' Pikey allowed his head to drop forward, and he frowned. 'No mate, she quit the job. Finish…finito.'

Despite all the noise outside, the three fell quiet. Then Raffles spoke again. 'Thought you didn't care?' he said to Pikey.

'Well I do' he responded. 'Actually, she was okay. *One of the boys.*'

*

Colours tried to re-orientate himself. The speed at which the helicopter could cover the ground always distorted his judgement. The observer spoke repeatedly through his headphones, exchanging information, but Colours thoughts were fixed upon the fields and woodlands below. Around them the perspex windows vibrated and drummed as the craft pitched nose downward and turned to descend. He could see the foliage yielding to the powerful downdraft. In the midst of all of this, words, lyrics, ran like a vivid thread through his mind. *'But I may as well try and catch the wind.'*

The Sergeant's fingers bit into his shoulder, and instantly his focus returned. He turned as he pointed down through the shuddering windows. Far below three men ran across a field of long grass and vaulted a stile gate. As he watched they broke into a run again, desperately seeking the cover of nearby woodland. 'They mustn't get in there,' he heard himself say. Then Mankowitz voice crackled loud through the headphones. 'Fucking hell guvnor!'

Colours watched the scene spiralling below them as the helicopter circled. The last of the three men on the ground dropped a black holdall. Then kneeling reached inside.

There was a puff of smoke and a flash. 'The bastard has a shotgun, he's firing at us.' The pilot veered sharply away as Colour's hand grasped his forearm. 'Get us down. *Get us down now.*'

*

'Good job that woman from occupational health picked her up,' began Gilhooley. 'I didn't like her just walking away like that. I didn't know what to say, what to do.' Cravetts thoughts were elsewhere. 'Okay Kieran, but right now I need to know where we are exactly.' As the news that a deployment was occurring had reached them, Cravetts and Gilhooley had abandoned the range weapons to the staff. They had seized the BMW estate abandoned by Colours and Mankowitz, and were now closing with Elstree.

'Left, left,' Gilhooley called, as Cravetts piloted the BMW into a narrow access. The car bumped and ground upon a surface that had once been churned mud and was now baked into a rutted track. 'There!' He pointed to where the helicopter circled high above. Like a bird of prey it wheeled, as if waiting. As they closed with it, across the top of a hedge the roof lights of an ARV stood as a flashing beacon.

They turned left into a field as the car bucked and protested under them. Before them stood an array of marked police vehicles. From the centre where Barry Mankowitz stood, Colours beckoned as he threw on body armour. As the nose of the BMW dipped he was already tasking its occupants. He dragged the sniper rifle from the back of the car and thrust it in Cravetts's hands, while Gilhooley unloaded shields and kit.

'They've gone to ground in that field of rape seed,' said Colours 'between us and the woods. Get up on the roof of the TSG carrier and scope it out. Spot them for us if you can. If they look as though they are about to shoot as much as a field mouse, drop them, okay? Cravetts nodded, his face a fixed and resolute mask.

'Hello guvnor.' Colours's focus was momentarily interrupted by a gravelled voice. From between two vans walked a Police Sergeant. Diagonally around his chest he wore a dark brown leather strap.

Much of his dishevelled uniform was adorned with tufts of fine hair, while behind him emerging from between the vans came a younger man, a Constable leading a young German shepherd dog. 'Are you going to let us play?' the Dog Sergeant asked, a grin spreading across his leathery face. Grey stubble betraying his age.

Colours struggled to make himself heard as a van rocked violently and from within it a large dog barked, its threat very plain. 'Pleased to have you along John,' he said 'I presume that's 'Bomber,' nodding toward the van.

'Yes sir,' he replied, a wry smile invading his features. 'Eight years old and still as mean as a snake.' He glanced back at the other dog handler. 'Bob, this is Inspector Bladen-Barras,' he said, nodding toward Colours 'An old soldier, like me.'

Barry Mankowitz appeared at Colours side, a sheaf of paper under his arm. 'Got some maps from the locals,' he said. He spread them across the bonnet of a nearby police car. 'Has he got that bloody hairy exocet with him?' he asked.

57

'Afraid so,' smiled Colours. 'That dogs bitten more people than Count Dracula.' His smile broadened a little… 'Most of them coppers.'

*

The field's boundaries were hedges, thorny and tangled. The curve of the land took it over a slight rise downhill toward the wood. A few clouds had gathered and were now scudding by on the light gusts of wind, a wind that might carry Colours's words away. He thought about that, he thought about many things. A long line of his men spread out to his left and right and he prayed the radios would not fail him.

Other armed crews had joined them, and men in blue coveralls, hung with guns and kit, disgorged from a large Mercedes van and an armoured Land Rover as a team of specialist firearms officers helped swell the numbers. He stood like an island and quickly briefed them all.

Now the responsibility was all his. He cast his eye back and forth one last time. The helicopter's rotors beat a distant rhythm high above, but it dare not expose itself to gunfire. The dogs barked, howled and whimpered with excitement, sensing the moment and Bomber's aggression reached fever pitch. The line was punctuated by the dog handlers, breaking it into three parts. Classic open country search formation.

'I have control, I have control,' Colours asserted through his radio as he moved to mobilise the search. Along the line, hands were raised in acknowledgement. He spoke again 'Sniper?' Cravett's voice whispered through his earpiece. 'Scanning sir, no movement.'

Colours took a deep breath 'Stand by.' Mankowitz appeared at his side, an MP5 carbine ranging ahead to protect them. Colours's weapon for now at least, would be his voice alone.

He paused again, clearing his mind of all else. The radio switch cupped in the palm of his now damp hand felt reassuring. His middle finger found the button as he heard his own voice forcefully giving the command. '*Odds up.*' Along the line every other man stood up from a kneeling position and began to move forward, carbines sweeping the field ahead.

The two dog handlers moved steadily forward, matching the line's progress and closely protected by the nearest armed man. Johnny, the Dog Sergeant, tugged hard on Bomber's lead and cuffed the baying dog's head. Then with a mutual acknowledgement both handlers released the dogs. They ran ahead sweeping left and right as the handlers whistled low, muttering their secret commands. Pikey hissed to Raffles in a low voice, 'Those bastards with guns are bad enough but that fucking dog terrifies me.'

'Trojan one from Johnny dog.' The voice of the dog handler, using his own familiar parlance, crackled through Colours earpiece. 'This rape seed stinks so much, the dogs won't get anything on scent,' he went on.

'Received,' and then 'evens up,' as Colour's voice barked another command and the second wave of armed men moved forward, the first dropped to the kneeling, covering their movements across the vast field of swaying, dazzling yellow. The voice of Chris Harding in the control vehicle, sweating it out in a car far behind them now at their RVP, confirmed and recorded it all. 'Received at Trojan control.'

'Trojan one from sniper,' Cravetts voice broke in.

'Go ahead but be brief,' Colour's reply was necessarily curt. 'Moving position to your right. Going to about point four.' Colours realised that Cravetts was moving his arc of fire from over their heads and positioning himself to their right.

'Odds up.'

He moved the line again, and to Cravetts replied, 'Received. Tell me when you're there. Two clicks please,' Moments later the earpiece crackled twice as Cravetts settled in.

The line moved relentlessly forward. 'Evens up,' Colours called as another voice imposed itself. 'Trojan one from 538, I see movement in the crop. About fifty yards from the line on your eleven o'clock.' John Munney's keen eye had found their quarry. Before he could reply Cravetts voice broke in.

'I have them. They're knees and elbows through the rape.' Then Colours voice, dominating. 'All units, hold the line stay in cover. Sniper give commentary.'

There was a long silence as Cravetts scanned the gently waving crop. A soft breeze gusted it in whisper like sounds. Only the subdued whimpering of the dogs, and a surreal bird song broke the silence. Distantly the helicopter powered on the horizon. Colours mind fought for clarity, balancing risk, resources, contingencies. He couldn't expose the aircraft to fire. He would have to risk the dogs.

'Sniper from Trojan one, can you update?' Colour's voice spoke in every ear. 'Trojan one from sniper, they're down boss. I can't see them. I know roughly where they are but unless they move again we're buggered!' He thought for a moment and then spoke into his radio again. 'All units stand by.'

Taking a deep breath he slowly stood up and shouted a challenge down the otherwise still scene. 'We are armed police, give yourself up now and you will not

59

be harmed. I say again, we are armed police.' Only the sound of hissing crops, the distant sounds now of police radio traffic and the helicopter wafting the hot air. From the robbers, there was nothing.

Colours spoke into the radio yet again. 'Johnny, run the dogs.' Across the line the Dog Sergeant stood up. He turned and faced Colours, knowing what this might mean. Then nodding to the other handler he tugged at the collar of the huge panting dog, now stood at his feet. He bent his head, leaning close to the animal, and whispered in its ear. 'Now don't you get killed out there, you mean old bastard.' He allowed his lips to brush the dog's ear.

His fingers slipped from the collar as the whimpering dog moved slowly forward, and then broke into a trot as his handler's command spurred him on.

'*Find Bomber...find*' Then both dogs disappeared into the mass of yellow. Back at the control vehicle, Gilhooley pushed his way through the gathering of local senior officers who were now besieging the control car.

He snatched up the keys of the armoured Land Rover, laying on the seat of the control vehicle beside where Chris Harding sweated over the radios. Their eyes met. 'Kieran, you wouldn't?'

Gilhooley's eyes hardened. 'If they shoot those fucking dogs I'll drive this bastard thing right up their arses,' he said. 'There's no gate,' the younger man pleaded.

'Oh there's a gate,' called Gilhooley as he turned... '*There's always a gate.*'

*

Through the scope Cravetts watched the dog's progress, appearing to him like invisible fingers drawing irregular paths in the sea of yellow, breaking the patterns made by the soft breeze. Here and there the dogs heads appeared as they leapt above the surface of the rape-seed. Then the fingers began again, drawing closer to each other, and ever closer still to where he had seen the last movement of his targets.

He stood now on the seat of the personnel carrier he had commandeered, steadying the weapon across its roof. He fingered the magazine beneath the Steyr rifle, where it nested his remaining rounds of point 762 millimetre ammunition. He could put in a two-inch group at 300 metres with this gun, and it could kill a mile away. For all its power, this was not a clinical range shoot and to succeed he would need a target. He had none. The dogs leapt again and again, growing closer to the danger and yelping ever louder. He cast an eye again along the gun. It was ready.

The distinctive sound of a V8 engine reached him as the Land Rover laboured along the rutted track behind him. Then the engine cut and familiar footfalls closed with him. 'Hey my Yiddo, it's your Irish uncle.' Cravetts would not shift his gaze, but turned his head a little. 'What've you brought that tank up here for?' he said through the corner of his mouth.

Gilhooley stood close at his side, whispering in his ear. 'Plan B...you have to have a plan B.' Softly Cravetts shook his head.

Seeing the growing distance, Colours began to move the line inexorably forward. He gave 'Odds up' through the radios and the process of relentless leapfrog began again. He walked the line, checking its progress while all the time Cravetts called out the distance from the perceived threat.

When Colours reached the Dog Sergeant he paused. He stepped forward and touched the man's shoulder. 'It's alright Guvnor, rather a dog than a man.' Colours saw the flush on the man's cheek, felt the knot in his own stomach. The animal had been 'Johnny dogs' faithful companion, his strength and perhaps his salvation for long years. Now it was likely to be sacrificed.

'Trojan one from India 99.' The helicopter observers disembodied voice spoke through Colours's personal radio. 'We can't get any closer, but if they break from the bottom of the field, there is a short meadow. We'll see them.' Colours lifted his gaze momentarily skyward. 'Can they break out to my left or right?' he asked. 'Hard to tell from up here sir, but I don't think so.' He had them in a net, but he was in it with them.

'Movement,' Cravetts voice cut in, uncharacteristic urgency in his tone. 'From your eleven o'clock toward twelve and one. Three traces going toward breakout at red and black aspects of the field. A deep-throated barking was followed by a terrible baying sound. Then the sounds of the two dogs combined as they took up a full chase.

Johnny dogs voice broke in on the radio. 'The dogs will be on them in moments boss.' To himself in a quiet, quavering voice he said, 'Take him down Bomber. Don't get killed and I'll retire you, I promise.'

Cravetts cut in again. 'Three men, one IC1, one IC3 and one IC4. Weapons are one revolver, shortened shotgun...' he paused 'Guvnor, looks like the lead man has an AK.' High velocity weapons and now the incident was running unchecked. In full chase, every man was running forward. Now it was down to them, he no longer had control. Drawing his handgun, he ran with them.

Cravetts managed to say only 'I've lost them,' as he threw himself down from the carrier. He heard Gilhooley churning the starter of the Land Rover and he ran toward it, the rifle in his hands.

Throwing it on to the back seat, breathlessly he turned to Gilhooley. 'Shot's not on any more. Chaos out there.' Then the sound of gunfire repeatedly seared the summer air, and was followed by a terrible screaming.

'Dog down'...Colours heard the call moments before he reached the point where the rape-seed was trodden flat, the boom of a shotgun echoed and then the mortifying sound of machine gun fire chilled him. The young Constable cradled the dying dog in his arms. Its coat was matted with blood about a terrible wound in its flank.

Several men stood mesmerized as its legs and paws thrashed for the ground it would never again feel. Bright crimson blood spread from its abdomen and then its mouth. Then its panting tongue ceased to move. The handler rocked back and forth, sobbing gently. Colours broke the spell. '*Wake up!*... that might have been you, it still could be.' In moments a line of armed men ran on toward the threat.

'They shot Bomber as well.' Johnny dog appeared at Colours's shoulder. Colours heart sank. 'John, I'm so sorry. Where is he?' The Dog Sergeant gave a weak smile. 'Dunno... The mad bastard got up and went after them again.'

*

'Kieran, you fucking maniac!' Cravetts clung to the fittings inside the Land Rover as it pitched downward toward the field. Gilhooley planted the accelerator on the floor as in four-wheel drive it thrust down into the ditch and up again to confront the hedge.

The screaming sounds of thorns and branches fevered clawing at its armour reached a climax as they burst into the field. Then trailing yards of vegetation Gilhooley powered onward. 'I said if they shot the dogs I'd drive this thing up their arses, and I will.'

Cravetts fought to keep his seat. 'I know you will Kieran, *I know you will.*'

The operator aboard the circling helicopter broke in again. 'Trojan one from India 99, they are running across the field now. The suspect with the automatic weapon is positioning himself at the edge of the wood. Colours's instinct, his training and experience took over. 'Get away from here, back right off or he'll bring you down.'

'Soldiers?'... Barry Mankowitz seized Colours arm. 'Ambush, classic ambush. He's creating a killing field.' Feverishly Colours dominated the radio. 'All units go to cover. Do not enter the field.' In the Land Rover Gilhooley cast a glance at Cravetts. 'Rifle?' he said. Cravetts nodded. 'My play now I think.' There was no cover from fire. Every man lay face down in the rape while short bursts of gunfire split the air. Colours chilled as he heard bullets ripping through the foliage. 'Don't crush our blokes,' Cravetts pleaded as the heavily armoured vehicle rolled and pitched across the ploughed ground. 'I can see them,' shouted Gilhooley as he span the wheel. Colours winced as the Land Rover passed within inches of him and burst into the meadow, smashing its way through a wooden fence.

Instantly it began to take fire. 'Close enough yet?' Gilhooley shouted as the clang and whistle of ammunition striking them resonated. Ahead of them two of the robbers lay down in the field, in no mans land. 'Good enough,' cried Cravetts and Gilhooley turned violently left, braking as he did so.

From the passenger door Cravetts dragged the rifle, protected from the automatic fire that raked the vehicle. Divots of earth and soil leapt around them. Gilhooley launched himself into the back. Then levering open a firing slot, raised his MP5. 'Say when, and I'll put some nine mil his way,' Cravetts spread the bipod legs of the gun and settled in behind a wheel. 'Go Kieran, go!'

Rhythmically Gilhooley began to pump rounds into the trees, knowing only that the gunman was within a limited area, but not where. Round after round crackled through the undergrowth, as bursts of automatic fire were returned. From beneath the Land Rover, Cravetts called loudly, 'Got him, behind the big oak tree at 1 o clock.'

'Make it soon Mark,' called Gilhooley 'or he'll put one through this slot.' From beneath the Land Rover came a sudden concussion. The automatic fire stopped. 'One nil to old bill,' muttered Cravetts. 'Fucking hell,' said Mankowitz, and he whistled low. 'I ain't *never* seen the like of this.'

'That's because you weren't a soldier Barry, and they both were,' responded Colours.

The Land Rover burst into life as Gilhooley powered down the field. Cravetts tracked them through the rifle's powerful scope as the remaining two robbers broke cover and ran. The man with a revolver turned and fired a futile shot at the armour. In seconds the vehicle was on him, tons of metal threatening his extinction. Gilhooley could see his face now, swarthy and bearded, a long grey coat swirling behind him. As he drew level he threw open the massive armoured door, knocking the man flat. The gun span from his hand.

Gilhooley stepped out and strode toward his prey, now rising to his feet. His massive fist curved upward to deliver a devastating uppercut. 'Ah the van wouldn't fit up your arse anyway,' he grunted to the prone figure, blood now oozing from between his teeth 'and that's for the poor bastard dog you and your mates slaughtered.'

Pikey, Colours and his Sergeant sprinted after the second man with a dozen others close behind. The black man fired the shotgun once and they threw themselves down. Then he abandoned the apparently empty weapon to run for the woods. As he disappeared from view a dark shape raced through the undergrowth from the left.

At the edge of the thick and tangled undergrowth they paused, not knowing where their quarry was or how he might still be armed. Loud crackling sounds issued from deep within the woodland as vegetation, dried from weeks of summer sun, clung to the fleeing man, tangling and containing him. Then a terrible scream was punctuated by the sound of savage, throaty growling as an angry dog took its revenge. 'Bomber'...Johnny dog appeared at Colour's side. 'Bombers got the last one.' Colours looked at him, finally at a loss. 'Are you going to call him off?' through rasping breath, Colours asked. The Dog Sergeant paused and wrinkling a brow replied,

'Yeah...eventually.'

*

The thundering sound of India 99 blotted out all other sensation as it settled in the meadow blowing loose, dried grasses into their faces. The turbulence from the last throws of the rotors were a cooling welcome relief. For a moment he thought 'a wind'... but then the cordon tape crackled under its power and Colours's mind instantly found focus.

Raffles appeared at their sides, handing out welcome plastic bottles of water that were desperately required. All around him sat physically and emotionally exhausted men. 'God, you want to see it up at the road boss' Raffles exclaimed. 'Three quarters of the Met and half of Hertfordshire constabulary are here. Never seen so many senior officers looking so lost in all my life,' he grinned.

'Jesus, look at the state of that!' Benny pointed to where paramedics led the handcuffed black man into the open, while John Munney covered. The glossy black tracksuit he wore was ripped and torn. His yellowed eyes were wide with anger and fear. The dreadlocks, his face and all of his clothing were spattered with blood and his hands torn and bleeding from endless puncture wounds. He moaned and cried out as he collapsed on to the waiting stretcher.

'Half that blood's Bomber's,' cut in Johnny the Dog Sergeant. 'The rest is his.

Apart from Bomber's contribution, the suspect ran headlong into the thickest set of angry brambles I've ever seen. It took us ten minutes to untangle him.' Colours frowned. 'More important than that animal, how's Bomber?' he asked. 'He's lost a piece of an ear and got some lead in him, but he'll live. No more of this though,' Johnny caught his breath. Then collecting himself he said, forcefully. 'Bomber is officially retired...as of now.'

Colours and Mankowitz walked to where the third man lay beneath the oak tree. In his lifeless hand an AK 47 assault rifle lay, impotent. One leg lay bent back under him. A thick black moustache above dark stubble covered his face. He wore a camouflage jacket and trousers. In the centre of his barrel chest was a massive bullet wound. From within the folds of the jacket a small blue book protruded. Colours bent his head and read the words 'The Noble Quran' on its cover. Nearby lay a 'Nike' shoulder bag from which cash money spilled. 'Arabs or the like, getting it on with a white man and a West Indian'. Colours slowly shook his head. 'It just gets worse.'

Mankowitz forehead creased. 'Like the IRA you are thinking? Crime to fund terrorism?' Colours stroked his chin. 'I reckon,' he replied. 'I wonder what this is all going to mean' he continued.

'I think,' mused Colours 'that this does not bode well,' and he stood for long moments, lost in thought.

'How are you going to write this one up boss?' asked Barry Mankowitz whimsically . 'Slowly' replied Colours. 'Very slowly...and very carefully.'

WIND AND SHADOW

Graham Lassiter threw his briefcase on to the cluttered desk and cast his eyes around a room that was to be his domain. It was nothing like the light and airy offices he had grown accustomed to at 'The Yard'. From his windows there, he had had all of London spread silently before him. Now just a pivoting oval of glass, almost too high to see through, permitted incessant traffic noise to intrude, permeated with the faint smell of exhaust fumes.

He sank into the aged swivel chair, all wood and green leatherette. Around him the room was coloured in a patina of cream, with only the woodwork encrusted with numberless layers of green paint and a grey filing cabinet to break the monotony. One wall bore photos, certificates and commendations, echoes of past challenges or successes. He sighed deeply.

From the desk he picked up a nameplate. The gold embossed letters read 'Chief Superintendent SO19 Eduardo Seredemigni'. He turned it in his hands. Unable to resist curling his lip, then he threw it into a waste bin, muttering 'arsehole' under his breath.

A sudden noise made him look up. A young Inspector stood in the office doorway. 'Morning sir. Welcome to SO19. Inspector Gordon! I will be your liaison officer for your first week. My office is just down the corridor.' He placed a folder in front of Lassiter, and proffered his hand. 'A sort of welcome pack sir.'

Lassiter shook his hand and smiled as the younger man spoke again. He cast a glance toward the waste bin. 'I hope you'll be happy here.' He paused, smiling. 'In fact I am sure you will be.' Then he turned and left. 'What's he like?' enquired the girl while her fingers played a staccato rhythm across a computer keyboard. Gordon smiled reflectively. 'I think he'll be fine. For my money he got off to a good start.'

The girl stood up, smoothing her skirt and ruffling the neck of her crisp blouse. 'I'll make some tea then sir, shall I?' She smiled knowingly.

The base-man was sinking fast. On the CAD screen in front of him, message after message began to scroll down while the voice of MP, the controller at New Scotland yard intruded through the desk-mounted radio, reminding him that cars were deployed in South London. In concert reams of paper rolled out accompanied by the printer's incessant ticking, while all the time angry telephones rang.

He pushed an empty cup and saucer to one side and bellowed through the door from which the busy sounds of an assembled relief were adding to his pain. 'Will somebody *please* give me a hand here and can I have a cup of tea?' There was no response, no respite and his anger rose.

'Yes…*yes sir*. We have a car on way. Trojan 511 is assigned.' He tore off his headphones and stormed through the door. '511 you are assigned to CAD 2381.' He stuffed a sheet of paper into the hand of the man nearest him. 'Regent Street' he said… 'and thanks for all the help, you shower of shit.' A chorus of 'Oh… someone's tired,' preceded peels of laughter.

The gabble of a dozen voices competing for supremacy filled the air, punctuated by the clash of crockery and the metallic sound of the huge aluminium teapot. There was a loud bang as the old and failed door spring allowed the door to slam viciously yet again.

The man nearest the base-room door stood suddenly to attention. He raised his voice to overcome the chaos around him. 'All correct *sir.*' The noise died suddenly away. Graham Lassiter stood still and erect by the door. Every inch of his uniform was immaculate. Even on this summer's morning he wore his tunic and hat.

Un-speaking his eyes surveyed all around him, alighting on the table, covered now with spilt tea and cakes. He allowed his gaze to trawl the sea of kit scattered across the floor, the pile of body armour and the assorted kit bags. He took a step forward to where an MP5 lay across one such bag. He picked it up, removed the magazine and pulled its bolt action to the rear, locking it. Then he tipped the gun and looked into its breach. Still he did not speak.

The room was deathly quiet. The base-man's head appeared around the door, puzzled by the sudden change. 'I don't think things are all correct, are they gentlemen?' began Lassiter. He turned to the man nearest him, still sitting stunned in an old armchair. 'Is this your weapon?' There was a long, empty pause. 'D'you think you might stand up when I talk to you?' Lassiter continued.

Instantly the whole relief rose to its feet, while men fumbled endlessly to hide their own indiscretions. 'No gentlemen, this is not what I want. What I want is for things to be done properly *before* I arrive. In fact all of the time.' He paced the middle ground between them, holding every eye.

To no-one in particular he said, 'Mag out, breach open, those are the rules.' He caught the eye of the man by the door. 'So things are not *All correct sir*...are they? Where's your Inspector?' he demanded of the same man. 'Lanzarote sir,' he replied, downcast, 'and your Sergeant?' asked Lassiter. 'In the armoury sir, booking out the weapons.' He paused again and span on his heels. 'Poor show gentlemen. Better next time...better next time or else.' Moments later the door banged closed behind him, the overworked door check long since rendered useless. He called back through the glass, 'and do something about that bloody door.'

*

Colours parked his car in the yard, threw the green kit bag over his shoulder and strode toward the stairs. As he passed the first landing, Lassiter appeared on his left. 'Good morning sir,' began Colours. 'Welcome to the department.' Lassiter drew a breath. 'Thank you Inspector Barras. Can you please come to my office right now?' Two Constables heavily laden with kit passed them, muttering 'All correct,' under their breath and with consternation on their faces. Thoughtfully Colours reflected that he had known Lassiter for years. This looked like trouble.

'Come in and sit down please Mr Barras.' Graham Lassiter leaned back in the swivel chair. He pulled a pair of slim reading glasses from the bridge of his nose, tossing them lightly on the desk. 'Coffee?' he enquired.

'Tea if I may sir, thank you,' replied Colours.

Lassiter walked to the door and called down the corridor, 'Elaine, could we have two teas please. Get them from the canteen. Tell them I will pay lunchtime.' Distantly the girl's voice responded. 'Yes Mister Lassiter. Anything else I can do for you?'

He snorted softly. 'Err! No Elaine ... Thank you. That will be fine.' He pushed the door closed, pressing it securely home. Then he tugged at his collar, loosening it at his throat and sat down.

'It's a long way from the charge room at Lewisham, isn't it Roy?' Colours paused, unsettled by this sudden change of mood. 'Well, yes sir, but that was another world.' Lassiter smiled softly. 'No Roy, I haven't gone over. I'm not the duty officer any more and you're not the custody Sergeant, but we are still the same men.' Colours smiled, memories flooding back. 'A bit risky in those days sir, but we survived.'

There was a light tap at the door. It swung open and the girl stepped awkwardly in, a tray with a teapot, two cups and a white jug spread out on a white cloth in her hands. She leaned forward, placing the tray on the desk in front of Lassiter, yet not glancing toward Colours. 'Is there anything else sir, are you sure?' she said in her sweetest voice.

The skirt rose up at the back of her thighs, a brief glimpse of white lace demanding Colours's eye. 'No that will be fine, thank you.' He pressed paper money into her hand. 'Get yourself something if you like. Please close the door for me.' Though a disappointment lurked in her eyes, she smiled and left, closing the door firmly behind her.

'Anything that reaches her ears will get networked faster than Broadband,' he said, softly shaking his head. 'And before you feel inclined, no comments about the privileges of rank. Tea for two might be better than a stained mug, but that girl is dangerous.' Colours smiled to himself. Lassiter was on to them all, as shrewd and enquiring as he had always been. Now it was his turn.

He poured the tea and pushed a cup across the desk. Colours nodded and took it. 'It was a fucking shambles downstairs this morning. Bloody T.V. blaring while bodies are draped everywhere. Wall to wall kit and guns all over the place. Safety rules broken, no supervisors. Tea, cakes, noise. What kind of a briefing is that?'

Colours sipped from his cup. Then he placed it on the table and spoke, stroking his chin thoughtfully. 'First of all that was not my relief. Mine aren't much better in that respect, but it's angels with dirty faces sir.'

Lassiter stood up. He turned and faced the diminutive window. 'You're going to have to do better than a few generalisations and platitudes Roy. What makes these people so different? Colours fell silent for a few moments, then walked to where Lassiter stood, staring across the city. 'Got a head for heights sir?' he asked. 'Maybe' said Lassiter uncomfortably. Colours smiled. 'Okay guvnor, come with me... and you won't need your hat.'

*

'I lied,' said Lassiter, 'I'm not going any higher.' Colours moved toward the last few steel rungs that would take them to the flagpole, the highest point of the building. Already they had clambered up the fire escape ladders, past the abseil frame and on to the flat parapet roof. A breeze ruffled Colours's hair while Lassiter's thinning scalp shone in the sunlight. He rocked gently as it tugged at his uniform. Below them traffic thundered along Old Street. Fighting with his own fear as Colours beckoned him closer to the edge, he walked haltingly forward.

'See that steeple,' he gestured to his right. 'Just about the end of this borough's responsibility. A couple of miles the other way, same thing.' Colours shifted, staring for moments at his feet. 'In the last couple of weeks my relief has shot and killed two men. They have been subjected to automatic high velocity gunfire, trauma, scrutiny and the loss of one of their own number back to borough.' He made a sweeping gesture toward the horizon.

'When they go out they have the whole Met at their feet. Really they can go anywhere. They are not hemmed into one safe little confine where they can be watched. I have to trust them. I trust them to be safe. I trust them to be tactical. I trust them to gather good intelligence for me, so that I can function. Without that my tactics and decisions look like crap.'

Then he turned and stared Lassiter squarely in the eye. 'And I trust them with my life. In terms of strict discipline, there is some trade off for that.' Lassiter pondered the moment.

'Okay… Let me make my mark. You know the rules of leadership. Start hard and then get slowly easier. There is no other way. I will listen, but there needs to be some tightening up. Agreed?' Colours nodded.

'Okay then' snorted Lassiter. 'Now let's get off this roof before I shit myself.'

*

'Gonna be a right bastard by the sound of it,' said Arthur. 'Apparently he ripped the arse out of A relief. All shiny buttons and creases in your trousers. That's going to work well here, don't you know?' John Munney was rummaging deep in his locker. Hearing Arthur's predictions he turned. 'Collared the boss on his way in I hear. Dragged him up into his office for a right bollocking it seems.' A voice wafted across the bank of lockers as Chris Harding contributed. 'So what's your source then, Arthur?' he asked.

'Well half the spare relief were talking about nothing else. Then I saw Elaine on the stairs as I came in. She told me about him collaring the boss. Took him in his office and shut the door. Then they went at it hammer and tongs.'

Harding poked his head around the corner of Arthur's locker. 'So you were following Elaine up the stairs again, were you Arthur? You are a grubby old bugger.' Arthur sniffed. 'Well that girl has got a lovely arse and a thing of beauty is a joy forever.'

Gilhooley's voice boomed across the room. 'Told you before, you lecherous old sod. There's no hope for you!'

*

Colours tapped on Lassiter's door. In a muffled voice he responded 'Come in.' Colours shifted uncomfortably on his feet. 'I would like to talk to you about Cravetts and Gilhooley sir, their suspension from ops.' Lassiter was seated facing him, turning a pencil in his hands. 'I know what you are going to say, and I sympathise.' He allowed the stern expression to fall from his face. 'We are all in this trap. It's the system.' Colours moved closer, gesturing at the chair facing Lassiter. 'May I?' he said. Lassiter nodded, softening his eyes. 'I know we can't change the system, but perhaps we can oil the wheels a little,' he went on.

'They are cornerstones of my relief. Could we not get Gilhooley cleared for ops. He hasn't shot anyone, even though he opened fire. Cravetts is a first class man. He's fit, reliable and sound. I don't want to lose him. The last thing I want is to find him on another relief a year from now, or have him get so pissed off he leaves altogether.'

Lassiter rubbed the palms of his hands together thoughtfully. Then he stood up. 'I'm going to a security briefing at the yard this afternoon. I want you to drive me there. It'll be useful for you and we can talk. Are you free?' Colours nodded. 'The relief is spare and my Sergeant is more than capable.'

*

'I'll be bloody glad when we move from here,' Arthur cursed and heaved at the old canteen window. It stubbornly refused to open more than a few inches, then tilted and jammed. 'You'll have a long wait. Word is we will be here for a good while yet,' said Benny.

'Wouldn't be the same.' Cravetts muscular form appeared over Arthur's shoulder. He wore black shorts and a vest. A small towel was draped around his neck and he was sweating heavily. 'There wouldn't be the atmosphere. You know, all that's gone on here, all the years, the incidents,' he paused reflectively, and then

71

seized the stubborn sash. With a grunt he pushed it at first down and then jerked it upward. It rumbled to its full height and cooler air swept the room.

Cravetts surveyed the group, pacing along behind Fudge who was seated devouring an enormous fried breakfast. He stopped, bent forward and put his face next to Fudge's jaw. 'Just furring up the old arteries a bit are you my boy?' he smirked. Fudge chewed a little harder, swallowed and turned to meet Cravett's eye.

'You're just jealous because you can't eat the bacon. Go away, you horrible, sweaty, hairy man. You'll put me off my food,' he said. Cravetts walked away laughing. He paused at the door. 'Another Jewish thing Fudge. Are you circumcised?' Fudge creased his brow. 'No… why do you ask?' Cravetts called back as the door closed behind him ' 'cos if you keep taking the piss, *you will be.*'

The sound of deep impacts was accompanied by ferocious grunts. Cravetts pushed the door of the gym open. Gilhooley swung punches into a bag that danced in submission, absorbing the massive blows. Sweat stains spread downward from the waistband of his dark tracksuit.

Cravetts sat on a wooden bench, wiping his brow. 'I reckon we'll be doing a lot of this,' he said, 'me more than you. I will be suspended from ops forever.' Gilhooley stopped, while the bag swung creaking on its steel chain.

He sat beside Cravetts and lightly slapped his thigh. 'You did well, my man,' he said smiling. 'Colours will do his best.' Cravetts took a deep breath, and he softly shook his head. 'It's going to be a crock of shit Kieran. You know it is.'

*

Colours stared straight ahead at his reflection, trying hard to study the expression of the vastly senior officer behind him. All around their images stared back from the mirrored interior of the lift. The man gave a shallow cough and dragged a finger across his brow, covering his gaze. He knew he was eyeing his gun. They always did. Lassiter turned his head and watched Colours's face. He read his eyes, reached for his thoughts. That was Lassiter's way.

'Third floor,' a detached voice wafted softy into their silence. The lift gently halted and doors slid back. 'Excuse me?…' The Commander brushed past them and his shirt-sleeved form pivoted left and he was gone. As the doors hissed closed, Lassiter spoke.

'Maybe I can do something about Gilhooley, Cravetts is another matter. Trials, Coroners, you know how it works. Perhaps if he takes an instructor's course in the mean time? Would that satisfy him?' he asked. They felt the lift slowing until it stopped. The soft, recorded female voice spoke again. 'fifth floor.'

They stepped out on to an austere landing. Turning left through double doors the atmosphere changed. 'I wanted you here for a particular reason,' Lassiter began, abandoning all other thought. 'There are some real problems coming our way, things that are beyond all our current expectations.'

From left and right and filing in from an ante-room came streams of people, men and women either in uniform or bearing distinctive identity tags. The two men joined the group that now filtered through a second set of doors into a vestibule. Instantly the atmosphere changed again to one of subdued hush.

Colours felt the deep rich red carpet beneath his feet. Around them pictures of past Commissioners stared down from dominating gilded frames. Display cases citing snippets of police history flanked them as they crossed a divide toward the auditorium. 'What is this what we're about to hear?' Colours asked. Lassiter nodded. 'This will profoundly affect everybody.' He pressed a forefinger to his brow. 'Eyes and ears,' he said.

An anxious-looking young Sergeant scanned the faces and I.D. of all that passed him as they filtered through and fanned left and right into the seating. Ahead a rostrum wide enough to seat several people presided, while behind it white boards and a blank screen dominated all. Everywhere wooden panelling and red upholstery prevailed.

From a side door figures emerged. A Deputy Assistant Commissioner, a Chief Superintendent and an apparently studious man and woman, the latter carrying a file of paper. As the screen lit up with the flag of the Metropolitan police they each found their seats and the general murmur amongst the assembly subsided. The D.A.C. rose and began.

'Welcome to this morning's briefing ladies and gentlemen. For those of you that don't know me, I am D.A.C. Wilson. This is Chief Superintendent Briars. Mrs Hadley is with us from the home office, and D.I. Peter Rose from SO13.' He opened a large file of papers, bound with a deep red ribbon.

'D.I. Rose will update you on current matters, but we will require a little more time from some of you today. The matters that will later be disclosed to you are of a most sensitive nature indeed. I therefore ask that you do not discuss the content lightly and that you apply the material advisedly.' A soft murmur ran through his audience, while the Detective Inspector stood and composed himself.

'First I'd like to draw your attention to a group called the Patriots.' He began. 'For those of you that don't know them, these are new and disturbing developments. They are a group of fringe motorcyclists, *Bikers* to their own fraternity. They consist mainly of ex-soldiers or paramilitary wannabees.'

He cleared his throat and went on. 'They have been a matter of concern as far as their involvement with the Gypsy fraternity and drug trafficking to the east of London and in the Home Counties are concerned. Their apparent and unsurprising pre-occupation with firearms is a particular worry to us all and SO19 in particular.' He broke off to cast a gaze to where Colours and Lassiter sat.

'Unfortunately they have developed wider interests now. Their connection to the ultra right-wing and Fascist group Combat 18 is one we have been aware of for some time. However the recent upsurge in anti-Semitic behaviour we are seeing throughout Europe has been linked to Palestinian and Islamic fundamentalist groups.'

'Incredible as this may seem and to whatever extent, they are able to get in bed together for this purpose at least. The result has been that internal conflict has arisen. What has developed is a power struggle, but sadly a cohesive faction has emerged that is targeting Jewish establishments, property and businesses.'

Lassiter shifted uncomfortably in his seat. 'Directed patrols, armed stops and all,' he whispered. 'I can see it all coming.' Colours smiled at him. 'Welcome to Disneyland sir, have a nice day.' Intelligence began to appear on the screen as the Detective Inspector and the D.A.C. related names, dates and places, the red dots of laser pointers dancing across the images. Finally the D.A.C. summed up.

'Thank you for your time ladies and gentlemen. Please break for coffee now.' He looked up directly at Lassiter and Colours as they made to rise. 'Would Mister Lassiter and Mister Bladen-Barras please return after coffee, along with any other officers from SO13. We have further business for you.' There was something in his tone and eyes, a sadness or a warning. Colours felt a cold alarm run through him.

He turned to Lassiter, but his eyes were downcast. There was something in Lassiter's face also, something he had never seen before, and it troubled him mightily.

*

'You know what this is about, don't you sir?' Lassiter placed two cups of coffee on his tray, grabbed some biscuits from the display and then proffered a handful of change to the woman at the restaurant till. 'Sugar?' Lassiter asked.

'No! No thank you,' Colours replied, a hint of frustration in his voice.

The two men strode to an empty table near the window. 'I had a view like this,' said Lassiter. 'In fact it was better. I could see all the way to the counties on a clear day. I used to look toward home and wonder what my family were doing.'

He gazed out of the windows, not turning his head to speak. All this time he stirred the coffee endlessly while Colours's impatience grew.

'You think I'm playing games with you, don't you Roy?' He turned to confront Colours, fixing his eyes. 'Well I'm not. I'm new to this department and I need your help as much as you need mine. That pratt Seredemigni has left me all sorts of problems.' He smiled. 'You won quite a victory there, d'you know that? Seagull was out of the nest before he knew it. He's not going to forgive you, not ever. He'll be plotting your downfall as we speak.'

Colours said nothing. He waited and listened, knowing this was a pivotal moment. Lassiter paused, taking a deep breath. 'I'm not over my head here but the water is deep. I have to absorb too much too quickly, and now this.' The two men sat for moments in silence, sipping the coffee. 'So what is *this*?' Colours ventured.

'I only know it's a threat to us all. Not just the establishment but this time each and every one of us. Not just politicians but their families also. Not because we respond to an incident, but just because we are there, because we exist. Because *we are the police.*' He paused again, taking a deep breath. His eyes fell to his coffee cup.

'You're a strong family man, aren't you Roy?' Colours nodded, lifting a questioning eyebrow. 'And that makes it worse,' said Lassiter, 'because SO13 and SO19 are at the top of the hit list. Now shall we go back?'

*

'Desert Wind and Shadow' the D.A.C. volunteered. 'That's what they are called by their fanatical following, Khamsin and Haab. Only a very limited number of people know who they really are.' Behind him in the now almost-empty auditorium a white board was plotted with names and circles. Between the circles ran connecting lines.

'World events of late have generated a new fanaticism. We have known of the existence of sleeper cells for a long time. They were always a threat but not in such broad terms. Nasser Medawhi is at the centre of all of this.' He pointed at the photograph of a Middle-Eastern man. He was slim and dark, with a full beard and moustache and dressed in traditional Arab garb.

'This photograph was obtained from American intelligence. We doubt if it's currently accurate. It was taken in Riyadh about three years ago.' He moved the pointer to a second photograph.

'This was his brother Wahlid. Wahlid joined a splinter group from Hammas and became a senior and a radical. He preached fundamental views and advocated ethnic cleansing on the scale of genocide. Informed opinion was that he was just this side of insanity, fanatical. Not a soldier, but a strategist. They were extreme and maverick. American intelligence located and identified a desert training camp in the summer of last year.' He poured some water from the jug on the rostrum and drank it slowly, measuring his words. 'The yanks used satellite technology to bomb the camp at night and at low level. During the last hostilities it passed almost unnoticed in the world at large, but not amongst his followers…or his family.'

'He wasn't killed. The destruction of the camp was total, but perhaps for some reason he was not as close as the Americans had wished. He was however terribly injured. He lost both legs and an arm. He was also severely burned. He died in a hospital after being returned to Saudi. He died in great pain.' Colours grunted under his breath 'Fucking shame.'

The D.A.C. held Colours's eye for just a moment 'Thank you Mr Barras' he said, before going on. 'Wahlid and Nasser Medawhi are the children of a Saudi woman who was Nanny to a hugely influential Saudi family. As such they were privileged and educated. Medawhi was trained as a civil engineer. He also served with the Saudi armed forces for a while.'

He stopped, casting his gaze around the assembled faces. 'His speciality was demolition and sabotage. He was seconded to the Jordanian army for six months. The fear is that he received further training and expertise there. When Wahlid died he disappeared. We know he's here. We don't know where.' They were moving him from safe house to safe house. Now he's melted into the Islamic community.

From behind Colours and Lassiter, a male voice posed a question. 'Don't we have anything from the Saudi authorities, can't they help?' The D.A.C's expression changed. 'I'm embarrassed,' he said. 'The Saudis are getting it big time. They don't know which way to jump. I think after the latest attacks we'll get more from them, but right now we're at a great disadvantage.'

'This much though, we do know,' he went on. 'They want to disrupt life in the capital. They have sworn to make politicians and their families targets. They consider any face of officialdom legitimate game. That includes all military and civil buildings and figures of authority. That means us…and our families, at work at play. *That's how bad this is.*' He paused; taking a deep breath he said 'I'm sorry.'

'There is one other thing you must know. There is a sister Jahwara. We don't have a photograph of her except as a child. She was a favourite with the Saudi royals until all this happened. Now they fear her more than any of the others. They called her the little Princess.'

'We know she's here and working in medicine under a false name and identity. Her hatred is as virulent as any, her fanaticism as great. She's powerful as much if not more than any member of the group. She is *Khamsin*.'

Colours studied the photograph. The dark eyes of a very young, innocent girl stared back at him. He thought of his own family, their young faces staring back, just like this girl. His stomach churned.

BROTHERS IN ARMS

'That animal is disgusting. Beth, why d'you *ever* consent to having him in your home? The dog snuffled as it shifted its snout from the food bowl to one brimming with water and lapped loudly, spraying water across the parquet floor.

There was a 'pharp' noise as it turned and trotted happily to the door, and tumbled down the steps to the garden. 'Oh my God! What on earth do you feed that beast.' The woman took a fresh handkerchief from her bag and pressed it against her nostrils.

'Mother, for pity's sake stop being so dramatic! He's a dog. Dogs do those things.' The older woman's face contorted in disgust. She had a kind of languid elegance that flowed from her exaggerated gestures, enforced by her height and mildly bohemian clothing.

'I had such hopes for you Elizabeth. You were such a cultured, talented child. You could have danced at the Royal ballet. Now look at you. You look like a cross between Charlie Dimmock and Jamie Oliver.' *'Mother...please...* I've got so much to do before this afternoon. I've got the food to prepare, a garden that is crying out for attention. Perhaps you would like to help me?' said Beth, raising a questioning eyebrow.

'You're like your father, d'you know that? You've inherited an unfortunately large number of that awful man's genes.' The older woman picked up a carton of sausage rolls and began to turn them in her hands. She lifted the thin spectacles that hung from a chain around her neck and placed them on the bridge of her nose, giving her a strange, bird like countenance. 'Aren't you going to make some nice, delicate little sandwiches? I always thought they looked so'...she tilted her head and smiled, her eyes distant 'refined somehow!'

Beth negotiated her way around her mother as she busied herself with endless plates and dishes, many covered with cling film stretched over colourful delicacies.

78

'Mother, he was a soldier. You were a dancer and an actress. Now! As far as I am concerned, you still are an actress. Would you please then dance into the garden and help prepare the tables?'

'Margaret?' Colours's voice boomed from the garden. He sensed the rising and inevitable tension between the two women. *'Margaret…* he called again, anxious as ever to avoid the growing confrontation.

'Would you please help me to lay out these trestle tables?' he asked. 'You have that wonderful way of folding the napkins. I never could master that.' She descended the steps into the garden with a flourish, the soft flowing fabrics of her dress accentuating her footfalls.

'Darling,' she said. 'It would be a pleasure. Do you think we can bring some culture to this assemblage of nasty rough men you work with?' Colours laughed. Arthur's face loomed large in his mind. 'I think you might struggle with one or two of them Margaret, but feel free to try.'

The sound of children's laughter issued from behind a garden shed as the bulldog scampered clear of some bushes, hotly pursued by two young girls. The first was about twelve years old and pushing a garden barrow in which an eight-year-old balanced precariously.

The table on which he had so carefully placed cutlery and serviettes rocked dangerously as the wheelbarrow struck it and then turned over, tipping the young girl out. She lay helpless with laughter as the elder girl squatted down on the grass, hooting so loudly that she could scarcely breath. A plate of sliced ham slipped off the edge to fall on the grass. In one deft movement the dog was on it, the ham devoured.

'Stuka you bad boy,' scolded the older girl. 'You are such a terrible thief!'

'Bethany, it's not his fault. It's you two. I swear you're boys really. I think your mother lied about you and Sarah.'

She wrinkled her nose. 'Well you used to bath us when we were babies. If you don't know, then who does?'

Then in mock outrage the two girls flounced off toward the house, noses in the air. 'Anyway Daddy,' Sarah called back from the house. 'We could still have a little brother…*If you tried a bit harder.'*

'Yes,' said the other. Mummy said if you were just at home a bit more…'Colours could stand no more. 'Sarah…*don't you dare'.*

'The way you are bringing up those children Royston! You really ought to be more authoritative.'

Colours felt the heat rising under his collar. 'Margaret, before you start your tirade about private education, state schools and young ladies with decorum…

Don't! If I can't afford it for all of them, then I can't afford it at all. End of!...' He picked up the wheelbarrow with an unusually forceful movement.

The dog belched and then with a flourish, relieved himself against a nearby shrub. Margaret sighed deeply, a despair in her manner. 'Let me please ask you just one thing then. Why did you have to give that awful dog such an aggressive name? Couldn't you have called him Bruce, or Fido or something?' she said dismissively.

Before Colours could answer a shrill voice interrupted from the terrace near where Beth laboured in the kitchen. 'I know why.' The diminutive form of his youngest daughter stood framed in the doorway. Colours winced, 'Amelia no!' he pleaded, but the little girl would not be deflected. 'Daddy called him Stuka because he says that whenever that dog drops a big one…everybody runs.'

There was a long silence while Margaret closed her eyes. She allowed her head to drop forwards and opened them again, staring at her feet. Then she merely uttered. 'Oh my *God*...'

*

'Nice house boss!'… Pikey stood at the gate, surveying the mock Tudor façade. 'All these nice trees in the road. Nice little villages I passed through to get here.' He took a few paces down the path, casting his eyes left and right across the neat lawns and colourful borders. 'This'll be the stockbroker belt then,' he smiled. 'Not too much like Rainham, but it'll do.'

'Nice to see you Dick. You're the first. Make your way around the back. I'll be there shortly. There are drinks laid out.' Beth stood at the gate. She smiled and exchanged a few words with Pikey's wife and young son before they followed him down the path. Colours slid his arm around her waist.

'Thanks for all your hard work,' he said. 'It is important to me. I want them to wind down. Things have been tense lately, and I think there may be worse to come.' Beth turned and caught his eye.

She gestured toward the muddy Land Rover parked half on the kerb, its paintwork patchy and faded. 'Pikey!' Colours volunteered. 'Sometimes he's a bit weird.'

'Do you really think there is a threat that we should worry about?' Suddenly her face was a pale mask. 'There's always been a threat, there always will be,' he said. Beth's face became animated. 'Don't stonewall me Roy. Talk to me, tell me...' He turned and faced her, looking straight into her eyes. 'That's all I know. If I

80

knew more, I would… I will tell you.' The sound of a car rounding the corner heralded more arrivals. 'Perhaps?' Beth said in little more than a whisper… '*Perhaps?*'

*

'Just about the loudest firework you can get,' Fudge beamed. From the boot of his black BMW convertible, he had lifted a huge cardboard box. Now it took centre stage on a trestle table in the rear garden as Fudge tore open the lid. An enormous circular multi-barrelled firework wrapped in clear plastic and marked 'For professional use only' stood in a veritable sea of smaller incendiary devices.

'How does he do it?' quizzed Benny. He ain't no oil painting, but he's got a gorgeous girl in tow, a flash car, nice clothes and now he's stealing the show. Dirty, lucky bastard!'

'Maybe he's hung like a donkey,' grinned Arthur. He sat astride a huge ornamental frog. In his right hand was a bottle of beer. In his left a chunk of French bread struggled to contain a sausage, while onions emerged at all points and a combination of mustard and ketchup escaped to flavour the lawn.

'Nah!' said Benny. 'I seen him in the shower. Just an ordinary bloke with extraordinarily rich parents.' He smiled, looking at Arthur's dilemma.

'That your idea of a balanced meal Arthur? A beer in one hand and a burger in the other?'

'No, that is.' Arthur nodded at the beautiful Eurasian girl on Fudge's arm.

She was pencil slim and the tight black dress clung to her every curve. 'I could eat that,' he chuckled. '*I would eat that.*' He thrust the mass of sausage and onions into his mouth. Shaking his head, Benny leaned forward and lightly cuffed Arthur's ear. 'If your Missus hears you, there will be one big squealing piggy on that barbeque.'

Colours placed a hand on Fudge's shoulder. 'Ray, will I have to inform air traffic control before you can launch that thing?' Fudge smiled. 'I thought it might liven things up a bit boss. The boy's have been a bit subdued since that *Desert Wind* thing came out.' Colours fell quiet as Fudge held his eye, suddenly intense.

'So speaking of fireworks, d'you think we really have something to worry about boss?' Colours nodded toward the empty terrace and the two men walked clear of the crowd. From beneath a bright-coloured awning, from which Chris Harding was serving drinks to all and sundry, Barry Mankowitz broke away, seeing the two men together and sensing the content of their conversation.

'You heard Lassiter's briefing,' said Colours. 'You all did. As to whether any of this becomes a reality, we'll have to wait and see. The threat is there though.' Mankowitz appeared at Colour's shoulder. 'There's poor intelligence on this group Ray,' he interceded. 'They've cut themselves off, so they can't be traced. They've got no contacts in the terrorist world. They've done this deliberately. SO13 say this is without precedent, that they have never known a group to be so secure, so insular. We won't know any more until they surface.'

Across the lawn Beth spied the three men. A weak smile on her face, she strode toward them as Colours caught her eye. 'Leave it now,' he said, turning to greet her. 'Not tonight boys,' she said, before they could speak. 'Tonight is for being happy.' Then she linking her finger in Colours and kissed his cheek. 'While we can,' she whispered.

Beneath the trestle table Stuka rummaged around with delirious fervour, as small pieces of meat and food fell to the grass. He nudged people and chairs aside with his broad shoulders, as the urge to gorge himself became overpowering.

'Royston, please take that Stuka thing of yours and put him indoors, especially before they light any fireworks.' Margaret's sense of etiquette was suffering its worst ever abuse. She sidled up to Colours and whispered softly. 'You might consider taking that awful Arthur person in there too. I have never met such a crude man.' A look of outrage crossed her face.

'He made the most *awful* suggestion to me.' Colours smiled. 'Can I assume that you imparted some advice on social graces to him then?'

'I merely pointed out that we had plates and cutlery for which there was no charge,' she said indignantly.

'I did warn you Margaret, I did warn you!' Colours replied, watching the group collecting around Fudge as he set the first fireworks in a hastily constructed pile of sand in a space near the foot of the garden.

He watched the delight of his children, the happiness of these men and their families for whom he deeply cared. He watched as Gilhooley lifted his child aloft so gently with those huge hands. He saw Cravetts now often-troubled face smiling for once and the responsibility for them all began to crush him. An enormous flash preceded a huge explosion high above them, lighting the sky. He saw the laughter and joy on their faces as charge after charge split the night.

The barbecue glowed and the smell of grilled meat was carried on the light breeze. All around him others happily ate and drank. He felt suddenly alone, cold. Beth's arm was there in an instant, circled through his. She turned to face him. 'You're a good man, Royston Bladen-Barras...*Colours*...' she said.

Then she led him from where he stood alone and reflective, toward the glow of the fire. The light danced from the bottom of Barry Mankowitz's glass as he lowered it. His eyes met Colours, smiling. 'Like your ol' man used to say Roy… *Manyana…* Quote, unquote.'

*

'Lima Kilo from 866, receiving over?' There was a long pause while the PC. drummed his fingers on the iron rail of the balcony. He turned to the woman in uniform who stood looking out across the estate, an expression of impatience and disdain on her face.

'Lima Kilo from 866, re: CAD 4193 to Battersby House, are you receiving *over*?' He dropped the radio to his side and began to pace impatiently back and forth. '866 from Lima Kilo, go ahead,' came the reply.

He stared intently at the girl, her attention grabbed by the radio traffic. He shook his head slowly and began again. 'Lima Kilo from 866, this is a false call. Number 46 Battersby House is empty. There are no occupants and the place is boarded up.'

There was a long pause. 'Yes… 866 we have a report of serious domestic violence. Are there any other premises nearby that could be the correct address?'

He grimaced, striking his thigh with the flat cap he now held in his hand. 'Lima Kilo, it's all-quiet here, someone's pulling our chain. This is a false call.' The voice through the radio spoke again. 'Received at Lima Kilo, will mark it up accordingly.' The two police officers strode along the balcony of the ageing block of flats, their footfalls echoing amongst the blackened brickwork. They reached a landing and turned to descend the stairs.

'I bloody hate that,' he said. 'Some stupid kid with nowt better to do has us running up and down these poxy stairs.' He cast his eyes around. 'I bet he's giggling from behind a window somewhere now, watching us getting pissed off and hot,' he went on. The girl reached for her radio. 'Lima Kilo one zero, can you pick us up from the base of Battersby House please, 762 over?'

There was a long silence. 'What the fuck is he doing?' began the man again. 'He knows we're here, he dropped us off.' He turned off the stairs to peer down into the courtyard. 'That's funny' he said to the girl. 'The van's still there.' He spoke again into the radio, now more forcefully. 'George, are you listening?' There was only silence.

'Lima Kilo one zero from 866, receiving over,' he said again, his voice rising. The girl peered over the rail. 'Broken glass,' she said, 'I can see broken glass around the driver's door.'

The squeak of his soft-soled boots echoed loudly as he threw himself down the stairs. He turned across the front of a parked car and slowed his pace. The van was facing away from him, the door open and slid back. 'George, have you checked your battery?' he called, slowing to a walk.

His pace fell to nothing as his legs became leaden. The police van driver sat upright, his chin on his chest. As the PC drew closer he could see a long glutinous string of saliva, red with blood and pendulous descending from the driver's mouth. A terrible entry wound had destroyed the driver's temple and blood ran profusely from his hugely-damaged right eye. The screen was splattered with blood and a spidery hole was visible high up. Shards of glass littered the floor.

*

'It's started' said Colours. The furore surrounding a shift change fell to nothing as the gravity in his voice lanced every consciousness. 'The driver of a police van was assassinated on an estate in Peckham last night. He was set up by a false call. While the crew were away he was shot through the head. He never knew a thing. Silenced weapon we believe. Nobody heard a sound.'

There was a stunned silence. Then John Munney's quiet and concise Welsh tones broke in, barely interrupting the reverent stillness. 'Any idea who's responsible?' he asked. Colours paced slowly back and forth, then sat on the arm of a chair, stroking his chin. 'Not local, maybe what we have feared. The dead PC had one epaulette cut off. The base-man found a photocopy of it this morning. *It was pinned to our front doors.*'

'Guvnor,' the base-man burst in. 'Can you speak to the Chief Inspector at M2VG urgently please?' Colours strode into the base room, taking the phone from the base-man's hand, huge concern etched in his face. 'Inspector Bladen-Baras here sir, how can I help you?' He could hear the man's laboured breathing. He was a senior and influential Essex Constabulary officer seeking cross-border aid.

'Can you send us some armed assistance? I have a massive search to do at Thurrock Lakeside and I don't have sufficient manpower,' he said. Colours knew there was much worse to come. 'We have security commitments to London sir. Can you clear this with Chief Inspector information room? I will help you if I can. How big an issue is this?' he asked.

'An ambulance crew were lured here on a false call' he began. 'On their return the vehicle was bombed.' There was a pause that Colours knew he must observe.

'The crew,' the man went on. 'The bastards waited till the crew were inside and then they blew them to fucking bits.'

*

As the car bucked over the flyover, Colours fought to steady himself against the violent movement. He strained to hear what was being said to him down the diminutive mobile phone that he had pinned to his ear. He hit the button to reduce the sound from the main radio, but still his ears were assaulted by the siren and the overwhelming tumult of an ARV in full cry.

'Say again!' he clamped his free hand over his left ear, desperate for information. 'Good God! What are we into with this?' Mankowitz risked a glance to meet Colours's eyes, his brow folded in an unspoken question. 'Where?' Colours asked, and 'Who's going?' He nodded and acknowledged point after point, scribbling notes on the log where he could.

The nose of the car rose as it climbed the flyover that led on to the stretch of motorway standard road, the last leg before Lakeside. Free of the congestion the speed rose relentlessly. Colours watched unconcerned. 110 miles per hour, a 120… 130… Now the mechanical roar began to overpower all else.

Mankowitz concentrated totally on the road ahead as they passed the world in a kind of unreal fast forward. 'They have taken out two fire appliances at Tottenham,' he shouted in Mankowitz ear. They took a false call and it looks like they hit them with RPG as the doors opened. His eyes fixed on the road ahead, Mankowitz manoeuvred for their exit. The speed fell a little as he hissed. 'For Gods sake.'

The noise began to subside as Colours added, 'Red team are running from the base. Brendan Harper will update us as soon as. Lassiter is on his way here.' A distant sea of blue lights greeted them. They slowed as a local PC lifted the cordon tape for them to pass through. Mankowitz piloted the car through an entrance to a car park and on toward a point where a plume of smoke rose as a sinister marker. They parked the car and walked forward past a mass of assembled emergency vehicles.

The shell of an ambulance lay amid a scene of devastation. Cordon tape created a massive exclusion zone where dozens of parked cars lay trapped, many singed or with windows shattered. A narrow corridor marked by fluttering blue and white tape led forward. Close to the scene stood a uniformed Chief Inspector, while white paper-overall-clad men and women crawled in line, examining every inch of the ground.

85

'Inspector Bladen-Barras sir, SO19. How can I help you?' As he turned, the man's face was ashen. Beyond him the ambulance smouldered. It was a shell. The roof had gone and its plastic and aluminium panels had melted away. The remnants of the cab were marked only by the steel seat frames, and the skeletal steering wheel and column. Intruder alarms rang incessantly, interspersed with those of the damaged cars.

Nearby a black body bag lay awaiting removal. In the contrived flower beds, masks and tubes hung bizarrely from the branches.

The stark outline of an oxygen cylinder stood out in the shrubs. Poignant reminders that this vehicle was an instrument of compassion, that these were the tools of mercy. The powerful smell of burnt plastics and rubber hung on the air.

Millions of blue and orange reflections shone back from the walkways where the shattered safety glass from doors and windows lay in untidy piles. Window displays were torn and blackened and swathes of soot rose upward to grasp at the once immaculate facades. A fallen mannequin lay half out of a window. From beneath a pile of fabrics it's hand reached plaintively upward, frozen in time yet beckoning.

Colours's eye was fixed. He could not drag it from the macabre figure that still sat in the remnants of the cab. Like some blackened creature of the night, it stood as a testament to the inhumanity of the scene. One hand still gripped the steering wheel. The feet still adhered to the pedals. Pink shining flesh appeared here and there through charred and melted clothing. Of the right arm, shoulder and head, there was nothing.

'Mr Barras…' A voice intruded into the netherworld he had entered. 'Mr Barras'…Another voice, this time it was Mankowitz. 'Boss, hey boss, snap out of it.' Suddenly Colour's senses returned. 'Sorry, I'm sorry sir,' he said, turning to the Chief Inspector. 'How can I help you?'

'Maybe just some manpower to do a walk through of the malls if you could,' he responded.' 'There's no way we can search everywhere and we all know they're long gone. I guess I called you a little late. It's all scenes of crime and forensic now.'

He lowered his eyes and placed a hand on Colour's forearm. 'I know, that's how I felt when I got here,' he said, exuding both strength and sympathy in his voice.

'Thanks' said colours. 'I'll get an S.F.O. team down here. You can have two car crews until they arrive, but I must have them back.'

'Seems like we're going to get our share too.' He nodded at Mankowitz, tapping the phone on his hip. The Sergeant nodded.

The blue lights of the RVP faded behind them as they sped Northward. 'It's been a long time since I've seen the like of that,' said Colours. 'Saw some bad stuff in Northern Ireland. You think you're immune, but you're not. D'you know, I have a friend who deals with people suffering from PTSD. She says that each time it's a brick out of the wall. Take enough bricks and the wall falls down.'

Mankowitz turned to look at him, even as the blue lights circled around them and the horns wailed. 'Yeah, I know who you mean,' he said haltingly. Colours caught his breath. 'Sorry! What did you say?'

The Sergeant stared straight ahead, pressing the accelerator to the floor. The engine note hardened. 'I said I know what you mean.'

Colours fell silent for a few moments. 'I feel like I've just seen the embodiment of everything I hate,' he said. 'I've never let it get personal, but now if I ever get the chance, I'd like to kill the bastard that did that myself. I'd like to watch them die slowly, to stare in their eyes and watch the lights go out.' Mankowitz took a deep breath. He sighed loudly, but said nothing.

*

The murmur in the auditorium fell into total silence. The Deputy Assistant Commissioner opened a file of papers and coughed to clear his throat. 'Ladies and gentlemen. I've called you here today because we're facing a new and unprecedented threat. Last night in London there were a series of attacks on the emergency services. In the gravest, two members of the ambulance service were killed.'

'In North London a device, believed a rocket-propelled grenade, destroyed two fire brigade appliances. Several fire fighters have been seriously injured. One is still critical.' He turned his gaze to where Colours sat with several officers from SO19. Lassiter lifted his head in a muted acknowledgement. 'There are those of you who have some insight in to the background to these matters. It suffices to say that we face a new sort of enemy and a new tactic.'

'That tactic is to destabilise the emergency response at a time when security matters are already at an all-time high.' He lifted a glass of water and sipped from it impassively, then continued, 'to dilute our ability to guarantee the level of security we are currently supplying.'

He turned the glass in his hands. 'The Commissioner has decided in consultation with Cobra and other senior officers, both within the Met and without, that we must identify and neutralise this threat and tactic at the earliest juncture. To that end extra funds and resources have been made available. Borough Commanders are authorised to place staff on a twelve-hour shift pattern forthwith and cancel leave wherever necessary. CO departments and SO19 in particular will commence such patterns at once.'

From a side door an Inspector in shirtsleeves approached the D.A.C. He passed him a document and whispered quietly in his ear. A soft murmur ran through his audience while Lassiter leaned towards Colours. 'Do you breed rabbits Mr Bladen-Barras?' he whispered. Colours creased his brow. 'Why, no sir?' he exclaimed. 'Shame,' he replied quietly, 'because I think I am about to be expected to produce them from a hat.'

The D.A.C. cleared his throat. 'Within the last few minutes British Transport Police vehicles have been attacked with incendiary devices at Kings Cross. Three have been destroyed.' He hung his head with an ever-greater solemnity. 'Far worse is that moments ago a civil servant was run down and killed in Broadway, outside this building. A note left at the scene indicates that the same group are responsible.'

'Accompanying each outrage have been faxes sent from differing points and arriving at various terminals within these walls. They are all photocopies of the assassinated Peckham officer's epaulette bearing the time and date of each incident. The typed logo Desert Wind appears on every one.'

*

'From this moment, all leave is cancelled'. From the back of the parade room Benny could not restrain his disgust. 'Fucking hell, boss I'm supposed to be in Tenerife tomorrow night. My missus is gonna go ape shit.' Colours and Mankowitz had returned to the base. Now it was time to tell the relief what they didn't want to hear, but tacitly expected.

Colours shook his head. 'Sorry, can't help that Benny. This is way beyond the norm. These directives are coming from on high.'

'Effectively the Home Office. In real terms that's the Prime Minister, so there's little good in entreating with me!'

Benny nodded, allowing his head to fall forward, he began to roll a cigarette. He took the silver 'makings' tin from his pocket and pulled a liquorice paper from the pack as he did his best to disguise his bitter disappointment.

'Expect to be working security patrols with the TSG at least once every week in addition to the twelve hour shift pattern that will be implemented as of today.

Those with compassionate grounds will have to see Mr Lassiter as a matter of urgency.'

He opened a folder, thumbing down the page he spoke again. 'I'm aware that you know now the background to this new breakaway group. You know about the brother and sister situation, but here is an update and a little hope. Although they seem self sufficient in weapons and are manufacturing their own explosive, they are vulnerable on one front.'

He reached for a remote control and gestured toward the ancient television set. 'This is the CCTV footage from our security cameras. You will see that the hooded figure who left the photocopy of the epaulette on our door is slim and very mobile.'

'The frequency and locations of the first incidents means it would be virtually impossible for just one or two people to have committed all of these outrages. Analysis of the footage suggests that this is a young woman. Other intelligence also suggests that they are recruiting from the Islamic student community.'

John Munney raised a hand from the back of the group. 'That doesn't narrow it down much sir, does it. There are thousands of them.'

'True,' said Colours. 'But every extra link in the chain means an increase in the chance of one being weak. The other point is that Muslim leaders in certain areas in West London are speaking out against these events and condemning the perpetrators for corrupting their young. All of this may work for us.'

Arthur slid his chair across to where Fudge scribbled in a notebook. 'Must be terrible for that lovely dark-eyed girl of yours, you having to work all these hours? You won't be able to satisfy her young and wanton loins,' he smirked. Fudge lifted his head but stared straight in front. 'So Arthur, you're about to proffer some grubby suggestion, are you?'

'Well, yes!' Arthur chuckled. 'Perhaps while we are all on extra shifts, we could all just stop by now and then and help you out. Personally, I'd be delighted to spare the odd half hour. Nothing's too much trouble for a mate.' Fudge turned to Arthur, curling his lip. 'One day Arthur, I am just going to spit in your eye.'

'No need for that kind of talk,' Arthur beamed toward his gathering audience. 'We'll all be a bit short of the old conjugal rights. I just thought we could kill two birds with one stone…as it were.'

CAT AND MOUSE

A bright crimson stain spread across the otherwise immaculate and glistening fabric. The sequined material picked up light from a thousand sources and sent it in fans of colour to confuse the eye. Above them the illuminated canopy of the club added to the kaleidoscope of colour. All the while the husky screams defied every effort to communicate.

'I need some latex gloves,' Raffles called loudly back to where Benny and Arthur were dragging kit and cordon tape from the back of the car. 'Get the first-aid kit and a field dressing.' The glistening silver dress had ridden up to the waist of the figure that writhed in agony in the gutter. The crowd was increasingly swollen by onlookers, as the bars and restaurants disgorged their customers and morbid curiosity took over. Below the pierced material an obscene gaping knife wound oozed blood into the gutter.

'MP from Trojan 511, Old Compton Street at the junction with Greek Street, West one. We have a female with serious stab wounds and a large and volatile crowd. Can we have further assistance from local units and an ambulance as a matter urgency.' Arthur's gruff voice was raised far above his usual gravely tones as he struggled to make himself heard.

All around the crowd closed in, driven by the excitement of the moment. A boy, perhaps eighteen years old, dark-skinned and swarthy, tapped Arthur on the shoulder. 'That ain't a woman,' he smirked. 'It's a tranny, y'know what I mean man?' The screaming reached fever pitch and rose above the sound of the music that resonated from a dozen different sources. The distant sound of the horns of approaching emergency vehicles grew relentlessly louder, serving to excite the crowd even more.

Arthur turned suddenly on the boy, somehow angered by his mocking expression. 'What did you say?' Arthur held his gaze. The boy tilted his head, the smirk turning to a sneer. 'I said he a she-male, you know? A transsexual, a cross dresser, *a gay boy!* Hey man where you been all your life?' he mocked.

Arthur drew close until his breath was in the boy's face. 'Thanks for that,' he snarled. 'And I been around things that would make you weep junior'.

The boy sucked his teeth. 'Yeah man, you already make me weep okay!' his eyes flicked downward and he began to nod gently, almost approving. 'Nice Glock,' he said, staring at Arthur's gun. The crowd parted and the boy melted away.

*

'Yes, I noticed,' Raffles muttered as Benny nudged him heavily in the back, nodding toward the very male genitalia that a tiny pair of black panties was struggling to contain. 'We have a severe and deep puncture wound at middle lower back,' he went on, 'and puncture wounds in the rear of the right thigh and left buttock. There is a slash wound to the right forearm, a defensive injury I suppose.'

The man on the ground was olive-skinned. The blonde wig he wore had fallen off and lay in stark contrast to the pool of blood that now soaked it. A thinly-strapped high-heeled shoe remained on his right foot, where painted nails matched the brilliant red blood. The left shoe was lost, trampled by the encroaching crowd. Now unable to speak, his eyes rolled in abject terror.

From below the man's back, blood pooled and now ran into a nearby grating. Benny's anger boiled over. He stood and turned on those who enclosed them so closely, jostling for a view and closing their working space down to a tight circle. 'Back off will you. Give us some room,' While those closest retreated a little, a jeering group of young men in football shirts mocked his anger at a distance.

He knelt beside Raffles, looking into the face of the terrified victim. He was about thirty years old. His head was close shaven and his face heavily made-up. The screaming had subsided as he choked and coughed, little flecks of blood appearing on bubbles of saliva at the corners of his mouth. Raffles turned to catch Benny's eye and nodded. 'Punctured lung,' he said.

Suddenly local officers forced their way to them, disgorging from a personnel carrier while to their great relief an ambulance crew appeared at their sides. The three men stood back, watching the crew go efficiently into life-preserving routines while the heated crowd was forced to disperse.

In a flurry of sequins and scarlet, a figure over six feet tall burst from the crowd. A dramatic feather headdress curved upward while he hobbled on high-heels as the tight scarlet dress and constraining hem bound his knees together.

'Sheba, are you badly hurt darling. Sheba my love!' The falsetto voice began to plead loudly with local officers, now cordoning the scene off. 'Please let me see her. She's not going to die is she? Why did this happen? We don't hurt anyone.' The three armed men picked up their kit and began to walk toward their car, the crowd melting away from it. A rotund local Sergeant stopped to speak. Raffles pre-empted him. 'Thanks for rescuing us,' he smiled. 'I don't like being in a crowded when I'm armed,' he confided.

The Sergeant lifted his eyebrows. His round face displayed an earnest and gentle quality. 'Our pleasure boys,' he said. 'You turn out soon enough for us when we need you, which is a tad to often nowadays,' he acknowledged. 'What d'you think this was about, a catfight?' asked Arthur, his gruff voice demanding attention.

'I doubt it,' said the Sergeant. 'A lot of the trannys aren't actually gay. Some are, some take customers, but they are a mainly just colourful. It's a bit of a carnival thing a lot of the time and people seem to like the spectacle of a six-foot plus showgirl mixing it in the street. They're rarely any trouble or have any enemies.' Arthur sucked a breath. 'Well this one did. You could have a fatal here.' The Sergeant nodded. 'Well leave us some reports on this, and C.I.D. will get back to you.'

From across the road, John Munney appeared with an anxious expression etched on his face as Gilhooley and Fudge hovered in the background. 'We just turned up to support you,' he said. 'It's all over thanks mate,' said Raffles with a smile.

'No it's not buddy,' said Munney, the gravity of his words etched in his eyes. 'Come and look at your car.'

The four strode to where the Vauxhall stood in the kerb. Dark red and brown translucent fluid streamed down from its roof. Arthur strode forward. 'What the fuck? Paint?' he growled, reaching for the door handle.

'No Arthur...don't touch It,' called Munney. 'It's not paint, it's blood.' He spread his arms left and right, preventing them from reaching the car.

'This will be a scene of crime boys, but look at the sheet of A4 on the screen.' Benny bent his head to read its content. 'What does it say,' growled Arthur, his anger palpable.

'It's a copy of that dead PC's epaulette again,' he said. 'Then there's some sort of Arab sword logo, some writing,' he paused for a moment...'and a Photostat copy of a point 762 rifle round.'

Benny dropped his chin on his chest. 'It's a warning. That they can kill, that they will kill. They're quiet happy to snuff that transvestite just to get us here.'

Raffles interceded, 'but that means they must have been following us, our car. They stabbed that man just to get us out in the street. They were behind us when we got out. Wind and shadow, that's what this is all about!' There was a horror in his voice.

'I'd like to blow a cold wind up the arse of whoever did this,' scowled Arthur, 'Followed by a few rounds of nine mil.'

*

'I've asked for someone from CO to come down and talk to each relief in turn.' Lassiter paced across his office, the morning sun casting his shadow across the desk and sparing Colours's eyes as he passed in front of the oval window. 'I want them versed in anti-surveillance drills and I want them to be used.' His voice carried an unusual depth of concern.

'They weren't followed,' reassured Colours. 'They couldn't be. They were expected though. Every Saturday night, you know as well as I do there'll be at last two cars running circuits through the West End to see the sights and bog the crumpet. Old Compton Street is a *must do*. They just laid in ambush. Forensic say it was animal blood.'

'I accept that,' said Lassiter, 'but it's just a first move. There were twelve false calls from vulnerable security targets all over the Met in ten days from this group and now this. They're going to pull our chain, tie us up.' He turned to face the window, his back to Colours. Then he dropped his chin to his chest and spun to face him. 'We have officers all over the Met as nervous as a cat on heat. They all think they are being followed home.'

'The Commissioner's climbing up the walls. The ambulance service, the Brigade and Borough Commanders are all talking about armed support and escort. Where the hell do they think I'll find that from?'

Colours shrugged. 'So you were dead right about the rabbits and the hat then sir?'

Lassiter sighed. 'Knowing that it's coming is not the same as being prepared for it. The DPG are already working every hour God created. Every lapsed shot has been re-authorised. They have even postponed one man's retirement. This is going off the scale.'

'This twelve hour shift business is going to cause us problems,' Colours volunteered. 'The blokes are pleased to have the overtime, but it soon wears thin and we'll be up to our ears in welfare issues before you can blink.'

Lassiter looked suddenly angry. 'I won't have endless whimpering over this. This is becoming a war and I need soldiers, not nursery nurses.' Colours smiled. In his mind's eye he could see the likes of Gilhooley and Arthur. 'Don't think that will really be *too* much of a problem sir.'

*

John Munney winced as the old green door yet again crashed closed behind him. He dropped a large green 'Bergen' on the floor and began to pour tea from the huge silver pot. 'They never will fix that bloody door,' he complained, lifting the steaming white and blue mug to his lips.

'*Parade*.' Pikey reacted as Lassiter appeared suddenly in their midst, Colours close on his heels. Behind them filed in Barry Mankowitz, a blue folder tucked securely under his arm. 'No gentlemen,' Lassiter volunteered. 'This is no time for formality.'

He removed his tunic and cast it on to a nearby table, a gesture of confidence. Then he reversed a plain chair to face the assembled relief. With his elbows crossed on its back, he motioned for the assembly to sit in a semi-circle around him. He waited till they had settled and then spoke. His eyes were downcast and his voice sombre.

'We all know we're in for a really bad time. I'll have to ask a great deal of all of you. The job has allocated a nearby car park for your exclusive use. It will be patrolled and I strongly advise you to use it.'

'Those of you that ride motorcycles, I ask you to use those as much as possible. You are thereby anonymous and almost impossible to follow. There'll be a team from the yard briefing everyone on anti-surveillance drills. Listen close and use them. Wherever officers wish to sleep at the base we will accommodate that and Paxton Street section house is being re-opened for anyone who wishes to use that facility.'

'How long is this likely to go on?' Chris Harding's voice rose anxious from the back of the room.

'The truth is we don't know,' replied Lassiter. 'What I do know is that the sooner we can nail these bastards, the sooner we can hope for normality.'

John Munney raised a hand. 'Sir, have there been any confirmed incidents of off duty police officers being followed?'

Lassiter shifted uncomfortably in his seat, lifting his eyes to where Colours and Mankowitz stood. Colours stepped forward and spoke. 'No John, there haven't. The thing is we all know how easy that would be, so we will prepare for that eventuality.'

He turned to catch Lassiter's eye. Lassiter nodded and Colours went on. 'We know they're targeting police vehicles on the streets, along with other branches of the emergency services. The tactic is to erode our ability to function against the backdrop of the other threats we face from bombing etc after the Twin Towers, Iraq and all that has followed. The school of thought is that the amount of resource they would have to employ in that fashion is much greater than to concentrate on the services on the ground. Why come to us when they can draw us to them?'

A murmur ran through the relief as Colours paused. Then Lassiter picked up the thread. 'Make no mistake, this has all been thought about and is very directed. The number of false calls is massive in relation to the number of actual incidents and yet they still seem to know when to strike for real at just the right time to keep us nervous. They want to stretch our resources to breaking point, and to do it very publicly.'

'What about directed patrols sir?' asked Pikey. 'Will they continue?' Lassiter pulled the slim reading glasses from his pocket and slipped them on to the bridge of his nose. Barry Mankowitz stepped forward and handed the blue file to Lassiter. At a gesture from Lassiter, Mankowitz began to speak.

'As of today there will be no recognisable pattern to your duties. Your assigned areas will be given to you at the start of each day. They may then be varied without notice by radio. You may also receive immediate notice that you are being followed by unmarked cars and motorcycles. They will identify themselves as police vehicles on the firearms frequency and direct you through surveillance filter points. A tactic has been devised to deal with that eventuality and you will be receiving instruction.'

'Wherever a vehicle is left at a deployment or for any reason in the street, an officer is to be deputed to guard it. A Local PC will suffice or one of your own crew if necessary. If that is not possible, a full old fashioned ground up mirror search will be conducted. Needless to say, refreshments will be taken at secure police premises only. There will be NO shopping expeditions, and obviously NO home visits. Impromptu requests from local units for armed support will be met wherever possible without formal reference.'

Lassiter rose to his feet. 'The only other point I wish to mention is that attacks may come from young student radicals, recruited by these mad fundamentalist bastards. Watch for them. SO13 seem to think that these *twist and go* motor scooters might be an ideal vehicle for them. Be aware! Teams of SFO officers will be patrolling in armoured Land Rovers in support whenever they are not otherwise employed.'

Then Colours added, 'and finally gentlemen, you will carry all weapons in '*condition one*' from this moment.'

Arthur stood up. 'May I say sir that I have found your briefing most disturbing.' There was a solemnity in his tone and he held every eye. 'I was okay with most of it except condition one. I ain't scared of no terrorist, but the thought of Pikey sitting behind me holding a gun locked and loaded scares me shitless.'

*

'Good morning sir' Colours looked up from the computer terminal into the eyes of a much younger man. He was about thirty years old and dressed in the immaculate uniform of a Sergeant. The chevrons stood out in a brilliant white tinged with gold in the reflected sunlight of the office window. 'My name is Martin Beckwith. Mr Lassiter has told me that I am to be attached to your relief.'

Colours stood up, proffering his hand and feeling a little bewildered. 'I should explain,' the young man continued. 'Mister Lassiter was unsure on which relief to post me. A couple are running light on Sergeants, as are you. I asked him to place me where I'd learn the most and learn it fastest. He said that would be your trademark.'

'I'm complimented,' smiled Colours. 'I confess I had no idea that you were arriving, but I'm pleased to have you on board. You couldn't have come at a better or a worse time, depending on your point of view I suppose.'

Beckwith smiled. 'I understand sir. My induction was hugely accelerated when all of this started to happen. I'd rather be here now than when things are quiet. May I say sir, that your reputation precedes you. I'm delighted with my posting.'

Colours smiled. 'Come to breakfast with me. I want to introduce you to my other Sergeant, Barry Mankowitz. He is hugely experienced and he'll be only too pleased to have some help. Oh! And yes. Flattery will get you everywhere.'

*

'Virgin soldier,' grunted Arthur through a mouthful of cooked food. Gilhooley and Fudge looked up from plates of egg and bacon as the relief devoured a 'fat-boy's breakfast'. They surveyed the young man in Sergeant's uniform who accompanied Colours to sit with Barry Mankowitz. They watched as Colours introduced them and they shook hands.

'Smart-looking bastard ain't he?' Arthur continued. 'Compared with you Arthur, Wurzul Gummidge was smart,' quipped Gilhooley.

'Bollocks,' Arthur responded, spooning more beans into his mouth. The assembled group studied the new man with professional interest, sensing that he would soon be another of their supervisors.

Beckwith still wore his full uniform. Sharp creases defined the line of his sleeves and trousers. His cap peak shone as a compliment to the gleaming shoes. An immaculate beard defined his jaw line and rose up over his top lip in a dark line. He contrasted Mankowitz's operational appearance, the shirtsleeves and the gun belt hung with paraphernalia giving him a purposeful, yet grizzled appearance.

'Looks fit don't he?' contributed Pikey.

Gilhooley swilled a huge mug of tea and then downed the contents. 'I guess we'll find out soon enough,' he said.

*

'It'll take an age to break that stuff in.' Barry Mankowitz watched in amusement as the young Sergeant wrestled with a black and shiny new gun belt. Across the counter the stores man fussed, muttering as he went about finding kit. He begrudged every item that left the stores, as if each one were his own.

He heaved a cardboard box up onto the flat, scarred surface and pushed it toward Beckwith. 'There you go young fellow,' he rasped. 'Everything you need.' Mankowitz stepped forward and rummaged through the box, throwing item after item on to a pile of discarded kit.

'Now you don't want our bright new Sergeant looking like a second hand rose, do you Ernie?'

The stores man screwed up his face. 'I ain't got much new stuff and that gear will last for ages yet.'

Mankowitz smiled. 'What about all the new equipment you have just taken delivery of?'

A look of horror crept across the storemans face. 'But that's me stores. I can't be storeman if I ain't got no stores, now can I?' The smile drained from Mankowitz's face. 'See that lovely big green Bergen over there. Well, fill it with nice new kit, top it with a nice new all-weather suit and...' He paused for effect, casting his eyes around as if in a furtive gesture'...I won't grass you up for all the gear you slide out of the back door'

'Is he that bent?' asked Beckwith as he climbed the stairs, the huge Bergen dragging him back. 'No. It's not a theft thing. He's just got some kind of syndrome that resembles kleptomania and crosses with the instincts of a shopkeeper from the Kasbah. You can get anything if you know how to threaten and barter. I think it's the juice of Ernie's life.'

They paused on a landing while the young Sergeant repositioned his heavy burden. Then Mankowitz pushed open a plain green door. 'Welcome to the inner sanctum,' he smiled. 'The Sergeants locker room.' He watched while Beckwith began to cram equipment and clothing into a large grey locker.

'Is he as good as they say, you know, Bladen-Barras?' Beckwith ventured.

Mankowitz took a deep breath. 'He's just a mortal man like you and me, flawed and not always right, but...' He again opened the door for Beckwith to pass through, down to meet his new relief, '...You fell on your feet with him, my man, believe me.'

*

'They want me to go to another security briefing at the yard Roy.' Lassiter leaned on the roof of the BMW estate into which Colours was loading his kit. 'You're taking Martin Beckwith out with you I understand?' he said whimsically. Colours ducked out from the rear of the car to face Lassiter with a smile. His respect for the man was growing daily. 'I was going to put him in the back seat crewing the car with myself and Barry. A kind of initiation day.'

'Seems fair,' said Lassiter. He turned toward the building and then paused. 'I tell you what Roy, let him come to the briefing with me. There won't be anything new that I can't relate to you back here later and it'll bring him right up to speed.' He turned to face Colours, raising a quizzical eyebrow. 'Okay sir, no problem as long as you don't mind it being a little crowded in here.' Lassiter nodded his approval.

Benny's gold tooth glistened in the bright sunshine as a broad grin spread across his face. He leaned across the driver's door of the ARV and drew heavily upon the self-rolled liquorice-paper-wrapped cigarette that was his trademark. 'Quite a pretty boy ain't he,' he said, smoke billowing from his mouth and nostrils. He nodded toward the doorway from which Martin Beckwith emerged.

'I reckon he'll give you a run for your money Fudge, maybe steal that pretty almond-eyed beauty away from you.' Across the roof of the car Fudge's head appeared from the passenger door as he placed the log and London atlas in the foot well. 'Raymond Bridgewater has no peers. The poor girl is putty in my hands. Anyway, the pretty boy new Sergeant has a young lady in tow I understand.'

'Bloody right,' Cravetts is on an instructor's course. He was up at Lippitts when Beckwith was on his final exercise. He reckons she's a bit of a J-lo, absolutely stunning,' said John Munney from somewhere in the rear of the car. 'My crown is secure,' stated Fudge. 'I am the relief seducer, I have no equals.' Benny groaned, his forehead creasing. 'Fudge…*Perlease…*'

The BMW'S muted exhaust note barely intruded into their conversation as the four men chatted informally. Barry Mankowitz piloted the car toward Bishopsgate where a brutal chicane of concrete marked the edge of the City of London area and boundary of 'The Ring of Steel'. A City of London PC tugged the peak of his helmet as they passed slowly through. Nearby a large white box van was being searched while police officers with carbines stood off watchfully.

'My old Dad would spin in his grave if he could see this lot,' said Lassiter. 'He was an Inspector at Whitechapel until he retired. He performed most of his service in the East End. He was a bit of an authority on Jack The Ripper. I doubt he could get his head around all of this.'

Martin Beckwith had remained subdued, content to let the more experienced men talk, to pick up their knowledge. He turned his head from where he had stared out at the towering buildings and broke. 'I came through here after the Bishopsgate bombing,' he said suddenly. 'I couldn't believe the power, the devastation. The things we are seeing these last couple of years. The number of shootings and guns. I went on a house raid in Forest Gate. We found guns that could bring down a bloody aircraft.' The men in the car fell suddenly silent.

Little more was said until the car entered Victoria Street and then turned right into Broadway, closing with the front door of New Scotland Yard. As they passed the armed and uniformed men guarding its perimeter, Lassiter broke the silence. 'Martin, you'll come with me. I'd like you to take notes on my behalf today, he smiled. 'That way you'll learn and I can just sit on my arse and listen.'

He lifted a buff-coloured file bound in a white tape and passed it to Colours. The file was marked 'Confidential'. 'Can you take this to Regency Street for me. It's Sally Galloway's file.' A strange silence descended yet again as Barry Mankowitz made himself busy with the car. Colour's expression paled, so much so that Lassiter creased his brow and asked. 'Is there a problem Roy?'

'No sir', sighed Colours. 'It'll be no trouble at all.' He looked down at the file. In red was hand-written a note. It said *For the attention of Clarissa Waters.*

As Lassiter and Beckwith strode toward the canopied entrance to New Scotland Yard, Mankowitz drove gently down the slope, turning left toward Victoria Street. 'So, Regency Street then boss?' he said quietly, his eyes fixed ahead of them.

Colours nodded. 'Yeah, Regency Street he confirmed. Then in a whisper to himself, beneath his breath, he uttered... *'Charlie.'*

*

Colours knew the voice so well. The carpeted corridor silenced his footfalls. The murmur of voices and the hum of the computers could not confuse him. Even with the harder edge of her profession driving it, it still transported him. The ground beneath his feet became sand, the murmur of the computers became the hush of sea upon shingle. Once again his mind's eye saw a near-naked girl glistening with salt water on her skin, a smile on her face and the very essence of life in her eyes.

Out of sight, he could hear Charlie conversing down the phone. 'Thank you. Could I have those reports by Monday next? Well, yes and if you could set up a meeting with her and her line manager, I'll come. Jill has my diary. That'll be fine. Bye, speak to you soon.' He heard her put the phone down. At his temples he could feel the blood pulsing, and he was afraid. He tapped lightly on the half-open door.

'Just a moment!' she said brightly. Paper rustled and a drawer closed. 'Please come in.' Her voice was softer now and that pit in his stomach opened to devour him again. He stepped into the office.

She looked up from her desk. The light in her eyes changed until they seemed to glisten. 'Roy!' she said, an emotional huskiness invading her words. 'Roy, what brings you here?' He gestured at a chair. 'May I?' 'Well of course...please,' she said, struggling to compose herself. She picked up the phone and pressed a button on the keypad. 'Jill, please hold my calls, I don't wish to be disturbed,' she said. She stood up and pushed the door closed behind him. Her slim form outlined in a grey pin-striped skirt and crisp yellow blouse. The pit grew ever deeper.

She picked up the file he had laid on her desk and walked back to her chair. Sitting cross-ankled, she smoothed her clothes.

'Sally, yes I managed to talk her into taking a career break. I don't think she'll come back though, but at least the door remains open.'

Colours felt his pulse slowing. She was beautiful. He had never understood why she made him feel this way. He had seen other women who looked so much like her, but she was always in some indefinable way, different. There was always something mystical, magical in her eyes, in her smile, in her voice.

For a while there was an awkward silence, then they both began to speak at once. 'No after you,' Colours cut in.

'Well, how's your family? Are you well?' she asked smiling, little creases, laughter lines enjoining the corners of her eyes. He struggled with his composure, his voice cracking.

'Yes, they're fine and growing, growing so fast, well you *know* how it is. I think they should have been boys though. They act like it.'

She smiled again. 'That'll change and then the trouble will really begin.'

'Yes it will,' he said. He stood and turned toward the window. 'Some things you know are coming. It's part of life and you just have to deal with it.' He turned again to face her. 'Don't you, Charlie!'

Her eyes fell and she clasped her hands on her knees. 'Don't Roy. You know this going to get us nowhere.'

Colour's face contorted, his emotions an agony. 'How did we do this, how did we make...make such a...' She broke in suddenly, 'such a fuck up,' she sighed.

Colours looked at her, shocked. 'I never heard you swear before, not ever,' he said.

Her emotions eased a little, a weak smile slipping across her features. 'No-one in the army fails to swear eventually, I just wouldn't do it in front of you.'

'So why now then?' he said.

'Because then was then and now is now,' she replied, suddenly assertive.

His eyes fell. 'So is this where I get some applied psychology, where all your training and counselling skills are applied?' he asked dismissively.

She took a deep breath. 'Please, let's not get angry with each other. We were very young; we believed things that weren't true, valued things that had no value. It's nobody's fault you know.'

On a tide of rising emotion, she stood up, continuing. 'I hate the thought that I was so young and stupid. I have never loved anyone the way I loved you. But I have to live with that now.' Her words began to quaver, *...and so do you.*'

She stepped closer to him, pressing her forefinger to his lips, and gestured toward the door. She caught her breath, and then said. 'Not here, not now! Let's meet and settle this, once and for all. You must be wise, there is too much at stake.' She composed herself and placed the file in a draw, pushing it closed with her thigh. Then she picked up a card from the green blotter and pressed it into his hand.

'Phone me tonight,' she said, cupping his elbow in her hand and guiding him toward the door. She reached for the handle and then paused. 'I cursed God almighty when I lost you,' she said, 'and I've lived my life so far with that memory. But we have to find a way. I will never hurt you or your family. I'd rather die.'

She kissed him lightly on the cheek and opened the door. 'Jill,' she called. I'll take my calls now. Please see Mr Barras to the door.'

*

'You know you mentioned your old dad used to have a saying,' said Barry Mankowitz as the car sped across Vauxhall Bridge.

'He had a lot of sayings,' said Colours wryly.

'No!' replied Mankowitz, 'the one about tomorrow, you know, wait and see… *Manyana…* '

.'Well my old man had some too. One was '*Don't just put a toe in the water. Make sure you know how deep it is before you jump in!*'

Colours stared at Mankowitz's eyes. 'So your old dad was a bit of a wise owl then, was he Barry?'

The Sergeant glanced back, a kind of mischief present in his eyes. 'Well no actually boss! In fact he was a bit of an old shagger.'

THE SWORD AND THE SCIMITAR

'What's wrong Roy?' Beth's voice wafted from the kitchen. 'You've done nothing but radiate brooding menace since you came home. The girls have noticed. Don't you think you should go and say goodnight?' He lifted the decanter of whisky from the drinks cabinet, softly cursing as it struck a glass and the clear sound echoed in the evening stillness.

'Sure, of course!' He poured three fingers of Irish whisky into a tumbler, and sipped it. Then he gulped the remainder down. Beth's head appeared around the door.

'Well go and say goodnight to your beautiful daughters. I'll see if I can think of a way to distract your thoughts?' A hint of mischief crept into her voice. Now something greater than terrorism, than work, than everything else populated his mind with confusion and it wouldn't recede. He couldn't think or clear it from his mind. Charlie's face, her words dominated his thoughts.

He refilled his glass and climbed the stairs, the thick carpet muffling his steps until they sounded like mere breaths. He turned toward the front of the house, mentally cursing as that same old board creaked and gave him away. 'Hello Daddy,' Bethany's soft voice issued from the darkness. 'You're very late. Has there been lot's of trouble?'

He drew a sharp breath. The hint of a young woman in his eldest daughter's voice almost shocked him. *'That'll change and then the trouble really begins.'* Charlie's words came again to his mind. He sat on the edge of her bed and stroked her long hair from across her eyes, his fingertips brushing her brow lovingly.

'No, no special trouble.' Her eyes held his in the half-light. 'I know what's happening Daddy. We all do. Every one at school asks about you. They want to know if you have killed any one.'

He hated this loss of innocence, this invasion of their intimacy. 'Shamila tells people that your job is to kill people and I hate her.'

Colours drew a sharp breath. 'Bee… It's not as simple as that and these are terrorists,' he said, yet again finding himself forced to discuss that which he wanted to avoid.

'Terrorists are bad, they're not the same as most Arab people. They are a few in a nation of millions. I don't like to think that that these things are poisoning your minds.' The young woman in his daughter reached out to him. 'I know that Daddy, but Sarah and Amelia are so afraid for you that they say they hate all Arabs.'

'Hate is very big word Bee… But love's a bigger one,' he replied. She relaxed her head back on the pillow.

'I know Daddy. I will tell them both again, I promise.' Then the little girl returned to her eyes. 'Give me a kiss goodnight,' she said, cuddling an old teddy bear.

He leant forward and kissed her eyes and then her forehead in turn. 'Night, night angel,' he whispered. From behind closed eyes she replied in a breath. 'Night Daddy, I love you.'

He tiptoed across the landing to where his younger daughters now lay. Kissing and blessing their sleeping forms, wrapping himself in the warmth of this moment and feeling suddenly and strangely calm. The creaking board betrayed him again as he made for the stairs.

'Daddy!' Bethany's voice whispered in the darkness of her room.

'Go to sleep love, it's late,' he whispered.

'Daddy,' she insisted. 'Mummy says she's going to make a big fuss of you tonight, because you are so stressed.' Colours smiled 'Well, that's nice,' he replied. 'Now go to sleep darling.'

'I will Daddy,' she giggled. 'And I won't come downstairs either. We would still like a baby brother you know?'

He smiled to himself in the darkness. 'Bee…, sometimes I wonder what I'm going to do with you.' Muffled laughter issued from below the bed sheets.

He passed the open door to his lounge where flickering firelight now danced on the walls and reflected back from glass and polished metals. 'I'm just going out to the garage,' he called back to his wife. 'I'll be using the Harley for a while now,' he added.

He opened the creaking garage door to where a large, gleaming motorcycle slumbered. He checked the oil and fluids then ran its rumbling engine for a few minutes. When he had done he took the mobile phone from his hip and punched in the word 'Manyana.' He typed in the number from the card in his wallet and pressed 'send'.

104

As he strode back to the house, the phone vibrated on his belt. The text message it displayed in reply said only, 'Okay.'

'Take a nice warm shower darling,' called Beth from the lounge. 'I'll lay out something for us to eat and a drink.' The hot water soothed him, massaging the back of his bowed head and neck, cascading downward, plastering the dark hair in patterns on his body. He raised its temperature, seeking greater comfort. On the tiled floor, delicate female footprints were outlined in talcum powder. The sweet smell of it hung on the air, mixed with her perfume.

Soon his bare feet felt the welcome softness of carpet as he descended the stairs, wrapped in a warm and deep red robe. The flickering firelight beckoned from the doorway of the lounge as he approached. He padded softly into the room. Beth sat naked on a duvet by the fire, her legs folded beneath her as she dried her hair. On the hearth a tray of food awaited, complimented by a small tureen of mulled red wine.

Soft music floated on the air. She patted the duvet beside her, bidding him to sit there. 'You look like the little mermaid,' he said, smiling softly. Her long hair tumbled down across her shoulders, brushing her breasts as she reached out to him, drawing her fingers down his chest, pulling the tie belt loose at his waist.

'Harlot,' he whispered.

'Pushover,' she responded.

She took a sip of red wine. Then pressing her lips to his, she kissed him, allowing the warm content of her mouth to escape, her tongue to flick at his lips. Her mouth followed the deep red tracks down his throat and then on to his chest. 'What chance do I have?' he whispered. 'I'm just a mortal man.'

Her hands clasped his thigh, her cheek pressed firmly to it as she curled into his lap. She looked up, the firelight dancing in her eyes.

'No, your not just an ordinary man Royston Bladen-Barras. In fact you are a very special one. Now your daughters want a baby brother, and I want a son.'

The firelight danced and crackled, the soft music wafted, mixing with their breaths. They were the only sounds.

*

In the early light he eased open the wooden garage doors, quietly cursing the creaking hinges. He rolled the huge machine out into the light. Minutes earlier he had dragged himself from their bed where the soft skin of her back had pressed against him as he held her. Studiously avoiding the noisy floorboard he deftly descended the stairs.

He had sat for a few minutes sipping coffee that washed down a little brown toast. As he did, he studied the tumble of textiles they had left in front of the now dwindling fire. The tureen that had glowed in the firelight now stood forlorn and near empty.

He threw the small rucksack across his back. When it was secure he mounted the motorcycle, allowing it to roll downhill away from the house before firing its big V twin engine. The sudden rumble somehow startled him and his thoughts turned to the day ahead. The greenery of Surrey lanes flashed by as the beat of the engine echoed.

He found himself checking his mirrors again and again. A white van loomed large and close, he caught his breath. The driver was a swarthy man with a dark moustache, while the passenger a fat younger man, studied him intensely. While his mind sifted evasive options it turned suddenly away.

His rapid breathing misted the inside of the visor and his heart pounded. 'The bike, they were looking at the bike,' he thought. He realised how fear was beginning to pervade his existence, despoiling his life and threatening his comrades. He opened the throttle and rode suddenly harder.

*

'Nice bike Mr Barras.' Martin Beckwith nodded his appreciation at the gleaming metallic red machine, dripping with chrome. Colours smiled in acknowledgment. 'It's my weekend toy really, but I guess it will have to earn its living for a while.' Beckwith's face split into a grin. 'Hey, don't go getting it wet Roy. It'll take you a month to clean it!'

Colours strode across the yard, the only sounds were the wooden footfalls of his boots and the creaking of his leather suit.

Then the steel gates clanged as others began to arrive. He turned toward the stairwell, wondering what this day would bring.

Chief Superintendent Lassiter thumbed through the file of information waiting on his desk. He adjusted his slim reading glasses as he turned page after page. The rattle of crockery broke his concentration as Elaine tottered in.

'I've put some biscuits on the tray, but can I get you something else. Some toast perhaps?' Lassiter pulled the glasses from his face and turned. 'No thank you Elaine. I understand Mr Barras is early turn today. Would you please contact him and ask him to call me?'

She placed the tray on Lassiter's desk. 'Certainly sir.' She smiled her sweetest smile. 'I'll do it right away.' She exited with a flourish, patting her hair. Lassiter slowly shook his head.

'You asked me to ring sir?' Within minutes Colours's assertive voice resonated through Lassiter's phone. 'Are you far away Roy?' asked Lassiter. 'Can you come in?'

'I'm just pulling in the yard sir' came the reply. 'Be up in two minutes.'

A short while later he entered Lassiter's office. 'Close the door and sit down Roy, please.' Lassiter placed a file on the desk in front of Colours. 'Another little problem for us,' he began. 'An Imam in West London has spoken out strongly against this new group. He was scathing and threatened to issue all kinds of edicts against them. The net result is death threats and we've been asked to come up with a plan for an armed guard.'

Colours drew breath through his teeth, musing on Lassiter's words. 'Where do they think the manpower for this is going to come from. Soon we'll have Muslims in street corner supermarkets demanding armed protection.'

'Lassiter's expression deepened. 'That's the whole thing Roy. The tactic, it's working. I can't deny this man our attention. His religious profile is too high, but I am worried about the knock-on effect.'

Downing the last of his coffee he called loudly. 'Elaine, fresh coffee please.' He looked directly into Colours eyes. 'We have to nail this down as soon as yesterday.'

He went on, 'SO13 are putting people in place to infiltrate the student radicals and recruiting from their ranks for big money. There's a price on the heads of this Wind and Shadow group you wouldn't believe.'

The door swung open as the girl entered, smiling. She picked up Lassiter's cup and placing it on the tray she backed away. 'For two?' she said eyeing Colours mischievously. He nodded his approval. Lassiter picked up the thread. 'You'll find our man's details in that file. He has some unpronounceable name. After coffee I would like you to accompany me to do the recce.'

Colours smiled, pleased at the degree of confidence that Lassiter was placing in him. 'I have a suggestion sir, with regard to the A.R.Vs. Can we have them patrolling in pairs wherever that's practical. Why don't we have them perform circuits and come up on each other from the rear, see if they can net something. They could do that on the hour? Twice a day? Whatever circumstances permit?'

Lassiter nodded his approval. 'Draw that up as a tactic for the instructors as well if you would Roy?' Colours picked up a green folder and placed it on the desk. 'If you'll excuse the presumption, I've already done that sir.'

Lassiter lifted his eyes from the folder. 'Can I assume, to what ever extent, you've also devolved this to the relief's?' Colours looked away embarrassed. 'To my own relief, sir,' he replied in hushed terms.

'Well then, you had best devolve it to the rest,' said Lassiter curtly. 'You always were a maverick Mr Barras.' There was a pause as Elaine entered, placing a tray of coffee on the desk. As she turned and left, Lassiter's face cracked into a wry smile. 'I expected no less.'

*

'Trojan 511 from Trawler three six, receiving over?' The radio in the centre consul of the ARV demanded John Munney's attention. His eyes turned to meet those of Chris Harding in the drivers seat. 'Trawler unit, go ahead.'

From the rear seat Raffle's voice echoed their collective thoughts. 'As you know I'm a bit of a betting man boys! Well I'll bet we have a live one on our tail.'

'Trojan 511, I have you in sight. I am the black Honda motorcycle in your mirror. I've a suspected target on your six, Peugeot scooter bearing index kilo five eight six, alpha alpha bravo. This is a false plate. Rider dressed red crash helmet, black bomber style jacket. Please give no indications. Minimise use of your mirrors and proceed toward Trawler filter point bravo five zero.'

'Trawler three six, all received,' Munney barked in response.

In the back seat Raffles was already on the case. 'Camden, head for Camden.'

'He's wired, I tell you he's fucking wired,' said Harding, snatching illicit glances in his mirror. 'He's got a bloody great coat on and it's steaming hot out there. He's a bomber, a fucking suicide bomber.'

'*Cool it Chris*, keep your head. If he attempts to draw level take him out with the car.' John Munney breathed deep, fighting to keep control. In his mind he wrestled with the possibilities. 'Make a plan, cover the contingencies.'

He turned to Raffles in the back seat. 'Andy, if it looks as if…' His words tailed off. Raffles had the map spread in front of him tracing their route. The Glock pistol lay in his lap. 'Turn right here,' he called. Then his eyes met Munney's.

'Don't worry…' Raffles smiled. 'I'm not that much of a gambler. If he reaches for as much as his dick, he'll have nowhere to put his hat come sundown.' He wound down both back windows.

'Trojan 511 from Trawler three zero. He's getting nervous. He saw you drop the windows. Be aware he's closing with you.' Harding pressed the accelerator gently. The bonnet rose in unison with the engine note.

'Trojan 511 from 533, we are on your tail. 500 yards and closing.'

'The cavalry are coming boys, let's suck this bastard in.' From the back seat Raffles added. 'One mile to filter point.'

'Trojan 511, Trojan 533, Trawler three six, all units to go to channel six, MP over.'

'Received MP.' John Munney acknowledged the voice of Scotland Yard's control room as they dedicated a channel. They listened as other units followed suit.

'Trojan 511 and MP from Filter point Bravo five zero, give me your headlights.' Chris Harding flicked the switch that controlled the alternate flashing headlights, casting light in their path toward the waiting ambush.

'Turn your next left,' called Raffles. The tyres protested as the heavy car lurched into the turn. 'Now right toward the old railway arch,' Raffle's voice rose in excitement. 'Is he on us, did he come through the turns?'

Harding's eyes ranged in the mirror. 'Two sets of bike headlights now, but I can't tell which is which.'

John Munney grabbed the radio handset. 'Trawler three six…drop out, drop out now.' Through the radio more voices, fighting for aural space. '511 from 533 we are on his arse.'

Then the controller at the filter point. 'All units from point five zero, all lights, all noise on *NOW*.'

John Munney shouted above the sudden cacophony of police sirens echoing through the ancient Victorian tunnel. '*NOW* Chris, go, go, go…' The tyres bit as the car rocketed forward. Blue and white light drew tracks around the darkened underside of the arch, while flashing headlamps combined to heighten the sense of unreality. '511 from 533, he's coming at you hard. Lose him, for fuck's sake lose him.'

Ahead of them concrete blocks narrowed the road while an armoured Land Rover and a personnel carrier sat at angles to their approach. The deadly snout of a sniper rifle peered across the Land Rover's bonnet. All around uniformed figures dived for cover.

The engine note began to scream as Chris Harding held the car's transmission in 'low'.

'Take the gap,' screamed Munney.

'That's the plan,' Harding replied, suddenly resigned. 'And then a handbrake turn. This bastard is going nowhere and the sniper can have him.'

'Chris, he's right on us, accelerating like fuck,' Raffles called from the back seat.

'I know, I know' Chris replied. 'That's the thing, those bikes are so quick off the mark.' The distance closed as behind them the second ARV screeched to a halt, the driver throwing into a 45-degree angle.

From behind the concrete blocks a brilliant light shone as they passed, directed into the scooter rider's eyes as the ARV rocketed through. Harding hit the brakes and then snatched at the handbrake as the car slewed around.

All three men broke from the open doors, rolling across the ground toward the welcoming safety of the concrete. Behind them a dark figure threw a 'stinger' across the road, its evil spines destined to destroy the scooter's tyres. The scooter slid and scraped its way along the cobblestones. Behind the protection of the Land Rover stood several coverall clad men. All wore respirators. Muffled shouts of 'armed police' filled the air as the scooter rider first rolled and then staggered to his feet.

'Keep your hands away from your body.' Frantically someone was trying to control the terrorist. Then the sniper stood clear, pointing his weapon at a target he could not miss. Despite the constraints of the respirator, he gave commands, clear, deadly and final.

The man in the red crash helmet staggered a little and turned to face him, his arms held wide. 'Keep your arms and hands clear of your body,' the sniper bellowed. 'Do not do anything until I tell you.' Behind the dark visor, eyes ranged left and right.

Then a clear voice rang out 'Alluha Achbar.'

Behind the concrete Raffles curled himself into a foetal position. 'He's going to blow, I'll bet you he's going to blow.' The sniper called again, hard and clear. 'No, do not move, *do not move.*'

The voice from within the helmet called once more, louder now. 'Alluha Achbar.'

As he moved to draw his hands to his chest a single shot rang out, its sharp retort drowned by a deafening explosion. A flash of searing light filled the tunnel, as all air seemed to be denied them. Behind the concrete barrier, pieces of cloth, plastic and glass began to fall endlessly, while smoke and dust pervaded turning the subdued light of the tunnel into almost total darkness.

An eerie silence descended. The three men stood up as a light breeze began to drive out the smoke and dust. Behind them their car stood blackened, windows transformed into a million fragments.

'Fuck me!' muttered Raffles.

They walked forward through the concrete chicane toward a scene of devastation. The sniper sat back against a wall where the blast had thrown him.

Others were dragging first aid kits from vehicles as they lifted the respirators from their faces. 'Red team,' uttered Chris Harding.

'You boy's alright?' The overall clad figure of the SFO team leader Sergeant Brendan Harper approached them. 'Apart from a little ringing in the ears and a singed car, we're fine. What about your rifleman and the rest of the team?' John Munney responded.

'Nothing that won't heal, said Harper. Can't say the same for that pile of pizza over there.' The crew of the second car ran to them, then all six men turned toward the dead suspect. He lay across the shattered remains of the scooter, its plastic panels melted and merged with the burnt fabric of the bomber jacket and blackened flesh.

His legs lay in a contorted and obscene tangle. One arm was reduced to a bloodied stump while the other lay twisted and broken under the torso. His rib cage was blown open and entrails cascaded from it into the wide pool of red blood, now turning black and glutinous.

'Where's his fucking head?' asked Chris Harding, his voice tremulous as he swallowed hard, fighting the urge to retch. The SFO Sergeant sauntered toward them. 'Don't go any further boys. I don't think first aid applies, so let's preserve the scene. Oh! The head's over there.'

He pointed to where the red crash helmet lay trapped against a kerb. 'I guess he wanted to ride safe,' he said drawing his forearm across his forehead, wiping away the sweat.

'Well you know what they say,' chipped in John Munney. 'If you wanna get ahead, get a hat.'

'Yup, if you wanna play safe wear a condom.' contributed Raffles.

The Sergeant lifted a gloved hand to Harding's shoulder. He picked a piece of material from near the epaulette and held it up. It was a fragment of bone with small ragged piece of flesh still attached. 'Don't think you'll want to take that home, will you young man?'

Chris Harding turned and vomited in the kerb. Munney lifted his eyebrows and quietly said 'whoops!'

*

'My dad misspent quite a bit of his youth over there!' Colours nodded toward the stark black and white Art Deco building. 'I think it's where I got the motorcycle bug.'

Lassiter looked up from the sheaf of paper on his lap. He pulled the glasses down his nose and peered through the window. 'Oh! The infamous Ace café. I never thought of you as some kind of Hells Angel,' he smiled.

'No, I guess I'm more a country lane man now. It's a nice escape. Sort of man and horse, if you see what I mean?'

Lassiter returned his gaze to the file on his lap, tracing his finger down the photostat copy of a small map. 'Left here,' he said 'then straight on for about a quarter of a mile. You should see a minaret as we approach. There should be a couple of DPG 'shots' outside, basic cover until we do our thing.'

Colours steered the black Rover around potholes in the broken asphalt until they sidled into the kerb beside two police officers, both wearing body armour and dressed in shirtsleeves. Each carried an MP5 carbine and a Glock pistol at their hips.

Colours stepped out first to speak while Lassiter made his way around the car from the passenger side. 'Who else is here?' Colours asked the nearest man, a portly individual, greying at the temples.

'All correct sir,' he began his reply. 'We've a man at the back of this building sir and us at the front. There's no public access to the rear and the office is separate from the main Mosque.'

Lassiter appeared at their side. 'How long have you been here?' he began. 'What arrangements have been made to relieve you?' The man became flustered.

'All in the hands of our duty officer sir. He's left a file for you in the lobby.' Colours frowned.

'Nice of him,' he said. 'Pity he couldn't spare the time to be here.' Lassiter grunted his agreement.

The DPG officer began again. 'You don't have to take your shoes off or anything here sir. Apparently the office is a quite different thing from the mosque itself. Saw the Imam a short while ago sir. He came out to speak to us. Seems a pleasant enough bloke. Asked me to tell you to go straight in.'

Colours and Lassiter turned toward the pale building, the entrance marked by double doors, glazed and panelled. It was surrounded by a classic arch. Behind the office building the mosque towered, culminating in the tall minaret.

Colours stepped forward first, opening the door for Lassiter to pass through. As they entered the lobby a tall robed figure emerged from a doorway on their right.

'Ah! Mister Lassiter and Mister Bladen-Barras. I am Saled Rahman. It is an honour that such ranking officers have taken the trouble to concern themselves with me.' He was about six feet tall. His face was largely hidden by a full beard and moustache.

His head was swathed in the same material as his robes. He clasped his hands together so that his forefingers brushed his beard and gently bowed his head. 'Gentlemen, please join me in some tea.' He beckoned them into an airy room, decorated in pastel shades and hung with fine textiles.

Low, striped chairs were distributed along one wall, opposite an impressively carved desk. 'Please be seated,' he bade them.

He rang a small bell on the desk and then broke. 'First, may I offer my condolences to the families of your colleagues in the emergency services. This violence is deplorable and quite against the ethic of Islam. I will help you in any way I can, and continue to speak out in opposition.'

A door opened and a woman carrying an ornate tray bowed low. Her head and face were hidden behind a black veil so that only her darting and dark young eyes could be seen. She poured three times into small and delicate cups while the Imam looked on impatiently. Then with a gesture he dismissed her. 'My daughter,' he said smiling, 'but I have sons.'

Forced to hold the delicate cups between finger and thumb, the two policemen drank from the tiny vessels. 'You will forgive me if I come straight to the point sir,' began Lassiter 'but we are under some pressure. D'you live here in the mosque, or do you have another home?'

The Imam smiled. 'I have another home in Hendon. I have a car and a driver. Very nice you see, as I never learned to drive. My life has been one of devotion.' Colours began to ask about his home, the times he travelled and the routes as Lassiter wrote furiously in the file.

'Do you have a family mister Lassiter? he asked, smiling again. Colours noticed that beneath the beard his cheeks were deeply scarred with pockmarks. Lassiter looked unsettled. 'Yes sir. I have a daughter. Just one.'

The Imam shifted his gaze to Colours. 'And you mister Barras. You have the feel of a family man.' His smile broadened while his eyes creased into narrow slits below his thick, dark eyebrows. 'A son I would wager, you have that about you.' Colours was disarmed, uncomfortable. 'I have three young daughters sir, but we are hoping for a boy.'

'Ah, yes a son to carry your name. Perhaps Mister Lassiter there is still time for you?' For the first time he laughed softly. 'And both garden of England men I would suggest. Stockbroker belt perhaps? I have friends in Guildford. Much better than Hendon. Perhaps one day then.' He smiled again, gently nodding his head.

113

Colours studied the man, disturbed by this intimacy. 'Not too far from Guildford,' he said guardedly.

Lassiter continued to write until he was satisfied while Colours commented and made suggestions. Finally they rose to leave. The Imam followed gesturing toward their waiting car.

'It has been a great pleasure and an enlightenment to meet you gentlemen. I am sure we will meet again soon. Very soon I think. These attacks, this is all a bad business. Strange how history repeats itself, isn't it. The Crusader and the Saracen, the believer and the unbeliever, the Sword and the Scimitar.'

The older DPG officer touched Lassiter's arm. 'Sir, there is a serious incident in Camden. I think you'd best ring the base.' The Imam clasped his hands as before and dipped his head. Colours for the first time noticed the thick gold rings on his fingers. 'Thank you so much. We shall meet soon *Enchala* …God willing,' he smiled.

Colours span the wheel in his hands as Lassiter punched the keys on his phone. 'Chief Superintendent here. What's happening in Camden?' Colours watched as Lassiter's face fell. 'We're on way.' He reached into the dashboard and trailed the cable to a magnetic blue lamp out of the window till it clamped to the roof. 'First contact Roy,' said Lassiter, staring straight ahead. 'Bomb detonation at a filter point, suspect is puree.'

*

'Won't be a lot of point in looking for an entry wound then.' Colours said out loud. He and Lassiter stood between the cordon tapes that marked the access route to where a blue-sheeted canopy enveloped the remains of the bomber. Lassiter's barely contained revulsion showed in his eyes.

He turned and looked at Colours. 'T.A.T.P,' he began. 'triacetate triperoxide with a tiny boost of C4 to kick it off. That's forensics early prognoses.'

Colours stroked his chin, feeling the first growth of a beard. 'So they're making their own stuff?' he speculated. 'That bears out the pattern of remaining isolated. Chancy though. It's so unstable.'

'You are so, *so* right,' replied Lassiter. 'I'm told that impact is enough to detonate it.' They turned and walked back along a corridor marked with blue and white tape that now swayed gently in a light breeze. 'Stinks in here, doesn't it?' said Lassiter.

Around them the process of scene investigation went on as men on all fours in white paper suits brushed the dust and debris with infinite care, searching for evidence between areas divided and sectioned with white tape. From time to time they marked a point or placed tiny items into sealed bags. Behind them a solitary figure logged every find.

Colours's head ached from the vapours of the explosive's residue. The air was pungent with the analytical fluids being applied to surfaces here and there. 'I think I need some air. I'm in danger of getting high or pissed on the fumes in here.'

Martin Beckwith strode toward them from a BMW estate car that sat ticking and cooling in the kerbside. 'Barry's with the lad, sir,' he said as Colour's eyes asked an unspoken question. 'They're at Hornsey. It's been designated for post incident procedures.'

'How are they?' asked Lassiter urgently. 'Pretty good sir, actually. Shocked but glad we came out winning. Young mister Harding was pretty badly affected by the corpse. Half the relief has turned up in support and I reckon they'll have him as pissed as a parrot before sundown.'

'Hornsey, that'll be our next stop then,' said Lassiter, striding back toward the black Rover. Colours dropped into the driving seat and cranked the starter.

'Spend some time with the boys and then we'd best jack up the security for the Ealing Ayatollah,' said Lassiter, and then, 'You didn't like him, did you Roy?'

Colours curled his top lip. 'He's bogey boss. I don't know why, but he is.'

Colours accelerated along Seven Sisters Road and turned left toward Hornsey police station. 'T.A.T.P. that should give us a starting point. They'll need to buy a fair quantity of ingredients to make a significant amount.'

'Agreed,' said Lassiter. 'The trouble is that they may have been stockpiling materials for a while. You can buy the chemicals from any number of sources. It's used in the production of fibreglass, hairdressing and photographic processes. Where d'you start?' He stared out of the window. 'We need another bit of luck here. Their factory is the clue. Where is it?' His eyes lifted skyward and his thoughts took him away.

Colours turned sharp right and then right again. As they entered the yard they were greeted by a wall of parked vehicles. 'Always the bloody same here,' his frustration rising. 'This yard was never big enough!' Lassiter blinked as he refocused from deep thought. 'Well half the cars here are your ARVs. Talk about closing ranks.'

Gilhooley leaned across the roof of a BMW. He caught Colours's eye as the car nosed in and lifted his fingers in a subtle and personal acknowledgement. Then he slid into the driving seat and backed up to make room. As Colours stood up from the Rover, Gilhooley closed with him.

'They're okay boss,' he smiled. Chris is a bit shaken but we'll sort it later. Leave it to the boys even if that pretty lady from occupational health is all over him. Quite jealous I was!' he said, smiling. Colours folded his arms, allowing his chin to fall on his chest, he let out a deep sigh. 'Are you okay boss?' asked Gilhooley. 'Early turn Kieran, I hate it!' Replied Colours.

Benny extinguished another liquorish wrapped roll up cigarette under his heel as he punched in the door code on the keys of the security lock. It released with a loud click and they passed through.

Lassiter and Colours climbed the stairs, while behind them came Gilhooley, Benny and Arthur. They crossed a landing and entered a teeming canteen through the double doors.

A long queue stretched back from a counter where two women slaved to serve the throng. A black man of about thirty scuttled back and forth from the kitchen with a procession of meals while numbers were called to their expectant diners.

Tables had been positioned end to end where a team of eight or ten coverall clad armed men now reclined drinking tea and coffee, a scattering of empty plates coloured in egg and sauces a testament to their indulgence.

Nearby ARV crews attacked large plates of food while others jostled in the queue. Everywhere the hum of raised voices pervaded. Near the tall narrow windows that commanded a view of the road outside, the SFO Sergeant stood up, proffering a hand toward Colours.

Barry Mankowitz tapped Colours on the shoulder 'Fat boy's breakfast and a coffee?' he asked.

'Thanks Barry,' came Colour's reply as he strode toward the window, leaving his Sergeant to place their orders. 'Tell me all,' said Colours, warmly seizing Brendan Harper's hand.

Lassiter disappeared into a gaggle of senior officers and then reappeared at Colours's shoulder. 'I'm going to show my face to your lads, but then get a lift back to the base. I've got to file this prot plan for our Arabic friend.' Colours nodded. 'You can cope.' Lassiter smiled.

'Lucky we were on our way back from an early morning dig-out,' began Brendan Harper. He tugged the neck of his coverall clear of his throat with the sound of ripping Velcro. 'If it hadn't have been for the respirators, I think my lads would have been more seriously injured. The rifleman's a bit bruised, but apart from that we were so lucky, as were your blokes.'

'Where are they now?' Colours asked. 'Mostly in here, that is with the exception of Chris Harding. He seems to have been more deeply affected. He's in the rest room if you wish to see him?' said Harper.

Colours turned his head to glance out of the window, replying, 'Of course, of course I do.'

*

'Guess you've been a little busy for phone calls?' As he grasped the door handle, her voice sent a cold shiver through him.

There was too much happening; He simply couldn't deal with this as well. 'Charlie I'm sorry. I can't find the time to breath right now.'

She looked up at him from the chair by the window. Through the opaque glass he could see Harding's outline in the room beyond. He was seated by a window, hunched forward protectively, sipping from a cup.

She let out a sigh that hinted at her disappointment. 'Roy! You don't have to explain to me. It's my stock in trade. Remember?'

He dropped his eyes in embarrassment. 'I'm so sorry, I had forgotten what a diamond you are,' he admitted, turning to look into her eyes, 'and you always were.'

Harding looked up as they stepped in. 'Settling down a bit now Chris?' enquired Colours. 'Just embarrassed boss! I threw up. I feel like a frightened schoolboy.' Colours put a hand on his shoulder.

'D'you know, most men that are soldiers never get to fire a shot in anger, never feel fear, never see a real bomb detonate or view a mutilated body. You've got nothing to reproach yourself about.'

Charlie touched Colour's hand. 'Hey big boy, you after my job?' she smiled.

'What happens now?' Harding enquired, his eyes uplifted toward them, almost childlike.

'Apparently the boys are taking you down the Barley Mow to get you pissed,' smiled Colours. Harding looked into the softness of the woman's eyes, seeking warmth.

'From my professional standpoint,' she said. I think you should let the boys take you down the Barley Mow and get you pissed,' and she chuckled.
Harding stood up and walked to the door.

'Deal!' he replied.

*

The car bucked over speed bump after speed bump. 'These bloody North London local authorities just love these things, don't they?' Mankowitz complained. 'I don't know why they can't let the surfaces decay like they do in most other places. Cost effective and the same result,' he grunted angrily.

Colours sat in silence. His fingers brushed the back of his own hand, remembering where Charlie's had brushed his skin such a short time ago.

'Cat got your tongue Roy?' Mankowitz asked. Colours turned to face him as they accelerated out into the Balls Pond Road, headed back to the base.

'Can you pull over for a minute?' Colours said, cupping his face in his hands. The car sidled to a halt outside a long terrace of Georgian housing.

He drew a deep breath. 'You know there's something going on,' began Colours. 'Me and Beth, you and Helen and all our children, we go back a long way Barry.'

Mankowitz stared intently into his eyes. 'You don't have to explain anything to me,' he said. 'I know that nothing in life is so simple. I know that you're a good man and you love Beth and the kids. You have your reasons. I will never judge, never comment and never speak of it.'

'I want to talk about it. Will you listen?' said Colours.

Mankowitz bowed his head, staring blankly into his lap. 'If that's what you want, if it will help,' he said.

'It goes back a long way,' Colours began. 'When I was a boy soldier, just eighteen, I met a girl. I loved her to distraction and now I know she loved me just as much. We were young and we were stupid. Life played us false and it just went wrong. Times changed and we went our separate ways,' he continued. 'Everything's different. Now we're half a lifetime apart. The thing is we've been thrust together again.'

His face grew more sombre. Mankowitz listened in silence.

'The thing is I love Beth and the kids. In a way I love these brave men I work with. I don't know of any measure that says you've not got enough love for a lot of people.'

'And you still love her?' said Mankowitz quietly. Colours dropped his head forward. Staring into his lap he whispered.

'Yes, I do.'

For long moments the two men sat in silence. Then Mankowitz clasped his hands gently together and pressed them to his own lips and chin. He turned to face Colours.

'You will do the right thing and so I believe, will she, whatever that thing may be. Until then I have been and I will always remain your friend.' Then he started the car and drove on.

*

As they entered the yard of the base, a sudden urgency became apparent. All around men in blue coveralls walked or ran urgently back and forth from the large white vans. They carried kit, ladders and weapons all coloured the same tactical matt black. Nothing must shine. Colours slammed the steel gate shut and walked back to the car.

'What the fuck is going on now?' hissed Colours, as the silence between them was broken. The baseman raced toward them. 'Mister Barras. Best you get up to Mister Lassiter's office straight away. He wants you and any other supervisors in the base for a briefing urgently.'

The office seemed ever smaller now that it was crowded. The meagre light from its window diminished by the press of men. Two Sergeants and an Inspector were already seated as Colours and Mankowitz entered.

'Gentlemen, we have two significant new developments beyond the Camden incident,' began Lassiter. 'There has been a major fire in Barnet above a butchers shop. The initial call was to an explosion and the brigade suspected a device. S.O.C.O was of the opinion that we had found our explosive substance factory. Since then spent canisters that had contained sulphuric acid, acetone and peroxide have been found bearing out his initial findings.'

A murmur ran through the group. Lassiter took a deep breath. 'Mr Barras, you're not going to like this.'

Colours looked up, 'It's been an interesting day so far sir, try me.'
Lassiter thought for a moment. Gentlemen, would you excuse us,' he said and then, 'no! Sergeant Mankowitz, perhaps you should stay.' Colours felt himself begin to tremble.

'For God's sake sir, what is it?' he could not contain his anxiety.

'Home is fine Roy,' said Lassiter, anxious to allay Colours's worst fears. 'It's nothing like that. Please sit down.' The three men sat quietly as Lassiter folded his arms on the desk, the thin glasses perched on his nose.

'The body of a man of Arabian origin was found beneath a flyover on the M1 at midday today. He had been tortured and mutilated and his throat was cut.'

Colours stared into Lassiter's eyes, hardly daring to think the unthinkable, less to speak it.

119

'He was Saled Rahman, the Imam for the Mosque we visited this morning.'

Colours face went ashen. 'But we had prot on him. We spoke to him. How can this be?'

Lassiter stared at Colours intently, measuring and anticipating his reaction. 'He'd been dead for at least twelve hours,' he said hesitantly.

Colours eyes widened. 'But…then who…?' he stuttered his response.

'Roy…' Lassiter continued. 'He fooled us both. He fooled the job, he fooled everyone. Think Roy, a man and a woman. Educated, sophisticated and eloquent.'

Colours stared at him open mouthed. Quietly Lassiter said, 'Wind and Shadow. A fax with the same epaulette, the image of a minaret, a sword and a scimitar has been received at C.O.'

Colours rocketed to his feet, clenching and unclenching his fists.

'He asked us about our children, our homes.' His eyes glazed as he spat out more words.

'If I ever get the chance I'll tear this bastard's heart out and feed it to him. I swear by almighty God I will.'

Then sat down abruptly, his face in his hands.

THE KILLING HOUSE

'Christ almighty', said Colours as he stared up at the charred remains of the flat. 'I guess you have your ways, but I'm buggered if I can see how they'll get anything from that blackened mess.' The sound of the diesel pumps forced him to shout. Four large fire appliances and two ambulances stood nearby while fire-fighters scuttled back and forth, stepping over the criss-cross of grey and silver hoses. In the rear of one ambulance Colours could see a seated elderly man. His head was bandaged over a bleeding wound. A car alarm sounded forlornly in the distance.

The street was flanked with shops of 1930s origin. Now they were corrupted into a hundred different uses. A small modern supermarket conflicted with an ageing shoe-menders, while an Indian restaurant nestled beneath an Art Deco façade. The colourful windows were strangely at odds with the patina of their surroundings.

The road dipped low between raised footways that were contained behind black iron railings. Here and there they were broken by granite steps, product of a quieter, more courteous age. Water cascaded over the paving stones and down the steps into gratings that barely coped with the torrent from the fire hoses.

Distantly the road rose up toward a wooded area, marking the visible end of suburbia. Above a butcher's shop, its interior now sodden and running with water the burned and destroyed flat looked somehow macabre. The vestiges of a window hung like trellis-work over a sill, the jagged edges of soot-stained glass projecting like shark's teeth from its edges. Sections of wall had blown out to fall on parked cars below, while others remained standing, larger swathes of mock Tudor rendering had fallen away to expose ugly brickwork.

Internal partition walls had burned through, allowing Colours to see right through the skeletal remains, to view the blue sky now misted by rising smoke and the roof trusses that were here and there naked to the world. Now and then the sudden hiss of steam marked where cold water found hot metal.

'Oh they will find plenty mister Barras. Residues, chemical fingerprints, burn rates, seats of fire. It's surprising,' the senior fire officer lifted an eyebrow. 'We're clever bastards,' he joked. 'Had years of practice.'

He leaned back against the dark red car. He was a Divisional Commander. The emblem of Laurel leaves surrounding an impellor stood out boldly against the dark navy tunic. He turned his flat cap in hands that were dark and hairy, a reflection of the dark growth at his chin and an equally dark moustache. 'Your boys will be in there next with our investigation team, bagging up all sorts. I reckon you can expect to get quite a lot from this site.'

Colours turned as Martin Beckwith approached him, his feet crunching on the shattered glass. 'I don't know how long it'll be before we can get in there,' he said as he closed with the two men. He looked at the fire chief. 'Your blokes reckon it won't be safe for hours.'

As if to bear out his words, a sheaf of slates suddenly slid off the roof to arch downward and impact on an already scorched Peugeot car, throwing a cloud of grey dust in the air. Beckwith shrugged his shoulders. 'Well, it is a double yellow line,' he said.

A masked and helmeted Fireman strode toward where they stood, silver bars on his shoulder. As he grew close he slid the mask and helmet off and shook his head. Sweat gleamed on his face and forehead. He sucked at the fresher, cooler air gratefully. 'Two bodies sir,' he said. The fire chief stood up, replacing the hat on his head. 'Go on. Age, sex, condition?' he asked.

'One's badly damaged, sir. Can't hardly tell the sex yet. Looks as if they were using camping-gas type equipment because some cylinders have gone off at the time of the main explosion. This bod was evidently a bit close. Most of him is still there while quite a few bits have been blown off. The rest is seriously barbecued.'

'And the other?' cut in Colours.

The fireman half turned toward him. 'He was in the toilet. The walls blew in on him and pinned him down. I don't care who he was. I hope the first blast knocked him out because he is still sitting there with his trousers around his ankles, baked like a Christmas turkey. You can't even tell what race he was, he's just cooked.'

'Fingerprints?' Colours asked urgently.

'Yes probably, DNA certainly!' the man replied. Colours nodded his approval to Beckwith. 'Hope,' he said 'We have a chance.' How long till they can take the prints? Beckwith asked.

122

'As long as it takes for the pathologist to amputate a dead man's hand,' Colours replied.

In all the heat Beckwith still shivered.

They walked back towards their car and to where a large crowd gathered at a barrier of cordon tape. Local officers stood facing them. Colours cast a glance over his shoulder toward the back of the Divisional Fire Chief's car. A vinyl sticker in the rear window read 'Get a smoke alarm…*before it's too late.*'

'Mr Barras!… Sergeant! The Fire Chief's voice boomed after them. He clamped a mobile phone to his ear. He beckoned them back while he continued to speak. 'Yes! …Yes!…okay.' He dropped the phone from his ear and flipped it shut as Colours and Beckwith closed with him.

'My blokes have cleared a path for your photographic boys and forensic. You can have a quick look at the scene before you go if you wish?' Colours nodded his approval, casting a glance at Martin Beckwith. The Sergeant's face remained grim but impassive.

'There's a steel fire escape at the rear,' the man went on. 'You can get up there safely by that route.'

*

Beckwith dropped his chin and turned his head away. 'That is just disgusting.' Around them cameras flashed amongst the rising vapours, nearby a single figure in green overalls worked diligently. His head was hooded and he wore thin transparent gloves.

The kneeling figure of the pathologist had a pale green sheet laid out before him, with gleaming razor sharp tools visible in an open wrap. A white cylindrical container stood open to his left, while the pungent chlorine-like smell of formalin pervaded the area around him.

'Foil-backed plaster-board,' said a voice. A leading fireman stood behind them, pointing to the pile of debris that lay upon the slumped corpse. 'The whole lot's fallen in on him and covered him in foil. He's well and truly roasted, but intact.'

Against the brick-built partition between this and the next flat, an almost conical membrane of material, charred and brown lay supported by a skin of dull silver, now assuming the shape of the dead man it enveloped.

At its lowest point the remains of the man's feet were visible. They were clad in grubby trainers and socks, the remnants of his trousers and underwear lay brittle across them. He had fallen forward, his chest upon his knees so that his left hand now hung claw-like beside the base of the white enamel toilet, a gold ring humanising its unreality.

The kneeling figure worked skilfully with a scalpel, his elbows rising and falling in unison with his deft strokes. From a zipped bag he produced a short bow saw and began to work feverishly until the severed wrist fell pendulant beside him.

He nodded to a photographer who snapped feverishly over his shoulder at an object he turned in his hands and then dropped into the container. He flicked the catches to seal its lid and then stood up, turning to face Colours, removing the gloves as he did so.

'We'll get you a report on this just as fast as we can. I think the fingertips are pretty well readable, so here's hoping,' he said.

'Thanks,' said Colours.

'Barely a drop of blood,' the man went on. 'Just about mummified him.'

Colours looked back at the mutilated limb, brown and wrinkled by the heat and appearing as if this were some mannequin, some alien creature. The pink flesh and severed bone exposed by the amputation reminded him that it was not.

*

Beth picked her way across the lawn, studiously avoiding the rotund animal that twisted left and right on its back, scratching some imagined irritation and baying with pleasure. Its ears and jowls flopped back and forth with each rising effort until it succumbed to the urge to sunbathe again.

'Modest, isn't he?' Colours laughed. 'Now that's how I think I should greet you when you approach,' he laughed. 'To see if I can appeal to your bestial side.' She closed her eyes and gently shook her head despairingly.

'You can perform some sort of primeval mating ritual if you like,' she said, now pressing her lips to his ear, 'but the mulled wine and the fireside were *much* more to my liking.'

She placed a tray on the garden table and began to lay out plates of hot food, interspersed with salads and delicacies. Nearby a barbecue crackled and smoked, delicious aromas pervading the evening air. Dressed only in shorts, Colours reclined in a garden chair shaded by parasol from a still strong if declining autumn sun.

Beth slid behind him; her body clad only in the smallest bikini slipping her arms around his neck. 'I had the hors d'oevres last night, tonight I want the main course.'

He turned to look into her eyes. 'Are you trying to make an old man very happy, or a happy man very old?'

She tilted her head on one side and he thought how pretty she was, how slim and vibrant. 'I want to make love, I want to make a wonderful man very happy and I want to make a son,' she said standing up and clamping a pair of barbecue tongs open and closed.

'Can't stop on an odd number,' she said laughing. 'But after that?' and she clamped the tongs firmly and finally closed.

'Argh... *NEVER*... he grinned. He reached up and tugged at the bow that held her bikini top.

'*That,*' she said 'is not on this menu...but talk to the chef!' 'Mummy...Daddy?' The sound of children's feet thundering on floorboards heralded his daughter's arrival. Beth began to apportion meals, her face reddened.

'Mummy! Amelia's fallen down the stairs.' Colours sprinted across the lawn and into the house to find his youngest child in a tumble of skipping ropes, croquet hammers and hoops. She was sobbing bitterly, a trickle of blood running down her shin. She stretched out her open arms to him.

'What have you done sweetheart?' he said. 'Where are you hurt?' She buried her head in his shoulder as Beth knelt beside them. 'I hurt my leg and my face,' She sobbed. He lifted her chin. Above her eye a deep red swelling was appearing. 'Oh dear,' he said in his most concerned tone. 'I think we might have a black eye coming this time.'

Beth scooted toward the kitchen. 'I'll get some ice,' she said as the bulldog plunged into the fray, wagging his tale with uncomprehending concern.

The mobile phone on Colours's hip began to ring. Beth re-appeared with a clear bag full of ice cubes and pressed them against the child's forehead, wrapping her arm around her in a comforting embrace.

She nodded at Colours as he reached for the insistently-ringing phone, his face creased in an angry frown he muttered 'bloody perfect,' and pushed the excited dog away. 'Hello, yes...yes.' Beth watched him suddenly concerned as his face betrayed his anxiety.

'Go on...yes. My God, what are they doing? Yes I will, straight away.'

Beth's face creased into an ironic half smile. 'Good job you haven't been drinking isn't it. Can I assume that Stuka will be eating well tonight?'

'I'm sorry darling,' he said. 'I must go in. Something's happened.' Standing up she drew the little girl into a close embrace, as the sobs diminished.

'You left the army so that you could be with us!' she said quietly, a hint of anger in her voice.

'You don't understand', he said, his eyes hardening. 'There are terrible things happening.' He bent and kissed Amelia's forehead. 'Mummy will make it better now darling. Daddy must go.'

'There are things happening here as well Roy,' she said. 'You won't lose sight of that, will you?'

He dropped his gaze. 'I'm sorry, I really must go. We'll talk later.'

She sighed and turned away. Dropping her head she whispered, 'Okay Roy…'

*

The exhaust note echoed back from the tall city buildings, the motorcycle's heavy beat hammering on glass and concrete alike. As he approached the base an ARV was just returning and waved him through the open gate. He swept into the yard and parked facing a wall amongst a sea of motorcycles. As he lay the heavy machine on its side stand, Barry Mankowitz approached.

'They have another address, Roy. They identified the burned bodies at Barnet and found an address book in the back of the foil wrapped corpse. He was not *most wanted* but still definitely of interest. Lassiter has two teams out and the hit's going in within the hour.'

Colours swung his leg over the Harley and stood up, dragging the helmet from his head. He rubbed his face and scalp with his hand and said. 'Did I hear right? They found T.P.U.s at Barnet?'

The two men strode toward the building while all around them the teams of specialist firearms officers were preparing their weapons, kit and vehicles. 'Just the remnants of one,' Mankowitz replied. 'The bods from the lab reckon that there wasn't the means to produce too much explosive in that flat, that there must be other places.'

Lassiter appeared in the doorway. 'Glad you made it Roy. Sergeant Mankowitz will brief you on the hoof. Grab an ARV and follow us. We're going to West Drayton.'

Without waiting for a reply he strode across the yard and climbed into a dark Range Rover. The distant clang of the gates heralded the exit of the first vehicles in a considerable convoy.

Breathlessly the two men climbed the stairs and burst into the locker room. Colours impatiently wrestled with his keys until the door swung open. As he pulled on his uniform the Sergeant devolved information and Colours listened. As Mankowitz finished, Colours looked up, holding his gaze.

126

'There's something wrong here. I don't think we have the measure of these people. Seems to me we're dancing to their tune and that's not our way.' He turned and banged his fist demonstratively on the side of the steel locker. 'This group, that man. They're under my skin. There is something so evil here that I can't wrest it from my mind. I have a bad feeling about tonight Barry.'

*

The car rose up onto the approach to the flyover. Colours turned and watched their reflections in the glass of Paddington Green police station as they howled past, their fragmented image shuddering across the windows. The traffic ahead jockeyed for the nearside lane as they closed with it, tracking the flashing blue lights of the convoy in the distance.

He watched Barry Mankowitz's face profiled by the images. The intense concentration etched there was plain to see, even in this visual confusion. Colours reminded himself that Mankowitz was younger than he. He felt responsible for his friend, he felt responsible for them all. He remembered the assembled faces of their families in the garden of his home.

He reminded himself also that there were people out there that would kill them all and would celebrate their dying. Suddenly the weight of responsibility blanked out all other thought, all sights and sounds as his mind turned inward in deep reflection.

'Where now boss?' Mankowitz pushed Colour's knee and the reflective moment was gone. 'They've topped a hill and I don't want to get lost. This is strange territory for me.' Colour's eyes fell to the 'geographia' on his knees. He traced a finger down the page.

'Left, left,' he said and the car lurched with sudden change of direction.

'Bit of a late call there,' said Mankowitz, a smile curling the corner of his mouth. The collective blue lights appeared again on the horizon.

The low, thunderous roar of aircraft began to intrude with regularity as they closed with the last Mercedes van. As they passed into West Drayton they were last vehicle in the convoy. Around them the land became more sparsely occupied. Housing gave way to open expanses of land, punctuated by reservoirs.

The lights of the distant motorways created strange auras while the incessant passing aircraft became ever more intrusive, drowning conversation. 'How the bloody hell does anyone live near this?' said Mankowitz, screwing up his face as the car vibrated below a passing airliner.

Colours shrugged, submitting to the noise and the futility of trying to speak. He pointed ahead to where the lead vehicle peeled off right and pitched downwards. They watched as each successive vehicle followed the beams of their headlamps ranging dramatically high and low on some unmade surface and were then extinguished.

They turned to follow. 'Shit,' Mankowitz cursed as the lights of the vehicle ahead went out and he was plunged into almost total darkness.

'Turn on the map light,' he said as he extinguished those of the car. 'Why are you whispering?' smiled Colours in the darkness. Mankowitz laughed softly 'Nerves I guess!'

Ahead of them a small torch began to range back from the van ahead. The car bucked and protested over an unmade surface while they fought for stability inside. The torch-light ahead went left. They followed and found themselves being marshalled into parking spaces by more hand-held small torches.

All at once every light went out, every engine stopped and between the passing aircraft, silence prevailed.

'Where the fuck are we?' said Colours.

'According to the briefing,' replied Mankowitz 'We're in a pub car park.'

The sound of gravel crunching underfoot prompted Colours to lower the window. The disembodied oval of Brendan Harper's face appeared framed against the night sky, the piercing lights of an aircraft distantly above him reaching ahead through low cloud.

He was clad from head to foot in dark blue and black, an oval ski mask framing his face. About him hung body armour and a tactical vest, slung with spare ammunition, radios, first aid kits and all the paraphernalia of his calling.

A Glock pistol hung from his belt and around his neck and body a Heckler and Koch MP5 A3 carbine. Behind him a shadowy figure hovered, only the dull gleam of a Remington 870 pump action shotgun breaking the otherwise matt blackness.

'Glad you could make it Roy,' he said. 'This is going to be some jamboree. Once we are all tucked in around the back, the licensee will turn on his lights as normal. We can kit check and re-brief inside, and go forward from there.' He looked back and winked. 'As usual, I'll see you in the bar, but as usual, you won't put your hand in your pocket.'

They stepped from the car as an ambulance picked its way carefully through the darkness. A police dog bayed and whined, as the handler cursed it into silence. Colours recognised the voice.

128

'How's Bomber? he whispered to his old friend. 'Home in the warm. Limps a bit, getting fat. Still a mean old bastard,' came the reply.

Colours smiled to himself. 'Good, as it should be.'

Inside Lassiter took an incongruous centre stage in the crowded bar, illuminated by multi-coloured bulbs, flanked by endless horse brasses and bottles. All around men in black coveralls creaked and chinked, muttering in subdued tones and checking their kit over and over again.

'Gentlemen,' he began. 'I do not intend to hold a full second briefing here. You're aware of the geography and of our intention. It suffices to say that all support services and contingencies are in place. May I remind you that we are obliged to pass a gipsy encampment to reach our target.'

'There are units cropped up near the target address and they will be aware of your approach. They've been in situ for only one hour, so current local intel is limited. Dogs may be a problem. If necessary the shotguns may be used on any aggressive animals once the search is progressed, otherwise long battens or Tazers.'

He turned to face Colours. 'Mr Barras, we have a set of coveralls for you to use. Sergeant Mankowitz, please drive the SFO kit van with PC Handley as your operator. You will follow the foot approach from here at a reasonable distance once called forward and set up a forward control.' Mankowitz nodded.

Lassiter smiled, 'No white shirts you understand!'

'Lassiter lifted his tone above the suddenly-raised voices. 'Form up in the car park at the front in three minutes.'

'You have to give him credit', Brendan Harper said as he passed Colours his coveralls. 'Most Chief Superintendents would be home in bed waiting for a phone call.'

Colours smiled. 'Lassiter? While this is going on? Over his dead body.'
'Show me on the plan what the ground is like and the configuration of the target premises?' Colours asked as he dragged the dark coveralls up his legs and fought his arms inside. Harper nodded and unrolled hastily drawn plans on A3 paper across a beer stained table.

'This is our RVP as we stand,' he said. He traced his forefinger along lines drawn in red and green felt tip pen. 'That's our F.U.P. We move off along this lane, which as you know is unmade. There's a ditch to the east and a large Gipsy encampment to pass on the west.'

'It sits well back but there is a chance we'll get pinged.'

Colours nodded, listening and watching intently.

'An initial vehicle mounted approach is out because of noise. The locals have the whole thing cordoned by now, so nothing goes in or comes out. It's about three hundred yards to a gate where we turn left and come in on the white aspect. There are four crop points roughly set up for eyeball equally spaced around and I've deputed six more units to contain the house from identified points as we approach. I have got two snipers out on night sights and plenty of night vision, but it's all only just gone in. We can't do a fly over check because the helicopter is banned from this airspace.'

'What about the house itself,' Colours asked. 'Have we been in there?' Harper looked up. 'No. It's a listed building apparently, a large Georgian farmhouse. It's boarded up to a point and semi derelict inside. English Heritage sent us some images by fax, but they are not very clear, all black ink and dark corners. What you can see is that there are three storeys, a tall narrow building.'

'The first two are galleried around a living area. A bit of old furniture, that's it really.' Colours shook his head and gently sucked on his teeth. 'Brendan! That entrance. It's a killing field. You'll be like fish in a barrel.'

Harper looked up as Colours buckled his gun belt on. 'Look Roy! All they have is a bit of intel from some snotty student. A vehicle attributed to the fried Arab from the Barnet thing was seen here and a few tracks. I reckon he might have been sleeping rough.'

'Personally I think we're clutching at straws, and we'll find fuck all. But hey! Its got to be done and so it's got to be done right.'

Colours sighed. 'How come Barry Mankowitz is here, who called him out?'

'No-one' replied Harper. 'He phoned in and when he learned you were going, we couldn't keep him away.'

*

The dogs whimpered and whined, as the handlers struggled to silence them. Johnny the Dog Sergeant clamped his hand over the young dog's snout. Pulling it back he pressed his mouth to its ear, whispering 'Shut up you noisy bastard.'

Ahead of him a single file of shadowy figures melted into a darkness broken only by the occasional flash of a torch, a beacon for them to follow. With each deafening pass of a huge aircraft, the line moved forward, using its roar to mask their footfalls as they stumbled on the unmade surface of dried, rutted mud and broken building waste.

Laboured breathing punctuated the momentary silences, while the muted sound of rattling gun clips, the buzz of radio earpieces was audible only to them.

Colours moved forward, his hand on Brendan Harper's shoulder. Another hand rested on his.

His feet stumbled on rubble and concrete, while the rutted tracks threatened to twist his ankles. The earpiece muffled outside sounds while beneath it the pounding of his heart filled his head and stole his resolve. He longed to ask how much further, but remained silent.

The shadowy images of trees appeared on his right, picked out in the reflections of a wide expanse of still water where a wildfowl broke noisily from a bank, cursing and flapping across the surface. A dog barked and the handler cuffed its ear.

A tiny torchlight painted a small circle that arced back and forth on the rough ground, indicating their path as they turned left. The tall building that greeted them looked almost spectral in the moonlight that peered between scudding clouds. All the while jet engines marked each passing minute.

Colours felt a hand on his arm as Brendan Harper guided him into a dry ditch, screened from the house by thick brambles. They dropped low and squatted as Harper pulled a small white cylinder from his tactical vest. He shook and broke it. An eerie subdued light now issuing from his hand. He held it above a sheet of paper, deflecting the light downward with his cupped palm.

'The full containment will be in any second now, then the team will move up to the front door. There's no other point of entry as everything is above ground level. Too many brambles and soft earth for ladders and nothing to be gained,' he went on. Colours looked at the detail of the roughly-drawn sketch of the building.

A dozen or more steps, wide at the base and flanked by an ornate balustrade, rose to meet a pair of large windowless wooden doors.

Windows to the left and right were of a high sash type, roughly boarded or covered with corrugated plastic. He rolled to the edge of the ditch, straining to see what he could through small binoculars.

'Spot on Brendan, but not good. No way at the back?' Harper shook his head. 'An old conservatory, rotten as a pear with floorboards missing. It'll just slow them down and make so much noise,' he whispered.

'What about M.O.E?' Colours asked.

'Enforcer should do it,' Harper replied. The local authority bod who checked it out last reckons just a few nails holding it closed.'

'So where did the suspect get in?' Colours asked.

Harper frowned 'No idea mate. The team will form up here, go forward while the containment covers, breach the door and challenge. No response and it's slow search to contact. Thank you and goodnight and we can all go home.'

131

Colours grunted, 'Optimist.'

Harper grinned. 'Lighten up Roy. I want to go home. I'm on a promise!' A voice broke through their earpieces. 'Red one from containment units, you have control.' Harper eyes hardened as he took responsibility. 'Red two from red one standby.' The voice of the team Sergeant, formed up somewhere in the darkness acknowledged. Harper took a breath. 'Red two...*go.*'

The sound of muffled steps accompanied the shadowy figures, Metal touched on metal and a dog snuffled. The movement stopped. There was an agonising pause and then the sound of a heavy impact and wood splintering. A voice rang out in the night, harsh and clear.

'You in the house, we are armed police! Come out of the house now, you will not be harmed.' There was a long silence and the call was repeated. Distantly a light came on in a caravan far behind them. The roar of a jet came and went, but there was no response.

Brendan Harper fingered his earpiece, pressing it firmly home, needing to hear every sound. He held Colours's eye in the glow of the 'Cylume.' In both their ears two clicks resonated as the Team Sergeant pressed his transmit button to tell Harper he had sent the dog in first. Colours peered through the brambles, watching the shadowy silhouettes. From left then right they swiftly entered until the last man vanished like the tail of a serpent.

'Soon be done now,' Harper whispered.

'*Support, man down,*' crackled in their ears as the sound of splintering wood rent the air. Harper made to speak, but Colours grabbed his shoulder, stared into his face. 'Don't take anyone off this containment yet Brendan...*Don't*'... Harper's face creased in disbelief. 'Brendan...it's a trap. Trust me.'

Colours stood up. 'Just you and me,' he said.

Harper called through the radio. 'All units hold, we will deal.'

Colours found himself running forward, the pistol in his hand. He had no memory of drawing it. The deep rasping of his own breath seemed deafening to him. Beside him ran Harper, an MP5 held high his eye ranging around the building. They reached the steps and flanked the door. From within the sound of men's voices, shouting and desperate mingled with other sounds.

Crackling and metallic noise. Heavy impact and moaning, a dog yelping. He heard the Team Sergeant desperately calling, 'Support medic.' Lights danced inside the grey dust-filled interior, its airborne presence solidifying the beams. The two men's eyes met and another jet thundered above, making communication impossible.

Colours held up his hand, signalling to Harper to hold. As the noise faded he called through his radio, 'Control, get an armoured Land Rover up here with six men off the containment. Get it up to a window. *No-one else is to approach the door.*' Harper's eyes were wide with realisation as Colours called. 'Brendan, it's a killing house!'

As the two men withdrew from the door there came a loud explosion that shattered timber and brick nearby, and threw them face down. Colours seized a handful of Harper's clothing, but Harper broke first. 'I know Roy. They're fucking watching us. When they couldn't get any more through the door, they closed it.'

Distantly headlamps pitched and rose as the heavily-armoured Land Rover made best speed over the torturous surface. Behind it the Mercedes Sprinter's tall bodywork rolled wildly. Barry Mankowitz fought the big van closer and closer to the house. The Land Rover paused by the gate as men ran to get in. Behind Colours and Harper the first hint of flame flickered within the building and then the rattle of automatic gunfire.

The Land Rover's V8 screamed in its lowest gear, powering the four wheel drive as the driver determined that nothing would stop its progress. The two men ran beside it until its bull bar impacted below the window crushing a mass of tangled vegetation, its bonnet at sill height. From the driver's door an 870 shotgun rose to range about the upper building as the driver screamed *GO, GO ,GO...*

The first man forward raked the remaining glass from the frame with a crowbar and picking up a short ballistic shield, burst into the room. He turned and dropped to his knees and then all fours as man after man stepped onto his back and down.

The overwhelming roar of gunfire filled the room, the stark hammering of a high velocity automatic weapon dominated from above, while from several places around them police officers returned fire, the sharper crack of nine-millimetre ammunition accompanied bright flashes that illuminated prone figures. Two did not move while one screamed and thrashed in pain.

Colours and Harper tucked in below a staircase. 'Brendan, we have to get them out and I want the 870. The hammering ceased momentarily and then all firing withered away. Suddenly the screaming of the injured man and the radio traffic dominated until yet another aircraft approached. Colours looked around. Upturned broken bottles and bubble wrap lay across the floor. Cans hung in groups at every door. Boards pierced with nails like fangs pointing upward to lance the dog's feet. At the bottom of the staircase, scaffold poles swung on long ropes.

133

A strange crackling, buzzing sound filled the air. He watched it descend as if in slow motion. He barely heard Harper's words as it exploded. 'Petrol bomb.' He heard his own voice, as if another controlled it, as if he were possessed. 'Give me the fucking shotgun.' The driver looked at him wide-eyed as he reached the window. 'What have you loaded?' he asked.

'S.G.' came the reply.

'Give it to me,' he said 'all of it.'

Brendan Harper lay on his back beneath the stairs, firing single shots upward from what little protection they offered.

Above him the staircase burned furiously. 'He's blinded himself,' he called. 'He can't see to shoot at us.' Colours lay beside him. 'When I open up with this, get them out,' he shouted, his mouth almost touching Harper's ear. Around them the screams of the injured man, the howling dog and the crackling flames combined in one tumult.

Harper nodded. Colours called. 'On my word go...'

He paused, then gave the command 'Standby...standby...GO...'

Selecting a clear area Colours rolled into the room and began to fire round after round toward the gun flashes above them, each discharge sending nine lead balls upward to shatter timber and plaster into fragments that descended on him. All around men scrambled to drag others to safety, some falling from the windows into the arms of waiting colleagues.

The dog was lifted clear as Colours felt suddenly wet. His eyes began to sting. 'Petrol,' he heard himself call. He threw himself out on to the bonnet of the Land Rover as it backed furiously away. Above him a flash seemed to momentarily precede a violent explosion. A cascading ball of fire descended within the building to consume it. In moments the building became a huge pillar of flame, lighting up the night.

The Mercedes van lurched toward him. As it stopped the door swung open and Barry Mankowitz leaned out, calling through the chaos. 'Get in Roy,...*get in*.' He held his eye, his face cracking into a smile. Behind him, beyond the gate, across the road and the ditch near the still water there came a brilliant flash. It lit up the trees in silhouette as Colours watched, so slow, *so slow*...

A spiralling projectile with a tail of spark and flame grew ever closer. It slammed into the back of the van. For a fraction of a second the van glowed from within while the two men's eyes were linked in horror, friendship and disbelief as it exploded, throwing Mankowitz face down in the dirt. Glass shards filled the air as the windscreen and windows blew out.

The air was alive with fragments that buzzed like flaming tracer and joined the burning debris still falling from the building. Then the fuel tank of the Mercedes exploded. Sheets of flame leapt from every opening. They reached out with hungry tongues.

A deepening roar voiced the power of the fire, as the van became the skeletal centre of the furnace-like heat, its panels melting and falling away. Mankowitz did not move as the ball of flame grew, spreading and lowering its embrace to where he lay. Colours ran forward but found himself grappled to the ground. 'No sir, you will be dead in seconds.' Colours stared into the eyes of a huge coverall clad policeman, his face bloodied. 'We'll get him.' Mankowitz's clothing burst into flame on his back, smoke rising from his body as the radiated heat began to destroy him.

Two darkened shapes crept forwards behind a ballistic shield, keeping low. Their faces etched with pain and terror, were orange in the light. While one manoeuvred the shield, the second reached out with a gloved hand and seized Mankowitz's wrist, dragging him clear.

Many more hands reached out to pull them back as Brendan Harper appeared, clutching his right eye, his face bloodied with many tiny cuts. 'Get him into the water,' he called. 'Kill the heat.' Colours scooped the smouldering figure up, the heat of his body searing his forearms.

Finding strength he did not know he had, he ran stumbling to the still water where as many hands helped him lower his friend into the cooling fluid. In the light of the fire he could see his eyes. They stared blank and uncomprehending into the night.

All around the distant sound of sirens grew louder, competing with yet one more aircraft. Paramedics scrambled down the bank, throwing open bags, baring the injured man's arms, putting in lines, stabilising him in the fight for his life.

Colours sank to his knees, then rolled and squatted on a grass bank. He felt the wet clothing about his waist and legs, the blood forming in droplets on his chin. He saw it mixed with the dirt and grime on his hands. His breath came in snatches as quietly and privately, he began to weep.

A COLD WINTER WIND

'It was my fault, I should have seen it coming.' Lassiter's anguish was etched on his face, his expression an agony of guilt. 'Mr Lassiter...*Graham*...please sit down.' The quiet sympathy of this vastly senior officer did nothing to quell Lassiter's agony. He turned and faced the panoramic window, vast tracts of London spread out like miniatures before him.

'I had a view like this from my old office window. I boasted about it when I arrived at SO19. Perhaps that's where I should have stayed?' The D.A.C. sat momentarily silent at his desk, touching his fingertips together. He reflectively dropped his head forward and studied them. With a sharp intake of breath he stood up and strode to the door.

'Hold any calls, I'm not to be disturbed until further notice and coffee please.' He smiled through the doorway at some unseen secretary. Then he closed the door firmly and returned to his chair. 'Mister Lassiter, Graham, I do like my visitors to be at ease. *Please...* sit down.' Lassiter returned from his thoughts, the agony remaining on his face as he sank into the folds of a deep leather chair.

'No-one including SO13 thought you were going to face anything like this. It's without precedent. I understand that traps were laid with great sophistication,' he went on, taking a moment for Lassiter to compose himself. 'Give me your personal take on this?' Lassiter drew his fingers across his forehead while a young woman laid out coffee and poured two cups. As she left he spoke.

'Not just sophisticated but cunning, wicked!' he began. 'The Barnet fire was a red herring. They burned two of their own just to make it look good. The expo has confirmed that the TPU was used to detonate a small charge of C4. It was intended to draw us to West Drayton. The calculating bastard knew we couldn't use the helicopter. He chose his ground perfectly.'

He sipped the coffee, wrestling with simmering emotion. 'They created a killing ground, a killing house and I allowed our blokes to waltz right in. I was there, I watched it happen!' The DAC allowed Lassiter another moment.

'That's right! You were there! Most other men of your rank wouldn't have been. I would not have been surprised to hear you had taken part in the entry, so stop reproaching yourself. Now,' he smiled gently 'go on.'

'They had boards with nails driven through them scattered around the floor, mostly to cripple the dogs. Bubble wrap under old carpets to give the team's movements away. They put jagged broken glass all over the floor,' Lassiter caught his breath. 'When the team went to cover, some of the injuries, they're horrific.' He drank a little more coffee.

'There were bunches of cans hung everywhere to make noise and they'd slung scaffold poles on ropes at the top of the first flight of stairs. As the remaining team members tried to climb up, the gunman released them. They swung down and did terrible damage. There were floorboards ripped up and disguised with sheets of cardboard'.

'They even put a charge on the door to stop them backing out. They meant to kill them all.'

'The hide from where the R.P.G. was fired had been there for days apparently,' the DAC began again. 'They had been laying for you for a long time. How is Sergeant Mankowitz?' he asked.

'It's very bad,' Lassiter said haltingly. 'He has sixty percent burns over his back and legs. He's in the specialist burns unit at Broomfield hospital in Chelmsford. His family are with him.' He paused, swallowing hard. 'It's doubtful he'll survive.'

The senior man stood up and walked to where Lassiter sat. He placed a hand on his shoulder and gripped it. 'I'm so sorry Graham. All this gold braid is fine, but under this uniform the skin's not so thick.'

He walked to the window and stared out. 'There wasn't enough left of the terrorist at West Drayton to fill a shoebox. The brigade and forensic reckon that he smashed open up to twenty one-gallon containers of petrol before the final explosion. The fanaticism, the venom is unbelievable.'

He turned again to face Lassiter. 'How's mister Barras?' he asked. 'Cut, bruised, shocked and beside himself,' Lassiter replied.

'And the team?' The DAC asked again.

'Just completely demoralised, drained. Those that aren't injured are in severe shock.' Replied Lassiter.

'A whole catalogue of injuries.' He went on, 'Cuts, broken bones and burns.

We've one shot through the thigh, one through the hand. It's only due to Mr Barras and Sergeant Harper that there aren't multiple fatalities. I've six of them in the nursing home. The staff there are bewildered by having dogs and armed policemen patrolling the grounds.'

'If there is anything the job can do, that I can do you're to ring me personally.' The DAC handed Lassiter a card. 'That applies to Mr Barras, to Sergeant Mankowitz's family of course, to anyone involved...and it applies to you. Occupational health have dedicated their best officer solely for this incident and given her extra staff and resources. She's very, very good. She dealt with P.T.S.D. effects from the Gulf. I believe you have met her. She'll be contacting you later.'

'This I must also tell you,' he went on. 'That I'll need your every resource. I'll get you whatever extra manpower I can. Those suspended from duty by post-incident procedures will be first, the process of returning them to operational duties will be hugely accelerated. The Home Office is right behind us on this.'

'We are looking at secondment from county forces. The S.A.S. are shadowing this whole situation and are at the highest state of readiness. We're one step away from militarising this situation. At the highest level though, that will be seen as a defeat.'

'But it's working sir, isn't it? They, he *is* tying us up in knots, spreading fear and alarm. They *are* disabling us, soaking up huge amounts of our resources,' replied Lassiter.

The D.A.C. leaned forward, balling his fists on the desk until his knuckles whitened. His measured manner gave way to a bright flame of anger, burning in his eyes. 'They've won a small victory,' he said, 'but we'll win the war.'

*

The moonlight filtered through the blind to draw vivid white lines across Colours's naked back, the cuts and grazes appearing black in the surreal light. From the refuge of their marital bed Beth watched him silently agonising. She saw his chest rising and falling with emotion, with tears he would not allow himself to shed and she knew he would not sleep.

She slipped from the bed and wrapped a silken gown around her body, her skin a shade of ivory, so pale and unreal in that same moonlight. She walked to him and knelt, looking close into his open, sleepless eyes. Gently she stroked his forehead. Her hands, her fleeting fingertips brushed the stubble on his chin where the very first hint of grey had begun to reside. She caressed his face, its surface now a road map of tiny cuts.

Her lips brushed close to his ear. 'You did everything you could. You risked your life. How many lives did you save?' In the corner of his eye the glint of a tear. Only here, in the dark insular silence of their bedroom, the very womb of their home, could he let go.

'He'll die,' he whispered. 'I have seen it all before. They talk back, even move. They can be as lucid as you or I, but the body can't sustain the fluid loss and they die. The kidneys fail.' He twisted the corner of a pillow violently in his closed fist, his knuckles whitening.

'Roy, things change,' she said. 'New advances, new drugs and treatments every day. This isn't some field hospital, not some poorly equipped facility in a backwater of the third world. He's a strong young man. Give him a chance, support him, believe in him.'

The door creaked slowly open. The diminutive figure of their youngest child stood framed in the doorway. 'I can hear voices?' Her tiny figure was draped in a long nightdress. Above her left eye a small plaster crowned a very black eye.

'Go back to bed Amelia,' Beth said gently. 'There is nothing wrong.'

'Yes there is Mummy,' said the child, her eyes drawn to Colours diminished form. Beth stood up and gently guided her away.

*

'Your clothing is most immodest,' he said. He allowed his gaze to scan her whole being repeatedly, up and down. His face filled with disdain and disapproval. The woman turned on him. 'You and I have lived on the fringes of western practices most of our lives. We have enjoyed its benefits and indulgences. If you want me to blend into this society, then I'm sorry but this is the way it will be.'

'Stop being such a hypocrite!' she continued. 'You can fool everyone else with your fundamentalist rantings, but I'm your little sister, remember that, Nasser!'

His mouth twisted in an angry curl. 'Yes you are. When this is over, I shall expect you to return to the old ways.' She turned and sat down on an old wooden bench, its slats carved and disfigured by a hundred different hands. They fell silent as a group of children passed, laughing and throwing stones in the water.

An elderly man on a cycle crunched the loose asphalt as a mallard scooted away across the water, cursing. To their right beyond a low bridge the gates of a lock were just visible, while the canal curved off eastward to their left.

139

He worked his jaw, the muscle in his face flexing, betraying his impatience, highlighting the deep pockmarks in his now clean-shaven cheeks. The woman studied her brother's face. A thick shock of black hair flecked with grey, crowned his head and descended as noticeable sideburns. A thick, untidy moustache dominated his face while his dark eyes darted back and forth constantly, as if scanning the surface of the water. Anger and malice dwelt malevolent within them.

'Where are you living?' he asked sharply, lifting his eyes. She shifted uncomfortably. 'I have a flat above a shop in Old Ford Road,' she replied. 'I think I have found work in a psychiatric unit within Goodmayes hospital. If I can get in-house accommodation I shall move there.'

He stood up and lit a cigarette, throwing the cellophane wrapper into the water. 'And will your cover work?' he continued.

'I know enough to keep this charade going,' she said. 'Anyway, most of the doctors are men. They are like children. Loosen a button, smile seductively and they melt. Nice teeth and good breasts are more than they can cope with.'

He threw her an icy glance. 'Sometimes I am ashamed of you,' he spat out the words. Her eyes met his, suddenly alive with anger. 'You think you are courageous to risk your mortality, in the hope of eternal life. I would allow the devil himself to penetrate me to taste revenge for our brother.'

'Perhaps I risk eternal damnation, *perhaps I have more courage than you.*'

The man's eyes fell.

'You have strength in your arm,' she went on 'but I have strength you can't begin to understand.'

He stormed toward her. 'Men have died,' he said, his eyes aflame. 'Yes they have,' she responded, 'and more will, fools that listen to your words, that rush to embrace death and your promises.'

'I don't wish to die,' she said, her eyes burning 'but I will if I have to. That's the difference between us Nasser. You have some hope. I have only hate. That makes me stronger.'

He turned sharply to face her, side stepping and placing his hands upon her shoulders until she stood at the canal's very edge, her heels above the water, her balance on the brink. She stared impassively into his face, a half smile slipping across her own.

'And then what?' she said quizzically. 'Who will help you, who will listen and comfort you? No big brother! I don't fear you like the fools who die for you.' She reached up and peeled his hand away. He did not resist.

'You have something for me?' she said.

He reached into his pocket, gave her a mobile phone and said, 'Only I will call you on this. Keep it with you always.'

She took it and walked toward a gate in the high wire fencing that led into a large park.

'Do not toy with me Jahwara' he growled low. 'There will be a price to pay.' She quickened her pace as the path turned away behind high vegetation, and she was gone.

*

'Don't take the children to school today Margaret,' said Colours. 'Stay here. I want to know you are all safe. It's just one less thing to worry about.' His mother-in-law's usually combatative manner was subdued. Whatever their past differences, she felt deeply for Colours, felt his sadness and concern. She saw the multitude of tiny cuts on his skin and the terrible deeper wounds that showed only in his eyes.

Beth descended the stairs into the hall, an overnight bag hanging loosely in her hands. She began to speak. 'Mother, if I need to stay...' But Margaret raised her hand and stopped her. 'Do what ever you must. I'll be here for just as long as need be,' she smiled. She embraced her daughter and whispered in her ear, so that Colours could not hear. 'I love you sweetheart. Take good care of him.'

Colours stepped toward her. 'Thanks for driving down at such short notice Margaret.' She turned and pressed her fingertips to his lips smiling gently. 'Don't worry about the girls, they will be fine.'

*

The lime green canopy of the last services of the A3 slipped by as Beth manoeuvred toward the nearside lane, anticipating the exit for the M25. They had not spoken for some time as Colours descended into a deep, reflective mood, running the events of the past few hours through his head over and over again.

He felt the mobile phone in his pocket vibrate. Reaching for it he flipped it open, pressing it to his ear. Beth fixed her eyes on the road, barely able to suppress her anxiety. Colours merely said 'Hello,' and then listened intently as Beth turned the black Four by Four east from the roundabout toward the descent on to the motorway. She heard him say just 'thank you, yes thank you,' and snap the phone closed, clasping it harshly in his fist.

141

The traffic lights changed to green and she accelerated along the slip road, out into the busy eastbound traffic, but still he did not speak. He stared blankly out through his window at the passing terrain, his face sad yet impassive. 'Roy, please tell me what's happening?' she pleaded. He lifted his right hand and placed it on her left where it gripped the wheel, turning to look at her.

'Put your foot down,' he said, managing a weak smile.

'I'm already doing eighty,' she replied.

'It's all right today Beth, you're on the firm's business. Drive as fast as you can,' he said, staring vacantly ahead.

The first rain they had seen for weeks began to drizzle on the screen, turning the lights of the approaching cars into broken, oily images. At first it barely moistened glass that had remained unsullied for so long.

Then the rain increased until it spattered like broken eggs and drummed on the roof like a thousand impatient fingers.

'The first autumn storm?' Beth ventured. 'I think,' said Colours catching his breath, 'that winter will soon be upon us.'

*

As Beth swung the heavy vehicle in through the hospital gates, the last of the heavy rain was fading, giving way to sporadic droplets that heralded breaking clouds and the first distant sunshine. The broad tyres splashed through deep puddles as the standing water still sought to escape through overwhelmed gratings.

Colours stepped down, shielding his eyes from the bright reflections this new sunlight cast upward from all around. 'I'll take that!' He lifted the overnight bag from Beth's grip as they turned toward the hospital.

At the door a local officer, a handgun at his hip, smiled a gentle welcome. 'Mr Barras?' he said.

Colours nodded.

'This way sir.'

He led them through a glass door and along a corridor bright with fluorescent tubes and flanked by endless notice boards. Distantly another armed officer stood respectfully back, almost embarrassed by the black carbine across his chest. Beyond yet more doors he saw Barry Mankowitz's family gathered in an anteroom. Colours felt the pulse at his temple pounding, his stomach contort into a knot. Beth slipped her fingers into his, squeezing them. With her free hand she rubbed the ball of his shoulder.

The officer pushed the door back. An elderly man sat expressionless and pre-occupied. He wore a long black coat and rocked back and forth almost imperceptibly. At his feet a small boy played with a model car, imitating its imagined sound. A teenage girl sat beside the old man, her hand wrapped in his.

She had plainly been crying. Her eyes met Colours's in a nodded acknowledgement. Then her gaze fell on Beth. She ran to her and began to sob, the two wrapped in each other's arms as Beth muttered words of comfort in her ear. Nearby another slim young woman stood motionless.

Colours stared at her as she whispered 'Family Liaison Officer, sir,' anticipating him. He motioned for her to step back into the corridor. 'What are they saying?' he asked.

'I'm not a doctor sir, I don't like to speculate.'

Colours fixed her gaze. 'Tell me what they are saying!' he insisted.

She dropped her eyes and stroked her brow. 'Fluid loss sir. He's not keeping up and they are pumping it in to him.' She saw the desperation in Colours's eyes. 'They're sticking with him mister Barras, they'll keep trying while his body catches up.'

He nodded. 'Where will I find his specialist?'

'Excuse me,' a woman's voice called from a doorway that spilled light across the floor nearby. Her face appeared around the corner, 'You're Inspector Bladen-Barras aren't you?' she asked. Without waiting for an answer she gestured for him to enter. She smiled at the liaison officer. 'Excuse us,' and closed the door.

'I'm staff nurse Sheila Halliday, I've been closely involved with Sergeant Mankowitz's care. The burns consultant, Mister Sharma, has authorised me to speak for him in his absence.'

'There's a great deal of pressure on him just now. They call you Colours I understand? I thought that was to do with some American gang identity?' she said, seeking to ease his tension.

'No,' he replied. 'I was a Colour Sergeant in the army and it just stuck.'

She sat down across the small room. Folding her arms she took a deep breath and spoke again.

'They think a lot of you, your men. There's been a constant stream of them since Sergeant Mankowitz was admitted. Their concern was for him of course, but every one of them has asked after you? I would call that a large endorsement of your character.'

'It's a dangerous job,' he replied 'and something like this really pulls people together.'

143

'I can understand that,' she paused and her voice changed. 'My husband's a copper.' She began to speak again, her words now measured. 'Sergeant Mankowitz has asked for you. We've minimised his pain.' She leaned forward, almost touching him.

'Much of the injury to the back of his calves, thighs and buttocks are third degree burns. There is little pain from that because the nerve structure has been destroyed.' She paused to allow him to absorb the magnitude of her words.

'His fluid loss is enormous… *Catastrophic,*' she emphasised slowly.

'You're telling me he's dying, aren't you?' said Colours, resignation in his halting words.

'We never give up mister Barras,' she said. 'We're fighting to balance the loss.'

'The other problem is that his kidneys were damaged by the blast. He's on a massive regime of anti-biotics, but the damaged and burned flesh needs to be removed. It presents a huge risk of infection. Mister Farouk is concerned about the effect of that surgery.'

Colours rose to his feet. 'You're telling me this will be the last time I will speak to him, aren't you?'

She reached out and touched his hand. 'No, but I am telling you that his life is in the balance.' Colours paced the room.

'Helen, his wife. What does she know?' he asked.

'As much as you now do', she replied. 'When's the surgery?' he asked.

'As soon as mister Farouk completes his current operation. Within the hour,' she said..

He span on his heels. 'When can I see him?'

She stood up and reached for the door. 'Now,' she replied.

Through the porthole glass of the double doors, he could see the collection of monitors, coloured bar graphs, insistently flashing lights and they alarmed him. He knew what to expect, yet he could not keep a fear from gnawing at his stomach. Clear bags suspended from frames all around the bed were conducting fluids into the injured man's arms where glass phials disappeared below white adhesive tape.

Helen sat with her head turned to share the pillow with him, her lips close to his face while she whispered softly. Her left hand gently stroked his hair. The nurse pushed open the door and then melted away. Colours felt like an intruder.

The injured man was lying face down, his head turned toward Colours. As he approached, Mankowitz's eyes brightened. His body was hidden beneath a tented framework of sheets. His arms were extended sideways from his body and downwards on extensions of the bed. He lifted his fingers in a gesture of welcome, as he whispered, 'Boss, hey boss!'

Colours strode forward, seizing the hand and yet holding it with a tenderness he would normally reserve for his own child. He bent forward and cupped Helen's head with his free hand and kissed her forehead. 'See what happens when you come to one of my parties?' Colours said, forcing a smile. Mankowitz lifted his head, his eyes flinching with the pain. Inwardly Colours recoiled at the hints of yellowed and pink fluid stained dressings visible through tiny gaps in the tenting.

'Next time there's a barbecue and pool party, I'll make sure I'm not on the menu.' He dropped his head back down to the clean white pillow. 'Anyway, you don't look so pretty. Can't you shave safely anymore,' he said, seeing the multitude off small cuts and abrasions on Colours face. 'Guess the old hands are getting a bit shaky, Roy.'

The door opened quietly behind them and Beth appeared at Helen's side. She lifted her gently from her seat. 'Come on,' she said. 'Leave the boys together for a little while…coffee, okay?' Colours heard the door hiss quietly closed behind him.

As he sat down, he felt the grip on his hand tighten. 'You know the score here, don't you?' Barry Mankowitz eyes hardened for a moment, sending a chill through Colours. 'Hey! Barry, give yourself a chance,' he found himself saying. 'I know I've a chance, but I know the risks,' he said. 'If it goes wrong, make sure the job looks after Helen and the kids for me.'

Colours's eyes grew moist while he could find no words. 'And never reproach yourself. I didn't have to be there. Remember that.' Colours found himself lost. He tried to speak but a strange strangled feeling gripped his throat.

'D'you know?' Mankowitz went on, 'that these past few years have been magic. I've seen and done so much. It changed my life. I wouldn't have missed it for anything.'

Then he smiled as if they were back in that car, listening to the sounds, seeing the whirling blue lights. 'Brothers in Arms,' he whispered and he gripped Colours's hand a little tighter.

The door hissed again, as a blue-robed porter walked in. Knowing what was next, Colours looked deeply into his Sergeant's eyes, leaned and brought his face very close. 'Do you remember what you said to me, about faith and friendship?' whispered Mankowotz.

He nodded as a nurse introduced a syringe into the tube leading into his arm. 'Until then, I have been and I always will be your friend,' the injured man continued, his voice barely audible. 'That's the way it is, the way it will always be.'

Colours replied. 'I'll get Helen.' Then he gently released their clasped hands and walked away.

*

'I'll stay. You go home to the children.' Colours stepped from the shower and wrapped himself in a warm, white robe. Through the door, Beth's misted image was emptying the small bag on to the double bed. 'D'you really think I'm going to leave you alone here tonight, that I want to be on my own in our bed without you while Barry's in surgery?' she said.

Colours squatted on the end of the soft hotel bed. 'No,' he replied. 'I should know you better.' He pulled his wife close, the warmth of her body comforting him as her arms encircled his head. The telephone beside their bed began to ring. Beth reached for it, pressing it to her ear she said, 'Mister Lassiter for you.'

'Roy, I've heard how things are. Don't worry about anything here, it's covered. Martin Beckwith is coping well. Cravetts is back to ops and I'm using him as acting Sergeant.'

'What ever happens, you're off for a while, no argument, okay?' Colours sat momentarily, digesting Lassiter's words. 'Okay sir. I'll keep you briefed as soon as I know anything. The hospital has my mobile number. Barry's family are here with us. There's nothing we can do at the hospital; it's likely to go on for hours. His wife won't leave though and I'm going back as soon as I've changed and eaten.' He passed the phone to Beth and she replaced it. 'And so am I,' she said. Colours held her gaze.

'No, please. I'll call you the moment something happens. Helen and I will need you to be rested, please don't argue.'

'Just for a couple of hours then,' she relented.

*

'You're Inspector Bladen-Barras,' said the old man. He spoke without looking up, his eyes fixed ahead of him. For the first time Colours studied him. The long dark coat was at odds with the warm room, yet the man seemed to wrap himself in it, to hide behind it. An untidy grey beard that accentuated the movements of his jaw, tumbled over the collar. 'Barry speaks well of you,' he said. 'I'm his father.'

146

The information stunned Colours and yet he could plainly see now, who the man was. He turned a trilby hat in his hands, his eyes now engaging Colours's own. 'My father was a fighter pilot,' he went on.

'He fought with the free Poles and then married an English girl at the end of the war. Many of them did. He was lucky. His wife, my mother, outlived him. I lost Barry's mother ten years ago. I miss her.' He dabbed a handkerchief to his eye. 'This is a bad business.'

Colours felt lost for words, clumsy. 'I'm so sorry sir,' he said.

'Mister Barras. There's someone to see you.' The staff nurse beckoned from the doorway. She led him to her office and walked away. Charlie was seated near her desk.

Colours closed the door behind him. 'Well, I have heard the term emotional roller coaster, but this beats all,' he said, slumping into a chair. Her face was impassive. 'No Roy, this is me being momentarily unprofessional. I've been given a whole team to deal with this incident. I could have sent any one of them here. I don't expect to become even slightly involved with the past or the future. I just needed to know how you were. I am still your friend.'

He felt himself crumble. 'I'm sorry. It's all too much just now.' He leaned forward, his elbows on his knees, his face in his hands.

'You look as though you have lost a fight with a very big bramble bush,' she said softly. 'I've never seen so many cuts and scratches, but that's not where you hurt, is it?'

He lifted his face. 'No, it's not,' he confessed. 'I hurt in the deepest part of me. I hate with a depth I cannot describe and it consumes me.'

Her face drained of emotion. She seemed to draw herself up, suddenly taller. 'Perhaps as your friend, I can promise you this? I will be there for you through this, wherever it goes. I won't let hate destroy you, or grief lay you low. That's what my job requires of me.'

She lifted his chin with the tips of her fingers. 'That's what my heart demands of me. If we'd married it would have been so. That part of what we had will remain. Be strong, I will be just around the corner, just over the next hill.' Then she left.

He sat for long minutes, the events of the last few days running through his mind. Examining and re-examining every facet, until his head ached. He saw faces again and again, the flashes of light, heard the voices. He saw the burned body, heard the explosions and the gunfire.

He rested his chin on his hands as the same words ran through his head, over and over 'I have been and I always will be your friend,' until the mercy of fitful

147

sleep took him for a while somewhere peaceful. He awoke with a start, struggling to clear his clouded vision against the bright fluorescent lighting.

Helen knelt in front of him, her tear-stained face so close to his. That face ashen, her eyes reddened. She parted her lips, but for long moments did not speak. She lifted her hands to his face. Her voice was cracked and tremulous as she spoke.

'Barry died a few minutes ago. His heart couldn't stand any more.' Then she buried her head in his lap and sobbed.

*

The old man's chin trembled, betraying the courage he fought hard to find. The same dark coat was wrapped against an autumn breeze that ruffled his whiskered, greying chin, but could not disguise his agony. He held the purple cushion ahead of him as he walked, the bright black and white checker band of the duty cap stark against it.

Colours watched the unfolding scene as if an observer, as if it were a dream. He watched Helen and he watched Barry Mankowitz's teenage daughter walking behind the coffin, held high by six immaculate pallbearers, their white-gloved hands gripping the flag draped casket that their shoulders now bore. He watched their regulated steps as the gravel crunched beneath their feet. He saw the small boy staring upward, uncomprehending at the assembly.

Each bearer had volunteered from the relief. Gilhooley, Cravetts, Raffles, Fudge, and John Munney. Arthur too had stepped forward. His manner now subdued, his dress immaculate. In close attendance, Martin Beckwith whispered his commands. Behind them the hearse was bedecked with flowers. Nearby four pristine motorcycle outriders sat quietly astride their machines.

The grounds of the quiet Surrey church were thronged with men and women in uniform. By the arched doorway stood the Commissioner, flanked by an entourage of senior officers. Distantly the cameras of a now respectful press flashed.

Colours knew there were guns. They weren't visible, but they were there. He looked up. Above them, high in the church structure, a rifle barrel ranged about. The clergyman's cassock stood brightly against the assembled uniforms and the aisle of the darkened church. Sally Galloway stood by the door, with Benny as an usher. She handed orders of service to all that passed. A smile gently crossed her face as Colours passed her.

As they walked on, the distantly familiar boyhood smells of the church filled his nostrils. The regular creaking of its aged floorboards marked their progress,

148

intruding into the quiet organ music and the girl's subdued crying. Helen clasped her close, her own face a mask of determination.

In the nave of the church, the party halted. Quietly and with practised motions, they placed their Sergeant upon the trestles and stood smartly away. The old man stepped forward. His trembling hands placed the cushion and cap atop the flower-strewn casket. Beams of autumn sunlight pierced the tall stained glass windows to throw patches of colour where Mankowitz lay.

Colours felt Beth's hand in his as his mind drifted. He saw the clergyman rise in the pulpit, saw his lips move but heard not a word. He felt Beth propel him forward and found himself climbing the few wooden steps that led to where a packed congregation anticipated his words.

He felt for the paper, the prepared speech in his pocket and then abandoned it. He took a moment for his eyes to scan the hundreds of faces that looked up at him, to absorb the love and the pain. Then from his heart, he spoke.

'I was a soldier for many years. I've served in theatres of war and in Northern Ireland. I know what conflict is and I know what comradeship is. I know what courage is also. If I didn't already know, I truly now understand what friendship is. It is simply the unselfish love of one human being for another. Today I must say goodbye to my, to our friend. He was a man with all of those qualities. He was an example of what a husband and a father should be. He was an example of what a good policeman should be. He died doing his job. He died because he wanted to help me in a time of great danger.' Colours took a deep, halting breath and went on.

'I shall never forget that. This is the most fitting memorial we can give him. Remembering the example he has set. Carry it with you all your lives. If we aspire to do half as well, we will have done much and he will be there with us, as he always was.'

Colours looked down at Helen and her children. He caught the old man's tearful eye and spoke directly to him. 'If I could have made my father half as proud of me, as you have the right to be proud of him, I would be fulfilled.' Then he turned and stepped down.

As he walked back to where Beth waited, Helen passed him, whispering softly, 'thank you.' As he returned to his place, her clear, tremulous voice echoed through the silence from where she stood in front of her husband's coffin.

'Thank you all for your friendship and support. Barry was a wonderful man, and I can't begin to think how I will live my life without him. Your gathering here is a measure of your love and affection for him. Believe that he carried as much for all of you. He loved this dangerous job of yours. Carry him with you in your

149

hearts always. That is what he would wish. Barry loved Elgar's 'Enigma'. He said it spoke of this land he loved. In a few moments you will hear it played.'

For the first time she faltered, a sob breaking her resolve. Gripping her daughter's hand, she gathered herself in one last effort. 'Before he went into surgery he asked me to do something if he didn't survive. As we leave there will be something from Barry to all of you.' Then she stepped quietly away.

The strains of Edward Elgar's masterpiece echoed through the building, filling every corner with its power. Then the clergyman gave his final blessing as the immaculate men in uniform gently lifted their comrade, one last time. As the coffin passed him, Colours's throat tightened and he could not keep control; tears welled up in his eyes. Around the ancient stonework, the strains of *Brothers in Arms* resonated as he turned toward the doorway and the churchyard.

He stood at a distance, watching the graveside service and respecting this, the family's last private moment. As the mourners drifted away, filing past him, he approached. Beth stood at his side as he embraced Helen once more. The two women stood to one side as the minister walked slowly toward them.

'Father,' Colours said, extending his hand. 'We've buried a very good man today. A very bad one killed him.' He gripped the clergyman's hand where it grasped the bible. His eyes met Helen's and he spoke with a force that carried every ounce of his being.

'I swear,' he said, his eyes burning, 'on all that is holy, I will hunt that man down and kill him. This to you Barry I do promise.' Then he turned from the shocked clergyman and walked away.

*

Colours didn't recognise her at first. The long, belted raincoat disguised the girl's outline as he approached Beth, now in the driving seat of the big black Shogun. Their conversation became more animated as Colours closed with them. He saw Beth smile and then extend a gloved hand to place it on the girl's shoulder. Sally Galloway turned sharply to face him.

Beth tilted her head and lifted a quizzical eyebrow, a warning to him. 'Sir!...' Sally began. 'Something happened for me in there today. What you said, about courage and friendship. I don't want to look back and say I missed out on all of that.' Colours brow creased in disbelief.

'If you'll support me sir, well then I would like to try again.' She turned to stare at Beth, anxiety etched in her face, then spoke to Colours again. 'It's not right, me asking you this now, not at this moment. But it's this moment that's made me see things clearly.'

She stepped back, leaving Colours drained, his face a blank canvas. 'I shouldn't have…I'm sorry,' she flustered, but Colours reached out and gripped her forearm, preventing her from turning away.

'This has been an awful, a terrible day,' he began, 'and yet even now I see things that hearten me. I see how my relief stands together. They took to you and they were sorry when you left.' His face descended into a watery smile. 'So was I!' He paused for a moment then said, 'Be at Old Street first thing Monday morning. I'll speak to Mister Lassiter.'

Sally turned away, sucking in a deep, sharp breath as she did. She took a few paces and turning to face them both, she spoke. 'I wanted to taste all there is in life, to feel it all and see it all. I suppose no-one can do all of that, but there is so much that matters here, that…I want to play my part,' her words tailed off like a sob.

Colours raised his hand, as if to silence her.

'I know,' he said. 'Of course I know.'

ANNA'S PLACE

'You can and you will. Anyway, you can't be seen in public looking like that. At least let all the cuts heal properly.' Graham Lassiter stepped down into the garden. He turned to where Beth sat drinking coffee at a table on the patio.

'I agree with you wholeheartedly,' she said. Lassiter slid a chair from beneath the table and sat down. He beckoned to Colours while Beth poured two more coffees. 'Look Roy, it's stretching things in the extreme to have you back on ops at all. I have to be seen to care for your welfare and moreover, you do need a break.'

Colours joined them. Dragging a wooden chair to the table, he sat down. He said nothing while his eyes drifted to where his daughters played happily in the autumn sun. 'Stuka!' he called to the bulldog that lay panting on the paving nearby, soaking up the warmth. The dog stirred and lifted its head. 'Lazy old bugger, come here.' Colour's firm tone brought the dog lumbering and panting to where he sat.

He slapped the dog's substantial body affectionately, lifting its forelegs he buried his face in the top of its head. 'We've walked a few miles in the last couple of days,' he said. 'Ol' Stuka and I have rarely had so much space.'

'Maybe that's what you need,' Lassiter ventured, his eyes meeting Beth's. She lifted an eyebrow, sensing Lassiter's meaning.

'I could ask mother to stay on a bit longer,' she said.

Colours turned to face her. 'You know I love your old mum dearly, but forty-eight hours under the same roof and there'll be a seismic explosion. They will read it on the Richter scale,' he grimaced.

'Precisely!' she countered. 'That's why you should take that bike of yours and get off for a while. Mother, I and the girls will be fine. There are such things as mobile phones you know!'

Lassiter nodded to her. 'Sounds exactly right to me! Roy!…there's nothing that we can't cope with for a few days. You need to give yourself a break. I'll need you to be sharp very soon. Best thing all round.'

Colours remembered the times he had enjoyed riding the Cornish roads so many years before, topping great hills that tipped down into tiny coves. For the first time in weeks, his heart lifted a little. 'If I take a week, then I can go back to work, and you'll sort Sally Galloway's reinstatement, Agreed?' He stared Lassiter in the eye.

'That's the minimum I'll settle for, but it's a deal.' Lassiter smiled gently at Beth. Subtly she nodded.

*

The events of the past few weeks still ran through his mind, but slowly an inner peace seemed to flow through him. Each hill, each curve that demanded his skill and concentration took him further away from the pain and closer to the man he had been decades ago.

The thundering exhaust of the big Harley Davidson had echoed over hundreds of miles. Hills and valleys passed by. Tumbling streams ran beside the road where he had stopped to listen to their calming sounds.

He had sat alone on his first night, reflective and thoughtful in the bar of a tiny pub in Combe Martin, while the mellow feeling created by a good beer had given way to melancholy. He had risen early to ride on, his spirits lifting a little more with each successive day.

The third day found him on winding roads in the early light, in damp and misty air. Lands End had seemed bleak and inhospitable, devoid of the luxuriant green of the early journey. The bare, bleak rocks tormented by the boiling sea below somehow twinned with an anxiety in him and he was pleased to leave.

Now the hedgerows began to embrace the roadside again. Twisting lanes passed tiny cottages and farms. Anticipation began to grow within him. It had been more than twenty years since he last rode here. Then it had been an old British motorcycle. He remembered the oil stain it left whenever it was parked.

There was no sign of it outside the aged frontage of the pub in Porthcurno. The same years that seemed to have reduced the building to an unkempt reflection of its former self, had long since washed away all trace.

He parked the Harley as close to the same spot as memory would allow. Its gleaming newness highlighted by the decaying backdrop.

The promise he had made to himself that he would sit and drink in the same bar would be broken. He was now a much older man. The old lady that sat at the bar each evening would now be long dead. Charlie was not here and he felt foolish and weary.

He sat astride the big machine, allowing it to roll down hill and away. Somehow he wanted to leave silently. When he reached the junction with the coast road, he started the engine. Its exhaust note seemed suddenly at odds with his mood and the quiet countryside.

A tight hairpin bend led him up over a steep rise. His thoughts span back through decades as he tried to remember how the old Norton had felt on these same roads, how Charlie's arms had encircled him, her soft hands finding his bare flesh within the folds of his shirt.

The branches of the trees hung so low and thick with leaves that the sign was barely visible. A gentle breeze lifted them momentarily away and his heart skipped a little as he read the words 'Lamorna Cove'. It was the same sign.

He leaned the motorcycle and turned, accelerating beneath the arch of tall green trees, along a road unchanged by the years and dappled in sunlight. The dry stonewalling echoed to the Harley's rumbling exhaust. As the descent toward the tiny harbour steepened, he allowed the machine to roll, its note reduced to a steady 'kertunk, kertunk'.

Small houses and cottages, protected by their own heritage were exactly as he remembered them. The aged pub nestled beside the road, totally as he had for so long pictured it. And then there was Oriental Cottage.

It was barely visible to the left of the lane. It sat near the stream in the lowest cleft of the deep valley, its roof barely level with the eyes of passing walkers, screened from them by a tangle of high hedges and the abundant hydrangeas. Colours wanted so much to see it again, to walk down that path. First though he wanted to smell the freshness of the sea, to stand upon that quay. To his left as he drew near, a ramp led down to the water's edge. Small boats would launch from there into the tiny encircling harbour.

He tracked the harbour wall, balancing the Harley along the narrow passage between a small café and a collection of tables, crowned with parasols, where its patrons sat eating or sipping coffee. The cobbled surface widened and rose into a parking area, now devoid of cars.

It commanded a view out across the sea, or down into the harbour some thirty feet below to his left. Hills rose to a great height behind it, barriers from the real world. Colours rolled to a halt. He propped the bike on its stand and left it leaning there while he unbuckled his helmet and climbed atop the stonewall that dominated the seascape spread out before him.

He sat there reflectively for long minutes, his heels tucked back and his chin on his knees. He was testing his memory, recalling moments and words from what seemed another age. A glance at his mobile phone prompted him to speak out softly, to no-one at all. 'No signal! How apt,' he smiled to himself.

At first it startled him, but he did not turn. His mind was playing him false he thought, tormenting him. Then the sensation of her fingers on his cheek was too real. He span and dropped on to his feet and she was there, looking into his eyes. Behind her the same hills, the same cottages. The same clear, green sea and the tumble of rocks.

He took a gasping breath, but he didn't, he couldn't speak. 'I've been waiting here for two days,' she said. The press of her mouth upon his took him into some parallel world. The passion moved his limbs outside the control of his mind. He felt wetness upon his cheek, salt on his lips.

'How can this be?' he said. Charlie stood there, where she had stood so many years before, her tears marking glistening tracks down her cheeks. 'I don't know Roy, I really just don't know.'

*

A gentle breeze had struck up with the turning tide. It tugged at the parasol above their heads, its fringe crackling from time to time. He sat with his elbows on the table, running his fingertip around the edge of a large coffee cup. 'How did you get here? Did you drive down?' She drained her cup, staring at him across its rim.

'I left my car in the car park of The Wink,' she said. He looked at her, puzzled. Her head tilted to one side, her eyes creasing with a smile.

'Typical man. The pub is called The Lamorna Wink, remember?' He cast his eyes downward, admitting his guilt.

He pointed upward toward where a promontory presided over the bay. 'I remember that house we were going to live in, the one at the end of the cliff road. That was a nice dream, wasn't it.' He drew a breath and sank the remainder of his coffee. 'Where are you staying?' he asked.

'Where else?' She replied.

The Harley rolled gently down the quay, past the parasols and tables, its exhaust note hardening as it powered its way back up the steep incline. A feeling of youthful excitement he thought he had forgotten filled his chest. Charlie rode helmet-less behind him. Once again her arms were encircling his body. Outside the cottage he swung into a recess and cut the engine.

Over the wall he could see the random stonework through the tangle of greenery. Without speaking Charlie walked toward the gate and turned in. She quickly disappeared down the granite steps and he followed. He watched her slim shape descending toward the familiar walls and could not believe he was there, that this was happening. But it was.

*

'Seredemigni? Well *fuck* that man. A more selfish, calculating, vengeful bastard never walked the face of the earth.' Lassiter stormed around his office, driven by a fury he could barely contain. 'To submit a report like this at this time is unforgivable. Does he have no other aim in life than his own betterment or his own vitriol.' He tapped his clenched fist repeatedly on the desk, barely able to speak, choking on his fury.

The D.A.C. sat impassively across the width of Lassiter's office, waiting for his righteous anger to subside. 'We have just lost one of our best officers,' he went on. 'We have several in hospital, injured and traumatised and more still convalescing at Goring. We have the worst terrorist situation in recent history and commitments we can't meet. Has this man got no soul?'

'He may not have,' said the senior man 'but I have to deal with it. D'you think we could have some coffee perhaps?' Lassiter called down the length of the corridor to where Elaine tapped at a keyboard.

Moments later she tottered in, balancing rattling cups on a white tray. Seeing the vastly higher rank of their guest, she retreated with barely a smile.

'Perhaps it's fortuitous that I'm here. Perhaps it is better that only you and I are aware of our conversation. I intend to confront Mister Seredemigni at the earliest opportunity. Plainly it would be better for the service and the department if this matter were dropped at the earliest juncture. I have to tell you that he submitted this report through a senior colleague and not to me direct.'

He rose and walked to the oval window. 'If he had come to me, we might not be having this conversation.' He turned to hold Lassiter's eye. 'He has intentionally made it well known in certain circles. He means to do harm. The only way he'll relent is if it'll harm him as well.'

'And might it?' asked Lassiter. 'Life is full of twists and turns is it not? But this is and will remain a delicate matter for some time yet,' the D.A.C. replied. 'I don't want this to become common currency. For now it's a matter of record that he has criticised the supervision of the West Drayton incident in the most graphic terms. As an ex-chief Superintendent of the Metropolitan Police Firearms Branch, it can't just be ignored.'

'Did you know,' said Lassiter, 'that where firearms are concerned, he couldn't hit the side of a barn with a garden spade?'

The D.A.C. paused at the door. 'I have heard as much,' he said wistfully.

*

Arthur slammed his fist down on the table so hard, the cup jumped, spilling coffee. 'The rotten bastard means to have the guvnor's guts. That fucking knob has never been on a live deployment in his entire life. Too fucking frightened. I swear if they suspend the boss I'll put my ticket in. If I see that fucking Seagull, I'll spit in the useless self-centred bastards eye.'

He slumped in his chair while the rest of the relief looked up stunned from their meals. Cravetts returned a fork laden with beans and egg to his plate, his mouth still agape. 'What do you mean?' he said, his dark eyes fixed on Arthur.

'Bloody Seredemigni has put in a report criticising Colours and Lassiter. He's blaming them for West Drayton, saying they didn't do a good recce, that they were irresponsible, that it was a crap briefing.' Benny looked up from his plate, a sneer exposing his gold tooth.

'I suppose we're to believe this has nothing to do with him getting busted out of the department?'

'No! Not fucking much,' Benny spat out the words.

'I move we all put our tickets in if they pursue this,' cut in Raffles. 'In the current climate, that will put the cat among the pigeons.'

Cravetts rose to his feet. 'Keep your voices down. Arthur, where did you hear this?'

Martin Beckwith walked back from the counter, a tray of steaming food in his hands. '*What*?'... The stony silence and air of anticipation were plain. 'Will somebody for Christ's sake tell me what's going on?' Arthur's gruff voice was unusually subdued. 'Seagull...Seredemigni has put a report in criticising the guvnor and mister Lassiter about West Drayton.'

Beckwith lowered the tray to the table, gathering his thoughts, measuring his words. He lifted his gaze, his dark eyes fixing Arthur's. 'And they came to tell you this first did they Arthur?'

The older man shifted uncomfortably in his chair, while every eye was upon him. 'Well, no sarge. I was just talking to Elaine, you know, and...' Gilhooley had sat silently listening, his chin supported by his balled fist until he could stand no more. 'So you've been sniffing around her mini-skirt again, and come up with this?'

The old Arthur they knew so well suddenly surfaced. 'Don't fucking matter where or how I heard it. The fact is it's a fact. Don't start taking the piss out of me, you lumbering great spud eater.'

Beckwith asserted himself. 'Shut up all of you. This is heavy stuff and I don't want it all over this canteen, never mind the department or worse, the press.'

He sat down and began to quietly eat his meal. Around him cutlery began to do its work. 'Mr Gilhooley?' he began. 'I have a task for you?'

The big Irishman looked up, his jaw working furiously at his meal. 'Certainly sarge. What is it?'

Beckwith cast his eyes around the assembled group. 'If they criticise or discipline either Mister Barras or Mister Lassiter, I will walk out of the door with you all.'

'In the mean time if ANYONE says another word about it, well!...feel free.'

Gilhooley grinned through a mouthful of food. 'Consider it done sarge.'

*

'Elaine'... Lassiter's voice boomed with uncharacteristic force along the corridor. 'Elaine'... 'Yes sir! Do you want coffee sir,' she squeaked. He lowered his voice. 'Elaine, come in to my office now.'

Her diminutive form sped along the corridor to the accompaniment of the tap-clatter of her high heels.

Graham Lassiter stood facing the window, while Martin Beckwith waited to one side, a spectator in what promised to be a very interesting exchange. 'Sit down Elaine. I want to ask you about a very serious matter, a breach of my confidentiality.'

She sat slowly down on the wooden chair, facing Lassiter as he turned. The first of her tears were already diluting the mascara on her lids. She pulled a tiny handkerchief from the pocket of a black, ruffled blouse.

'I shouldn't have told Arthur sir, I know. I was just so angry. That Mister Seredemigni, he's so sly. I'm sorry sir but he is! I really liked him for a while sir, I really did and then he just changed. He's like that with everyone. He just uses them

158

and then throws them away.' She caught her breath and began to cry, leaning forward till her face was on her knees. Beckwith caught Lassiter's gaze, creasing his brow quizzically. Lassiter shrugged his shoulders.

'Do you know this could amount to a discipline offence. You could lose your job,' said Lassiter gruffly. 'She looked up, black streaks now running down her face. 'I don't want Mister Barras or you to be in trouble because Eddy's been horrible,' she said. 'I know that I'm a bit dizzy, but I didn't mean any harm sir.'

Lassiter took a deep breath. 'Don't cry any more Elaine. Let's see what we can do. If this doesn't get much further I might be able to help.' He looked at Martin Beckwith. Lifting an eyebrow he mouthed 'Eddy?'

*

The stream tumbled over rocks and around large boulders. It skated across small plateaus of pristine gravel and around tight bunches of rippling weed. The sunlight pooled beneath the overhanging trees where dragonflies dipped and skimmed. It was just as he remembered it.

They sat upon the decking outcrops beneath which the water flowed down to the harbour. All around the hydrangeas stood tall, their broad leaves still dripping with the dampness of the night. Behind them to their left Oriental Cottage nestled against the hill, while below it again a pristine new cedar chalet looked down at the chuckling water. Colours sat with his legs dangling over the edge, tossing small pebbles. 'The chalet is new, but everything else is just as I remember it,' he said.

Charlie leant against a tree. 'Many things look the same, but so much has changed, hasn't it Roy?'

He sighed. 'I'm sitting here feeling that time hasn't moved. It's as if all that has happened is not real. Maybe that's what I want for a while. To be the person I was twenty years ago. I knew then what I wanted and what I had to do to get it.'

She cast her eyes downward. 'I thought I knew that much as well.' She stripped a small branch from the tree. Walking toward the edge, she threw it in the water and watched it tumble away. 'I had everything in my hands and I let it go, just like that. When I looked for it again it was gone, like that branch. Gone down to the great sea of life and lost in its wide ocean.'

Colours caught the glimpse of a tear in her eye, but knew he should wait, say nothing and allow her to empty her heart. 'It's such a big thing, an ocean. You can stand and stare across it, looking for something that's small and dear to you upon its great, endless surface and feel hopeless. Then you give up and walk away.'

159

'And then one day you turn a corner and the world is upside down?' said Colours.

'*Charlie*'. A woman's soft, delighted tones wafted down from the steps. Her clothes and manner spoke of a love of her surroundings, gentle and natural. She seemed to float across the grass divide to where Charlie stood, extending a hand and kissing her cheek.

In her voice culture and wisdom seemed at once modestly concealed, yet undeniable. He thought how she belonged so completely to this house.

'This is Roy, a very dear friend of mine,' Charlie began, a hint of embarrassment in her voice. 'Roy, this is Anna. She has been my host many times in the last few years. We've become close friends. He smiled and shook her hand. 'That'll be your wonderful motorcycle up on the road Roy. Pleased to meet you.' She smiled warmly. 'Come in for coffee.'

They entered through the unlocked half door, into a kitchen that was hung with herbs, brass, large wooden spoons and vessels. 'Your home is lovely,' he ventured. He was resigned to making no mention of the past.

They crossed a small hallway into a lounge. The smell of sandalwood pervaded mixed with perfumed candles, pot-pourri and the stone and timber of the house. He loved it. The aroma of coffee completed his delight as they sat on furniture spread with fabrics of every kind, and Anna swept in. 'Have you been here very long?' she asked.

'Just an hour,' he replied smiling.

Anna stared down into her cup, as if embarrassed. 'And will you be staying?'

Colours paused, taking a deep breath. Then he looked at Charlie, holding her eyes, silently questioning her. 'Yes, I will if I may,' he said turning his eyes again to Anna.

'Of course,' she said brightly. 'I'll be away this evening. Would you like me to make up the spare room.' There was a long, uncomfortable pause. Charlie stood up, and placing her cup on the tray and said.

'No… but thanks Anna. We'll be fine.'

*

'What do I do about this?' Lassiter paced the carpeted floor, the shadow he cast from the oval window rising and falling across his desk. 'Sorry sir?' Beckwith stood by the door.

'I was thinking out loud,' said Lassiter 'but as you are here and you heard all that, I shall swear you to silence, but what *do* you think I should do?'

Beckwith turned, using the time to measure his thoughts and his response. He closed the door and gestured toward the chair. 'May I, sir?' Lassiter nodded and he sat down.

'If I may say so, I think Mister Seredemigni's behaviour is beneath contempt.' His lip began to curl with contained anger. 'I also think he deals from the bottom of the deck. Personally, I would have no compunction about using any means within my power to do him the maximum amount of harm.' He settled back in the chair, a soft satisfied smile on his face.

He took a breath and spoke again. 'Perhaps if you allowed me to have an informal conversation with the young lady?'

Lassiter turned a file in his hands. He looked at Beckwith over the slim glasses that perched on the bridge of his nose. 'And to what end?' he said. 'Tactics sir!' said Beckwith. 'I propose that we cover every contingency.'

Lassiter tossed the file on the desk and dropped his glasses on it. 'And do you think we can cover them all?' he said. 'If you're prepared to lead this particular operation sir.' replied Beckwith 'I won't fail you.'

Lassiter smiled wickedly. 'You can count on it.'

*

The chalet had a charm of its own. It nestled below overhanging boughs that trailed damp leaves across its roof, almost embracing it. A massive hydrangea all but concealed its doorway. Broad green leaves that moved gently in the breeze veiled it. Balls of white flowers drew the eye away.

Inside Anna's unmistakable touch was everywhere. A small radio and a kettle were the only concessions to the outside world, while earthy paraphernalia abounded. The aroma of pot-pourri here also, now competed with tangy pine. Two single beds covered in warm fabric were strewn with cushions. A single electric radiator stood by the window that looked out over the stream, its chuckling sound ever present.

Colours threw the saddlebags from the motorcycle upon a bed. Then he un-slung a rucksack from his back and placed it on the floor. He sat down on the edge of his bed, facing Charlie. She stood by the window, staring deeply into the tumbling water outside.

'The last time we were here, it was a much more decrepit shack than this one.' she said quietly. 'It didn't matter then,' she went on. There was a long, empty silence before she spoke again. 'I remember the sound of the water so well. We washed in that stream, do you remember?'

161

Colours smiled. 'Of course' he said.

She turned to look at him, a deep resolve in her eyes. 'If we are to steal this night, to have and keep this moment, then we agree now. No regrets. No anger. No recrimination. I have no rights in your life, you have none in mine.'

'I have no rights in your future, but I have rights in your past and your present, as you have in mine or we wouldn't be here.' She turned her head away, casting her gaze downward. 'Do we agree?' she whispered.

He reached out and took her hand, drawing his fingertips across hers. She turned again so that their eyes met. 'Blue eyes,' he said. 'I remember that we both have blue eyes,' He took a sharp, emotive breath and then released it in barely a whisper.

'I agree.'

*

Martin Beckwith eased his way into the small office. Behind a monitor, Elaine typed furiously. She hid her face, but the short, shallow breaths betrayed her distress. He drew the tops of his fingers along the line of his jaw thoughtfully, rustling the immaculate beard.

'Would you like a coffee,' he said, turning to the trolley upon which a kettle and an array of jars resided. She stopped typing abruptly. Without speaking she placed two clean white cups and saucers from a cupboard beside her in front of Beckwith. Never once did she raise her eyes to meet his.

'I'll take that as a yes then, shall I?' She nodded, her eyes flashed momentarily to meet his and then downward again.

'Listen to me Elaine,' he said. He hit the switch and the kettle began to creak and click as the heat took hold.

'Best check there is enough water in that,' she said, turning her chair to face him.

He placed a restraining hand on her bare forearm. 'It's heavy,' he said 'plenty in there.' She drew closer, drawing her hand back until it cupped his and then placing the other upon it. Tears flowed once more while she fought to articulate powerful emotions. Beckwith's discomfort grew as she leaned forward to speak in hushed tones. 'You're a nice man, Martin Beckwith,' she said. 'Your wife's a lucky woman. I always hoped that I would find someone to share things with, to be kind to me, to care for me. All I ever got was men with wandering hands and short memories.'

She stood up, dabbing the tears from her eyes. Composing herself she straightened her clothing, checking her face in a small mirror.

'I'll make the coffee, Martin,' she said. A tiny defensive mechanism triggered deep within him at this intimacy. He felt ever more vulnerable as she pushed the door closed, her overt sexuality carried on the strong scent of her perfume.

'Sugar?' the sound of spoons and crockery were unusually loud in the silence that had descended. While he sat uneasily by the door, she spoke again, her back to him. 'I understand more than you think,' she began.

'Now you're afraid that I want to attach myself to you, to drag you into my bed like some black widow.' He sat stunned by the sudden directness, the incisive words. 'I've been a fool for a dozen men, more...' her voice quavered at this admission.

'Sergeant Mankowitz was a lovely man too, wasn't he?' Beckwith found himself lost as the exchange turned in ever more different directions. 'I hardly got to know him,' she said, 'but I liked him immensely. So many people are heartbroken at his loss, so that must be true.' She nodded thoughtfully, measuring what she would say next.

'I know! I was at the funeral, but I stayed at the back. What his wife said, it really made me cry. Mister Barras, he was so good, standing there with all those cuts still on his face. He made me feel sort of proud as well, about being part of this place.'

'When I type reports about people, the things I see on the Chief Superintendent's letters and reports.' She looked piercingly into his eyes. 'You'd be surprised how much I know. I'm not important I realise that, but I'm very proud to work here.' Tears began to well in the corners of her eyes once more. 'I don't want to lose my job.'

She reached into a drawer and lifted out a small black folding album. For a while she faced Beckwith slowly turning the pages. Watery smiles appeared, rising and fading on her face. 'D'you like this one?' She said turning it around for Beckwith to see. 'We had a wonderful weekend.' a strange fragile tone in her voice.

He stared incredulously as Chief Superintendent Eduardo Seredemigni's smiling face looked back at him. The man's left arm was curled around Elaine's waist.

Her hair was tangled by the same strong wind that powered the rough sea behind them. Distantly a burned and decrepit pier stood out in the distance. 'Brighton?' he asked.

'Yes,' she replied. 'We had the best of everything. We stayed at the Grand Hotel. I have never been in a place like that before,' she went on. 'It was wonderful. We even had a view of the sea in the morning and breakfast on a balcony. He said he was going to leave his wife. I was so stupid.'

Her eyes held a terrible secret, something she wanted him to know, but could not bring herself to tell. 'He was brutal, you know…*like that!*' She turned and faced the window, unable to look at Beckwith any longer. She placed her hands on her hips and then slid them forcefully down the outside of her thighs, as if bracing herself.

'He didn't come to the hospital either.' Beckwith rocked in his chair at the enormity of all that he was hearing. 'Do you mean he hurt you? He assaulted you?' he said.

She turned and faced him, braced for this moment. 'No, he didn't hurt me like that, but he has hurt me a great deal in other ways. Please don't judge me too harshly,' she said, her eyes now reddened. 'I won't let him hurt any one else.' She took a deep breath, lowering her head until Beckwith could no longer see her face. 'He made me pregnant.'

*

'I don't think the inside of this place has seen a lick of paint since the last time we were here.' Colours scanned the bar for any trace of change, but could find none. On the gnarled furniture a clean tablecloth disguised decades of abuse. 'A good Merlot,' he continued, filling her glass, 'I was right about that if memory serves me well.'

'Jack Daniels if mine is as good,' Charlie replied, a soft smile on her lips. 'Maybe Jamieson's nowadays,' he replied.

'I had a wonderful, magical day.' she said, her eyes whimsically dancing around the room. 'To be back on those beaches, the green unspoilt sea. It was all I had hoped for.'

While an elderly man cleared their table, Charlie walked back from the bar balancing two small glasses of whisky.

She slid one across the divide to him. 'To the past, the present and the future, whatever that may be,' she said, raising hers.

He stared at her, the soft candlelight wiping away the intervening years. 'To the life that is and to the way things might have been,' he replied. The same light reflected in the whisky as their glasses touched.

'Have you noticed that they seem to have more stars down here?' she said, smiling as they walked back along the darkened, descending lane.

He looked up at the night sky that became infinity with the distant horizon. The clear night hosted a full moon in wonderful stellar clarity. 'I guess London has too many gases hovering above it. Here it's so clear,' he said.

She turned and descended the steps, their outline stark white in the moonlight. 'It's a perfect night,' she replied. As Colours turned the key in the pine door, his heart beat hard in his chest. 'I won't be a moment,' she said, and turned suddenly toward the house.

For what seemed an age he lay naked between the sheets, listening for her footfalls. There were none as the soft, damp grass cushioned her bare feet. Her shadow at the door drew his eyes. She stood in the doorway, framed by the moonlight and tugged at the towel until it fell at her feet.

He watched as she padded silently toward him, the squares of moonlight from the window caressing her body, turning its every feature porcelain until she stood above him, bending to kiss his face.

His thoughts span and his body ached with desire as her skin grew ever closer and she slid beside him, pressing a finger to his lips. Her face nuzzled his ear, her breath warm against it and caressing the nape of his neck. She whispered 'Manyana! You say that a lot, do you know that? *Now leave the rest of the world 'till Manyana.'*

Her hands began to torment his chest and nipples, moving down and across him, as her lips pressed bruisingly upon his. He felt her silken thigh, then the warmth of her whole being upon him. She moved deftly until he lost himself in the soft, warm folds of her body. Only the moon watched as they crossed into another consciousness.

While passion racked his body, he embraced her tiny waist, caressed her soft buttocks. She held his face in her hands.

Kissing his eyes she tasted the tears that pooled there and then mixed with her own. 'You were the love of my life,' he said in gasped whispers. 'You were always mine,' she responded.

Her fingers bit into his cheeks as her body arched in orgasm, a huge wave of sensation and emotions carried him with her until they lay quiet. As she curled in his arms, he stared out into the moonlit night, the only sound the chuckling water. He felt peaceful, and yet so sad.

*

He woke to the sound of tapping on the door. 'Mr Barras...Roy, it's Anna. Would you like breakfast?' He struggled to clear his head, to remember where he was as brilliant sunshine dazzled him through the glass. 'Yes, yes please Anna. Can you give me twenty minutes?' He heard her turn from the door.

'Fine,' she said. Beside him the other bed remained unused and pristine. All of Charlie's clothes and bags were gone, as if she had never been there. He wrapped a towel around his waist and climbed down till he stood knee deep in the crystal, tumbling water.

He paused, knowing that he would be washing away the very last traces of her on his skin. He whispered, 'Over the next hill, just around the next bend.' Then he pulled the towel from his waist and sat in the crisp water and lay back, immersing himself.

'A cooked breakfast, or continental style? Fruit, coffee and croissant,' Anna said. 'The cooked breakfast please,' he replied, knowing there was a long ride ahead. He could hear Anna clattering with the pots and pans as he approached the door of the open kitchen. The smell of the bacon caressed his senses. 'When did Charlie leave?' he asked.

Anna looked up. 'Would you mind if I joined you at breakfast,' she said brightly, and then 'she left before daybreak.'

The coffee was very welcome as it washed down mouthfuls of food. Anna cut small pieces of fruit and ate them slowly and delicately. 'I've come to know Charlie very well over the last few years,' she said suddenly. 'I knew who you were even before we met. Not by name and not by face, but as an entity when we spoke as women sometimes do, about the deepest things.'

She shifted uncomfortably on her chair. 'She's asked me to tell you something. I hope I can convey this in the right way, if that's possible.'

She paused to collect herself. 'Charlie is married.' Colours stopped eating. He let his head fall into his hands. Anna drew close, pouring fresh coffee into his half empty cup. 'Are you okay?' she said softly. He looked up. 'I have no right to feel anything, no right to comment.' he said.

Anna knelt before him, her hands clasped almost as if in prayer. 'I love Charlie as a close friend. Lots of people have stayed here and their liaisons are none of my concern. I have no thoughts about the two of you other than this. I have never encountered a more poignant story and I can feel what is between you.' She stood up. 'She loves you enough to want you and so much that she will leave you. There's a letter on your motorcycle.'

*

166

Colours tossed the saddlebags over the Harley, then picked up the cream envelope. He tucked it into the front of his jacket and started the bike, riding then down to the same harbour wall to where she had first gently touched his face. He sat in the same place and slowly tearing open the envelope, he read her words.

My darling Roy,

Please forgive me for not telling you about Alec.

We have not lived together for many years. He is a Major engaged in covert operations abroad. He rarely comes home. It was a mistake. I wanted what you and I had and I thought I could substitute it. I couldn't.

One day maybe, I will sit with you and explain it all. One day maybe this hurt will all be put right. Between us there is something quite magical. What a wonderful life we might have had. Last night we placed all the rules and conventions on one side and took something life perhaps owed us. If my life had ended at that moment, joined with you in the darkness, I would have been complete. Take all of that love and lavish it upon your wonderful family. Perhaps we were robbed by our own foolishness, but we have that moment to savour, to remember. Now you must embrace them.

I will see you from time to time I know, fate has dictated that. But whatever, I will never do harm to you or them. That is the measure of my love.

Take care, my most beautiful man.

Always…Charlie.

He fought back his tears, remembering her words by the little stream that fed this harbour, that ran out in to this great sea, this ocean.

'It's such a big thing, an ocean. You can stand and stare across it, looking for something that is small and dear to you upon its great, endless surface and feel hopeless. Then you give up and walk away'.

He took the letter in his hand and brushed it across his lips. Then he threw it out on to the ebbing tide and watched it carried out to sea.

VENGEANCE

As the Harley pulled him relentlessly higher and clear of the valley, his mobile phone vibrated as the world outside intruded once more and endless messages demanded his attention. He tilted the big machine steeply downhill while the endless panorama of blue sea spread below to his right and descended into the tiny village of Mousehole, rolling to a halt by the harbour.

Punching in his code he listened to message after message. Martin Beckwith's voice sounded surreal, a link with a harsh reality while all around was the vision of another age and gentler times. 'So we are going after Seagull with all guns blazing. Ring me soon. Take care sir.' The voice clicked off. He watched a great, greedy gull balancing comically on the harbour rail, looking for food, and thought how apt the nickname was.

Then Beth's loving voice whispered in his ear. 'Hello darling,' she began. 'The girls send their love. There'll be a big steak with all the trimmings for you when you come home. Tell me when you're close. I hope you're having a wonderful time. I love you Roy. Phone me soon.'

Above him the gulls circled and screeched and he felt utterly wretched, then at once easier, like coming home, as if a page had been written and turned. He started the Harley and rode on, determined now that he would ride until he was there.

*

The old transit van lurched from the holding area into the auction hall. Its white panels were stained brown here and there, where hidden rust seeped through its cheap spray job. 'Hey fella,' the young gipsy grinned wickedly at the olive-skinned man that eyed the van, looking into its cab, opening its rear doors.

'You'll not be bidding on this old shitter?' he mocked, casting a glance at the other gypsies that were his audience as he derided the young Arab. 'I've a mind to take it home me self, so I have,' and he smiled, baring teeth broken and missing in some fight. 'So you'll not be bidding against me now?'

The man turned, his young face uncomprehending. 'Thank you sir.' He clasped his hands, and bowed. 'I wish only to buy a van sir, thank you.' The gipsy shook his head, 'Mad fucker,' he said looking to his mates.

'A twin wheel transit van, believed five previous owners,' the auctioneer began. 'No service history. Do I have an opening bid here of £250.00.' The young Arab raised his hand. Beside him the gipsy laughed raising the bids by fifty pounds at each gasp of the auctioneer's rapid-fire lead. 'Three hundred pounds, do I have three hundred pounds? Four, I have four hundred. Four hundred and fifty. Five... I have five hundred pounds.'

In the hall all eyes fell on the contest between the two men as the bids began to far exceed the van's worth. The young Arab reached into his shirt, revealing a tight roll of new bank notes, several thousand pounds. The gipsy turned and spat on the ground at his feet, malice in his eyes. 'Fuck you.' he said as his entourage mocked him.

'I have five hundred pounds on this vehicle. Going once, going twice, *sold*,' and the hammer fell, echoing around the hall. 'Take your bid to the cashier's window,' said the auctioneer, sensitive that the proceedings were alien to this odd bidder. The young Arab took his slip of paper from the assistant and walked away as another sale began behind him.

He stood nervously by the glass portal while the cashier fired questions at him. 'Name?...'

'Mohammed Farouk' he replied. He reached for the roll of money, peeling new note after new note until ten £50 notes lay on the counter. 'Surcharge thirty five pounds,' added the cashier. He peeled off another fifty. Barely waiting for his change, he tucked the still thick roll of money into a 'bum bag' around his waist.

He signed the top copy of the document proffered to him and walked toward the lot with it tightly in his grip. Handing the slip to the waiting attendant he climbed into the van. He placed the bag on the seat beside him, pinning its straps beneath his thigh. Then he drove the coughing, rattling vehicle toward the exit, where a drop-down barrier barred his way.

From the booth beside him an attendant emerged smiling and carrying a hand–held bar code reader with which he scanned a label on the screen. As the barrier rose, the young gipsy appeared by his window.

Several others emerged to stand in front of him, barring his way. 'Ye're making a fool of me, are ye?' The gipsy reached in and grabbed his loose, Hessian shirt. 'And you with all that nice new money too.'

In the driving seat, the young man's face remained impassive. He turned slowly as the gipsy pulled violently on the shirt, dragging him head and shoulders out of the window. Others moved toward the passenger door. In the booth the attendant reached for a phone.

At the van door the two men were almost nose to nose, the broken toothed gipsy in full flood, a tirade of saliva-ridden abuse issuing from his lips. He fell silent as the Arab jammed the old Browning pistol into his eye socket, pinning his arms to the door. Then he spoke in a low, deadly whisper.

'You are filth, *scum*. What would you die for thief? I will die for Allah, but you will die for nothing.' He jammed the pistol deep into the man's eye socket and twisted it, and he fell to the floor. With his hands cupped over his injured eye he began to scream in agony, as blood flowed freely through his fingers. Then the young Arab turned to the others, ranged across the front of the van, showing them the gun. Dragging the whimpering man with them, they backed away.

Within the booth, the attendant could see little of this, but knew the situation was dangerous. As the van pulled away he continued to speak down the telephone. '… I don't know, but he scared off a whole gang of Gyppo's. One of them is hurt pretty bad I think, but they just put him in their truck and drove off. I got some numbers.'

*

The parade room was as chaotic as ever, it's disarray worsened by the deluge of manpower that was passing through it, as the Metropolitan Police struggled to maximise their resources. Benny stepped over a discarded kit bag, lighting his cigarette as he went. 'D'you have to light that disgusting roll of horse shit in here Benny? Can't you wait till your outside.' Arthur's face creased in a look of disgust.

'Shut up Arthur,' Benny derided. 'You sound just like my ol' woman.' 'Sound like her? You look like her,' laughed Pikey.

'Careful junior,' Arthur rounded on him as Cravetts entered from the base room, a clipboard in his hand.

Arthur smiled, his eyes fixed upon the two chevrons that Cravetts sported on his shoulders. 'Was going to say its nice to have you back Mark, but I see you have gone over.'

'No,' said Cravetts, his words clipped, 'same old me, same old you, same old shit.'

Arthur smiled 'Yes Sergeant…oh! sorry…*acting Sergeant.*'

'No! Stay where you are.' Graham Lassiter swept into the room, a sheaf of paper in his hand. John Munney and Raffles had made to get up, but dropped back into their chairs as the rest of the relief gathered round, aware that some revelation was imminent. Lassiter sat on the corner of the table as Benny burst back in, the pungent aura of his cigarettes following him as the old wooden door slammed loudly closed. Lassiter eyed it knowingly.

Cravetts passed him a steaming blue and white cup, brimming with tea, and he nodded his thanks. 'Gentlemen,' he began. 'Yesterday there was an incident of note at Chelmsford car auctions. A young man of Arab extraction bought a van there. I have his description and that of the van on these handouts.' He passed out several sheets of paper.

'The cashier remembers him particularly well because he was so ill at ease. He had several thousand pounds in new notes on his person.' He took a deep swallow from the cup. 'There followed a confrontation at the gates with several members of the local gipsy fraternity. The Arab male produced a handgun and made off, not before threatening them all with what was probably a Browning.'

'Nice old gun that,' cut in Benny. 'I carried one for a while.' Lassiter caught Benny's eye. 'We are pretty sure it's a Browning by the gouge marks in the gypsy's eye socket. He turned up at hospital in Harlow. Otherwise they would have told us nothing. SO13 say he looks really pretty now, half his teeth missing and half blind.'

He shifted himself a little. 'I anticipate the vehicle is intended to be used as a device.' He stopped, silently demanding every eye. 'You should also know that a Manchester firearms team were attacked last night. They were drawn to a farmhouse in the Ramsbottom area on false drug information.'

'The place was laced with petrol and T.A.T.P again. They lost a team member and a dog handler. Several officers are severely burned.'

'The Wind and Shadow terrorist campaign is being widened.' The room fell totally quiet. 'Where's Sergeant Beckwith?' Lassiter asked. 'In the armoury, sir,' answered John Munney. 'Ask him to come to my office please.' Lassiter responded.

Lassiter paused by the door. 'I know of course, how much grief and trauma this relief has suffered lately. I want to tell you again how much that affects me personally as well. I'm sure you'll be pleased to hear that Mister Barras will be back at work with you within days.' He watched as an infectious smile spread throughout the assembled men. For the first time in days, he felt just a little better. It was small comfort.

*

'Nasser wait! Do not do this thing.' Her dark eyes met his as they burned with bottomless anger. The knife drew blood from the young man's jowls. It ran crimson along its razor-sharp blade and over fingers that held it tightly, so tightly the knuckles turned white.

His face contorted with anger, saliva glistening on his bared teeth as he spat angry words into the terrified man's face. 'I told you to buy carefully, anonymously.' With his left hand he tore at his hair until his head bent so low it impacted loudly with the edge of an old sink, the sinews and tracks of his arteries showing bare in the light.

'This will only make things worse.' she said cupping her brother's face. 'Another death here will be hard to hide. You will turn others against you. Think… *please think!* Do not let your anger be blind.' His chest rose and fell with his angry breath as slowly the fire in his bloodshot eyes diminished. He lifted the knife a little and then placed it against the man's cheek. A spot of blood began to spread from its point.

'How will you make amends, my disciple,' he hissed. Then he threw the younger man to the floor. He lay there clutching his face where red tracks of blood ran through his parted fingers. 'Do not speak my name here.' Medahwi turned on her. 'You are Khamsin, I am Haab. It is enough.'

'Lord Haab, forgive me. My life is yours.' The man began to crawl toward Medahwi, his fingers reaching for his feet. 'Please allow me to atone. Let me sit with the prophet.' The eyes of brother and sister met. She nodded gently. 'We have enough,' she whispered.

He turned and looked down on the cowering figure. 'You may redeem yourself yet. Even this dog that bites the master's hand may be forgiven. If the Imam should bless you, are you ready to be martyred.' The crouching figure nodded, fearing to raise his eyes.

Medahwi lifted him to his feet. He took a dirty cloth from the sink and wiped the smears of blood and tears from the young man's face.

'So be it then. You shall be blessed.' The young man began to cry as Medahwi looked deep into his sister's eyes. A weak smile chanced across his lips, an imperceptible nod as she turned away.

Colours stopped at the top of the hill, by the old school and looked down at the village. In a few moments he would turn into his own drive, re-enter his own world and all that had passed would be like a dream.

He wondered how he would cope with his emotions, with the knowledge he had been unfaithful. He had never lied to Beth, not a real lie. His stomach knotted. He sat for a long while, examining his feelings, weighing these huge issues that were the cornerstones of his life and felt drained.

A loud, rasping voice startled him. 'Can't be lost? You must be thinking?' A bearded, red-faced man appeared at his side, a broad grin on his face. 'Ain't seen you down the pub in a month of Sundays,' he said. 'Guess you're a busy man with all this trouble, Roy.' Colours collected his thoughts. 'No Peter your right! Maybe I will soon. Certainly need to.'

'Nothing's different,' he thought, as the man's rotund, tweedy figure retreated into the trees. He found himself speaking softly to no-one at all. 'Some of me belongs to the past, some to the future. You just put one foot in front of the other and keep walking.' Then he started the Harley and rolled down the hill toward home.

*

It was a strange feeling as he cut the engine. Its last resonant note faded into silence and he was home. Looking around the garage, it was just as he left it, his private cobweb-embroidered refuge. Beth had left it open. He could see her by the patio doors, setting a table. Perhaps the music she played, the fact the he had barely coasted in had suppressed her hearing. But if she didn't know he was there, the old bulldog did.

Through the side window he could see Stuka pounding down the path, his pendulous tongue flinging saliva left and right. In a moment the side access door burst open. Colours dropped to his knees as the dog's considerable bulk hit him square in the chest.

He found himself in a tumble of saddlebags, garage dust and a hugely excited bulldog. He fought for air as the animals hot, wet tongue lashed his face repeatedly. 'Stuka, you great, gormless oaf,' he laughed, hoisting the dog aloft in a hug as it fought to continue the salivating facial.

173

'Daddy!' …Three barefoot, excited girls ran down the lawn toward him. Their loose pyjama's rustled in the evening air, as tiny Amelia struggled to keep her waistband in place in her haste. 'Amelia, is that how you greet your daddy, by baring your bum?' He strode forward and bent his knees as the three embraced him and he drew them into his enfolding arms. All the while the dog circled, barking hysterically.

'Now that!…' said Beth from the steps of the terrace 'is what I call a welcome. Your best mate to greet you, and an entourage of young girls hanging around your neck.' The sheer white wrap was tied at her waist. The light from the house lifted the red in her long hair. It gathered on her shoulder as she tilted her head and smiled. Her bare feet looked small and china-white against the dark timber beneath them.

'Big steak, just as I promised' she smiled. He strode across to her, Amelia on his arm. The height of the decking brought them face to face, and he drew Beth to him, burying his face in her shoulder. While Beth wrapped his head in her arms, his family closed around him.

*

The steam from the shower filled the room, the autumn air giving it substance until the panels and mirrors misted over, and he could hide there. He didn't want to see himself, to look in his own eyes for a while. He didn't want to see the pink tracks that marked the last of his now healed wounds. He didn't want to look into his own eyes, to see his own image and dislike it. How could anything be normal whilst this great chasm he felt inside waited to consume him?

He heard Beth call from somewhere beyond its mists. 'Roy, come down. You have a visitor.'

Colours towelled himself down, and, pulling on a loose track suit, descended the stairs. Martin Beckwith waited in his lounge, sipping coffee as Colours padded barefoot across the hall. 'Forgive the intrusion. I won't be stopping long,' he said. 'I just wanted to bring you up to speed on a particular issue before you heard it from anyone else.'

'As you know, Chief Superintendent Seredemigni has put in a highly critical report concerning the West Drayton incident. Before you react in any way or hear more from anyone else, I just want you to know that there's nothing to be concerned about.' Colours brow creased quizzically. Beckwith stood up to leave.

'I can see I'm interrupting your privacy and I'm on my way home.' He turned and faced Colours. 'I just feel quite confident that he'll be withdrawing it.' He winked as Colour's consternation grew, questions beginning to frame in his mind. 'That bastard. There aren't words to describe how I feel about him.'

'Then perhaps you should enjoy your steak and your evening a little more,' Beckwith said. 'Good to have you back sir. Oh! And Sally Galloway passed her back to ops shoot. One weeks re-familiarisation and she's back with the relief.' Then he nodded to Beth and left.

'What was that about?' she said, concerned. 'Whatever it is it'll wait until tomorrow.' He smiled wistfully to himself. *'Manyana...'*

He could hear Beth as she placed the last few dishes in the washer. Then the sounds of the coffee jar preceded the pop and hiss of the machine. He sat turning a glass in his hands, watching the candle light flicker in its amber contents. 'Brandy tonight,' he whispered low, 'not whiskey.'

'Did you say something darling?' Beth emerged with a tray of coffee. He placed a hand on hers. 'You do know that I love you very much, don't you?' he said. She turned to face him.

'Yes, of course!' she replied, and sat down, keeping a grasp on his hand. 'What is it Roy? I feel I don't understand everything, as if there is something more you want to say?'

He looked deeply into her eyes. 'Only that this is a complicated world in which it's sometimes not enough be right. That the rules don't always fit the game.' He dropped his head forward and stared at their linked hands.

'I just want you to know that my love for you is unqualified, unlimited. That I have enough love for a lot of people. I needed to tell you that.'

She sat for several moments staring at him, as if searching his eyes. Then she drew a deep breath and hesitated before she spoke. 'You didn't need to tell me what I already knew for my sake, but perhaps you did for your own. If that helps with all that has happened, then good.'

'You have lost a best friend, seen some terrible things and been the rock for so many others. You're entitled to be troubled by all of this. I married a most exceptional man. You are a hero to your children and a hero to me. We are rock solid, and always will be. Now I wanted to tell *you* that.'

She stood up and walked to the hearth, where the dog slumbered, baying quietly. 'And now I want to tell you something else.' She pulled her self up to her full height, as if to make some great statement.

'It's late.' Colours looked her with puzzlement. He shrugged his shoulders. 'Okay, if you say so!'

175

His eyes lifted to the clock. 'Beth, it's only ten pm?'

She smiled gently. 'No...*It*...is late. Fourteen days late actually! So I ran a little test.' His eyes creased in realisation.

'Yes, you dummy... I'm pregnant.'

*

'What the hell do you think you're doing here?' Seredemigni's face bloated and reddened with rage. 'I shall report your visit, and don't think I don't know why you're here. You are going to try to influence me, to try to corrupt a complaint investigation... Well, don't waste your time.' He spat out the last words.

Lassiter smiled. He pulled up a chair and sat down opposite Seredemigni, across the desk. 'Eddy. Oh Eddy!' he began, 'You do get so emotional, and why so presumptuous? I merely wish to query a mileage on one of the fleet vehicles. Now, you won't mind helping me out on this, will you?'

Seredemigni's face began to drain of colour, a whitened pallor creeping across it. 'I'm sorry,' he said, but I can't possibly remember every journey I made.' Lassiter opened a black logbook. An entry was highlighted in pale yellow. 'You'll remember that rather nice black BMW we had on contract? 'Well there's this weekend of the third and fourth of August last year. A hundred and fifty three miles unaccounted for. The garage man swears blind you had the car. Says he remembers it well.'

'Fuck you Lassiter,' Seredemigni hissed. 'You've always hated me.'

Lassiter stood up, the palms of his hands on the desk in front of his now sweating adversary. 'Oh no Eddy, I wouldn't have it said. Actually, it took me several minutes.'

'So what does that prove. I did some visits and I forgot to book the mileage, that's all.' Seredemigni hissed. Lassiter bared his teeth and opened a blue file that he pulled from his case. 'Nice photo Eddy. That'll be you with your arm around Elaine. Is that Brighton pier I can see? How pleasant.'

He threw a scrap of paper on the blotter in front of Seredemigni. 'That is a copy of the bill at the Grand. I like your style. American Express gold card. Guess that's the account the wife doesn't know about.' He drove his finger into the paper. 'That is *your signature*...isn't it Eddy?'

Seredemigni began to sweat more heavily and rock in his chair. 'One last thing, you unscrupulous, soulless bastard.' He found himself shouting. 'Apparently they keep samples, so they can get DNA from an aborted foetus.'

176

He leaned across and seized the man's lapels, pulling him upright. 'And if you ever come near or after me again, we will settle this another way, in uniform or out, you complete wanker,' and he threw him back in the chair.

The door opened and a flustered-looking Inspector peered in. 'Is everything alright gentlemen?' he ventured. Lassiter straightened his uniform. 'Well, is it, Eddy my lad?'

Seredemigni stuttered a reply. 'Yes, Inspector. Everything's fine. Thank you.' Lassiter pulled himself up and walked to the door. 'One last thing. If you ever find a decent bone in your body, do me a favour and give it to the dog. Wouldn't want it to spoil the rest of the set, would we?' Then he slammed the door.

*

The Harley chuntered to a halt by the steel gates, its last notes echoing up the side of the building. He swiped the access card and the lock released with a loud metallic clunk. As he turned back he noticed the dust that still clung to his bike. He reflected on the long journey that had put it there.

Minutes later he was descending the stairs, almost time-warped as if so much that had happened were just an imagination. A young uniformed Inspector climbed toward him. He was new to the department and Colours could not, to his great embarrassment, recall his name. He stopped on the stair and caught Colours's eye. 'I just wanted to say how sorry I was about Sergeant Mankowitz.' He extended his hand and shook Colour's own warmly.

Moments later he pushed open the old wooden door. His entrance was announced as it slammed loudly behind him. Benny looked up, a broad smile exposing the famous gold tooth. Arthur rose to his feet. 'I hope this means you will demote that bloody ego maniac Cravetts,' he said dryly.

Before he could speak, every man in the room stood up. He looked around him on a sea of smiling faces. Fudge, Raffles, Chris Harvey, John Munney and Pikey. At the door to the base room, Martin Beckwith stood smiling with Cravetts gripping a clipboard at his side. Gilhooley strode forward and seized his hand in a crushing grip, then slapped him on the back.

Suddenly they closed on him. Everywhere the extended hand of friendship and the face of fraternity. He sat on the corner of the table, drinking from the mug of tea that Chris Harvey had thrust into his hand. He dropped his eyes, unable to respond to this wave of affection.

Arthur stepped forward. 'I would just like to say sir, that these men will follow

177

you anywhere.' He paused and took a breath. With a smile he gruffly added…'But I think it's mainly just curiosity.'

Cravetts gently intervened. 'Mister Lassiter phoned down. He would like to speak to you in his office when you are free.'

Colours acknowledged him and then spoke, raising his voice above the hum of general conversation. 'I've served with all manner of men, in the army and in the police force. Sometimes I think you lot should be living in the hills and sending out raiding parties. Overall though, you're not a bad bunch. Thank you for all your support, particularly at the funeral.'

There was a long empty silence, until he spoke again. 'We will not forget Barry, nor will we rest. Perhaps now some payback? We must hope so.' The soft murmur of agreement rose slowly in many voices as Colours walked into the base room. As he passed through the door, he called back, 'now get out on the streets. The public aren't paying you to drink tea and scratch yourselves!'

Gilhooley subtly caught his sleeve and spoke, his soft, husky words for Colour's ears only. 'A moment sir, if you wouldn't mind, *in private.*'

Colours nodded walked out into the fresher air. He stopped by the brooding menace of an armoured Land Rover, lurking in the darkened corner of the yard, pulled at the heavily steel-plated door and climbed in.

Moments later the vehicle dipped as Kieran Gilhooley climbed in beside him, darkening the cab. 'Sally sir… PC Galloway. May I say something?' Colours was unsettled. Gilhooley was rarely this observed and he knew at once that this was going to be difficult, that Gilhooley was agonising, just as Colours had. But the agony was right. The stakes of this game were too high for lesser deliberation.

There was a long, pregnant pause while they watched their colleagues walk by, oblivious to the two men darkened as they were by shadow, and the thick, misting, ballistic glass of the windscreen. Gilhooley traced a finger thoughtfully across the dashboard, then lowered his head. 'I like her a lot sir, not just because she's attractive you understand…' Colours rocked back in the seat, smiling while Gilhooley's face turned to thunder.

'No, you see guvnor, that's the trouble. Everybody sees the girl thing, and yes, she's got that in spades, but there's so much more…' his voice trailed off.

'So spit it out Kieran, say what you feel,' Colours continued. 'There's no-one else in here.'

The big Irishman took a breath. 'She cracked sir, on the range, she told me she could never do this job again. You're going to back her, aren't you'?

'And you don't agree?' Colours snapped.

178

'It's not so simple.' Gilhooley countered. 'I don't know what I feel. Sure if I was a single bloke things might have been different. But I ain't sir and this ain't what I'm on about. I do care what happens to her though, but it don't make putting her back to ops right.'

'So what is right?' Colours retorted. 'She did the right thing when it mattered, on her first day on ops. That's a whole lot more testing than a fucking range, don't you think?' he said, instantly regretting his words.

'Look, I'm sorry, I didn't mean that to sound like a reflection on you. I know that was beyond your control.'

Gilhooley's mighty fist crashed on the dash top. 'And I know I couldn't have done nothing else, but it don't stop the bad feelings,' he turned to stare into Colour's eyes. 'Does it boss?'

'Forget the 'boss' for a moment Kieran. I'm just a man like you, just as flawed, just as fallible.'

'If we swapped hats, neither of us would find the other's job easy. I have to discuss this with Mister Lassiter, but yes, I'm going to recommend that after a trial period, Sally goes back to ops. I guess the truth is that when you have to open fire it's just as bad every time. You and I both, the army service and all, we know that.'

'She did right the first time, I have to give her the chance, I have to take the chance that she will be equal again. Isn't that the name of the game? Don't we all wonder if this time, next time we will do the right thing? Don't we all wonder why sometimes we're scared shitless when it's all going on and then the next time, when you really should be, your not. Who knows why Kieran? I reckon she deserves the chance and we must gamble on her as much as we gamble on ourselves…every day, every time that sick old serpent, fear, raises its head!'

Gilhooley let out a long, sad sigh. 'Poetry or politics boss, you could be good at both. Reckon you'll make Commissioner yet. It's not my decision and you've got the brown gloves. Maybe I don't have the courage for that and that makes you braver. Thanks for listening,' he took a few paces and looked back. 'And for what it's worth, if it's good enough for you, it's good enough for me.' Then he strode off.

*

'How did you manage that?' asked Colours. Lassiter paced back and forth across the green corded floor of his office. 'Something had to be done. You sorely pissed off Seredemigni. He hates you for getting him posted, he hated me for filling his place, and now he hates me with a real vengeance for squaring him up. The thing is he can never move on us knowing that he's vulnerable. Don't ask me what motivates that man. I can't begin to grasp what goes on in that scheming cesspit of a mind.'

Colours leaned forward in his chair, stroking his chin. 'I've only the outline of what happened.' Lassiter sat down at his desk, leaving the bright autumn sunshine through the oval window to silhouette him, searing Colour's vision. 'Seredemigni couldn't resist the temptation and the proximity. He started an affair with Elaine.'

'They went away several times apparently, but one weekend he took her to Brighton. He did the whole thing. The Grand Hotel, the firm's Beemer. Breakfast on the balcony and photos on the beach. Unfortunately for him, the whole thing included getting her pregnant. For an allegedly intelligent man, he has been utterly stupid. I merely brought these matters to his attention.'

'And Elaine?' Colours asked. 'Only you, me and Martin Beckwith know all about that,' Lassiter said. 'If we can keep it that way she is secure here. I am aware that although she almost blew the gaff, she also saved the situation at great personal embarrassment and cost. I won't forget that.'

Colours nodded his agreement. He lifted an eyebrow. 'Beckwith's young, but he's a good man sir. I am pleased to have him.' The mobile phone on Colours's hip began to ring. He answered it, listening intently as his face grew ever darker. 'Yes, I understand. On my way.' He turned to Lassiter. 'D'you wish to ride with me sir? They've just detonated a suicide bomb in Bishopsgate.'

*

Gilhooley strode to meet them as Colours guided the BMW to a halt at the line of cordon tape closing the road. The morning traffic had descended into chaos as local officers fought to contain it. The impatient horns of frustrated commuters competed with the distant wail of sirens as emergency vehicles fought to get through.

'It's a partial,' said Gilhooley. 'The van's still loaded with explosive.' Distantly Colours could see a white van in the centre of the road, at the point where City of London police officers manned a checkpoint, the 'Ring of Steel.' A pall of smoke rose from the van's windows and doors, but it remained largely intact.

An armed City of London officer was being lead around a corner to a waiting ambulance. He was blinded and blood streamed from between his fingers as he clawed at his face, agonised, guttural sounds issuing from his lips. Nearby several others, some also armed sat with their backs to a wall, looking pale and shocked.

'Control is in Folgate Street sir. Cravetts is the man. They let him loose on the public again,' he chuckled. 'The expo is there with all and sundry. They'll brief you.' Then he turned and scanned every aspect around them, looking for the 'third eye.' The bomber's back up.

Lassiter sat impassively in the passenger seat. Colours tapped the Glock pistol he had hurriedly strapped on as they left the base. 'Expecting trouble then sir,' he smiled.

Lassiter turned slowly, his lips parting to reveal bared teeth. 'Wouldn't want to miss out if it happened, now would I? Anyway, there's the man who really expects it.' He pointed at a figure dressed in a huge padded suit.

'Now for my money, that's heroism. I wouldn't want to do his job at any price.' Several men in dark coveralls and heavily equipped stood nearby in a huddle around the ARV, its bonnet covered in papers. Cravetts sat in the driver's seat writing furiously as plans were made, contingencies formulated. Behind them were other cars, an ambulance and a fire appliance. More emergency vehicles were arriving by the minute.

Next to the explosives officer stood a small tracked vehicle, equipped with a camera head and a remote mechanical arm. As Lassiter and Colours approached the expo turned to greet them, Brendan Harper stepped forward. 'How's the eye?' Colours enquired. 'I thought your imitation of Moshe Dayan was impressive.'

'How are you?' Harper countered. 'You didn't look too pretty for a while there.'

'Good afternoon gentlemen,' the expo interceded. 'The plan is to send the probe in, get the door open and see what we have. Then if we can be reasonably safe, I'll go forward with the team in an armoured Land Rover and neutralise the device. Are you happy with that?' Lassiter nodded his approval. As preparations were made he turned to Colours and said quietly 'What do you suppose his idea of reasonably safe is?'

'What about the bomber?' Colours enquired. 'If he's dead, we'll leave him there' the Expo replied. 'If he's not we won't.' Colours shook his head. 'Most pragmatic if I may say so.' Harper turned toward Bishopsgate and laughed.

*

The probe edged forward. Looking like a miniature of some ancient armoured tank, it bumped and wobbled toward its target. Behind the armoured Land Rover, its bonnet now projecting into the main road, Colours and Graham Lassiter nervously watched its progress. Above them through the windows of an obliging office, Kieran Gilhooley viewed the scene in detail through the telescopic sight of a .762 rifle.

Where the chicane of plastic cones marked the crossing into the City of London proper, the van stood alone. Only the diminishing haze of smoke and a distantly visible carpet of fragmented glass marked the explosion. Above them the helicopter circled at a safe height, while only distant traffic noise and the occasional bark of a radio intruded.

Far beyond the van, Bishopsgate and the approach to Liverpool Street station were ghostly silent and deserted. The whine of the probe's electric motor became audible, as Gilhooley's voice broke in on the radio.

'Control and all units from sniper, I have movement in the target vehicle. Stand by.' As the probe tottered ever closer, imperceptibly the van began to rock. The click of the door lock seemed amplified by the silence. Then the door swung slowly open. Gilhooley brought the crossed hairs of his gun sight to bear.

'All units from sniper, I have him. I have control,' as his finger softly embraced the trigger. In a moment the smouldering figure of a man rolled out of the door. He fell on to his knees and began to crawl blindly away, reaching out left and right with his free hand, feeling his way in this world now for ever darkened to him.

His blackened form was almost naked. Vestiges of clothing hung from his body. Elsewhere great swathes of skin were burned away, leaving glistening flesh and muscle exposed to the light. Colours leapt into the driving seat of the Land Rover, cranking the starter. *'Come on…let's go…'* Beside him Brendan Harper slammed shut the massive armoured door.

In moments they were on him, while others cleared the suspect van. Harper and Colours lifted the pathetic figure almost tenderly into the back of the Land Rover, racing back to where Lassiter waited with the paramedics. As they squealed to a halt the medics were there even as the doors were opened, with bags of saline in their hands and ready.

'He looks like some obscene goldfish,' commented Pikey as he peered at the convulsing figure, the injured man's mouth working open and closed soundlessly. 'All pout, pout and shiny skin,' he said, a gleeful hatred in his voice. Colours stood over the figure as it was transferred to the ambulance.

'Burned are you? Blind are you? Now you know my friend's pain, you bastard. Don't you die. Not yet, not until you tell me where I'll find your boss. Then I'll redefine vengeance.' Lassiter allowed his head to fall forward until his chin touched his chest, sighing deeply.

KHAMSIN

Medahwi's angered, bellowing voice echoed around the arch. The mug of brown, milk-less tea spiralled through the air, its content left glistening on papers strewn across the untidy desk. It struck an old filing cabinet and shattered. The harrowed face of a mechanic appeared at the small office door, blackened smears of grease mingling with the dark stubble on his chin.

'Haab, what is wrong?' he enquired humbly. The girl appeared from his right, placing herself between them. 'There is nothing for you to be concerned with. The Haab has great anger, but it will pass.' The mechanic nodded and returned to his labours. 'You are a fool Nasser,' she began. 'You are a slave to your anger and it will be our downfall.'

Medahwi slumped into an old swivel chair, brooding menace etched on his face. He drew his knuckles back and forth across his dark moustache while his eyes returned to the small television set that crowned a stack of books. Images taken from amateur video footage showed the scene in Bishopsgate. 'Why am I surrounded by incompetent idiots? That fucking moron could not even manage to die successfully.'

'*Shut your mouth,*' The girl rounded on him as a train passed above them, its rumble echoing around the blackened brickwork. She bent over him until her breath was at his ear. When the rumble faded, she spoke again in a measured, forced whisper. 'You are Haab to these your followers. You scorn them and yet they are your lifeblood. Show them the weakness of your adolescent anger and we are lost. Now you use the profane language of your enemy. Stop and think... *think!*'

He turned his head to face her, eyes wide with menace as they met hers. 'Do not think to threaten me. I have no fear of you, you should know that,' she said. 'Now you need me now more than ever.' He stood up, suddenly calm and she

183

backed away. 'I will have my revenge,' he hissed. 'I have a new plan. There are others who martyr themselves for Allah. We still have their strength.'

'We fight for our people, our ways, but you must be wise,' she pleaded. 'You have strength, but also you have weakness. It is so with all men. The boy you sent to die for you still lives! If he speaks, he can tell them much.'

'We have striven to be Wind and Shadow. To be unseen and untouchable. It is our cloak and our shield and this boy may strip it away.'

He began to work his jaw, the muscle pulsing in his cheek. 'Then I must kill him,' he said. He strode out of the office past the mechanic who struggled beneath an ageing Ford Sierra. She followed him out into the bright, crisp sunlight and on to the cobbled roadway.

'Only I can reach him,' she said. 'He will be in hospital and they will guard him. They will expect you to go after him. I am a nurse, remember?' He turned to face her. 'And do you think you can do this thing? Can you look at this boy and blast the life from him? Could you look into his pleading, pathetic eyes and snuff out his life, have real blood on your hands?' he said mockingly.

Her eyes clung to his, wide and burning with defiance. Slowly a smile creased his face. 'Yes, you could, little sister. I see that now. I will give you a small gun.' She shook her head. 'I need no gun and I'll know where to find him.'

His smile broadened. 'And how will you kill him, little one? Will you beat him to death, stab him?' She reached into her handbag and retrieved a small syringe. 'With this,' she sneered as she walked away. Slowly he turned away, smiling and shaking his head. 'Very well,' he responded, 'so be it and I will strike another blow.'

*

'Makes you see things in a different light, doesn't it?' Colours nodded toward the elderly couple embracing in a small anteroom opposite him where they stood in the hospital corridor. The man's head was nearly bald. Thin strands of hair stretched across the sallow skin breaking up shiny reflections from the fluorescent lighting that played mischief on his scalp. He wore a long black, un-seasonal coat.

The shine matched those of tears upon his cheeks. His wife's face was buried in his shoulder as she sobbed in his arms as they both rocked gently back and forth.

'I'm surprised you've got any compassion left after all you've been through.' The young Sergeant extended his hand and grasped Colours own. 'My name is John Stillwell MacKenzie,' he smiled. 'A Scot of course!'

He was dressed in coveralls and the paraphernalia of an Essex Specialist Firearms Officer; the only clue to his rank the embroidered blue chevrons on his shoulders. Across his lip was a thick, dark moustache, perhaps an attempt to give his fresh face maturity. 'He could be my doctor, or my corner-shop keeper,' he said, staring intently at the old man.

Colours proffered several sheets of paper toward Mackenzie. 'I reckon you'll need at least six men on this at all times. Until you're up and running I'll leave four Met S.F.O officers. I've recce'd the place and these are my suggested deployments. The final choice is yours of course,' he said.

'We've laid false trails to other hospitals, but it won't keep the press off for long. There's a limited number of specialist burns units, it's only a matter of time. I guess that applies to our terrorist's too.'

Martin Beckwith appeared at Colour's shoulder. 'I've deployed our blokes as you suggested Mr Barras.'

Colours looked toward his young counterpart. 'I've told them that it's your responsibility, that they're to re-deploy if you so desire. Mr Lassiter is negotiating cross border co-operation, so I expect you'll be getting further aid from the Met before too long.'

The young Sergeant huddled by the exit with several of his own men. He gave them directions and returned to Colours's side. The three men then walked toward an open set of double doors, beyond which a team of white-coated doctors worked feverishly on the injured man. Colours glanced at the Essex Sergeant, realising that for reasons he couldn't define, he would like and trust this man.

The young Arab's ravaged body lay on a crash trolley. Grotesque wounds open and shining, looking plastic and contrived in the artificial light. Above him several bags of clear fluid were being piped into his veins. Heavily sedated and opened-mouthed, his form appeared less than human.

Martin Beckwith dropped his eyes and looked away. 'Their parents scrimp and save to send them to university to learn wisdom.'

'All they listen to is the voice of hate whispering in their ears,' said Beckwith.

'We have his name as Farid Al-Hammani,' said Colours. 'His parents run a small post office in Stoke Newington. I think they sold their souls to pay for his education. How wasted. The doctors believe he'll live, but he'll be terribly scarred and blind. The adhesions caused by the wounds will take years of plastic surgery.'

An armed Essex officer appeared at their side. 'Excuse me gentlemen, but Mister Lassiter's here. He'd like to see you.'

As their feet crunched upon the gravel of the car park, Lassiter stood up to greet them, a large rotund man of about fifty at his side. The man was perhaps six feet tall. A drooping moustache flecked with grey dominated his face. Untidy black and equally flecked hair surrounded an otherwise bald head.

'*Colours!*' he bellowed, extending a huge hand. 'Who said you can't fool all the people all of the time,' he continued, his gruff east London accent clear. A smile lit up his reddened face.

'What does that mean?' Colours replied, anticipating him.

'It means I am thinking fuck me, he's still got a job,' the big man chuckled.

Colours turned to the two young Sergeants flanking him. 'Let me introduce you to a legend in his own living-room. Gentlemen this is Detective Sergeant Billy Burrows, SO13. He's known far and wide for many things, but mostly by his nickname. This is Bingo.'

Colour's hand disappeared in the hairy grasp of Bingo's crushing handshake. With the other he slapped Colours heavily on the back. Then he turned to shake the hands of the other two men. 'I've known Mister Barras since I was slim,' he said 'and that's been a fucking long time.' The peel of his laughter echoed across the car park.

'Almost as long as you have had that suit,' Colours retorted.

*

'Medahwi smiled as the boy nervously entered the office. Behind him the rattle of the air tools competed with the whir of escaping compressed air. The sounds amplified and echoed in the confines of the arch. 'Please shut the door,' he said. The boy pulled closed the glazed metal door behind him.

'That is better,' Medahwi said gently, allowing his face to soften. The boy dipped his head. 'Haab,' he acknowledged humbly.

'The Imam speaks well of you,' Medahwi began again.

'He tells me you would wield Allah's sword. By coming here and meeting with me you have taken the final step, you understand that?' The boy dropped to his knees, clasping his hands together. His face was fresh with the barest wisp of a beard trespassing there, as he sought manhood.

He was barely eighteen years old. 'My life is yours, Haab,' he said, his voice trembling. He cleared his throat. 'I give my body and my honour. It is my Jihad.'

Medahwi walked around the desk and stood above the boy. 'Jihad is not for you to declare or decree. But the Imam, the Haab and the faithful call upon you, and you are honoured. Your place in paradise will be assured.' He placed his fingers lightly on the boy's head.

'You are not to leave here until I place that sword in your hands. You will strike the infidel and the un-believer very soon. Then shall rise a golden dawn for you, and you will see paradise. Your ancestors will embrace you.' Then he opened the door and melted into the noise and dust of the workshop.

Only the greasy overall-clad legs of the mechanic protruded from below the van. Medahwi lightly kicked his feet. The man slid out from beneath, his look of annoyance fading to fear. 'Haab,' he said submissively. Medahwi thrust paper money into the man's greasy hand.

'Buy him food. Eat with him and watch him. His time is coming this day. Do not allow him to talk with any one. Disconnect our phone and do not allow him to leave. I shall look to you alone for these things. My blessing or my anger will be for you alone, do you understand?' The man nodded fearfully. Medahwi acknowledged him, a smiling menace in his eyes. Then he walked out into the midday sunlight.

*

The old man sat rocking gently back and forth. A trickle of saliva escaped from the corner of his mouth and tracked downward through growth of white stubble on his chin. His eyes remained transfixed by the light from a tall sash window while he murmured endlessly.

'Hello, Harry.' She knelt slowly beside him, pushing his sleeve back and baring his forearm. He did not reply, nor shift his gaze from the window as she swabbed his flesh.

Deftly she pushed the needle into his vein and pressed the plunger until the syringe was empty. She cleaned the puncture wound and applied a small dressing. 'There you are, Harry,' she said. 'All done!'

Imperceptibly he grunted very low, and the trickle of saliva began to string from his mouth and hang downward. He was immune to her olive-skinned beauty. Few men would be. The ward sister passed behind her, and paused to speak.

'Koo! Please cover Mister Wallis up. His dignity is very much on show.' She looked down at where the loose pyjama's bagged open, exposing the old man's genitals. She studied the thin vascular nightmare of his lower legs and his swollen and discoloured feet, barely contained within grubby wine coloured slippers. 'I

187

shall not live to grow old,' she whispered quietly to herself. 'In this at least my mission is a blessing.' Then she pulled his clothing closed.

*

As he walked into Three Colts Lane, the sound of Medahwi's mobile phone was almost lost, drowned by a passing train above the arches he had left behind him. He strode toward Cambridge Heath Road as he rummaged in the pocket of his coat, then pinned the phone to his ear.

'Jahwara, what is so urgent that you ring me on this phone?' He sucked his cheeks inward with impotent anger.

'I have some medicine for a sick friend,' she said. 'I will visit them in hospital later today. I think things will be much better then. Do I have Haab's permission?' His face twisted gently into a half smile.

'You are resourceful my sister, and you honour me. What will you need?'

She paused and then spoke again. 'A car and a driver, that is all.'

'Keep this phone with you. It shall be done. What name will reach you on the ward,' he said, turning on his heels back toward the railway arch. His eyes were cast downward and fixed, a bitter smile on his lips.

'Ask for Koo,' she said. 'Nurse Khoulad Al-Hassan.'

'I understand,' and he snapped the phone shut.

Moments later he re-entered the arch. 'Jamal...'

The mechanic's eyes squinted as he looked up at Medahwi, the strip lights dazzling him. 'Take the boy to the railway station as I have instructed you. Then you will pick up another passenger. Drive her wherever she requires you. Fill the tank of the oldest car with fuel. When you have finished, burn it.'

He strode to the office where the boy knelt, rocking in prayer. Picking up a khaki rucksack he placed it in front of him. 'This is your sword,' he said 'and today for Allah you will wield it.'

*

Benny looked the young black boy hard in the eye, moving slowly forward and pushing him until he was pinned against the dirty brickwork of the bridge. 'Listen carefully to me,' he hissed in the boy's ear. 'See this gun on my hip? Well it's real. It's not like that stupid fucking replica you've been fooling with, showing off to your mates.' He lifted he boy's hand until his fingers brushed the butt of the Glock.

188

'So can you tell the difference?' His voice rose as genuine anger mounted within him. 'I don't know you from Adam, so take this as real. I don't want to live the rest of my life with knowledge that I've shot and killed some young snot like you, just because you've got one of these things.' The boy's eyes rolled, then fell upon his three friends who watched open mouthed.

'Now, we can have your mum and dad down the nick and sort this out, or you can see if that poxy thing floats. What's it going to be?'

Chris Harvey stood by the car stunned into silence. From the driver's seat John Munney called loudly, 'Do what you're going to do and get in the car. We've got a call.' The boy turned slowly and threw the replica over the bridge parapet into the canal. His eyes returned to engage Benny's, anger and shame burning there. Distantly it splashed into the water.

'I like your attitude,' Benny said, his voice now controlled as he dropped into the passenger seat and the car moved off. From the kerb the boys voice tailed off after the accelerating car, spitting the words through his teeth. 'Fuck you...'

'Nicely handled Benny,' said John Munney as he span the steering wheel through his hands. 'I reckon there'll be friction burns on the front door of Shoreditch nick, his parents will be in such a rush to complain.'

Benny grinned, his gold tooth glinting. 'Nah! He ain't told them he's got that replica Beretta, so he won't be telling them it's at the bottom of the Regents Canal now, will he? End of problem. Now what's this call?'

Munney turned left from New North Road and into City Road, then left again into Old Street. He strove to make himself heard above the their noise, and the incessant radio traffic. 'It's in the log. There's a British Transport copper on a district line train coming in to town. He's sussed an Arab boy with a rucksack that he's convinced is a bomb. Says he's been reading from a pocket Qur'an and muttering prayers all the way.'

'Five one one are running to it and the R.V.P. is outside Aldgate East Station. They reckon to stop the train there.' Benny began to plan. He braced himself against the car's interior as it pitched and rolled. 'I've had one of these before, at Embankment station,' he shouted above all the noise, now heightened by the screeching of the tyres. He grabbed the handset and began to speak.

'MP from Trojan five three one, receiving over?...'

'Go ahead five three one.' The operator high in Scotland Yard's Information Room responded.

'Re: your message C.A.D. 786, can I have fire brigade, paramedic ambulance and expo to R.V.P. with us and Trojan five three one outside Aldgate East Railway

189

Station? Our E.T.A. three minutes. I also require India nine-nine on standby, and traffic and local units to implement road closure of the Aldgate one-way system.'

The car rolled as John Munney turned sharply left into Commercial Street, and Chris Harvey slid across the rear seat, a mobile phone in is hand. Many miles away, Colours was listening to Bingo's assessment of their information, as his phone rang.

'We can narrow the corridor of investigation down on the basis of the mileage on the van's speedometer. The auction house have it on record and the dashboard of the van is relatively intact. Using number plate recognition and CCTV on the A12, I reckon you're looking at the moment at an evidence gathering catchment area between Tottenham and the scene, perhaps five miles wide.'

Colours turned away, cupping the phone to his ear as a light breeze muffled its sound. Bingo stopped, seeing the concern in Colours's eyes.

'Yes, yes! I understand. I'm at the Broomfield hospital in Chelmsford. Get an S.F.O. team down there, and another Inspector. We'll run to Bishopsgate.'

'Another one!' Colours said.

Bingo looked directly at him, his comical, untidy persona swept away as the professional kicked in. 'Go. I'll get whatever else I can from here, and catch up with you later.'

'How fast can you drive?' Colours asked Beckwith as the car tipped out into the main thoroughfare.

'Warp speed Okay, sir?'

Colours shifted in his seat, tucking the seat belt securely around him.

'I want to be in Aldgate *now!*' Beckwith stamped on the accelerator as the mournful rise and fall of the siren heralded a high-speed journey of mythical proportions. Beside him Colours scribbled in the logbook, gathered scraps of information from his mobile phone or the radio. Neither of them took any note of the old red Ford Mondeo that passed them at the entrance, heading for the car park. Such a car with a middle-eastern man driving would be common here, like an old minicab. Likewise the pretty olive skinned girl in a nurse's uniform that was his passenger.

*

Trojan five three one turned out of Commercial Street into Whitechapel against the flow, yet there was no traffic. City of London and Metropolitan Police officers had worked with great speed to seal the area and make it sterile.

190

As John Munney rolled up, a local duty officer, an Inspector was there to greet them. His silver Vauxhall stood at an angle to the kerb, its blue lamp rotating. Distantly other police cars, cordon tape and foot duty officers marked the incident boundary. From the direction of the City, an ambulance, a fire appliance and another A.R.V. closed with them from a break in the cordon.

Trojan five one one sidled to a halt beside where Benny was becoming the centre of attention. Arthur raised his eyebrows in surprise. 'They're on the case here. Look at that lot.' From the station entrance a stream of commuters appeared, marshalled away by increasing numbers of police officers as Territorial Support Group carriers began to arrive.

He stepped out of the car and walked to Benny's side, while Kieran Gilhooley slid from the driving seat and Raffles from the rear. They closed with Benny who now held every eye, surrounded by officers of every rank as he laid out his plan.

'We have a suspect on a central line train, believed to have an explosive device in a rucksack on his person,' he began, updating all present. 'He is described as a man of middle-eastern origin, aged early twenties or younger, with a fine chin beard. He's wearing a black 'Puffa' type jacket, jeans, trainers and a black baseball cap with white designer logo on the peak. He is slim and about six feet tall.'

'Currently he's being kept under observation by a British Transport Police officer travelling in the same carriage. He describes him as being agitated and murmuring constantly, which he interprets as prayer. Delaying tactics are being employed and we are speaking direct to the PC on his phone from this car.'

'Currently the station is under evacuation by B.T.P. officers. We estimate we have about twelve minutes until the train is in the approaching tunnel. The plan is to halt it on a pretext of signal failure. Using the driver's cab phone we'll feed it into the station one carriage at a time. Whatever SO19 units are available at that time will deploy along the platform and deal with the suspect. There are other units on way including a depleted SFO team, but we have very little time.'

The distant echo of two-tone horns along the high sides of Commercial Street marked the arrival of a firearms team as a black Range Rover turned the corner, the blip of blue light issuing through its darkened windscreen. Four men in dark blue coveralls hung with guns and equipment, burst from its doors and ran to Benny's side. One carried a high-powered rifle.

As the last of the passengers were ushered from the station, Benny quickly appraised his additional manpower. Arthur, Raffles and Gilhooley dragged kit from their car. Behind him Chris Harvey followed suit, while from the driver's seat, John Munney ran the control, besieged by radios and telephones as he scribbled furiously in the incident log. At high speed and far away, Martin Beckwith was trying hard.

'I wonder what the speed cameras would make of this?' he shouted above the raucous bellowing of the engine. Colours bent forward as the noises of the car, its horns and the radios combined to threaten all aural communication. He turned speaker volume to its maximum.

'If you go any faster, we'll travel back in time,' Colours shouted. 'What speed are we doing?' Beckwith chanced a glance at the dashboard. 'A hundred and forty three miles per hour.' Colours fell quiet, breathing deeply. His phone rang and he pinned it to his ear, squinting with effort to hear. 'Duty officer...Yes, thank you. Our E.T.A?' He paused, watching the world pass by in a blurred fast–forward. 'About ten minutes. Keep me updated. He turned to Beckwith and shouted, 'They're deploying now.'

*

The red Mondeo sidled smokily to a halt in a quiet corner of the car park. An armed Essex Police Officer, a carbine across his chest, moved toward them. Jahwara loosened the top button of her blouse. 'Wait for me here Jamal. Do not leave the car, and try not to look so nervous.'

'Yes Khamsin,' he replied, bowing his head in a subdued gesture.

She stepped out, greeting him with mischief in her lovely dark eyes. She allowed her lips to part in a sensual half smile. 'I won't be long,' she said, smiling sweetly. 'I have left my study notes in the office.' The man's eyes softened as he succumbed to her sexuality.

'I'll walk you to the door,' he said. 'Please be quick, there is a high-security operation in place here.'

'I'll be right back,' she smiled, tipping her head coyly. 'The cab is waiting and it'll cost me a fortune.' He walked beside her to the door, while in the Mondeo the driver sat fearful and sweating.

She swept in through the double doors, her crisp uniform rustling as she walked. 'The young lady just wants to collect some paperwork from her office.' The armed man had opened the door to the surprise of his colleague who stood motionless at the access to the nearby corridor, a gun on his hip.

'I am confused,' she said smiling. 'I entered from the ward last time and I can't get my bearings. Where is sister's office from here?' The second officer pointed along the corridor toward intensive care. His brow creased with suspicion as she passed through a second set of doors.

'You sure about her Jack?' he asked the first.

The first man nodded gently, watching her swaying form turn right and disappear. 'Sweet meat mate, good enough to eat. Proper little angel of mercy.'

His mouth creased into a smile. 'I might have to go and get myself a small burn,' he continued. 'Nothing too big, just so she'll kiss it better.' In the office the girl slipped on a white coat with an identity tag on its lapel. She lifted her skirt and removed a syringe and phial attached to her thigh with tape.

She filled it from a small ampoule placing it in the coat pocket, and picking up a clipboard, attached a few clinical papers from the desk to it. Then she opened a second door. Carefully, and, checking the corridor was clear she began to follow the signs toward the intensive care facility, the clipboard under her arm. She passed another armed man unchallenged as he nodded and smiled.

As she turned into the side ward where the burned man lay, she caught her breath at the sight of a further armed Police Officer sat at the foot of his bed. Quickly she read the name on the identity tag as he lowered his newspaper, nodding to her. 'I'm Doctor Hassan. Has he stirred at all?' she asked, her fingers feeling for the injured man's pulse.

'No, doctor, the officer replied as he returned to his newspaper. She turned her back to him and disconnected the drip. Then fitting the syringe into its place she pressed the plunger fully home. She reconnected the drip and pausing to check the monitors, said 'thank you.' Smiling, she walked away.

'What fucking woman Doctor Hassan?' said Bingo. 'The only Doctor Hassan I know here is a little Indian bloke. Proper dapper character, nice as you like,' he growled. 'Ask reception if they have such woman.'

'We do not,' the rounded figure of a woman in nurses uniform appeared at the door, a tray full of medication and syringes in her hands. 'I can guarantee that.'

Bingo galvanised. 'Fucking hell you idiots, she's probably done him by now. Check the prisoner.' He ran toward the exit, bursting through the double doors into the car park. Distantly he could hear the old Mondeo coughing into life as he shouted at the armed officer. 'Jack! The Mondeo, the girl! It's a hit on the suspect.'

The carbine rose as the man turned and ran through a chicane of parked vehicles toward the Sierra, his voice ranging above them. 'Armed police, stay where you are or I will fire.' As he cleared the last car a bright orange flash stole his vision.

A colossal impact and great pain stole him away into blackness as the bullet hit his chest. Bingo emerged breathless from around a large van as instantly a searing pain pierced his face and gum, clawing around his head and neck as a white blur confused his eyes.

Jahwara drove the syringe ever deeper into his face, her screams of animal fury, matched only by those of Bingo's pain. He grabbed the trailing coat she still wore and span her around, slamming her into the side of the van, knocking the wind from her. With all his remaining strength he punched her repeatedly in the face until she fell bloodied to her knees. The voices of other armed officers echoed around him as they desperately strove to find them. Then a terrible impact and a searing pain both knocked him down and stole his every breath, as a bullet tore into his lung.

'Khamsin, you must come.' Jahwara saw the blurred vision of the driver's face as he dragged her to the car, the old revolver still smoking in his hand. Her world span as she tasted blood. She lay across the back seat of the car as a loud but remote concussion showered her with glass fragments.

There was a deep thud and then a cracking sound as a red and white barrier arm span past the car. Then the fading sound of chaos behind her as the car's engine screamed and she embraced the blackness that closed all around her and there was silence.

DISCIPLES

'*Fuck me!*'... Colours could not contain himself as the car hit the flyover hard at High Street Stratford. The nose dipped violently as the springs compressed to their maximum, their rebound accentuating the climb. The sounds echoed ever louder, contained within the parapet walls as the car then leapt on to the down slope into Bow, its wheels leaving the ground to impact with yet another heavy thud and a shiver ran through its whole fabric.

'I don't care what I face after this,' Colours shouted. 'I can never be this scared again.'

Beckwith's face cracked into a soft smile as he fought the car through a chicane in the traffic. 'You did say as fast as possible sir.' Colours braced himself against the windscreen pillar. 'I promise you,' he said, turning his head to stare at Beckwith's intent face 'that I will *never* say that again. You're enjoying this aren't you, you mad bastard?' The smile broadened.

*

John Munney raised his hand to stop the Inspector speaking. Beside him now sat a young woman police officer, frantically logging messages as the pace of events quickened remorselessly. The Inspector leaned into the car, eager for more information, while Munney kept his phone link with the British Transport Police officer who now watched the young bomber within the train carriage with rising anxiety, fearing he would detonate, fearing the phone link might fail.

Munney spoke into the radio, clearly so that the Inspector and the young girl could hear. 'Benny from control, receiving over?'

Benny's gruff voice buzzed through the car's speaker. 'Control from Benny.

Just about set here. I can see the train down the tunnel. Tell the driver to bring it in until the first carriage only is on the platform. Is that clear?'

'All received Benny.' Munney looked up at the Inspector. He nodded and began another conversation with a B.T.P. Sergeant beside him, who issued instructions through a radio link to the driver. 'Be aware that our man on the train says the X-Ray is becoming very anxious and agitated,' said Munney.

In the carriage the officer sat impassively reading a newspaper. He held it high. His face remained calm. Only the imperceptible trembling of his hands gave any clue to the depth of his fear. He made it a rule never to travel in uniform. Today he was glad he did. A small earpiece connected a wire from his mobile phone that trickled down his cheek to a microphone, hidden from the bomber's eyes.

An excited group of visiting teenagers jabbered incessantly, standing between him and the threat. Their accents seemed to be Dutch and their noisy chatter allowed him to speak unnoticed. The temperature in the carriage rose relentlessly as the driver's voice broke in on the intercom. 'Transport for London wish to apologise again for the delay. This is due to an electrical fault and resultant signal failure. We do anticipate that matters will be resolved once we have passed Aldgate East Station and we wish to thank you again for your patience.'

From behind the newspaper the officer saw the young Arab's rising fear. He watched him finger a prayer band that was barely visible below the baseball cap. From there beads of sweat ran down his cheeks. He muttered constantly, his lips barely moving and all the while his chest rose and fell in panted breaths that grew quicker as the fear and emotion gripped him. Then he moved his hand to the jacket pocket, fingering and turning something within it.

'This bloke is definitely game on.' Munney heard the officer's voice down the open line. 'I'm sure he's got the trigger in his right hand jacket pocket. I thought I saw some wire. It's as hot as Hades down here and he hasn't taken off that jacket or rucksack. We don't want to be too much longer over this.'

The train gave a gentle jolt and began to move forward, the slow, regular clunk of the rails marking its progress. The distant lights of Aldgate East Station now illuminated the sides of the tunnel. From between the chattering teenagers a woman of about thirty emerged and sat down beside the police officer. She had a pert, gentle face and a bobbed hairstyle. She smiled and spoke, gazing at the floor. 'My English is quite good,' she said. 'You are a policeman, and we are in great danger, aren't we?' His eyes fell. 'Please do not give any indication of your fears,' he said.

'I must protect these children,' she replied. 'They are in my care. Their parents, they have trusted me. Please, I want to take them into the next carriage.

Let me take them through the adjoining door, *please.*' she replied, fear etched on her face.

John Munney's voice broke into his earpiece. 'I can hear this. For Christ sake don't let her blow it.' He still held her gaze. 'I won't,' he said, his reply intended for Munney. Suddenly she began to raise her voice, panic rising within her. 'You can't tell me that. These are children, let them go! You have no right to tell me that.' The train shuddered to a halt.

From behind a ballistic shield, Benny's unbroken gaze stared further down the train, hungry to know what lay just a short distance away. Arthur slipped quickly into the driver's cab, while Gilhooley and Raffles entered the first carriage, guns raised. On Munney's directions, the coverall-clad men ran to the second, eastern entrance. When the train came in, they would be behind and above it.

Gilhooley pressed his forefinger to his lips as the first wave of passengers were cajoled, escorted and even carried by sweating Territorial Support Group Officers in to the street above them. In the penultimate carriage, the officer's fingers bit into her thigh. They bit so hard she winced. 'There's a man in this carriage with a bomb,' he whispered, his mouth now to her ear. 'If you make a fuss, if he suspects that I know, that the police know, he will detonate it and we will all die.'

Her eyes rolled in fear. A tall, slim young man in their group turned and saw her distress. Gently the train shuddered on and stopped again, as one more carriage disgorged its passengers. The young man spoke in his own language, his voice accusing as he eyed the seated police officer nearby. The woman replied, her voice tremulous and the group fell quiet.

The sweating young Arab looked up. 'Don't look at him. Please don't look at him', the young Police Officer vainly hissed, but first one, then another, then all the teenagers turned to stare at the sweating, shaking figure. For the first time the boy's eyes met those of his adversary and he slowly rose to his feet, glistening sweat highlighting his brow.

His fearful eyes engaged those of the officer, who eased out a breath. 'Oh God! We're blown. He's seen me, he's seen me, he knows!'

*

'*Get out of the bloody way.*' Martin Beckwith's cool persona finally broke in a tidal wave of frustration. The narrow barriered confines of Whitechapel Road contained them as the car passed the Royal London Hospital and the traffic bottlenecked. 'Jesus,' said Colours 'It's happening now...'

On the station platform Benny ducked low behind a ballistic shield as Munney's voice crackled through his earpiece. 'Benny we are live, we've blown it. Some tourist woman has shown out. The target's moving.' Benny gritted his teeth. All around him armed men, some in uniform and some in coveralls sought whatever cover there was behind the tiled columns.

Over a rail above them a sniper steadied his rifle. Cravetts appeared from the eastern entrance. Dropping to his knees, he pushed his earpiece firmly home and became the sniper's eyes and ears, as the man's sole focus became the small circle of vision that is a telescopic sight. He settled in, his weapon ranging through the wrought iron work above the west bound platform as he defined his field of fire, considered his backdrop.

The young Arab turned nervously and opened the doors to the adjoining carriage. With little more than a backward glance he walked through. 'He's gone into the last carriage.' John Munney heard the words down the open telephone line.

From the control vehicle in Aldgate, Munney relayed the changing scenario to Benny on the platform far below. He reacted. 'Bring it in, bring the whole train in now.' In the driver's cab, Arthur was beyond pleasantries. 'Get this whole fucking train in the station as fast as you can.' His gruff voice and glazed expression leaving the driver in no doubt.

'SO19 duty officer! Open the bloody cordon now,' Beckwith shouted. The pre-occupied Constable at the cordon tape was shocked into real time as the BMW slewed to a halt beside him. The blue lights and horns had numbed him, and he reacted clumsily.

The blue and white tape was lifted high above the car's roof as Martin Beckwith propelled it the last few yards and skidded to a halt beside the control vehicle, where John Munney laboured.

Colours was beside him in a moment. 'Tell me all,' he said, but then fell silent as he absorbed how crucial the next few moments would be. Martin Beckwith appeared at his side. Below their very feet, fate played fast and loose with so many lives.

'Come on, bring it in Arthur. Bring the whole train in now.' The time for caution had passed as Benny committed them to confrontation and the train began to lumber slowly forward. In the last carriage a few frustrated passengers would finally discover the cause of their torment.

The door slammed behind him as the Arab boy, now wide-eyed and beyond reason, ranged insanely through the carriage. A black man in postal uniform, an elderly couple and a man carrying builder's tools, his face dusted white, watched in awful anticipation as the boy careered through the carriage until he could go no further. Then he turned to face them and they knew that death had come to call.

As the train halted for the last time, Benny burst into the second from last carriage, four armed men behind him. '*Where?*' he called to the B.T.P. Officer, now the only man standing. All around him passengers cowered, or were herded rapidly toward the street. He stood, his warrant card held high.

'There!' and he pointed to the connecting door to the last carriage. 'Control from Benny,' he called. 'Entering last carriage. Sniper, are you ready for target acquisition?' In his ear he heard two distinct clicks. They ran through the carriage, passengers cowering at their presence until they grouped at the door.

Gilhooley opened the first and then grasped the handle of the remaining connecting door, the door that might lead to the very gates of eternity. For a fleeting moment the two men's eyes locked, accepting that pain and blackness, perhaps the end of all things awaited them. Then with a nod that spoke more than a lifetime of words, Kieran Gilhooley swung the door open.

At the second set of double sliding doors, now open to the platform, the Arab boy stood frozen. His tormented gaze seared Benny's lethal, determined eyes. 'Armed Police, show me your hands,' Benny called, as his master eye drew the concentric rings of the carbines sights together, fixing the single pole of the foresight in the centre of his face.

He knew he must kill him instantly, that he must not live long enough to move even a finger. As the boy lifted his hand, Benny fired. A bright yellow flash interrupted the dull lighting of the carriage and a shell case struck the carriage window, tinkling to the floor. A woman screamed. A huge eruption of glass and noise issued through the door where the Arab boy stood, thousands of fragments showering him and the nearby platform.

In the street above, Colours torment increased as the words 'shots fired,' issued from the car's radio speaker. He resisted the urge to run forward, to add to the chaos below him. Martin Beckwith turned to him, open-mouthed. Colours looked down at the gun he now held, and had no recollection of drawing.

As the boy leapt on to the platform, Benny cursed 'fuck it.' Ahead of where the boy had stood, an aluminium upright was dented and bent, its glass shattered. Then he called again, frantically 'Sniper, you have control.'

On the platform Raffles centred the sights of his carbine on the boy's head, settling himself, concentrating. 'Armed Police,' he called 'keep your hands away from your body.' The boy stood suddenly still, engaging Raffle's eyes and facing him, becoming strangely calm as the sweat trickled down his face. 'Allah is merciful,' he said.

A sudden, deathly quiet descended. Within the carriage the remaining passengers lay prostrate on the floor, the only sound that of a woman sobbing, the last distant scramble of feet on the stairs to the exit. Benny and Gilhooley took up point of aim at the boy's head through the open doors. Above them the coverall-clad sniper settled in, the telescopic sight centred on the boy's skull. Raffles desperately fought to dominate his target.

'Look at me, only at me,' he said, loud and assertive, while all else fell quiet. 'Keep your hands away from your body. Do only what I say, and only when I say it. Do you understand?' The boy smiled softy. With his hands held wide from his body, he began to turn, so that the rucksack was presented toward his tormenter. Silently his lips worked, reciting verse.

'I did not tell you to move. *Stand still...*' Raffle's torment increased as he watched his fate unfold, and yet he could not bring himself to fire. He needed something more, something imminent.

The words '*Only when a man is armed, or otherwise so dangerous,*' echoed in his head as years of training spoke to him and stayed his hand as the boy called 'Haab.'

'Keep your hands away from your body. Do not move, do exactly as I say,' Raffles heard himself scream as the boy's hands began to descend toward the pocket. Raffles felt his finger tighten on the trigger as from above and behind him a powerful concussion assailed his senses, resonant in the white-tiled confines of the station. Seemingly in slow motion a mist of reddened fluid filled the air. Then as if the strings of life were cut from a puppet the boy dropped, his legs folded beneath him as his face exploded and all that was his being was instantly extinguished.

He fell on his knees and elbows and lay hunched. From what remained of his eye sockets, nose and mouth, a blackened red pool began to spread, gelatinous and glistening. Above the wispy beard that shone now with his life-blood, his mouth remained open in a final prayer. Gilhooley placed a giant hand on Raffle's shoulder and turned him away, facing him as Raffles whispered, 'Oh! Jesus Christ.'

'He's not seeking Jesus,' Gilhooley said 'He's seeking Allah. Perhaps now he's found him.' Benny broke the awesome spell as silence followed the shock of gunfire. 'Get them out, everybody out. There's still a bomb in here.' The sudden reality struck as Colours appeared on the stairs, his voice dominating. 'Everybody out until the Expo has done.'

Benny, Gilhooley, Raffles and Arthur sprinted for the stairs, the firearms team close behind. Walking towards them the ballistic-suited figure of the Explosives Officer imposed himself, stoic and methodical. Cravetts and Colours lifted the shocked sniper to his feet, running him into the street.

Alpha Eight Two, the City of London bomb car deployed toward the station, three men in their C.B.R.N. suits, carrying an X-Ray facility with them ran down the stairs toward the platform. All around the flash and whir of cameras competed with a multitude of blue lights.

The relief gathered around John Munney as Cravetts appeared from a sandwich bar with a huge tray of steaming drinks. He placed it on the bonnet of the car next to Raffles, who sat on the front wing, ankles crossed.

Cravetts pushed a coffee firmly into his hand, and he looked up. 'You did well Andy,' he said.

In the corner of Raffles's eye a tear began to form. 'I didn't fire. He might have killed us all. I hesitated.' Cravetts smiled gently. 'You would have, we all would have. Just timing mate! It's always a bad trip, whichever way. Believe me, *I know.*' He placed a hand on Raffles's shoulder. Colours caught Cravetts eye and nodded his approval. Far below them the expo edged closer to where the boy lay, his feet slipping in the ever-widening pool of congealing blood, while behind him the crew of Alpha Eight Two waited seeking cover at the staircase.

With a watchmaker's care, he cut each strap on the rucksack and lifted the flap. At each movement he peered into its interior with a brilliant pencil torch. He beckoned them forward, and they gingerly set up the contents of the black suitcase like equipment around the dead boy.

Lassiter's car sidled to a halt. He stepped out and strode toward them, speaking to the assembled group that now faced Colours in a semi-circle. 'I'm sorry I wasn't here sooner. I have been at the nursing home with the boys from the West Drayton thing. Made my best time lads, I promise you. Everybody okay?'

'One nil to the Old Bill sir.' Arthur's gruff voice cut in. 'You have a way with words Arthur,' smiled Lassiter. 'Keep all your weapons in battery. Don't unload anything and wait for the S.O.C.O. to bag them up. We will go back to…' His voice trailed off as the crew of Alpha Eight Two burst back on to the street.

Close behind them the explosives officer was framed in the doorway, hindered by the heavy suit. 'Timer,' he called. 'They've got it on a timer.' A sudden flash silhouetted him as a shock wave accompanied a huge explosion. Glass fragments showered them as the air filled with dust and debris and the blast propelled them skyward from the station below. Everywhere paper began to float and descend as a newspaper stand was blasted into the air. In the distant crowd, women screamed.

*

Below the Canary Wharf tower, the girl clutched the paper bag to her chest. The steaming hot coffee and salt beef sandwich laced with mustard promised her a respite from the tedium of her office. Above her, millions of tons of steel and concrete housed the offices of multi-national corporations and newspapers. She enjoyed being here, in the hub of all this.

She settled on the bench and smiled at familiar faces, her back to a planter filled with broad green leaves. So many others had enjoyed this now waning summer, while they sat by the old docks on warm, sunny breaks. Now as the days cooled, still the open subterranean walkways appealed. The smell of food and coffee wafted on the air from the shops around her. Their glass fronts and the bustle of life provided her with free entertainment, as she chatted and ate with friends.

The figure of the woman in strict Islamic garb was unusual. The girl studied her dark eyes. They darted nervously back and forth, not settling. They seemed so sharp and clear, so young. The rest of her entire form was tented within the black gown, a single silver band about her head. The girl watched with growing apprehension as the bulky figure paused, then sat awkwardly on the bench beside her.

She sipped her coffee, making real eye contact for the first time. At first it was the eyes and glimpses of her feet as she had descended the stairs, and now the hands of this strange figure appeared so young, so at odds with the bulk and waddling demeanour that rendered her almost as a caricature. The woman raised those hands, as if in an act of prayer, and faced the girl, her eyes suddenly alive with hate and mockery.

She opened them for the girl to see. Through her palms ran red wires, soldered to the gaudy rings on her fingers. The girl gasped loudly a few words, the last words she would ever speak. 'Oh God. *Please no!*' The man beside her turned in alarm. 'Are you alright Miss?' his face gentle with age. The woman in the Burqua closed her hands. The rings met and they all died.

The blast roared up and through the bowels of Canary Wharf, where glass and dust showered out through the doors. At the bars and at tables people screamed or perhaps sat silently disbelieving.

A coffee bar, a Pret a Manger and a salt beef bar were gone, turned to dust and glass.

A glass-fronted wine bar turned into a million fragments and a sea of fluids. Paper cups and plates, the remnants of food mingled with burned and ragged body parts. The girl was gone.

*

The Explosives Officer lay bleeding in the kerb, where the blast had lifted and thrown him. As Colours and Beckwith ran to him, the distant resonant boom of a second explosion assailed their ears. The Expo raised himself to a seated position, blinking to clear his vision. 'Close,' he said, as Colours steadied him. 'A bit too fucking close!' He took another breath. 'And that will be a another one?' he sighed forlornly.

Colours's phone began to ring. He snatched it angrily from his belt. 'Duty Officer,' he barked. Martin Beckwith watched Colours's eyes ranging angrily, his mouth becoming hardened and bitter. As the call ended, his head dropped forward and he sighed deeply, as if he were drained. He sat on the kerb beside the injured Explosives Officer as his men gathered around him, shocked and bewildered.

'Bingo's been shot. He's bad. An Essex P.C. took a round in the chest, but his body armour saved him. They injected the prisoner with something lethal. The second bomb was Canary Wharf. There are massive casualties and fatalities. We're losing, he's winning.'

In the base room at S.O.19, a fax machine began to chatter. As the baseman studied it, the image of a Police Officer's epaulette emerged. Then the words 'Allah be praised...'

*

Medahwi's mobile phone rang. Above the clamour of the railway arch workshop he fought to hear Jamal's voice. 'Haab. I have killed two policemen I think. Your sister has stabbed the boy with a great needle and I think he will die also. She is very sick my Lord. The policeman has beaten her face and there is much blood. She cannot speak.'

Anger and elation ranged in Medhawi's thoughts. 'Where are you?' he said.

'By a water tower, Haab, in a road called Beehive Lane. Shall I burn the car?'

Medahwi erupted. 'No you fool. Every police car for miles will be drawn to you. Wait there till I come for you. I will bring the blue van.'

'Keep the telephone with you and wait. Hide, do you understand?' Meekly the man replied. 'Yes Haab.'

*

Colours nervously entered the side ward where Bingo lay. His greying hair was a matted tumble about the crown of his head. One side of his face was enormously swollen. Profiled against the light of the window, it was covered now in stubble. His chest rose and fell in rapid breaths as he wrestled with his pain.

A white sheet had slid down to his groin, losing the unequal struggle to cover the huge girth of his stomach. Tubes of pink fluid tracked down into waiting bags while another was half filled with urine. Above him other bags hung from chromium frames to pipe blood and fluids into his veins. Monitors clicked and bleeped. A nurse fussed nearby.

Colours shuddered as he saw the plastic tag on Bingo's wrist, the words *William Burrows* written in blue ballpoint. He remembered how often he had seen plastic tags on pallid, lifeless flesh. He remembered Barry Mankowitz's face, staring at a night sky with unseeing eyes. He didn't want to lose another friend.

'Roy!' Bingo curled his fingers to beckon Colours forward. He realised that Bingo had watched his silhouette, tracked his reflection in the glass of the facing window. As he turned to face him, the extent of his suffering made Colours's heart first sink, then ferment with anger.

Half of his friend's face was crimson and swollen beyond recognition, his left eye closed. His jaw line was defined in the blackness of massive bruising. With shallow breaths, he forced tortured words from the corner of his mouth. 'She paid for this,' he said lifting his huge fist. 'I got about six hits in on her before some bastard shot me.' He began to cough shallowly, and painfully.

'You always talk too much Billy, and now you're even more ugly. Didn't think it was possible.' Bingo's mouth curled in a tortured smile. 'She ain't so fucking pretty right now.' He took a breath, silently waiting for the pain to recede. Then he spoke again. 'I got her D.N.A. all over my fist. Also they recovered the syringe and the ampoule.'

'She done him with insulin so he would die slowly. She thought she could slope off but I got her. The doctors filled him full of glucose and he survived.'

204

'So like a good detective, you collected the evidence. Couldn't you have done it in a less painful way?' Colours asked.

The big man began to convulse gently. 'Don't make me laugh.' he said. 'It hurts when I laugh, but yes I did. I got it done…Bingo!' Painfully he turned his head, holding Colour's gaze with his one open eye. 'And I ain't going to die. Planning see! If your gonna get shot, make sure it's outside a hospital.'

'I should hope not,' Colours sighed, a sense of relief flowing through him. 'It's your round! One more thing! They shot you with a very old revolver. Apparently they wanted to use something from your own era.' Straining to track Colours's progress toward the door, Bingo called softly again. 'Roy!'
Colours stopped. 'What is it mate?' he smiled. Bingo beckoned him close. Then in a whispered breath he said, 'Fuck off.'

*

'You will need to see a doctor.' Medahwi stared at his sister's bloodied and swollen face in the light of a small but piercing torch. Dried, blackened blood had congealed around her nose and mouth. Her beautiful eyes were now bloodshot and yellowed, while the first discolouration around them had begun to spread from a badly broken nose. Semi-conscious, her breaths came in rattled spasms as blood and mucous filled her mouth.

He turned to the trembling figure beside them, which still clutched the ancient revolver. As their eyes engaged, the man dropped his gaze fearfully. 'Haab,' he whispered respectfully. 'You have done well Jamal,' Medahwi responded. 'Lay my sister on the blankets in the back of the van. Then bring me the small box from beneath the driver's seat.' Jamal nodded submissively and lifted the woman's limp form.

Taking a pair of short cutters, Medhawi reached below the car and ruptured the petrol pipe. The fluid began to trickle on to the ground below. Jamal returned with a small wooden box. Medhawi opened it, screwing down an electrical contact. The ratcheting sound of the timer seemed strangely loud in the silence of the abandoned gravel pit.

'Drive!' The headlamp beams ranged both skyward and then downward as the van pitched and rolled on the unmade road and Jamal fought with the steering wheel. 'Stop,' Medhawi barked. They sat in silence while his unbroken gaze searched the night's blackness. Jamal flinched as a loud explosion heralded a fireball and the old Mondeo was consumed.

Medhawi did not flinch. The orange glow flickered in his eyes, giving them a demonic light, playing evil shadows across his cratered face. 'Shall I drive now, Haab? Where shall I go, Haab?' Jamal said fearfully. 'Go to London, as if to the arch. Then we will visit a friend. I will tell you where when we are close. If you ever speak of it, ever speak his name, I will kill you.'

Jamal did not reply.

*

Beth woke with a start as the telephone beside her began to ring. The last embers of the fire she had lit to ward of the late autumn cold were barely glowing. 'Thank god you rang,' she said at once, hearing Colours warm voice. 'Go to bed,' he said 'I'm fine. There's a whole lot happened. I guess you'll have seen it on the news. But I'm fine. Loads of paperwork but I'm on my way home.'

She tucked the wrap around her legs as she felt the first chill. 'I'll be right here in this chair until you get home. Then we will go to bed together.' Colours pleaded with her. 'It's three a.m! Go to bed, *please.*'

Beth picked up a log and threw it on the fire. 'Sure! See you soon.' She lifted the bottle of Irish whiskey from the cabinet and laid out two glasses. Then she returned to her chair and curled up to wait.

RELUCTANT MARTYRS

Bottomless fatigue washed over him as the last beat of the Harley's exhaust faded away, and he rolled into the garage. In the darkness he could hear Stuka's claws on the paving, beating a path to where he would assault Colours in a tidal wave of affection.

Beth's shape was outlined against the lights of the house, framed in the doorway. The dog launched himself, pinning Colours against the garage wall. He barely had the strength to resist. 'My turn next' Beth called. The dog snorted and snuffled at his feet as he walked leaden to where Beth's extended hand proffered the small glass of whiskey. 'Shower's running,' she said.

The hot water soothingly cascaded over his head and neck. She picked up the clothes he had abandoned in the urge to lose himself in the welcome warmth. She slipped off the wrap, and Colours felt a gush of cooler air as she ducked low, then rose up between his arms, pushing her soft cool body against him.

He opened his eyes and her face was so close, barely touching, her hair now plastered wet to her head. Her pretty eyes looked deeply into his. He sucked in a deep breath. 'It's such an ugly world,' he said, 'but you're so lovely.'

'Make the most of this,' she replied blinking in the force of the cascading water. 'Soon something will come between us.'

His brow creased and then he smiled. 'Oh yes! No show yet then,' he said, as he slid his hand across her smooth stomach.

'No,' she smiled softly. 'Business as usual!' Then she pressed her soft lips to his. Deep within him a confused agony twisted his emotions

*

'Hello boss! It's Martin. Sorry to disturb you on your day off, but I thought you might want to have an update.' Beth sighed, releasing her grip on Colours's arm as his attention and his mind wandered far away. She picked up a stick and threw it beyond where Stuka ferreted and snuffled through ferns that were now tinged with the brown of autumn. In his inimitable way, Stuka ignored it completely.

'Bloody phone,' she uttered under her breath as she kicked at the first of the countless damp, brown leaves beneath her feet. They stuck to the mud on her boots the coming winter was already demanding. Quietly she was angry at how much of a beautiful summer they had already lost to his work.

The laughter of their daughters echoed through the Surrey woodland around them as they ran and played nearby. The first damp breath of this changing season saw them wrapped in woollen sweaters. Soon the ground would be a sodden mush, then frozen hard as her body began to swell with a new child. When could they, could *she* have his heart and mind for herself alone? Her anger grew.

'They've recovered the Aldgate bomber's phone. They found it in a sleeve pocket of the puffa jacket he was wearing. His arm was still in it, but it wasn't connected to the rest of him.' Beckwith went on. 'It's damaged, but technical support reckon they can salvage the sim card and will have some phone numbers to work from within hours.'

'Where and when?' Colours asked. '4am Monday morning.'

'I'll be there,' snapped Colours.

'So will I boss. Wild horses...'

Beth turned to confront him angrily. 'Don't you dare!' she said. He smiled back at her. 'No! Not today love. Early tomorrow!' His face creased into a smile. 'Today's all ours. So a pub lunch and the rest of the day at home?'

Her face softened. 'You were lucky. I'd have come after you with a blunt and rusty razor blade if you'd left us today.'

He wrapped her in his arms and swung her around until her boot flew off, nipping her ear until she squealed. 'Your not so tough,' he laughed. Then he curled up in a ball amongst the ferns as three little girls, a grown woman and a bulldog assaulted him.

*

Danny Cohen sauntered back across the road with a plastic cup of steaming coffee in one hand, a large burger in the other. He turned left across the front of Mile End Station and past the first in the row of cabs waiting at the rank. 'Hey Danny, is that meat kosher?' called a voice in a strong Irish accent.

The driver of the first cab smiled wryly at him. 'I should worry if it's Kosher,' he laughed. 'If it's low calorie, that'd be much better, Yes?' He slapped his ample belly.

'My wife and my children, they all say Danny, you are very fat. Hey! life's too short,' he chuckled. He walked on calling back, 'Maybe you should drink less Guinness?' Then he swung into his cab, burying his face in a magazine through his pebble glasses. They perched on his broad nose and dominated his face below an old chequered cap. Then he devoured his food.

Medahwi and Jamal climbed the stairs from the eastbound platform. They walked out through the foyer and paused at the pavement. Jamal moved toward the line of cabs. 'No Jamal, the third one. We will take the Jew. Perhaps our brothers in Palestine will hear of it and thank us.'

Danny was shaken from the pages of his magazine as the door opened and the cab tilted as the two sallow skinned men climbed in. 'Sorry gents,' he said, struggling to centre his vision through his thick spectacles and the sliding glass divide. 'The cab at the front's first. The driver won't like it!' His throat closed with fear, almost choking him as Jamal pointed the old revolver at his back. 'You will drive now,' said Medahwi.

The cab swung out from the queue. Danny was sweating heavily as the Irishman cursed him. 'Please,' Danny said. 'I'm an old man. I've got grandchildren. Take my cab. I won't say nothing! Let me go home to my Maria. Please, I beg you,'

Medahwi smiled. 'Drive to Bethnal Green. I will tell you where. Be silent and I may let you live.'

He picked up his mobile phone and rang the arch. 'Open the doors in two minutes.' Soon the tyres rumbled over the cobblestones and then swung right through the corrugated iron gates that slammed behind it. 'Fit the plates,' said Medahwi to the waiting mechanic. He reached in the cab and pulled the breathless old man out and pushed him ahead, toward a derelict van. 'Get in,' he said, spitting words alive with hatred. As Danny struggled to step his bulk up into the van, Medahwi pulled the green oval badge from his neck. He passes it to Jamal. 'Wash it before you wear it,' he said scornfully.

Then he pulled the old revolver from Jamal's belt and centred it in the old man's terrified forehead. Relishing the moment he paused, drinking in the fear and agony on Danny's face.

'Will Maria miss you?' he hissed. 'Will your grandchildren grow to oppress us again? You will never know.' Danny lifted his hands in a final defensive plea. Medahwi raised the gun and fired. The crash of the gun resounded with shocking violence within the bricked confines. 'Put all the explosive in the cab's boot, in two suitcases in the front,' he said, unmoved by the old man's death.

209

'Yes, Haab.' Jamal and the mechanic fearfully obeyed. As they lifted the oil drums and boxes into the cab's boot, the mechanic raised his eyes, watching Medahwi place a prepared charge on the diesel tank of a half-dismantled lorry. On its flat bed back stood several jerry cans full of petrol. 'I have known men that look for a reason to kill, but this Haab, he needs a reason not too,' and he shook his head. Jamal nodded. 'Ibrahim, be silent,' he hissed. Between the closed rear doors of the van, blood began to pool. It seeped through the gap in the doors and dripped on to the step, turning it a deep and violent red.

'Drive toward Ilford,' Medahwi commanded. He handed the mechanic a mobile phone. 'Khamsin will telephone you. She will tell you where to hide the cab until the morning. You will not leave it. Do you understand? He turned and centred his gaze on Jamal who then dipped his head obediently. 'Yes, Haab.'

Far away Jahwara paced the muddy ground impatiently. The mobile phone startled her from her thoughts. She pulled the veil from her face and winced as she pressed it to her ear. 'Nasser?' she said through swollen lips. 'Wait ten minutes and then ring the other phone. Tell them how to find you. I will bring the blue van. Have everything ready for loading,' he said.

'I understand,' she replied curtly.

She redrew the veil to hide the mass of dressings that criss-crossed her broken nose, and her bruised and battered face. Drawing her fingers across her injuries, she winced at the pain and the anger grew until it consumed her, burning in her chest, unquenchable.

She turned to the pile of weapons that awaited transportation. The ragged assortment of handguns. The assault rifles, grenades and the rocket launcher. The boxes of C4 and Semtex expolsive.

She thought of the volatile homemade explosive that Jamal and Ibrahim the mechanic, were even now bringing closer. The corners of her mouth curled in satisfaction as in her mind's eye, she saw her revenge in fire, blood and terror. Then she rang Jamal's mobile phone. 'Khamsin,' he said reverently, knowing before she spoke that it could be only her.

'Take the Romford Road until you reach Hampton Road on your left. Turn in there and look for a sign that says Aldersbrook Joinery. Drive around the block three times to see if you are followed. I will be watching. I will open the gates and tell you when to enter.'

'I understand,' said Jamal. Ibrahim the mechanic turned his eyes rearward, toward the drums of volatile explosive fluid rocking gently in the boot behind them. 'Go softly my brother,' he whispered.

Lassiter sank the last of a steaming mug of tea while he waited for the briefing room to fill. Behind him a white board was covered in information, hurriedly scribbled there in red and green dry-wipe pens. As Colours entered the room, the names Medahwi, Khamsin and Haab now seared his mind, and anger began to surge in his chest. For a few moments he forgot the cold that had chilled him as he rode hard in the early morning darkness and mist. Martin Beckwith plunged a cup of hot coffee into his willing hands.

'Thanks Martin,' he said, shivering slightly. 'Security or not, I think my car will re-appear soon.'

'Let's hope that after today, it won't be an issue,' Beckwith replied.

Behind them, row after row of men in dark blue coveralls fanned out, the low murmur of their conversation broken only by the occasional comment or jest. Around the floor, kit bags, weapons, styrene cups and plates were muddled together as men sought a snatched breakfast at this early hour.

'Gentlemen…' Lassiter's voice rose above it all, demanding attention. Quickly silence descended.

'Good morning. Today's operation, codenamed 'Lancer' will be a combined effort including ourselves, SO13, firearms teams from West Midlands, Manchester and the home counties.'

'There will be four separate addresses in North London. Three will be briefed at the south base. Our concern will be one major address in Bethnal Green. Our information is that an arch below the railway in Cudwell Street is both a base of operations, an armoury and perhaps a bomb factory. Technical support have worked with the phone manufacturer and recovered the last dial numbers from the Aldgate bomber's mobile. The telephone number of this venue features prominently.'

'In addition the perception amongst the Islamic student fraternity that their friends are being sacrificed wantonly is being fuelled by the anguish of their parents. Their distress was televised last night, and has led to several phone calls being received. The tide is perhaps turning.'

Lassiter took a sip from his coffee and continued. 'The premises are used as a repair facility for vehicles owned by local traders, predominantly from the nearby Bethnal Green Road market. The occupancy varies, but there are usually up to three mechanics at work there at any one time, in addition to our suspects. I cannot stress strongly enough that this group, and Nasser Medahwi in particular, are singularly ruthless and vicious. They are suicidal in their intent. Our hope is that he at least is sleeping in the premises.'

Lassiter cast a glance toward Colours. 'Mr Barras?'

Colours stepped forward and continued. 'I must stress that our information is scant and being updated by the moment. As Mister Lassiter has stated, we believe that principal members of the Wind and Shadow terrorist group are sleeping in and using these premises. Our intention this morning is to covertly surround and contain the premises, and arrest or otherwise neutralise the occupants. An armoured Land Rover will ram the gates and the firearms team will fill the premises with CS gas. ARV crews will provide the containment while Sergeant Harper will go forward with members of Red and Green teams to search and clear the arch.'

Brendan Harper took over. 'Your individual postings and responsibilities are listed on the board behind me. The time now is 5.17am. I want the convoy ready to roll at 5.30 to R.V. at Bethnal Green police station for final checks and briefing at 5.45. Expo will be waiting. The combined operations are timed to go in at 6.30am. There is no leeway.'

Lassiter stepped forward. 'So gentlemen, let's make it happen.'

*

'Where is the boy?' stormed Medahwi. 'Soon it will be sunrise. I am surrounded by fools and cowards.' He paced the floor of the old workshop, stepping over discarded timber and window frames. The muted sound of the first train of the day clattered slowly by. He turned suddenly on Jamal, waking him from a fitful sleep. 'Load the van. I want to be ready to leave in an instant. Put the guns and some grenades in the cab. Do it now!'

Jahwara stepped forward, blocking his path. 'Curb your anger brother. It is your great enemy. You are a hero to so many young believers, but you spend their lives cheaply. Their faith is shaken. Too many mothers and fathers are mourning at home. Now it is happening here. You should not have killed the holy man. That was foolish. There are voices now that speak out against you. After today we begin again in another city, but you must be patient, you must be wise.'

Medhawi's eyes burned with anger. He lifted an assault rifle from the pile of weapons and shook it above his head. 'I'm not afraid to die. I will shed my blood now, today,' and he fired a shocking, loud burst into the timber, sending fragments and splinters flying, filling the air with dust and the smell of the gun.

212

Jahwara stepped in front of him, pressing her breast against its hot barrel. 'Would you then waste my life now, as you would waste yours? Shall the whole world be woken by your foolishness and we die here in the dirt for nothing? If we die, it is for our brother and our people. Spend your life, but do not waste it.'

'Then another must sacrifice himself today,' he said and turned, his eyes fixed upon the cowering mechanic. Ibrahim began to tremble violently, fear assaulting his already cold body.

He was seated with Jamal on an old mattress pressed against the wall of dismal brickwork that formed the workshop. His eyes, glistening with tears were cast upward, pleading with Medahwi.

'Lord Haab, I am a simple man, a mechanic. I have a wife and children. Please Haab, I am not a fighter. Have I not served you faithfully? Nasser Medahwi squatted in front of him, stroking is chin, cradling the assault rifle. 'It is your time Ibrahim. Our people call to you, and you must answer.'

Jahwara watched him intently, until her mind pushed the pain in her face aside and her hate and fanaticism ruled. 'Now even your lap dogs are to die for you Nasser,' she said through her swollen lips. 'Perhaps one day soon even you and I will die. If this is to be so, we must be legend. We must be Wind and Shadow. Then they can never kill us.'

He stood, lifting the veil, his eyes staring intently into hers, studying her bruised and swollen face. 'You have suffered but a little. Our friend Muhktar is a fine doctor. You will heal and seduce men's eyes and minds again. It is our path to give much more. Tomorrow it will be Ibraham that will seek the face of the prophet. But you are right, our time will come soon enough.'

She glared at him, her expression fixed and angry. 'I have watched you grow and I know your very soul. They are as fearful children, and I am not. We are bound not by love, but by hate. I follow the same path not out of fear, but for vengeance. Do not patronise me,' she spat out the words. Angrily he began to work his jaw. Then he smiled. 'So be it little sister.' He turned sharply again to face the two men. 'Prepare yourselves. We are leaving.'

*

'Got some updates here boss!' Martin Beckwith slid into the passenger seat of the BMW with a sheaf of paper in his hands. It was parked now in the shadow of the old police station. 'SO13 have been trawling the health service records. A psychiatric nurse called Khoulad Al-Hassan from Goodmayes hospital hasn't turned up for a few days now.' Colours listened intently, while his eyes scanned the mirrors, watching as armed men checked their kit near the vehicles behind him.

'They ran checks and the I.D. and references are all false.' Beckwith continued. 'They got down there P.D.Q and guess what? Phials of insulin are missing. Bingo...! as your man would say. By the way, he's doing well.' Colours smiled his approval. 'Jahwara Medahwi?' he mused.

'Looks like! Also a cab driver called Danny Cohen is missing, complete with his cab.' Beckwith continued. 'He didn't come home last night and the family panicked because he's been hiding a heart condition. Just angina, but it was enough to worry them. The locals have been down to the rank, and one of the drivers reckons that our Danny picked up a right dodgy looking pair last night. Says he jumped the queue, which was out of order and out of character.'

Colours stared blankly ahead, lost in thought. 'Martin, take the wheel will you?' He got out and strode back to where Lassiter was pulling on body armour, surrounded by the relief. 'Guvnor?' he called, forcing Lassiter's attention. 'D'you know about the cab?'

Lassiter turned to face him. 'Yeah, as soon as we're done here, I'll give it more thought. It's been circulated. Maybe we'll get lucky and find the cab and him at the arch.'

Colours stepped into Lassiter's path, stared hard into his eyes. 'Medahwi is no fool. He isn't taking this into or through the city and the security barriers there. The bridges are manned, the tunnels also. He'll know we'll be looking at cabs by now. What's he doing?'

Lassiter nodded as he wrapped the Velcro fixing around his chest. 'Okay. So he's moving on something. There are countless black cabs in London. He's sure to have cloned a number plate. Where do we start? Maybe ANPR will pick it up.'

Behind them Brendan Harper's voice resonated in the early air, crisp and clear. 'Mount up,' as black clad, masked and armed men climbed aboard the Land Rover.

A darkened Transit ticked quietly in the kerb nearby. Colours eyes widened as he saw Sally Galloway's pretty face profiled for a moment by the interior light. 'Guvnor?' Colours quizzed Lassiter.

'Hair of the dog,' he replied. 'She passed on the range, so Brendan's keeping her under his wing for a few days. Just driving, no involvement.'

Harper turned and walked back to where Colours and Lassiter stood. 'We've had a crafty eyeball over the gates. They are just corrugated iron and wood. I'm putting the armoured Land Rover straight through them and then gassing the place out with ferret rounds through the main doors.' He turned to Lassiter. 'You'll have control sir. We have eight minutes to reach the form-up point and then deploy.' He turned to Colours, and seeing his concern said. 'Don't worry big fella. We'll look out for her.'

Colours was deep in thought as Gilhooley, Cravetts and Arthur checked their equipment and weapons. All around the rustle of uniform and the rattle of the gun clips were amplified in the quiet air of this bright morning. His mind wrestled with so many things. What would Medahwi do next? His anger burned ever more intensely.

A milk float hummed quietly by, its driver wide-eyed as the bottles rattled and chinked. An old man passed. Waving a rolled newspaper, he called low. 'Good luck, sir.' Colours knew instinctively he was an old soldier.

As each vehicle filled, a hand extended giving thumbs up. Brendan Harper's voice broke in on the radio. 'Are we set? Count off, one to six.' Successively the numbers were called until he was ready. 'Right, let's roll,' Harper's voice in the radio again as in an instant the lead van lurched away, followed by successive cars, the Land Rover and a paramedic ambulance. Somewhere within the convoy a police dog barked.

The van slipped quietly into the kerb beneath a high-vaulted railway bridge. One after the other, vehicles sidled to a halt, only the rustle of the tyres, the squeal of their brakes betraying them. Silently man after man stepped down, closing every door with infinite care and each knowing his appointed task. They formed a line, the leader at the very corner.

The dark coveralls melted into the shadow of the wall, breaking their outlines so that they were almost invisible to the sun-dazzled eye. The muffled sound of their voices was barely audible through the black respirators they wore, their breathing marked by the 'suck-blow' sound of the valves. Their trunks were swathed in body armour and hung with ammunition and grenades. All wore handguns, and carried carbines or a shotgun.

Martin Beckwith fell quiet beside Colours as he guided the BMW silently into the kerb.

Gilhooley stopped the second car level with them, ready to deploy and contain the target. Beyond them another car appeared crewed by Pikey, Fudge and John Munney.

For agonising moments the cars stood impotent, only the hiss of their engines betraying their presence. Nobody spoke while men checked their kit one final time. Harper's voice ran a shock through them all. 'Stand by.' Beside them

Gilhooley slipped the car into 'drive' and it jolted lightly. Beckwith watched Colours fingering his gun.

He knew! He knew this was not their fight, their operation. He knew that they were there to observe. He knew that if Colours had the smallest chance he would kill Medahwi in an instant.

*

Jamal fumbled with the controls of the cab. 'Drive smoothly today, Jamal, or we shall see paradise together,' Jahwara smiled wistfully as the taxi's diesel engine rumbled into life. The swelling on her face had begun to recede. Around her eyes her skin was tinged yellow as the bruising faded. Nasser Medahwi opened the boot. Jawahra watched as he placed a shoebox sealed with packing tape between the drums of deadly fluid.

She turned to him, hiding her words, meaning them for his ears alone. 'What have you done, Nasser?' she said. He scowled, 'the fool's courage will fail. The package has a pager wired to a detonator and a charge of C4. The message will read *Allah be Praised* as the Mayor of London dies.' Her eyes softened and flicked to where Ibrahim cowered within the cab.

'This is a war Jawahra. Men will die,' he said.

'She took a sharp breath. 'And perhaps women,' she said softly.

'Perhaps,' said Medahwi. Then he stepped into the cab and Jawahra followed. Ibrahim faltered, then climbed in. He pulled down the rearward-facing seat and sat opposite, his eyes downcast and fearful. Around him was the mass of explosive that would end his life, rip him into countless shreds. Jamal started the engine.

*

'Go'... Harper's voice barked through Colours's earpiece. The firearms team stood tensely waiting, their weapons held low and ready. At the word they nodded and moved stealthily forward, the weapons now raised, their thumbs caressing the selector levers. The pace of their footsteps increased until they ran. As they closed with the yard gates the ARVs broke cover and the crews burst from them to contain the area.

The churning, rumbling of the oncoming Land Rover heralded the onslaught of three tons of armour. As it reached the gates it turned suddenly right as the driver floored the throttle. It pitched violently left and right as a rear wheel clipped the kerb. The roar of its V8 engine conspired with the scream of tortured metal, as the ancient gates were crushed and split like paper and matchwood.

The heavy vehicle ploughed onward, sweeping all in its path, driving aside a half-painted mini with disdain. The bull bar impacted with the workshop doors, ripping the padlock and hasp from its bolts, as calls of 'armed police' resounded everywhere. Dark, menacing armed figures suddenly flanked the Land Rover.

The crash of two Remington 870 pump-action shotguns hurling gas projectiles through the fabric of the doors was repeated again and again, punctuated by the racking of the shotguns and the sound of breaking glass, all adding to the crescendo of noise. Deep inside the thud of detonation heralded swirling gas that escaped through broken windows. From within, there was no other sound, no response.

As the Land Rover backed off just a little, the team melted together like liquid mercury and filtered methodically through the door. Again the calls of 'armed police' filled the air, resonating from within. In the street outside, Colours stepped from the car, the knot in his stomach driving him forward.

Within the misted confines of the arch, the team searched cautiously, alive to every potential threat as they covered each other's movements, the beams from the powerful torches made solid in the gas and dust filled air. Brendan Harper felt a grip on his shoulder as a team member, anonymous in the haze, gestured left and forward, his gloved hand held vertically, slicing the air.

The van stood in the corner, its rear doors confronting them. With his carbine held high, Harper closed with the ominous shape. The air was slowly clearing behind them as the circle of light from the torch-mount below his gun danced across its doors, sending reflections from the rear windows to play like wisps on the brickwork around and above them.

Through the lens of the respirator he wore, strange confusing shapes made surreal in the artificial light, danced in the air before him, and his stomach tightened. As he stepped closer, the revulsion he felt within him spiralled, as insect after insect thudded into his respirator and body.

He stared through the gun sight at the darkened red/black putrescence that oozed from between the doors and reflected from where it pooled on the step. Everywhere, flies buzzed insanely. The beams of other torches joined his as he extended his trembling hand, turning the scene bright.

A feeling akin to panic gnawed at him as he turned the handle, dark sticky blood stringing from the rubber seal as he opened it. A revolting mass of flies billowed out and upward to shock them all. Danny Cohen was kneeling where he fell, as if in prayer. The deep plum colour of his sweater matched the congealing blood that pooled wide beneath his face.

The chequered cap remained on his head. He still wore the pebble glasses and his bloated face was half turned to greet them, the skin pale and yellowed in death. One eye still belatedly pleaded for life. The other was a blooded pit of glass and flesh where the bullet had passed through.

Radio messages buzzed in Harper's ear, but he was oblivious to the pleas for information. He was riveted, fixated by what he saw, unable to draw his eyes away as the image was burned into his memory forever. Then a hand fell again on his shoulder, shaking him. A muffled voice through the rubber that encased it, pleaded with him.

'Brendan! Get out!…Device…*Brendan!*… The voice called again, ever harder. 'Brendan, for Christ sake get out…*They've left a bomb…*'

REDEMPTION

Mark Cravetts stood transfixed, staring into the van while white-paper overall-clad figures stepped around him, bemused by his presence. Colours appeared at his shoulder, watching him finger the Star of David that hung from his neck. From about Danny Cohen's neck a gold chain trickled downward to where such a star lay half immersed in his blood.

'Come away Mark,' Colours said softly, 'this is a crime scene now, we shouldn't be here.'

Cravetts nodded, yet his mind was far away. 'My great grandparents died in the ghetto, did you know that?' he whispered. 'I have distant relatives in Israel. It never stops, does it?'

Colours put an arm around his powerful shoulders, guiding his diminished figure back into the sunlit street. He lifted an eyebrow to Gilhooley, who sprang to their side. 'Get Mark a coffee Kieran.' Gilhooley nodded knowingly.

'Mr Barras?' Lassiter stood with the Expo, a look of anticipation on his face as he beckoned him. 'Our expert here has some revelations and a plan for us.' The diminutive figure of the bomb disposal expert suddenly grew in stature as the resolve in his nature filled his eyes. 'This was just a very small charge of plastic explosive. The intention was to rupture the diesel tank and in turn ignite all the petrol.'

He held a cheap mobile phone in his rubber-gloved fingers. 'It's intended to destroy the evidence and create a distraction while our boy is busy elsewhere. He wanted to control the timing in relation to whatever else he's planned. He just rings the phone and fires the detonator. Only now he can't.' A grin of satisfaction slipped across his face. 'You were too quick and fortunately, it wasn't booby trapped.'

Colours's eyes widened. 'That's right, Mr Barras. As soon as he rings we can extract the caller's number and plot where that phone is. Hope that he uses his mobile, and that'll lead us to him.' Colours excitement grew. 'Can we get saved numbers and last dials from this phone?' he asked. A second figure appeared, a bespectacled black man in his thirties, dressed in blue overalls.

'If we dismantle the phone now, we risk missing the call. We have to forget forensic considerations for the time being. I have spoken to the phone company. They will have up to the minute records and be back to us directly.'

He smiled. 'Sorry! I'm David Clark, technical support.' He extended a hand for Colours to shake.

'Thanks very much,' Colours replied, his thoughts gathering pace. 'I'll organise a contingency response now. Let me have as much notice as is possible.' He paused for thought, breaking his stride toward where Brendan Harper sat pale amongst his team, 'and could you let me personally have that number as soon as you get it.'

Martin Beckwith had watched the whole episode. He turned Colours's words in his mind. *'Personally'...'* He knew what that meant.

Brendan Harper looked drained. 'How are you doing?' Colours asked. 'That was a bad thing mate, but brace yourself. We may have to go again.'

Harper's face creased into a smile. 'How about you introduce me to that nice lady from occupational health? I bet she could sort me out!' For a micro-second Colour's mind escaped. 'Don't think she's available buddy,' he replied, dropping his eyes.

Colours gestured to the ARV crews, now huddled together drinking some tea Sally had magically scrounged, and they gathered around her. 'I want two cars fully kitted and ready to go on my word,' he began. 'You're likely to be after these bastards again at any time, so the highest state of readiness. Tanks full, kit on and engines running. Do I make myself clear? Bottom line is that you have the fastest cars?'

Cravetts rose suddenly to his feet, his teeth bared and fixing Colour's gaze.

'I understand Mark,' Colours said. 'We all do, and myself in particular. I want him so bad I can taste it.'

Cravetts seized Colour's hand, pressing it firmly. 'Sorry sir! How could I be so?...'

Colours stopped him. 'It's okay'.

*

It was an unusual thing for the crewman to see. Cabs rarely used the ferry. It burned meter time and took them away from their best customers. It was so early!

He stared for long moments at the swarthy driver, catching glimpses of the green oval badge around his neck. The silhouette of a woman appeared shadowy in the rear compartment.

'Female logic,' he thought. Why not get out and hail another across the water? Then his mind dismissed it all, as it descended into the insular fog of early morning sloth. Close by Medahwi and Ibrahim walked ahead, masquerading as foot passengers.

Distantly the broad, flat bulk of the first ferry of the day raised brownish white foam in its wake. It backed away from the southern pier, churning thunderous grey water as the engines were reversed, the sound a muted drumming across the river to where Medahwi waited staring. It eased out to cross the main channel. Nasser Medahwi reached into his pocket. He cupped the mobile phone in his hand, turned it on and punched in a number. Ibrahim trembled as he watched, the cool morning breeze chilling him through his light clothes, while fear racked his whole being, sapping his breath and strength.

*

From within the blue technical support van, Clark's voice rang out. 'Got it! We've got it!' Colours ran to where he sat, a telephone handset pinned to his ear. A fever of anxiety produced beads of sweat on the black man's brow. 'Yes! Good. Give me the map reference. Thank you. Stay by this phone please, stay on the line. Tell me if the phone moves.'

Colours hurriedly opened the 'geographia' that lay nearby, as Clark called out the numbers. 'one six five, five four three, one seven nine.' At the door, men in uniform gathered, waiting for information that might soon test all their skills and resolve. Brendan Harper appeared, all traces of shock and exhaustion wiped from his face by a wave of adrenalin. Cravetts stood close, a bitter resolve in his eyes.

Colours flicked the pages, then ran a finger along first one grid, and then another. '*The ferry*! They're getting on the Woolwich Ferry. *Go, go, go!*' The scene around him galvanised as the crews leapt into the cars. Engines screamed and tyres shrieked.

The lumbering kit van rolled forward as everywhere the air became alive with sirens and chirping, tortured tyres. As Colours hit the passenger seat, Martin Beckwith already had the car moving.

'As fast as I can sir?' he asked. Colours paused, turning to face him, a half smile on his face.

'Yes, Martin! As fast as you can!'

Behind them David Clark stepped down from his control van and placed a hand on the Expo's shoulder. 'Must be something I said,' he quipped, glancing around the now virtually empty street. The second man turned to look at him. 'Has he got the phone number?'

Clark raised his dark brow. 'What do you think?'

*

The crewman listened as a recorded female voice repeated yet again sentences that punctuated his every working day.

'Passengers are reminded that they must remove their vehicle from the craft at the end of each crossing...'

The recording reminded him that another long day awaited, that thousands of tons of vehicles would pass across this watery divide before his day was done. Beneath his feet the craft vibrated as the huge diesel engines reversed the shafts, the propellers churning the water brown and grey as the captain skilfully nosed the craft gently to rest. A bump tugged at his lower limbs.

High above, the hiss of the descending ramps announced the descent of the 'spans', the ramps by which this first contingent of the day would exit north. He loosened the chain barrier as a colleague beckoned a motorcycle and then the first cars to leave. Moments later, Medahwi stepped aboard. His fierce, angry eyes danced everywhere, meeting the crewman's and quickly moving on. Ibrahim followed, downcast.

The rattle of the taxi's diesel engine faded as it crossed clunking on the wooden planking of the deck to stop close to the exit, leaving the grey-green water stretched before it. The deep rumble of the lorries faded, giving way to the softer note of the cars and the rattle of the wooden planking until the deck was full. The ramps rose high above, the water churned below and the ferry moved gently away.

The recorded voice began again, monotonously punctuating their day.

'In the unlikely event of an emergency evacuation you will hear a series of blasts followed by a long blast on the ships whistle. The ship is fitted with buoyant apparatus...'

*

'MP from Trojan one, receiving over?' High in Scotland Yard's Information Room, an operator reacted. 'Go ahead Trojan one, MP over.'

'We are in Blackwall Tunnel Northern Approach Road, travelling toward the Woolwich ferry,' Colours continued. 'I require paramedic ambulance to attend the Woolwich Ferry northern jetty, and India nine-nine on immediate standby. Please direct the firearms team aboard Trojan nine-zero-one to the same location.'

'Received Trojan one,' came the reply. 'This incident now dedicated as CAD number 5783, northern Jetty as RVP. The incident room is being opened and a D.S.O. allocated.' Colours fought to steady himself as the car slewed left. Martin Beckwith wrestled the car into the slip road, desperately fighting to get to the northern jetty. In a hell of noise and lights, Trojan five-one-one passed them and plunged into the tunnel, headed break-neck for the southern jetty, to throw a net around Medahwi. To catch him, cage him. Perhaps to kill him.

Everywhere horns echoed, blue lights circled and tyres screamed. Radio traffic engulfed the airwaves as Colour's phone began to ring. 'Go ahead.' He struggled to write a phone number in the car's log. Then as he was thrown forcefully against the door, he rang it.

'Sorry! Who are you?' Seated quietly in his office close to the southern embarkation point, the Master Captain of the Woolwich Ferry was shaken from his thoughts. 'You want what? Who are you again?'

Colours struggled to make himself heard against the noise in the car. 'You may have a bomb on your ferry. It will be in a cab. I'm Inspector Bladen-Barras of the Metropolitan Police firearms branch. If you have them on board, don't let the ferry dock. Keep it mid-stream. We'll be with you very soon.'

As Colours and Martin Beckwith barrelled through Connaught Way and into Albert Road, Trojan five one-one with Pikey, Fudge and John Munney was screaming along Woolwich Road, closing with the southern pier. Munney squinted as the headlights and strobing blue of the following ARV driven by Kieran Gilhooley tailgated him, the combined horns of the cars drowning out all other sounds.

Beside Gilhooley, Arthur wedged himself in, scribbling furiously in the log. He cast his eyes back to where Mark Cravetts sat in silence, a dreadful menace in his eyes, immune to the violent contortions of the car and lost in his own vengeful thoughts. 'Keep a handle on it,' Arthur said, feeling Cravett's anger. 'We must do this right.' Cravetts dark eyes flicked up from the torment of his thoughts and they met Arthur's. 'I will,' he said. *Be sure I will...*

*

223

'Something is wrong, my brother'. Jahwara appeared at Nasser Medahwi's shoulder. His eyes turned on her, burning with anger. 'I told you not to speak to me on the ferry. They must not know we are together.' He bared his teeth between his pinched lips.

'Look above you Nasser, look at the captain! He clings to the radio. He speaks and his eyes are everywhere.' Above them in the high bridge that spanned the ferry's decks, a man's face peered anxiously down at the mass of cars and lorries. On his shoulders he wore patterned epaulettes, and a dark braided cap sat on his head. Others joined him, their gaze scanning everywhere. They began to point, focussing on the cab.

'He knows we are here Nasser. Look up!' She pointed skyward. Distantly the force helicopter, India nine-nine skirted the horizon. 'Look at the lorries that queue for the ferry.' Medahwi fell silent, his expression filled with anger and dismay. 'They stay back. They do not wait by the ramps. Behind the walls, hidden from our eyes there are police cars. Watch closely and you will see the heads of men running. Nasser... *We are trapped*.'

*

'Yes sir. I'll keep us in mid-stream. I'll announce a mechanical problem'. The captain's eyes were filled with dread. He stroked his chin anxiously, then picked up a mobile phone. Below him a crewman answered. He moved to where the rear of the cab was visible to him. 'Thank you Joe. Don't show out. Don't do anything unusual.' Picking up the radio again the captain spoke to his senior, frantically now staring out from the shore toward the main channel. 'The cab's number plate's been changed. It doesn't match the small print on the licensing disc. This is for real.'

Medahwi's eyes burned wide and angry as the vessel shuddered beneath his feet, and began a slow turn. A dry voice began to bellow from the speaker system. 'The captain regrets that there will be a short delay while a technical problem is dealt with. Please do not be alarmed. The vessel and passengers are in no danger, and I thank you for your patience.'

Medahwi's face settled, as if resigned. 'Yesterday we spoke of death, you and I. Today we are called.' Jahwara lifted the veil from her battered face, leaving it framed in the black material. She smiled softly, as if in acceptance. 'How shall this day be Nasser my brother? For Wind and Shadow how will it end?'

He turned to the rail, a light breeze tugging at his dark and now greying hair dropping his gaze until it fell on the churning grey-green water below. 'Wind and

224

Shadow are eternal, are they not? They exist for all time.' Jahwara stood beside him, pulling the cloth from her head. Letting her black hair tumble in the wind, she tore the dressing from the bridge of her injured nose.

'What will you do, Haab?' she asked gently, her gaze now following his along the surface of the ancient river, tracing it back toward the very heart of London. 'We will take the ship,' he said, his jaw working in that same way, as anger rose in him. 'We will take the ship to the heart of their vile city and blow it up.'

*

Brendan Harper appeared at Colours's side. 'We can't just bring it in, can we?' Harper said, knowing he was stating the obvious. 'There's another team coming down river from Wapping on a RIB. Nine-nine is waiting for our directions.' Colours turned to him. 'My blokes'll have it bottled up on the other side, but you know we'll have to get on there covertly don't you, and the RIB will show out instantly. He'll maim, kill and then detonate. The bastard is pure evil.'

Colours seemed detached, staring blankly through the iron work of the massive jetty at the ferry, now wallowing in the soft swell, it's engines barely keeping pace with the flow, it's bow trailing a line of foam. 'We won't use a RIB,' he said suddenly, his mind reaching for a plan.

'How many private boat yards do you suppose there are around here?' Brendan Harper's eyes were suddenly alight, as if with mischief.

'I don't know,' he replied, 'but I damn soon will.'

*

'Perhaps it is not just your time, perhaps it is time for us all.' Ibrahim's fear was manifest in the sweat on his brow as Jahwara appeared at his shoulder. He stood by the bow, pretending to have heard nothing of their conversation. Fearful of discovery, still he had clung to Medahwi's every word.

Placing a hand on his shoulder, she turned him to face her. 'Go to the cab. Stay with Jamal.' He walked away, disturbed by the bruising on her face that had until now been hidden. He was shaken by this demonstration of their mortality. If they could bleed, they could die. Khamsin was as vulnerable as he. Haab was not a god, not a myth. Just like Ibrahim himself, he was just a man. He felt suddenly angry.

225

Mark Cravetts clutched the mobile phone to his ear. 'I understand sir. Yes there is. A private marina about a half-mile away to the east! Let me try, I've trained for this.' Gilhooley watched in frustration, burning to know the full content of this one-sided conversation. The phone buzzed at Cravetts's ear, but he could not decipher what were evidently the words of Colours's plan.

'Yes, sir! Leave it to me. I'll pick a beauty.' Cravetts turned to Gilhooley and Arthur, a grin on his face. 'Come on boys. We're off to steal a boat.'

'You don't need to,' cut in Arthur. 'There's a nice little launch bobbing about on a jetty beside the ferry terminal. I saw it when I was nosing around just now. It's perfect!'

Kieran Gilhooley held Cravetts's eye as he shrugged his shoulders, and Arthur's rotund shape scampered from the car and across the tarmac. Moments later he returned breathless but excited, his reddened face beaded with sweat framed in the car's window. 'The launch belongs to one of the ferry skippers. It's fuelled and ready to go.' His face cracked into an even broader grin as he raised his right hand into view, bright metal glinting in the sunlight clasped in his stubby fingers. 'And I got the keys!'

*

Colour's feet slipped and stumbled as they refused to carry him fast enough down the steel-nosed spiral steps that led down to the Woolwich foot tunnel. His footfalls squeaked and clattered, the echoes reverberating around the tile-faced brickwork of the Victorian tunnel workings. While his right hand clasped the MP5, with his left he feverishly grabbed at the handrail, stabilising his headlong descent. The sounds magnified and were confused by those of Martin Beckwith and Brendan Harper, racing downward. Close behind a firearms team grabbed the barest kit and followed, but Colours would be first, no matter what.

He pinned the carbine to his chest and prayed that his kit would remain in place, not wanting to concede even a microsecond. Medahwi was close, so close he could taste him. In his head he remembered his graveside promise to his dead comrade and it drove him on. The long white walls of the foot-tunnel seemed to stretch into infinity, first downward and then levelling out beyond his view. If they were to board that ferry, he meant to be there.

His lungs began to sear with pain as the pace increased, threatening to run him off his feet, but the insane anger bore him up, the insatiable thirst for revenge sustained him. He cursed with breath he could not spare as his mobile phone worked loose and fell, skidding along the ground. Barely stopping he scooped it up, suddenly aware of Martin Beckwith beside him.

Beckwith paused, bending forward and gasping for air, his hands on his knees. 'Fast as I can sir?' he rasped, a half smile on his face.

'Faster than that!' Colours replied. Toward them came several figures, walking north. A black woman with two young children, a group of building workers and a post man pushing a cycle, a limp satchel across his back.

Colours seized the cycle from the postman as he and all the other pedestrians threw themselves back against the walls, and the children began to scream. The sight of the approaching armed men running full tilt had terrified them. He stepped on to one pedal and scooted the cycle along the down slope, the rush of cooler air turning the sweat on his face icy cold.

As he reached the tunnel's lowest point, the momentum was lost and he slowed. He stepped off allowing the cycle to career into the wall and clatter on to its side, its bell scraping loudly along the ground.

Seamlessly he broke into a run. Grateful for the short respite, his lungs felt sore and angry as he called again on his deepest reserves. Ahead the tunnel rose toward the distant gates of a lift, beside which a spiral staircase would lead from the surreal confines below the river, up into the reality of the day.

More figures emerged from the lift gates as they clattered back. As Colours approached, fear and disbelief were etched on their faces. He ducked between them. Unwilling to trust the lift or suffer its leisurely pace, he stepped on to the staircase that wound its way upward around the lift. Pausing momentarily to look back, he saw Martin Beckwith closing fast.

Beyond him again the dark bobbing mass of the firearms team, sweating beneath coveralls and body armour. Steeling himself, he began to climb.

*

The small launch bobbed in the swell as the second ferry began to churn the murky water around the jetty that hugged the waterline, far below the towering superstructure of the south terminal and the larger craft's bulk. Its exhaust burbled first loud and then subdued as it was pitched above, then below the water's surface. The noise interrupted the fevered argument that raged between Arthur and a barrel-chested man in a white shirt and black trousers.

'It's my fucking boat. If you want the boat, I go with it. End off…!' Arthur's face turned crimson. 'You ain't got a gun, you ain't a policeman, so you ain't coming out there!' The second man drew himself up to his full height, pulling in an ample stomach.

'I'm a ship's captain, a qualified navigator, an ex-marine and the boat's owner. I know the tides; the currents and I know this old boat inside out. Without me you ain't going nowhere. *Right!*'

He stood closer to Arthur, creasing his brow and holding Arthur's eye through bushy eyebrows. 'I think you should listen to him,' interrupted Cravetts. 'You could be out of your depth here,' he smirked. 'Very fucking funny,' Arthur snorted, turning away.

Colours emerged blinking from the foot-tunnel doors out into the sunlight, sucking in air that was disappointingly warm. His clothing clung wet with sweat to his body as his radio became live again, free from the subterranean confines.

He took a moment to compose himself as Martin Beckwith appeared at his side, propping his back against the aged red brickwork. 'The bike! Nice move boss! *Faster…* you were right!'

They turned and broke into an exhausted trot down some steps and on to a gantry that led to the embarkation area and the ramps. Behind them sweating, panting armed men emerged into the sunlight, some squatting to regain their breath. As the two men turned onto the broad, tarmaced area, the bright reflective markings of two ARVs greeted them. By a low wall TSG carriers disgorged large numbers of uniformed men and women. Police dogs barked and ambulance crews stood close to their vehicles.

A uniformed Inspector confronted Colours as he approached. 'I'm Inspector Howard, scene Commander,' he said pompously. He stared at Colours dishevelled figure, the sweat running down his face.

It moulded the whiteness of his shirt almost transparent on his limbs. 'What options d'you have for me?' the local Inspector said contemptuously. 'Watch and learn,' said Colours, his anger flaring. 'When I need you, I'll tell you. Until then, sit on this fucking riverbank and command the scene,' Then he turned toward the cars.

'With your permission, sir?' Gilhooley lifted the rifle from the back of the car. He pointed to a flat roof high above the surrounding ironwork dominating the river.

'Up there! And if I may say so, sir?' his Irish brogue somehow dominant, 'You look like shit.' A wry smile curled the corner of his mouth.

Colours turned breathlessly to Fudge. 'Go with Kieran, take the binoculars. I want you to update me on every move on that ferry out there. Spot for him.' He turned to a TSG Sergeant, watching with fascination as Colours's dominance swept all before it. 'Give me two of your officers to help my man run the control from here. Pens, paper, phones, radios. You know the requirements.'

The young Sergeant looked at him transfixed. Colour's eyes flared '*Go*,' he shouted, and the man was galvanised.

As Cravetts emerged from the top of the walkway that led down to the small boat, Colours leaned into the car where John Munney laboured. 'Get this right for me John, and I'll be '*Owen*' you…a great deal.' Munney nodded.

Brendan Harper appeared glistening with sweat at Colours's and Martin Beckwith's side; a phalanx of black-clad and sweating armed men behind him. He opened his mouth to speak, but Colours was already in full flood. 'Give me a man on that parapet wall with a radio to work with my control car here. I want him to liase with the boys on the RIB. I'll need them as a distraction while we board the ferry from the rear.'

'No point in arguing that this should be a team assault I suppose?' said Harper.

'None at all,' Colours snapped angrily. Then he turned sharply toward the walkway that led down to the where the small launch nestled against the jetty, hidden in the lee of the ferry and between the iron stanchions and the shore.

Near the launch, Arthur had made his peace with its owner as Colours strode down toward them. 'Good job the tide's up, that will help,' the man said.

Arthur looked at Colours eyes; saw the resolve and hatred that resided there. 'I reckon the surf's up, never mind the tide.'

Cravetts picked up on his words. 'More than the surf Arthur. It's the blood that's up, his and mine.'

*

Nasser Medahwi's eyes were calm, resigned. All thoughts of pretence abandoned him as he walked toward the cab. 'Arm yourselves,' he hissed at Jamal and Ibrahim. Close by, the driver of a lorry turned sideways in his cab, stretching across the seats. He punched in the numbers nine, nine, nine on a mobile phone, clutched in his trembling hand. Jamal and Ibrahim dragged the suitcases and bags from the cab, arming themselves with assault rifles, grenades and handguns.

'I'm on the Woolwich ferry,' the driver said, his words feverish with fear. 'There are three blokes and a woman, Arabs I think. They're near a cab.

They have guns and grenades, and God knows what else. I was in the Green Jackets; I've a fair idea of what I'm looking at.'

'They have AK 47's and grenades, self-loading pistols and explosive charges I think. The girl seems to have a medical kit.'

*

The small launch rocked dangerously in the swell from the single remaining ferry as it ploughed its way back and forth while its sister stood impotent and distant, matching the river's flow in mid-channel. Colours studied it as it bumped the fenders of the jetty. 'How close can you get us to the ferry out there?' he asked. The white shirted man's face cracked into a smile. 'Right up to her,' he pointed up at the ferry docking beside them as the jetty beneath their feet rocked softly and the craft impacted with the stanchions.

'See those openings? We call them the gun port doors. They're always open at the sides. You can't see them from on deck, and if we have enough lorries on board, the screening is even better.' He turned and faced Colours. 'Joe Simpson. Good luck with this. I don't envy you.' Colours smiled and extended his hand.

'Some risk for you too. You don't have to do this you know'. The man just smiled, a certain resignation in his tone. 'No! I do. Call it a sense of duty, shall we?' and he stepped forward.

'If we go out with the second ferry, I can stay on its blind side until the last possible moment. Then turn onto the first ferry's stern and come up on the doors.' He nodded his approval while Brendan Harper studied the launch. Its wheelhouse was roofed and glazed on three sides. From the waist down, its pilot was hidden.

'Four men in the forward cabin keeping low, four under a tarp in the well.' Colours nodded again in agreement, then spoke. 'Bring the RIB into view as a distraction. What else can we do to get his attention?' he said, allowing his thoughts to become words. 'Nine, nine,' said Harper. 'I know we shouldn't expose it to fire, but what about landing the helicopter at extreme range and make a fuss as if we are going to assault the boat by air. That should get him rattled.'

*

Kieran Gilhooley burst breathless from the doorway out into the sunlight. Fudge's footsteps echoed in the darkness behind as he fought himself upward. The sudden

230

bright daylight stole Gilhooley's vision away as he cupped his hand to shade them, waiting for them to adjust.

'Christ almighty it's hot up here,' Fudge croaked breathlessly. The light grey asphalt that covered the roof reflected the sunlight, and felt sticky beneath their feet as the mid-morning sun heated it. Fudge strode forward to a low parapet wall, the panorama of the Thames and the Woolwich reach laid out before them. 'I can see for bloody miles,' he began, until Gilhooley grabbed his shoulder, and thrust him down.

'You daft bastard,' Gilhooley ranted. *Shape, shine, silhouette.* If they see movement, we're in big trouble. Do you want them throwing .762 at us up here? I want to see them, I don't want them to see us.' His eyes fell on two old oil drums, close to where the staircase emerged in a small blockhouse.

'Roll those over to the edge, but keep low.' He picked up some sacking that lay nearby. With the drums in place they draped the sacking over it to create a hide. Then Gilhooley slid the rifle from its cover, opened the bipod legs and positioned it so that he could dominate the scene in mid-river.

With Fudge beside him they settled into the minimal shade their makeshift hide offered. While Fudge scanned the ferry with the binoculars, Gilhooley adjusted the telescopic sights, working himself into some degree of comfort upon the body armour he had spread out beneath him. He lay his radio close to hand and began a long wait.

*

Jawahra struggled to pull the dark clothing clear of her body within the confines of the cab. Then she slid the camouflage coloured suit up her legs and torso. She pulled on black trainers and stepped out into the air, bundling her black hair into an equally black baseball cap. Nasser Madahwi stared at her dispassionately as she picked up her pistol and the small black bag.

'If I am to fight, I must be able to move,' she said, anticipating Medahwi's thoughts. He turned and faced Jamal and Ibrahim, his body hung with ammunition and explosive, an AK47 hanging loosely in his hand, a rocket-propelled grenade launcher slung across his back.

Each of the two men wore a red band around their foreheads, and camouflage combat jackets. By Medahwi's feet stood a small suitcase. 'This is our mission. We take this ship into the heart of London and blow it up. We are honoured and we shall meet again in paradise.'

Then he raised the weapon double-handed above his head and called ever louder as Jamal and Ibrahim joined him 'Allahu Akbar, Allahu Akbar'. Close by the lorry driver peered down in silent horror, as the group split and moved about the ship.

*

'Control from Trojan one, do you have communication with the team on the RIB?' Trojan one over.' He paused impatiently while beside him Cravetts, and Brendan Harper joined the pilot in the wheelhouse of the launch.

'Trojan one from control.' John Munney's voice crackled in response. 'They're on standby just beyond the Thames Barrier. They've strict instructions to stand off until called forward. India nine-nine are standing by on Woolwich Barracks Fields. They will make a show of landing well back in the south using New Ferry Approach.'

'I have positioned three un-manned TSG carriers and some support vans along the wall as cover from the river as they land. I trust that meets with your approval sir?'

'Well done,' said Colours. 'Take everyone off the second ferry when it docks, but leave all the vehicles where they are. Get a contingent of TSG officers aboard for the return journey. Give a set of body armour to the ship's Captain and get some shields and a ballistic blanket up there for him. Is that all clear?' Munney acknowledged. Martin Beckwith nodded to Colours. 'I'll see to it,' he said, and turned away.

Colours turned to Arthur. 'Go back with Martin to control and make it happen. I want you on the bridge of the second ferry as my eyes and ears,' Arthur's eyes were downcast, as Colours smiled gently. 'You're a tough old bastard Arthur, but maybe waterborne assaults might be a bit much. Anyway, I need your grit and a your good tactical mind on that ferry, okay?'

Arthur smiled weakly. 'Can I register my protest and just say one other thing?'

Colours put a hand on his shoulder. 'Sure Arthur, what's that?' Arthur grasped his hand and shook it firmly. 'Just… *Fuck it…* with respect sir'. Then he turned swiftly away.

Brendan Harper leapt on to the swaying launch, ducking into the wheelhouse, while its white-shirted pilot donned body armour. More coverall clad armed men clambered aboard, passing a shield forward to protect the pilot, or working their way down to lie low in the well of the launch. Then they pulled a tarpaulin over them.

Colours turned to gaze across the river. Distantly the second ferry began a slow turn back toward him. He pressed the transmit button that he held cupped in the palm of his hand and began to speak. 'Control from Trojan one. Get India nine-nine airborne. Are they on the firearm's radio link yet?' Munney's voice was there again. 'Trojan one from control, yes they are, and they're running up now.'

'Okay,' replied Colours, 'Tell the team on the RIB to start showing themselves, but to keep their distance.'

The mobile phone on his hip rang. 'Mister Barras? This is the Inspector at Information Room. We have a lorry driver hidden in his cab on the ferry. He has a mobile, can you write down the number?'

Colours felt the sweat on his skin going cold in the shade of the superstructure above him. Brendan Harper threw him a dark bundle, some coveralls. 'Put those on,' he called. 'If you are going with the team, you should look like one of us... and you're shivering.' The radio began to bark in his ear, suddenly startling him. 'Trojan one from sniper,' Gilhooley's steady voice called to him.

'On the ferry sir! They seem to be rounding up hostages, corralling them near the prow.' Gilhooley used the magnification of his telescopic sight to study the scene unfolding below him.

Distantly the thundering beat of the helicopter reached Colours's ears. Close by the racking sound of weapons being made ready. A cold breeze chilled him and the weight of it all suddenly made him afraid, like a small boy in the darkness.

He stopped, the coveralls hanging from his waist and stared into the dirty water below his feet, while all around him fell away, all sound was lost and his thoughts withdrew into the darkest recesses of his mind. He felt the heat of Barry Mankowitz's burned body in his arms, the water about his waist. He saw the blank gazing eyes.

'Are you okay, Roy?'

He was drawn back to reality as Harper's fingers bit into his forearm. Instantly all the force and anger flooded back through his being, driving out the cold and the fear. 'Yes, I'm fine,' he said, turning to hold Harper's gaze. 'I'm fine really. Maybe someone just walked over my grave.'

Then he smiled and pulled the dark material up over his shoulders.

*

The two crewmen hid in the galley below decks. One steadied himself against the swell and poured hot water into stained cups, while the other sat at the table, desperately punching numbers into a mobile phone. 'Can't get a bleeding thing,' he protested. 'Too much metal, I can't get a signal.' He was a heavy-set man, red faced and with bloated cheeks. The other, a much younger and slimmer man, offered him one of the steaming mugs. 'Well keep trying. If they see this on telly at home, they'll freak.'

The steel door swung open, prompting the younger man to gasp. The mug of tea fell to the floor, its dark contents running like thin, sprawling fingers across the deck as the ferry gently rolled.

Nasser Medahwi dominated the doorway. He raised the AK 47 and ranged it around the cabin. 'Where are the diesel tanks?' he hissed.

'We can't go in there, not while the ships moving', replied the younger man, his face a mask of fear and incomprehension.

The concussion shocked the room as automatic fire deafened them and smoke filled the air. The older man was driven back off his seat as a foul confection of blood and tissue splattered the walls, leaving them glistening.

He slumped back onto the seat and then fell dead to the floor beneath the table, a crimson red pool spreading rapidly across the steel floor, mingling with the spilt tea. Medahwi levelled the weapon at the younger man's face. 'You will take me to the diesel tanks now', he growled through clenched teeth, his expression impassive and unmoved by the life he had just extinguished.

'Shots fired.' Gilhooley's voice suddenly dominated the air-waves, but the echoing sound of automatic gunfire had reached them all.

'They have a large number of people massed by the front of the ferry on the car deck. There's one suspect with an AK covering them. The girl's climbing up toward the bridge. The target is acquired.'

'Kieran, keep her in your sights, but don't fire. They'll slaughter the hostages.' Mid-stream the second ferry ploughed toward him, passing its sister ship now wallowing in the wash, still marking time against the river's flow and facing toward the Thames barrier and London's heart. Colours dialled the number he had so hurriedly written down moments earlier, praying the lorry driver aboard the now high jacked ferry would answer.

'Who is this?' the man's voice was a husky fearful whisper. 'I'm a Police Inspector' Colours began. 'My name is Roy. We're here to help.' There was an awful long silence before the driver replied. 'Well I hope you've got some serious firepower, because these bastards certainly have.'

'What's your name?' Colours asked. 'Billy,' the driver replied. 'Billy! I was a soldier, and I sense you were too,' said Colours. 'What are they armed with?'

'Ak's, self-loading pistols, grenades and an RPG,' he replied. 'They have all kinds of stuff in this cab beside me. I reckon I'm laying next to a bomb, but I can't show myself.' Colour's thoughts span. 'I'm going to give this phone to another officer. Stay on the line, and he'll relay for me. okay?' Colours handed the phone to a breathless Martin Beckwith. 'Keep me constantly briefed on live updates,' he said. Beckwith nodded his acknowledgement.

Deep in the bowels of the hi-jacked ferry, a burst of automatic fire reverberated around the engine room. Nasser Medahwi stood astride the dead and bloodied body of the young crewman as he opened the suitcase, set the timer and closed it, pushing it against the fuel tank. Then he turned and walked back toward the deck, bloodied footprints marking his every step.

*

'Get out.' On the bridge high above Medahwi, above where Jamal now terrorised the collected hostages, the captain cursed his mate. Together they had watched Jahwara and Ibrahim climb toward them. Now they were just a few feet away. The chance to escape the immediate threat lay with the descending steps on the other side of the bridge, but the captain could not leave the controls.

'Get off my fucking bridge you fool. It won't help me if you stay here. *Now go.*'

As Jahwara's hand extended toward the door handle, the mate broke and ran, his footsteps clattering on the ironwork. In a breath she stepped into the glazed confines of the bridge. While the Captain's skilled hands worked the levers, she raised her hand and plunged a syringe into the nape of his neck and he cried in pain.

'Potassium Nitrate,' she purred through curled lips. 'If I press this plunger you'll be dead before you hit the floor. Do you understand?' The captain nodded.

'Then take your ship up the river. *Now.*' Then she turned to Ibrahim, who stood pointing his pistol at the fleeing mate's back. 'Kill him,' she cried. Ibrahim's eyes were wide with terror, his hands shook violently. *'I said kill him,'* Jahwara screamed. The pistol jumped in his hand, a sharp retort coinciding with the flash from its muzzle. The mate fell forward. He lay on the iron walk-way, his eyes glazed. With each failing breath, blood pooled from his mouth. Ibrahim stepped forward and stood over him, shocked and open-mouthed.

Below them Nasser Medahwi emerged on to the deck threading his way through the parked cars and lorries. He headed to where Jamal was corralling the terrified passengers at the prow, parading them before the world. Jamal stood high upon the bumper of a lorry, dominating the cowering assembly before him. Men, women, children. He ranged the muzzle of the AK47 across their upturned faces, a deranged smile residing there. 'If you fear God, then pray to him,' he called. 'Soon you will learn that Allah is all powerful.'

'The radio broke through Colours's earpiece. 'Sir! I think they are winding up to something really serious with the hostages. There are two men covering them now.' From high above them Kieran Gilhooley's steady tone related the scene through his gunsight. He lowered his tone until it echoed with foreboding. 'I have a terrible feeling about all this.'

Colours watched through the lower reaches of the ironwork as the second ferry closed with them, making its final turn to berth into the south terminal. High above the unmistakeable sound of the helicopters thundering presence signalled its approach.

'Control from Trojan one.' Colours began to play his hand. 'Tell the team on the RIB to begin to tempt the terrorist, but at extreme range.' He felt the structure shudder as the second ferry impacted with the fenders. John Munney's voice crackled in response. 'Trojan one from control, the RIB is on the move.' Above him the sound of running feet as the ferry was evacuated, the passenger's exchanged for police officers. 'Trojan one from control. We have press and media at the cordons.'

Truly it was beginning.

*

'You'... Nasser Medahwi forced his way through the ranks of the assembled hostages, now herded against the bow. A woman screamed and children cried, but he was unmoved, their fear fuelling his violence. His extended hand clamped the lapel of an old man's jacket, forcing him back against the rail. Jamal slipped into the cover provided by the lorry, now between him and the South terminal, while Medahwi sheltered himself amongst his terrified victims from Gilhooley's eye, trained now upon Medahwi's every move through the rifle's telescopic sight.

'Trojan one from sniper.' Now Fudge broke for Gilhooley, whose eyes and mind had only one focus. 'We have lost target acquisition on suspect believed Nasser Medahwi, now designated X-Ray one. He is using hostages as human shields, sniper over.' Colours's hatred intensified, but his face remained impassive. 'All received,' he replied. 'Continue to mark your target and report.'

Fudge's voice broke in again. 'Control from sniper, receiving over.' Munney's steady tone responded, 'Go ahead.'

236

'Control from sniper, I think our radio battery is failing. Can you get a replacement up here... and some water. *The heat...*'he tailed off.'

As the launch laden with armed Police Officers, turned from the jetty, Martin Beckwith leapt aboard, the impact rocking the craft and the impetus carrying him forward until he collided with Colours in the cockpit.

'You weren't going without me, were you boss?' he gasped breathlessly. Colours's face grew grim. 'I've lost one Sergeant...' He paused... 'and a good friend to this bastard. I don't intend to lose another.'

A silence descended between them all as the skilled hands at the wheel guided the launch into the lee of the second ferry, and hid it from Medahwi's eyes, as yet again it journeyed north back across the watery divide. The drumming of the larger craft's diesels competed with the sharper engine sounds of the small launch, as its garbled exhaust note spoke from above and below the water as the craft pitched. Martin Beckwith whispered huskily. 'Here we go.' The only other sounds were the rush of bow water, and the rising sound of helicopter rotors.

*

'What are they doing?' A desperation entered Jahwara's voice, and she levered the needle in the Captain's neck, seeking to torture the truth from him. 'They're just crossing back, just as normal,' he replied in agonised tones while he cramped his shoulder and neck together, desperately trying to ease the pain. 'You lie... *You lie,*' she screamed. 'They know! They would not cross knowing we are here. They are going to attack us, aren't they? Tell me the truth,' and she drove the needle deeper.

'For God's sake I don't know,' he pleaded, his head cranked against the terrible pain she was inflicting. 'I've been here with you. How can I know?' he said as his voice trailed off into an agonised whisper, and he dropped to one knee. 'If they board this ship, you will be the first to die, do you understand? Turn to face them, turn now.' she said.

On the prow Medahwi pushed the old man until his back was bent over the rail as India nine-nine dropped ever lower behind the barrier of parked vehicles that John Munney had arranged as cover.

Medahwi screamed into the breeze that had risen with the changing tide. 'You want death, I will give you death.' He drove the AK47's barrel violently up under the old man's chin, as the man gasped and gurgled, and around them the passengers screamed and cried. Then he fired. Blowing the man's face apart. He lifted the old man's legs and tipped him over the bow.

'Trojan one from sniper. He has begun killing hostages. We don't have a shot.'

In the hide between the oil drums high above on the roof of the south terminal, Fudge spoke desperately into the radio, while Gilhooley fought to maintain his concentration. Sweat increasingly ran down his face and into his eyes, and he cursed.

'Trojan one they are turning the hostage ferry away from us.' From the bridge Arthur's usually implacable tones were rising through Colours earpiece. 'You must go now sir.' Without waiting for a reply, Colours struck the pilot's back with the flat of his hand. 'Go…*GO NOW.*'

With her free hand, Jahwara beat on the glass screen with a pistol, desperate to gain Medahwi's attention, but the sound was lost. She turned to Ibrahim who still stood transfixed on the walkway, his face stained with tears as the freshening breeze tugged at his clothing. Jahwara raised the pistol toward him, while the captain agonised as her movements levered the syringe in his neck. 'Tell the Haab now. Tell him they are coming.' Ibrahim stared at her blankly until she fired yet another round into the dead man at his feet, shocking Ibrahim back to reality. '*Go NOW…!*' She said, levelling the gun at Ibrahim's eyes.

Nasser Medahwi turned and looked up, his face now stained and flecked with other men's blood. He saw Jahwara gesturing, he saw Ibrahim clumsily descending the steep-laddered steps. He turned and watched the helicopters measured descent and then he un-slung the rocket launcher from his back. '*R.P.G…*' Fudge blurted out the words through the radio as he watched Medahwi aiming the weapon toward the shore. Gilhooley lay bathed in sweat, concentrating hard on his sight picture. 'No shot! The shot is not on,' he said calmly.

The launch swung out from below the stern of the second ferry, breaking for the open water between the two larger craft, and being tossed in their wake. Colours turned, calling back, 'Everybody up. If he sees us now it's a fire-fight either way.'

From beneath the tarpaulins, armed men emerged raising weapons toward the captive ferry that now began to turn, threatening to expose them. 'Get us along side now Joe, it must be now.' The launch pitched in the swell, dirty brown water splashing over the bow and flecking the faces and the dark blue coveralls of the armed officers.

Its engine note hardened, burbling harshly in and out of the swell as the pilot harnessed all its power, driving relentlessly for the gun-port doors.

From the cockpit of the launch Colours watched the spiralling, flaming projectile reach out for the land, its vapour trail lying heavy on the air.

He remembered in that instant how it had stolen his friend's life that darkened night, now many months ago.

*

'Fucking hell.' John Munney's expletive was carried down the airwaves to every ear, and all knew its significance. Beside Munney and his helpers a TSG carrier erupted and bucked in a sheet of flame. Glass fragments showered all around them, tinkling and tapping as they fell on the ARV that was the control point. All around men and women cowered, some bleeding from small cuts.

The helicopter dropped abruptly but safely on to its landing gear. 'Control from Trojan one, sitrep your location.' Desperately Colours sought to know the extent of the damage.

'A bit deafened,' broke in John Munney. 'Minor injuries to a few TSG officers, flying glass mainly. Ambulance on scene and LFB dealing with the carriers. Three are now burning.'

*

Jamal pitched forward, the AK47 spilling from his hands and clattering across the deck. Behind him stood Billy the lorry driver, a long steel bar in his hands. As Medahwi turned, Billy threw it with all his power at Medahwi's face and dived for the loose weapon. Again the rattle of automatic fire racked the air, while the hostages cowered and screamed.

Near the front of the lorry, Billy writhed in agony, the blood from his stomach wound mixing and diluting with the green tinged fluid from the lorry's bullet-punctured radiator. Medahwi walked close and stood over him, the barrel of the gun inches from the wounded man's face.

'You're in great pain.' Medahwi looked down, sneering. 'Lie there and die slowly. Soon all here will join you.' He leaned forward and lifted the mobile phone from the lorry driver's belt. He picked up the loose weapon and thrust it into Jamal's chest where he lay gasping.

'Boss!' Martin Beckwith thrust the mobile phone into Colours's hands and he cupped it to his ear, desperate to hear against the launch's now bellowing diesel engine. 'This is Inspector Barras, who am I speaking to?' he said. There was a long menacing silence. Then Medahwi spoke.

'Mister Barras. We met once across a desk. You could not better me then, you

239

shall not now. You could not better me when your friend died. How is your family Inspector? Safe in your nice Surrey home?' he gloated. Every fibre of Colours's being became inflamed with anger and hatred beyond anything he had ever known.

'You will die today. Not as you would wish, but at my hands I promise you. I'm coming for you.' Medahwi laughed. 'Yes mister Barras. I can hear your engine. I can see your pathetic boat. Now I send you my greetings.' Then he strode to the bow and opened fire on the distant firearm's team. The staccato rattle of gunfire echoed in the metal confines of the bows. Shell cases tinkled as they danced across the deck. The firearms team's Rigid Inflatable Boat distantly bobbed about in the swell near the cover of anchored barges, their only vestigial cover. The shock of gunfire no longer generated a reaction in the terrified hostages as they cowered low. 'I see you are out of my reach Inspector', he laughed, returning to the mobile phone. Then he began to reload the rocket propelled grenade launcher.

'He thinks we're on the RIB. The bastard still doesn't know we're here. Get us on board now.' The radio crackled again in Colour's ear. 'Trojan one from sniper, I have target acquisition. He is reloading the RPG.' Colours's reply was immediate. 'Do not fire. If you miss they'll slaughter all around them. I'll deal with him.' Beside Gilhooley Fudge shuffled uncomfortably. 'D'you think you would miss from here?' he said dryly. 'No' replied Gilhooley. 'But I don't think the boss will either.'

*

The launch bumped lightly with the side of the ferry, its smaller size making it pitch faster and deeper than the bigger craft it now joined. Colours dragged himself over the rail and aboard, anger multiplying his strength but clouding his judgement as he drove himself on, ignoring the pain from his shins as they scuffed across harsh metal. Only one aim in life now, only one wish this side of eternity.

On the upper deck Ibrahim's whole being shook as he clumsily negotiated the last few rungs down from the bridge. Fear racked his being, stealing the strength from his limbs and the breath from his lungs. He gripped the handrail to steady himself, even the gentle swell of the larger craft challenging his quaking legs.

Hours before he had been just a working man, skirting only the very edges of the dark world of terrorism. Now he was one of them, a killer himself and soon to die. His mind drifted to his family, the children that he would never see again. His eyes filled with tears, his breath snatched gasps.

From the rail near the gun-port doors, Brendan Harper fought with the line, desperately trying to keep the launch alongside, but the power of the ferry as it turned began to tear the rope from his hands. The distance between the two craft widened as Cravetts clambered aboard, dragging Martin Beckwith after him as he hung perilously close to the churning water.

In turn they both grabbed the arms of the last coverall-clad man who leapt after them, his flaying legs submerged to the thigh as he hung from the ferry. Then the force became too great for Harper as the rope burned his palms, and the launch broke away. They watched it turn. They had lost half their number.

Emphatically, Colours waved them away, knowing their presence could only alert Medahwi, and place them all in greater danger.

*

Inside the control vehicle, the radio broke in again. John Munney abandoned a telephone and grabbed the handset. Beside him a young woman officer scribbled frantically, desperately trying to log all the events, the radio transmissions that filled the air. The squeal of brakes announced the arrival of the kit van nearby, as Sally Galloway ran to them from the driver's door.

'Go ahead,' barked Munney, as Fudge spoke on the airwaves. 'Control from sniper position. X-Ray one and X-Ray two at the bow have numerous hostages standing up at the rail. They are trying to use them as shields. Men, women and kids.' Munney swallowed hard, suppressing the emotion.

'Fudge from control,' he replied.

'Do you have a shot, is the shot on?'

Fudge's voice replied, cracked with the tension he sought to disguise. 'We have target acquisition at times, but the shot is not on. We need to take them both at once. We have one female terrorist on the bridge.'

'She has a syringe in the Captain's neck. Fourth X-ray is between decks. We do not have eyeball.'

Benny seized Sally's arm. 'Take some spare radio batteries up to the roof,' he said, thrusting them in her hands and pointing the way. 'Grab some water from the T.S.G. if you can and take that with you.' She smiled and nodded as she turned to leave, but Benny held her arm a moment longer. 'Keep your head down,' he added solemnly, 'You're still non-ops, remember.'

*

Ibrahim retched, and then convulsed as he vomited against the painted steel work. He lifted his head to walk forward, then staggered and fell into the pool of vomit as the butt of Brendan Harper's carbine crashed into the base of his skull. He fell face down, coarse snorting noises issuing from his lips. Colours held Harper's eye, mouthing 'Dead?' Harper shrugged, in turn mouthing a reply. 'Hope so!'

'Go up the river now!' Jahwara levered the syringe again as a blooded circle began to stain the Captain's white shirt. His face, whitened and sallow with shock, was etched with agony as he fought to stay in control, knowing his life would be forfeit if he failed. She watched the launch scurrying for the cover of the second ferry, knowing what it meant, but unable to warn her brother.

Within the confines of their hide high above the river, Gilhooley sweated heavily. Beside him Fudge shifted uneasily, the blessing of movement easing his discomfort. Kieran Gilhooley would not break his concentration for a moment, even though the stinging, tormenting salty fluid invaded his eyes.

It trickled down his face to hang pendulous from his nose and chin. Through the gun-sight he allowed his eye to scan the scene across the captive ferry far below them. He licked the moisture from his lips. 'Tell control I'm concentrating on the woman on the bridge,' he hissed to Fudge.

'Let the guvnor and the team deal with the rest. I will not initiate fire unless instructed or there is a compromise.'

On the ferry Colours placed a hand on Martin Beckwith's shoulder, tapping his earpiece as Gilhooley's words were relayed. Then successively he raised five fingers, pointing at each man in turn. Colours would lead, then Harper, Cravetts, Beckwith and the only team member to make it aboard would be last.

Colours took a moment to place a hand on Cravetts's arm, and draw close enough to whisper. 'Let's do this right Mark. Keep a handle on your anger.' Then he turned toward the steps and began to climb toward the car deck, knowing he could barely contain his own.

Gilhooley agonised. As the ferry turned again toward the city his view through the windows of the bridge was progressively masked by the steel superstructure as it made a long, slow turn, bringing it closed and closer to the southern terminal. '*Shit, shit, shit...*' The words hissed through his clenched teeth as Jahwara's form was shielded by solid steel.

'Jesus Christ,' Fudge could not contain himself. 'If the guvnor goes now, she'll kill the Captain.'

'Control and all units from sniper. The shot for the bridge is not on.' Fudge's voice seared the air-waves. 'The ferry will need to travel up river about fifty yards. There may be an opportunity through the window to the side door, but it is very tight.' Colours paused near the car deck as Harper touched his arm and then tapped his earpiece.

Colours nodded and mouthed, 'I know.' Then he shrugged and began to move forward as Brendan Harper let out a long, rasping yet almost-silent breath.

His heart pounded in his chest so hard it boomed in his ears. Ahead of him was a man who would not be deflected. He chanced a glance back to where Cravetts's hard eyes were empty of all but hatred and the burning need for revenge. Behind him again Martin Beckwith looked lost, almost bewildered. Then Harper turned once more toward the upper deck, leaving his life and mortal soul to fate, he checked the carbine in his hands, tucked the butt into his shoulder and stepped up and onward. Behind them blood issued from Ibrahim's nose and mouth, colouring the vomit in which his face lay. A small trickle appeared in his ear, but his eyes slowly opened.

*

'I demand to know what your officers are doing right now.' The young Inspector banged the flat of his hand on the windscreen in front of John Munney's face.

'Best we let him concentrate sir!' Benny's gruff voice carried an air of threat. 'Lots going on right now, and my colleague desperately needs to concentrate.' He forced a smile, the gold tooth turning it somehow into a snarl as he moved between the Inspector and where Munney laboured.

'Are you threatening me?' The young Inspector stepped back, angered. Benny smiled again. 'Well no, sir,' he whispered, his mouth now close to the Inspectors ear. 'It's more of a promise. Any of my colleagues get killed or injured as a result of your interference, and I'll break your fucking neck...with respect...*sir!*'

*

On the bridge of the second ferry, Arthur was beside himself with anxiety, as he watched the remainder of the armed officers crossing the deck below him. They had clambered on board from the launch that now powered its way back toward the southern jetty. 'Get us up close,' he said to the captain, and he pointed at the captive ferry ahead of them. 'I want to be near enough to board or take people off in a moment.'

243

'What if they fire at us?' the captain said as the bow of the craft turned up river toward the city. 'He won't sink a thing this size with an R.P.G. now will he? Arthur replied, knowing full well the risk he was exposing them to, that they could be raked with high-velocity fire. He paused for a moment before continuing. 'But I will put the remainder of our blokes in the bow, ready to respond. The captain smiled weakly and replied, 'How comforting.'

From his vantage point above the developing confrontation, Fudge watched in an agony of emotion. He glanced at Gilhooley beside him, saw the sweat that trickled down his brow and glistened in the autumn sunlight. His eyes fell again on the deck where the hostages cowered as Jamal panned his weapon back and forth to threaten them, and he saw Medahwi at the bow, the R.P.G. at his shoulder.

Billy the lorry driver writhed in agony behind them, his fingers clawing at a stomach wound that spilled his blood crimson across the deck.

A spiral of sparks and smoke tracked a second round as it skimmed the water to impact with a barge close to where the R.I.B. sheltered. Fudge could see Colours at the top of the steps, and he watched as he led his team toward the maze of parked vehicles on the deck. He felt remote, helpless. He knew what was coming, and he knew he could do nothing more to prevent it.

Beneath his feet Colours felt the drumming of the diesels intensifying as Jahwara commanded the captain to increase power, to take the ship swiftly up river. The green sheeting around the bulk of a laden lorry flapped in the breeze where ropes contained it, lashed to the steel loops on the chassis. It crackled and slapped the load as Colours beckoned his team forward. Distantly he could hear Jamal and Nasser Medahwi chanting in Arabic as Cravetts's reassuring hand fell on his shoulder.

The sudden rattle of automatic gunfire stole Colours's breath away. It was so shockingly close that he seemed to feel its concussion. Screams and cries echoed between the avenues created by the parked vehicles. Cravetts beat his fist on the side of the lorry, fearing that more executions had begun.

Fudge's voice rang desperately through the earpieces of their radios. 'Control and all units from sniper, X-Rays have fired over the hostages heads, but now are closing with the group. More fatalities appear imminent.' Colours turned his head, just enough so his whispered command could be heard. 'On my command we go. Direct assault.'

From the bridge above them all Jahwara watched in desperation. She dragged the captain from the bridge and his controls, working the needle of the syringe in his neck. Colours winced as a round ricocheted along the deck beside him.

244

Cravetts span about, searching the skyline, but unable to find a target. 'Nasser!' Jahwara called loudly from the walkway beside the enclosed bridge where she now stood. As the ferry passed below them, Gilhooley stood up, throwing the sacking that both hid and shaded them aside. In his haste he shouldered an empty oil drum that fell and rolled noisily across the roof. He closed the bipod legs that supported the weapon and rested it on the safety rail. The ferry was now passing so close that he needed to depress the rifle at an extreme angle, almost vertically downward. All his preparation, his careful aim had been lost. Now he had but seconds to settle himself.

The captain knelt helplessly beside her paralysed by pain and fear. Jahwara tucked herself in behind the protection that the open steel door and the waist-high steel frontage of the walkway to the bridge offered. Then she peered out, shouting with all the force she could muster.

'Nasser, they are behind you, they come for you! *Nasser my brother.*' She called desperately as with one hand she controlled the syringe in the Captain's neck, while with the other she fired the pistol wildly towards Colours and his group. A searing pain burned Colours's inner thigh as a bullet found its mark. Then a strange, cold feeling washed down the limb as Cravetts supported him, and lowered him gently to the ground. The sharp, regular crack of the pistol ceased, while the distant bark of a rifle rose triumphant above it all.

From where he knelt cowering, the captain felt a sickening confection of blood and tissue shower him, warm fluid pouring down the side of his face. He felt the syringe ripped away in an agony from his flesh as Jahwara slumped kneeling beside him and fell against the rail. She had dared to expose herself for a moment, and that moment was enough.

The aged paint of the steel plate was smeared with bright blood where her cheek slid down it. She stared at him, her gaze fixed and impassive. Her face became a bloated death mask as blood issued from her eyes and nose. With each fading convulsion, each diminishing pulse it gushed from her lips until she slid to the floor. Gilhooley's bullet had done its work.

Through the gun-sight, he watched her fall. The .762 round had penetrated the top of her head and passed down and through the whole length of her body. A strange feeling of disbelief numbed and paralysed him. He had never wanted to kill a woman.

He felt himself knocked sideways as Fudge barged him down on to the warm asphalt roof. The steel rail rang with impacts and fragments of concrete flew all around them as Medahwi and Jamal returned a hail of automatic high-velocity fire. Beside them an oil drum boomed and rocked as a round ripped through its edge, rupturing the seal. With a sinister hiss, it loosed a suffocating, chlorine-laden breath into the air to sear Fudge and Gilhholey's eyes and lungs.

Far below them Cravetts used a pocket knife to cut open the material covering Colours's wound as he lay with his back against the wheel of the lorry, blood staining Cravetts hands. 'It's not too bad boss', he chanced a grin. 'Another couple of inches and she would have shot your balls off.'

Colours pulled the material aside, examining the gouge in his inner thigh. Then he wiped off the blood on his hand across his chest, and stood forcefully up. Only the slight squint of his eyes betraying the burning pain he would not submit to. 'Okay. Full assault now.'

Medahwi's face contorted with anger. His eyes glazed with insane hatred. 'Kill them, kill them all', he screamed and he pointed toward the cowering hostages. A young mother began to sob, pleading for the children she gathered to her breast. A boy who still clutched his cycle stared blankly, unable to believe that his life was about to end. Others clung together in groups. A slim black girl began to recite the Lord's prayer.

Jamal released the empty magazine from below his gun, allowing it to fall and clatter on the deck. He pulled another from his belt, locking it in place with a metallic click. Then he turned toward the terrified captives as Ibrahim staggered from behind a car. Blood ran from his nose and ear and his face was stained wet with tears. His clothing glistening with his own vomit. He stood desolate before Jamal, his hands hung loosely at his sides. In the right he held a pistol.

*

Colours gestured to his team. He and Cravetts would cling to the left of the narrow passageway between the parked vehicles. Harper and Beckwith to the right. The remaining man would track them, facing rearward to deal with any threat from there. As Colours nodded they moved forward, their weapons ranging left and right, Medahwi and Jamal's chants of 'Allahu Akbar' fell away.

Now Ibrahim's single tremulous voice cried out, its pitch higher than the collective sobbing of the hostages. 'It is enough', he pleaded. Ibrahim placed himself between Jamal and his intended victims.

'He is not a God, not a myth.' He turned his eyes and anger on Medahwi. 'You bring our people only shame and death. Now I am as you are. I have killed. My

246

life and my family is lost in the shame and filth in which you dwell.' He raised the pistol.

Colours's voice cut through the mass of radio messages to assault John Munney's ears in the control vehicle. 'One female X-Ray down on the bridge, believed dead. There is a confrontation on the bows near the hostages between the remainder. The ferry is out of control and drifting, full assault imminent.'

*

As Sally appeared on the roof the smell of chlorine hung heavy in the air. A wisp of vapour was carried away and beyond the roof to spend itself in the river below. She felt her throat tighten, her nasal passages stinging with the last of its diminishing presence. Gilhooley clawed at his eyes as frantically she began pouring drinking water from a large plastic bottle into his face.

She opened another and thrust in Fudge's hands and he feverishly poured into his. 'I can't take the shot Sally,' said Gilhooley as his coughing and retching began to subside. 'I can't see. It's up to you. I'll help but it must be you.'

Sally caught her breath. 'It's happening again, isn't it?' she gasped. Fudge appeared at her side. 'There's only you,' he croaked, rubbing his streaming eyes with his forearm. Then he picked up the rifle and worked the action and a fresh high-velocity round slid wickedly into the breach. 'Kieran will talk you through, but it's your eyes, your call.'

'Come on, you can do this.' Through his pain Gilhooley dragged himself up, his streaming eyes an agony that seemed to her as rivers of tears. 'Take it,' he bellowed but Sally hesitated. 'I've never fired a rifle, not ever' she said, her words halting as she fought with her emotions.

'It's just another gun,' Gilhooley agonised, desperately trying to inspire some confidence in the few seconds left to them. He levelled his speech, painfully measuring his words while Fudge looked on helplessly. 'Take the rifle, rest it on the parapet and look through the sights.'

*

'*Go*'... Colours bellowed as the rattle of automatic gunfire shattered the air once more. The hostages screamed and cried again as Ibrahim fell kicking and writhing in his own blood, and was still. Jamal stood stunned for a moment, staring uncomprehending at Medahwi, now profiled at the bow.

Smoke wafted from the barrel of the AK47 as he swung towards his helpless captives.

*

'Sally, move your head back and forth until the shadows have gone from the telescopic, find the middle of your target and pull steady, like down the length of the range. Take a breath, hold it and let it out slow and controlled.' Gilhooley caught Fudge's streaming eyes where a world of anxiety dwelt.

Sally struggled with the heavy, cumbersome weapon as it slipped on the rough surface, tilted now at an extreme angle it threatened to plunge to the water so very far below. 'Steady... Steady...' he exhorted her. 'Pull steady, exhale slowly, sights clear...' Her heart thundered in her chest, each pulse like the rush of a huge wave in her ears and she thought she might burst.

She felt her clothing and face becoming wet as the fatigue of the climb began to tell and fear and her own adrenaline took over. She saw her target so far below ranging in and out of her vision as Jamal swung the weapon he held all around him as if to terrorise entirely those he meant then to kill. He stopped, deciding as if he were God, who would die first.

The glass of the telescopic sight grew misty with the heat and dampness of her sweat, or perhaps from the vapour her breath produced. The crossed hairs of the sight traversed the figure below again and again as her very soul cried out for it to be steady for that one crucial moment.

'Now Sally, now,' Gilhooley croaked, his throat tight from the chemical burn. She found her self grinding her teeth, exhaling in a long hiss as a colossal force impacted her shoulder, driving her back. There was a sudden, violent explosion of sound that seemed to echo across the river.

Jamal fell to his knees, blood cascading from his chest as a rifle bullet ripped through him. He fell forward, lifeless and face down in his own spilt body fluids. Far above them Sally stood frozen to the spot as Fudge, his eyes still streaming, gently took the weapon from her hands, pulling her down into cover. Then he poured more water into his and Gilhooley's eyes. He made to speak but Sally raised a hand. 'I'm okay,' she said. 'Really I am okay.'

'Not tough enough?' Gilhooley rasped. 'Not bloody much...' as his huge hand cupped her face, his glistening features cracking into a pained smile. She pitched forward to bury her face in his chest.

As Colours and his team burst forward, Medahwi opened fire, bullets ripping into the assembled vehicles. Before Colours could return fire, he found himself thrown face down. The sound of tortured, grinding metal filled the air. Muted crashing sounds rang as from behind them as parked vehicles were shunted together, the impact driving them forward. As the ferry collided with the anchored barges, Medahwi tipped backwards over a capstan and fell from view. 'Get us close.' On the bridge of the second ferry, Arthur's adrenalin caused his heart to thunder in his chest, his breath to rasp. 'You must get us alongside.' He seized the Captain's arm, his fingers biting deep.

Colours rose to his feet, his eye ranging through the sights of an MP5, seeking a target. Beside him Cravetts steadied himself against the bonnet of a car, the carbine levelled at where Medahwi had fallen. To their left and right, more carbines waited to snuff out Medahwi's life.

'You could not better me once before Mister Barras. You will not better me now.' His mocking voice issued from behind the capstan. He turned and slowly stood up, his arms loose at his sides. In one hand he held a pistol, in the other, and far more menacing he held a mobile phone. Blood streamed down his face from a head wound, earned somewhere on the metalwork of the ship.

It mingled with the dark stubble on his face and intruded into the corner of his mouth where a sneer resided. The muscle in his jaw worked incessantly. He began to speak again.

'Shoot me Mister Barras. Go on! Will the shock be enough for my finger to press this button? Then you will all die, I can blow you to pieces. Soon I will. I shall die this day, but this serpent has many heads. Cut off one and another will grow. I shall be a martyr to my people, an avenger for my brother. May your widow and your cursed children weep long and painfully this day and ever after.'

He raised his hand, holding the mobile phone high and away from his body. A smile began to track across his face. Colours felt lost, unable to move or think.

The focus of all his fear, all his hatred was so, so close, but he dare not strike him down.

A sudden shocking explosion concussed the side of his face. Medahwi screamed as his hand was thrown back, disintegrated in a shock of crimson fluid. Beside Colours, Cravetts carbine smoked. The shattered, blood stained remnants of the mobile phone span across the deck.

Like a wounded animal Medahwi struck out, firing wildly with his good right hand. A fusillade of fire returned, every weapon striking him at minimal range, driving him back as impact after impact ripped into his chest. The firing withered away as the bloodied figure sat back against a rail.

Colours could not be sure if he were dead or alive. He moved forward, his aim sighted in the centre of Nasser Medahwi's forehead, where it hung down toward the deck, his chin on his chest. From a multitude of wounds, blood tracked down his body and limbs.

A sudden jolt tugged at Colours's legs as the second ferry impacted lightly alongside. Medahwi's form rolled backward, his eyes cursing Colours from beyond death as his body pitched backwards and was lost in the murky waters far below.

Colours ran to the rail, but Medahwi had gone, churned beneath the massive bulk of the craft. He froze there, while all around him men shouted and called. He heard only Medahwi's last words. *'You could not better me once before Mister Barras, you will not better me now.'* He felt the heat of his gun, he felt the knowledge that he had pumped bullet after bullet into Medahwi's form as it stood there at the rail, moments ago. He found himself shouting and cursing at the dirty brown water below.

'But I did better you, you murdering bastard. This is for my friend.' Then he spat into the river, *'Fuck you.'* Suddenly Arthur was there, breathless. Cravetts was at his shoulder as they dragged him away.

'The explosives boss! We have got to get everybody off. He probably put it on a timer as well, just like at the station. You must come away now.'

*

From the bow of the distant second ferry, Colours watched the explosion, deep within the wounded craft they had abandoned. It bucked, sending a wash across the river, then settled ever lower in the water until it reached the car deck, while the bright orange tongues of fire licked upward from doors and windows. Fire roared and hissed as the river quenched its power. Vehicles began to slide across the tilting deck, cars and lorries alike, until the deadly laden taxi slipped overboard bumping the rail, and disappeared to join them. It floated a short distance, rotating in the current, and then sank from view.

All around him sobbing hostages sat trembling. Cravetts and Brendan Harper dressed the stomach wound of the grievously injured lorry driver.

As the ferry turned toward the shore where a myriad of flickering blue and amber lights beckoned, Martin Beckwith placed a hand on Colours shoulder,

250

standing resolute at his side. 'You have evened the score sir. Sergeant Mankowitz loss has been paid for.'

Colours turned to him, his face sallow and tired. 'Did you hear what he said. The serpent has many heads. I think perhaps we have not evened the score. Perhaps Martin, we have merely opened the game.'

EPILOGUE

The roads were damp. The sheen reflected from them mirrored the Christmas lights that hung between the lamp posts, signalling a warning. The Harley's wheels hissed in the moisture, or splashed through shallow puddles. He pitched the big motorcycle right from Putney Bridge into Lower Richmond Road and then down onto the Embankment.

As the engine chuntered to a halt, he swung out the stand to leave the bike close to the river. Locking his helmet to the side of the bike he strode toward the steps that led up to the bar. Distantly Bingo's voice boomed.

'So how's the eyes now boys? Any long term effects?'

As Colours climbed the stairs he could hear Gilhooley's reply. 'Fine thanks Billy. The effects wore off after about a week. Ruined me voice though. Got me thrown out of the choir. I so wanted to attend midnight mass tonight! How about you? You're a shadow of your former self.'

Bingo slapped his waistline with both hands. 'Working on that, soon be up to my fighting weight,' he chuckled. 'Fucking stopped me smoking though, it did!' he rasped. Worse for several whiskies a grin spread across his stained teeth. 'Every time I took a drag, I 'ad a smoke ring puffin' out between me shirt buttons.' Then he let out a roar of laughter that descended into a hacking cough.

'That's a hell of a diet you've been on.' Colours smiled as he entered the bar. Bingo's enormous girth had diminished considerably, his ravaged body drawing on every reserve as he recovered from his grievous gunshot wound. Privately it shocked Colours, but he knew Bingo's inner strength would sustain him now.

The mischievous glint was back in his eye and endless Guinness and curry would ensure that Bingo's full 'persona' would soon return. 'Ruined your favourite suit too. You got married in the old one, didn't you?' he continued.

'Well buy me a new one for Christmas,' Bingo countered. 'You Inspectors earn buckets of money.'

Bingo sat next to one of the large windows that looked out from the Star and Garter above Putney Embankment, across the Thames and the gently bobbing, anchored boats beyond the plane trees and near the pier they dominated. Above his head tinsel and paper decorations adorned the drapes and appeared around the bar and nearby tables. It was 'themed' now in a kind of thirties Italian style but fully dressed for the festivities. Like so many things over the years, it had changed.

Colours mused to himself that it had changed so much it disappointed him. When he had frequented it as a probationer so many years ago, it had been wood panelled and atmospheric, a reflection perhaps a gentler age. He decided it would always retain, for him at least, its old identity.

'Have a beer will you?' Bingo said insistently. 'Can't have you being teetotal like young Mark here, can we?' Cravetts lifted his gaze from where he sat beside Bingo turning a small glass of orange juice in his hands. He looked up smiling through his eyebrows as was his habit, to meet Colours's gaze, but said nothing.

'I'll have just one drink with you today. I'll lift a glass with you all. Are we agreed?' Colours replied. Around the gathering he held every eye. Gilhooley's massive hand held a glass of dark ale, while Sally more delicately fingered a glass of red wine. They were all there.

It would be unforgivable to miss this moment, and none would. Benny with his liquorice-papered cigarette hanging unlit in his mouth and Arthur surrounded by drink and food, a ridiculous pair of mock antlers clamped to his head. Young Chris Harvey was there, John Munney, Pikey, Fudge, Benny, Raffles and every one of those faces that meant so much, that had endured it all with him were present, lightened by odd pieces of festive decoration attached to their clothing.

Graham Lassiter hovered in the background. Conscious of his rank he tried at once to be supportive yet invisible. By choosing this location Colours allowed them all, just for a moment, to share something very personal with him. Whether they knew or not, they still sensed it and it hung in the air.

'Jamieson's, no ice. That's right isn't it boss'? Martin Beckwith pressed a glass into his hand. 'We'll have you propose the toast then,' he went on.

Colours rocked on his feet gently while his eyes for a moment descended. 'This past year, the ferry and all. Thanks for being professional, for doing it right and for staying the course. I couldn't have asked for more and I couldn't have done it without you,' he said in subdued tones.

'I guess you never stop learning and I've learned a lot.' Without raising the glass he said, 'May I wish you seasons greetings and a happy new year. Please carry that back to your families.' Then he raised it and looked up. 'To absent friends,' he continued and whispered under his breath, 'wherever they may be,' as the sentiment echoed through the group and the glasses were drained.

'Now I'm going home, I've a house full of women, a pregnant wife and a hungry bulldog calling to me,' he said, smiling again. Sally Galloway stepped forward and touched his arm, saying 'thank you,' through a soft smile. Colours returned the smile and then slapped paper money on the bar.

'Always the way, the guvnor ends up paying,' He said, quietly smiling. Laughter followed him through the door as he stepped out into the crisp night air. Gilhooley made to follow, but Martin Beckwith stopped him. 'There'll be something he'll want to do Kieran. Best leave him now.'

As he walked toward the slipway, a cold wind tugged at his clothing and ruffled the feathers of the old swan that eyed him suspiciously from the shallows below. The same wind tossed the last of the leaves from the plane trees into spirals, or sent them scudding along the darkened river's surface to collect in greasy-looking trails here and there.

Behind him familiar voices rose in collective laughter, contrasting the subdued sound of water splashing around the bows of the anchored craft. A myriad of coloured lights reflected on glass and on the river now so close to him. He walked slowly across the damp tarmac and down the ramp toward the river's very edge, treading carefully on the wet and slippery surface.

Reaching into his pocket he retrieved a packet of peppermints. Peeling one off he slipped it into his mouth then threw another at the swan's feet. The bird cursed and swam off, disappearing between the anchored boats.

Colours smiled to himself. 'Guess he's learned since we were here last, Barry,' he said. There was no one to listen but it didn't matter. He had resolved that he would speak to his friend throughout his life at moments like this. He had resolved to keep that faith, and in it some small hope that in some way, some time?... He picked up a rounded stone and cast it out into the channel. 'Perhaps... Perhaps *Manyana*, my friend,' he whispered.

He watched as the waters of the old river Thames flowed as they had for centuries, disappearing now below the arches of Putney Bridge as the shimmering light of the city he fought to protect shone back, as if to acknowledge him. He remembered that it was upon these waters that fight had become so very manifest. He remembered also that as great as this river was, it would soon be lost to a greater sea, and that sea into an ocean.

'It's such a big thing, an ocean. You can stand and stare across it, looking for something that's small and dear to you upon its great, endless surface and feel hopeless. Then you give up and walk away.'

The words, her face came suddenly to his thoughts. In a flurry the events of the past few months and weeks ran wildly through his mind and then fell blankly away, leaving him suddenly empty yet calm when he turned to walk back. As he mounted the motorcycle, only the pain in his thigh connected him with it all. As it faded he started the engine.

Pushing the thoughts away, he rode for home.

GLOSSARY OF TERMS

ACPO – Association of Chief Police Officers

AFO – Authorised Firearms Officer

Area Car – Fast police car, with two-man crew. Operating within the limits of a particular borough or district.

ARV – Armed Response Vehicle.

Asp – Extending steel baton.

ASU – IRA Active Service Unit, or Air Support Unit. [Helicopter]

Baby – Portable door opening ram.

Ballistic Blanket – Large, heavy, flexible sheet containing bullet resistant material.

Ballistic Shield – Bullet and projectile resistant shield

Bergen – A large rucksack, usually military green with multiple pockets.

Birdshot – Shotgun round containing a multitude of small lead balls.

Blue on blue – Accidental armed contact between friendly forces.

Blues and twos – Driving to a call with blue lights and two-tone horns employed.

Boarded – To go before an interview board of senior officers.

CAD – Computer Aided Despatch.

Call sign – The title by which any police unit can be identified, usually prefixed by the area or department from which it works.

Carbine – Short rifle-type weapon. [e.g. MP5]

Carrying – Armed.

Casevac – Casualty evacuation.

Check Zeroed – Range testing and adjusting a weapon until it is deemed sufficiently accurate.

CID – Criminal Investigation Department

Clock face – Means of determining a position of armed containment.

Crops – Covert rural observation point. [Cropped up].

C4 – High explosive AKA Semtex.

Cylume – Polythene tube containing chemicals that produce subdued light when broken, shaken and mixed.

D6 – Title of the first Metropolitan Police firearms unit.

D11 – Title given to the firearms branch subsequently.

DA – Deliberate action.

DC – Detective Constable.

DCI – Detective Chief Inspector.

DI – Detective Inspector.

Dig Out – Term used to describe an early morning armed raid to affect an arrest.

DPG – Diplomatic Protection Group.

Dragon light – Powerful hand-held lamp.

DS – Detective Sergeant.

D.S.O. – Designated Senior Officer.

End-ex – End of exercise.

Enforcer – Second generation door-opening ram.

ER – Emergency response.

Expo – Explosives officer.

FAP – Final assault point.

Federation – Police officer's union.

Ferret Round – Gas projectile, fired from a shotgun.

FME – Forensic Medical Examiner.

Forward control – SO19 control point.

FUP – Form up point. [Prior to assault].

Geographia – Metropolitan Police's London wide map book.

Glock – Austrian firearms manufacturer.

Glock 17 – 9mm self-loading pistol, now carried by virtually all armed officers within the Metropolitan Police.

Heckler and Koch – German firearms manufacturer, now multi-national.

HEMS – Helicopter Emergency Service.

IA – Immediate Action… planned armed intervention.

IEDs – Improvised Explosive Devices.

India 99 – Call sign of the force helicopter. [Nine nine]

IR – Information room. [Central control, New Scotland Yard].

Job (The Job] – Generic term for the police Force

Lab – Forensic science laboratory.

LAS – London Ambulance Service.

Lee Enfield – British firearms manufacturer.

L.F.B – London Fire Brigade.

Mag – Magazine to contain ammunition for a specific firearm.

Met – Metropolitan Police Force, or reference to its area.

MOE – Method of entry.

MP – Call sign used when addressing information room over the radio.

MP5 – Heckler and Koch. Sub-machine gun with many derivatives Used commonly as a single shot carbine in this country.

M2VG – Identifying call sign, Essex Constabulary command and control.

M2MP – Identifying call sign as above, but Metropolitan Police.

OIC – Officer In Charge.

OP – Observation point.

PIRA – Provisional Irish Republican Army.

Pinged – Seen by your adversary, noticed, cover broken.

Plasticuffs – Plastic handcuffs strongly resembling industrial cable ties.

PR – Personal radio.

PTSD – Post Traumatic Stress Disorder.

PT17 – Forerunner of SO19.

RVP – Rendezvous point.

Relief – A group of police officers who regularly work and are rostered together.

Remington – American firearms supplier, famous for the manufacture of pump-action shotguns.

RIB – Rigid Inflatable Vessel.

RPG – Rocket Propelled Grenade.

SFO – Specialist Firearms Officer.

SFO Team – A team of such officers who commonly work together.

Shot – [A shot] Police speak for a firearms officer.

Slot – To slot an enemy. Military slang term to describe shooting and killing.

Smith and Wesson – A very well known American firearm manufacturer, famous for revolvers.

Stick – Broad term to describe a small file of men, usually preparing to go forward, or batons, truncheons or staves.

Strapping – Filling in on a team or relief.

Tazer – Firearm that discharges electrical conductors. Designed to disable and incapacitate a suspect or dangerous animal. Described as less lethal and unlikely to cause permanent injury.

TI – Target indication. A means to describe a firearms incident for tactical purposes. [Colour code]
Tooled up – Armed.
TPU's – Time and power units. Triggers or detonators for 'IED'S' [Improvised explosive devices... Home made bombs]
TSG – Territorial Support Group.

CHARACTERS

Colours

- Royston Bladen-Barras.
- Ex-Colour Sergeant with a strong military background
- Married, devoted wife and children.
- Currently an Inspector supervising an ARV relief who have a deep respect and admiration for him.
- He has several years police experience.
- Served as an SFO Supervisor and a Tactical Advisor.
- Deep thinker, combatative, Faithful friend, unforgiving enemy.
- Currently heads an ARV relief.

Barry Mankowitz

- Polish origins. Grandfather a free-Poles Spitfire pilot. Father an academic.
- Fit, athletic, strong young family man. Devoted father.
- Loyal, pragmatic. Worships Colours.
- Home in Surrey.

Martin Beckwith

- 28 years old. Smart, keen. Single + girlfriend. Chin beard and immaculate, manicured. Wants it all. New blood that wants to succeed, and he will.
- In awe of Colours and sees Mankowitz as a role model.

Arthur

- Short, untidy, very strong in a squat way. Said to resemble a post box in uniform. About 40 years old. Comes from Sunderland and has the accent. Ex merchant seaman then Royal Navy. Crude and lecherous. Absolutely awful, wicked sense of humour.
- Has and needs to have a forgiving wife. Worked for a while in the funeral profession and makes references to 'being in the trade'. Brings in his own pickled onions at Christmas that are almost uneatable.
- Refuses to discuss the recipe. Goes everywhere by bus. Much wiser than his demeanour suggests. Rifleman. Hidden qualities.

Eduardo [Eddy] Seredmigni[[Seagull]

- Chief Superintendent.
- Devious, self-interested, selfish.
- Post-graduate entry with a degree in psychology. Thirty five years old accelerated promotion man. Strong Catholic origins. Family originated in Tuscany. Married a nursing sister who converted to Catholicism but is resented by the wider family.
- Uses buzz-words and pretends to know the job but it's bluff. Tactically useless. Wayward daughter.
- Cares about targets, resources, directives, but never the 'troops'.

Andrew [Andy] Blake [Raffles]

- Tall, willowy character. Thirty eight years old. Married but no children.
- Inveterate gambler. Will gamble on…
- Raindrops down a window pane.
- Horses.
- Dogs.
- Live or die.
- Anything.

Karl David Benjafield ('Benny')

- Wisecracking ex-soldier. Cropped hair, tattood. Seen action. Falklands vet. Married late. Malayan wife and very young children.
- Boxer, one gold tooth. Runs for miles even with a full Bergen [rucksack] Smokes revolting rolled cigarettes in liquorice paper. Allegedly pipe tobacco but Arthur says 'It's horse shit'.
- Challenges authority. Difficult but reliable. Father was a soldier before him. Sees things through.

Graham Lassiter

- Wise old owl. Vast experience and an old colleague to Colours. Served all over the Met. Huge public order [riot] experience.
- Tall, languid, well liked, moral man. Grounded, solid, tactical, involved.
- Volvo estate. Golf. Adult family. Public school educated. Children at 'uni'
- Not to be crossed. Good friend, bad enemy.

Kieran Patrick Gilhooley

- Irish man-mountain. Nineteen stone of fit muscle. Married, young family. Ex-soldier, ex-boxer. Disqualified but never beaten. Can be ferocious but can be caring. Smiles a lot.
- Came to the relief from C.D. [West End Central] with a fearsome reputation as a 'bar clearer'
- Loyal. Disciplining influence on his colleagues.
- Rifleman / sniper. Another good friend, bad enemy.

Sally Galloway

- Slim, dark-haired ex-territorial Support Group [TSG]. Road runs a lot. Was an good amateur in athletics.
- Single girl who shares a flat in Wimbledon with another female officer from Fulham. Comes from Kent.

- Quite driven 'Girl in a man's world'. Well liked. No ties but close to her family, sister, parents.

Clarissa Waters [Charlie]

- Languid beauty in her late thirties. Long dark hair with a hint of red. Mischievous eyes. A sparkle in her voice.
- Tall, slim and intelligent. Met Colours through the armed forces many years ago. The relationship failed. The army came first. An authority on P.T.S.D [Post Traumatic Stress Disorder]. Now employed as such and a counsellor to the Police.
- Caring, professional, mature and very attractive.

Chris Harding

- A young blood. Fair hair that falls across his eyes. Came to the police force from the retail industry. Driven, eager to learn, eager to please. Loves the department. Loves the relief. In awe of Colours.
- Teenage gymnast. Proportioned, powerful physique. Plays rugby. Drives a Toyota MR2.
- Single. Small flat in Putney. Rides a high-powered motorcycle. Fitting in well.

Mark Pearson Cravetts

- About 5'10". Slim dark. Twenty eight years old. Short cropped hair with matching chin beard. Quiet, looks at everyone through his eyebrows. [Looks up from his thoughts]. Always a half smile when he speaks. Very reflective.
- Jewish, wears a Star of David but never refers to it. Grandparents escaped the Ghetto but some distant family members lost to the holocaust.
- Loves motorcycles. Shrewd, tactical. Sporty. Squash addict.
- Family in North London but there is an Israeli connection.
- Also has a nice car and a beautiful girlfriend.

Raymond George Bridgewater [Fudge]

- 'Life is not a rehearsal' … Larger than life. Parents live in the Surrey stockbroker belt. Fudge doesn't need the money. He just loves doing the job for the sake of it.
- Late twenties, stocky and jovial. Drives an expensive convertible with a personal number. Always has sweets, hence the nick-name. Plays golf well. A string of women in tow and yet he's no oil painting.
- Single man's apartment in Wimbledon. No respect for the establishment. Wicked gleam in his eye. Excellent shot, sound tactician. Pragmatic when it matters but flippant when it doesn't.

Richard [Dick] Pike. [Pikey]

- Scruffy, late, unkempt. Tall, willowy man who speaks slowly. Drives an old Land Rover with which he tows a caravan that he fills with his many children, almost as many as his dogs. Keeps the caravan and another derelict Land Rover on the frontage of his house.
- Married to an enormous woman who is an 'Earth Mother' to many. Always has his sandwiches with him that he famously carries in a Harrods bag, the endless source of which is a mystery.

William [Billy] Burrows [Bingo]

- Detective Sergeant and a contemporary of Colours, if a little older. Approaching fifty Billy is the epitome of an old time 'seen it all' CID officer. At 6 feet tall and nineteen stone he is a loud and unavoidable presence. His depth of knowledge and experience garnered from years of police work, are unparalleled.
- His dress code is deplorable and the suit and tie have suffered much beer and curry over the years. Fierce, formidable and divorced. He has a Thai girl as his partner and is proud to advertise the fact.
- He might appear comic, but he is not to be underestimated.

John Stillwell MacKenzie

- Young, fit Essex Constabulary Firearms Sergeant. Fit and eager. Wants to impress and knows both the game and to respect seniority and experience.
- Colours likes him. That speaks volumes.

John Owen Munney

- Welsh origins. Small village along Cardigan Bay. Fiercely patriotic. Formidable. Fluent in the Welsh language. About 30 years old. Good tactician. Slim, tall and dark haired. Wry sense of humour.
- Two children, boy and girl school age. Doting wife.

THE TRIBUTE

Within the last few days I have been welcomed again by my old colleagues at the headquarters of London's Armed Police Department. This book is a fiction based in recent times but perhaps reflective more than current. That I hope is understandable, given that I have now been retired for several years. Certainly we were a little more rough and ready, make do and mend at a very formative point in SO/CO 19's history.

Though I recognise far fewer faces now, even though the surroundings have changed, the atmosphere, the conviction and the devotion remains. The equipment is much advanced while the regulation and scrutiny grows ever more daunting. However, these very professional people are not deterred. *Not for a moment!*

The dreadful tactic described herein is just a fictional example of where the terrorist mind might stray. Capital cities in Asia have been attacked by armed groups! The establishment struggles endlessly to outflank the terrorists mind in this grim game of chess. Any perceived error is trumpeted as an abuse. Since 9/11, 7/7 and beyond the stakes rise. The recent successes of Greater Manchester Officers are to be deeply admired. How many lives were spared?

Few successes in the huge range of operations and intelligence gathering that go on constantly are visible. By the very nature of that work, those successes must remain covert for the most obvious reasons. Remember also that in the decision making processes, the judgement to go or not in any scenario is much harder. Miss a bank robber and you can hope to catch him next time. Miss a terrorist and people die. In all of this there is the constant aside of armed crime and that great consumer of human life, domestic violence.

I trust you have read and enjoyed this book. I hope also that you take something thought provoking away with you.

We aren't no thin red 'eroes,
Nor we aren't no blackguards too,
but single men in barricks,
most remarkable like you,
An' if sometimes our conduck'
isn't all your fancy paints,
Why, single men in barricks
Don't grow into plaster saints,
While it's Tommy this an' Tommy that
An' "Tommy fall be'ind',
But it's "Please to walk in front sir'
when there's trouble in the wind –.
There's trouble in the wind my boys,
there's trouble in the wind,
O' it's please to walk in front sir,
when there's trouble in the wind

From Tommy by Rudyard Kipling